IN ALL SHADES

By GRANT ALLEN *author of* *"What's Bred in the Bone," etc.* . . . .

NEW YORK AND LONDON

STREET & SMITH, PUBLISHERS

IN ALL SHADES

CHAPTER I.

ABOUT one o'clock in the morning, by a flickering fire of half-dead embers, young men of twenty-five are very apt to grow confidential. Now, it was one o'clock gone, by the marble timepiece on Edward Hawthorn's big mantelshelf in King's Bench Walk, Temple ; and Edward Hawthorn and Harry Noel were each of them just twenty-five ; so it is no matter for wonder at all that the conversation should just then have begun to take a very confidential turn indeed, especially when one remembers that they had both nearly finished their warm glass of whisky toddy, and that it was one of those chilly April evenings when you naturally cower close over the fire to keep your poor blood from curdling bodily altogether within you.

'It's certainly very odd, Noel, that my father should always seem so very anxious to keep me from going back to Trinidad, even for a mere short visit.'

Harry Noel shook out the ashes from his pipe as he answered quietly: 'Fathers are altogether the most un-accountable, incomprehensible, mysterious, unmanageable creatures in God's universe. Women and horses are mere child's-play compared to them. For my own part, I've given up attempting to fathom them altogether.'

Edward smiled half deprecatingly. 'Ah, but you know, Noel,' he went on in a far more serious tone than his friend's, ' my father isn't at all like that ; he's never refused me money or anything else I've wanted ; he's been the most liberal and the kindest of men to me ; but for some abstruse and inconceivable reason—I can't imagine why—he's always opposed my going back home even to visit him.'

'If Sir Walter'd only act upon the same principle, my dear boy, I can tell you confidentially I'd be simply too delighted. But, confound it all, he always acts upon the exact contrary. He's in favour of my coming down to the Hall, in the very dampest, dreariest, and dullest part of all Lincolnshire, at the precise moment of time when I want myself to be off to Scotland, deer-stalking or grouse-shooting ; but he invariably considers all my applications for extra coin as at least inopportune—as the papers say—if not as absolutely extravagant, or even criminal. A governor who shells out freely while remaining permanently invisible on the other side of the Atlantic, appears to me to combine all the practical advantages of the governor, viewed as an institution, with none of its painful and objectionable drawbacks. *O fortunatus nimium tua si bona noris,* my dear Teddy.'

'Ah, that's all very well for you, Noel ; you've got your father and your family here in England with you, and you make light of the privilege because you enjoy it. But it's a very different thing altogether when all your people are separated from you by half a hemisphere, and you've never even so much as seen your own mother since you were a little chap no bigger than that chair there. You'll admit at least that a fellow would naturally like now and again to see his mother.'

'His mother,' Noel answered, dropping his voice a little with a sort of instinctive reverential inflection. 'Ah, that, now,'s a very different matter. Fathers of course are our natural enemies, we all admit ; but the man that goes back upon his own mother isn't worth salt to his porridge.'

'Well, you see, my dear fellow, I've never seen either my father or my mother since I was quite a small boy of eight years old or thereabouts. I was sent home to Joyce's to school then, as you know ; and after that, I went to Rugby, and next to Cambridge ; and I've almost entirely forgotten by this time even what my father and mother

look like. When they sent me home those two photographs there, a few months back, I assure you there wasn't
a feature in either face I could really and truly recognise or
remember.'

' Precious handsome old gentleman your father, anyhow,' Noel observed, looking up carelessly at the large
framed photograph above the fire-place. ' Seems the right
sort too ; has what I should call a benevolent shelling-out
cast of countenance, which ought to be strictly encouraged
in the breed of fathers. Fine air of sterling coininess also,
I remark, about his grey hair and his full waistcoat and his
turn-down shirt-collar. A man of more than fifty who
wears a turn-down collar, I've long observed, is invariably
coiny. Real old solid mahogany father, I should be inclined to say ; good all alike throughout ; no veneering.
Calculated to cut up very respectably.'

' Oh, Noel, please ; don't talk that way ! '

' My dear fellow, it's the course of nature. We fall as
the leaves fall, and new generations replace us and take
our money. Good for the legacy duty. Now, is your
governor sugar or coffee ? '

' Sugar, I believe—in fact, I'm pretty sure of it. He
often writes that the canes are progressing, and talks about
rattoons and centrifugals and other things I don't know
the very names of. But I believe he has a very good
estate of his own somewhere or other at the north end of
the island.'

' Why, of course, then, that's the explanation of it—as
safe as houses, you may depend upon it. The old gentleman's as rich as Crœsus, I'll bet you any money. He
makes you a modest allowance over here, which you, who
are an unassuming, hard-working, Chitty-on-Contract sort
of fellow, consider very handsome, but which is really not
one quarter of what he ought to be allowing you out of his
probably princely income. You take my word for it, Teddy,
that's the meaning of it. The old gentleman—he has a
very knowing look about his weather-eye in the photograph
too—he thinks if you were to go out there, and see the
estate, and observe the wealth of the Indies, and discover
the way he makes the dollars fly, you'd ask him imme-

diately to double your allowance; and being a person of unusual penetration—as I can see, with half a glance, from his picture—he decides to keep you at the other end of the universe, so that you may never discover what a perfect Rothschild he is, and go in for putting the screw on.'

Edward Hawthorn smiled quietly. 'It won't do, my dear fellow,' he said, glancing up quickly at the handsome open face in the big photograph. 'My father isn't at all that sort of person, I feel certain, from his letters. He's doing all he can to advance me in life; and though he hasn't seen me for so long, I'm the one interest he really lives upon.'

'Oh, you excellent young man, Teddy, how deliciously green and fresh you've managed to keep yourself! Do you really mean to tell me you still believe all that ridiculous paternal humbug? Why, my governor always says precisely the same things to me in precisely the same language. If you were to believe Sir Walter, his one aim and object in life is to make me happy. It's all for my own sake that he stints me in money; it's all for my own sake that he spends every penny he ought to be generously showering upon me, in building new cottages and mending fences and improving the position of the tenants generally. As if the tenants wanted any improvement! They prefer to pig it, while I prefer to have my money.'

'Well, Noel, I certainly did think it very queer, after I'd taken my degree at Cambridge and got the Arabic scholarship and so forth, that my father didn't want me to go out to the island. I naturally wanted to see my old home and my father and mother, before settling down to my business in life; and I wrote and told them so. But my father wrote back, putting me off with all sorts of made-up excuses: it was the bad season of the year; there was a great deal of yellow fever about; he was very anxious I should get to work at once upon my law-reading; he wanted me to be called to the bar as early as possible.'

'And so, just to please the old gentleman, you left your Arabic, that you were such a dab at, and set to work and mugged up over Benjamin on Sales and Pollock on Mortgages for the best years of your lifetime, when you ought to

have been shooting birds in Devonshire or yachting with
me in the *Princess of Thule* off the west coast of Scotland.
That's not my theory of the way fathers ought to be
managed. I consented to become a barrister, just to pacify
Sir Walter for the moment ; but my ideas of barristering
are a great deal more elastic and generous than yours are.
I'm quite satisfied with getting my name neatly painted
over the door of some other fellow's convenient chambers.'

'Yes, yes, of course you are. But then your case is
very different. The heir to an English baronetcy needn't
trouble himself about his future, like us ordinary mortals.
But if I didn't work hard and get on and make money, I
shouldn't ever be able to marry—at least during my father's
lifetime.'

'No more should I, my dear fellow. Absolutely impossible. A man can't marry on seven hundred a year,
you see, can he ? '

Edward laughed. 'I could,' he answered, 'very easily.
No doubt, you couldn't. But then you haven't got anybody in your eye ; while I, you know, am anxious as soon
as I can to marry Marian.'

'Not got anybody in my eye l' Harry Noel cried, leaning back in his chair and opening his two hands symboli-
cally in front of him with an expansive gesture. 'Oh,
haven't I ; just dozens of them. Only, of course, it's no
use a poor beggar like me, on seven hundred a year, talking
about getting married, or else I'd soon take my pick out of
the whole lot of them. Why, by Jove, there was a pretty
little girl I saw last Wednesday down at the Buckleburies
—a Miss Dupuy, I think, they called her—by the way, a
countrywoman of yours, I believe, Edward—from Trinidad ;
or was it Mauritius ? one of those sugary-niggery places or
other, anyhow ; and I assure you I fairly lost the miserable
relics of my heart to her at our first meeting. She's going
to be at the boat-race to-morrow ; and I'm a Dutchman if
I don't think I'll run down there in the dog-cart incontinently, on the spec. of seeing her. Will you come with
me ? '

'But how about that devilling of Walker's ? '

'Oh, nonsense. Walker, Q.C., may devil for himself,

for all I care for him. Leave him alone for once to take
care of himself, and come along with me.'

' What o'clock ? '

' Eleven. A reasonable hour. You don't catch me
getting up at five o'clock in the morning and making the
historical Noel nose, which I so proudly inherit, turn blue
with cold and shivering at that time of the day, even for
the honour of the old 'varsity. Plenty of time to turn in
and get a comfortable snooze, and yet have breakfast
decently before I drive you down to-morrow morning in
my new dog-cart.'

' All right. I'll come with you, then.—Are you going
out now ? Just post that letter for me, please, will you ? '

Noel took it and glanced at the address half unintentionally. ' The Hon. James Hawthorn,' he said, reading
it over in a thoughtless mechanical way and in a sort of
undertone soliloquy, ' Agualta Estate, Trinidad.—Why, I
didn't know, Teddy, this mysterious governor of yours was
actually a real live Honourable. What family does he
belong to, then ? '

' I don't think Honourable means that out in the
colonies, you know,' Edward answered, stirring the embers
into a final flicker. ' I fancy it's only a cheap courtesy
title given to people in the West Indies who happen to be
members of the Legislative Council.'

' Legislative Council ! Better and better. My dear
Ted, the governor's coiny, you may depend upon it, or
else he wouldn't be admitted into the legislature of his
native country. A man who has so much tin to spare
that he can afford to throw some of it away in attending to
the affairs of the nation—which means, after all, somebody
else's business—is certain to be coiny ; absolutely certain.
Bleed him, my dear boy ; bleed him wholesomely. As a
son and a citizen, it's your plain duty to bleed him without
flinching. Think for a moment of the force of the example ;
think how eminently undesirable it is that governors
generally should get into the habit of skulking away in
remote corners of the uninhabitable tropics, on purpose so
as to chouse their own children out of their proper reasonable allowances. It's an atrocious proceeding altogether,

I tell you, and, for the sake of the whole community, it ought to be put a stop to immediately without any question.'

Edward paused for a minute, still seated, and poking away nervously at the dying embers; then he said in a more serious voice : ' Do you know, Noel, there's a district judgeship in Trinidad going to be filled up at once by the Colonial Office ? '

' Well, my dear boy ; what of that ? I know a promising young barrister of the Inner Temple who isn't going to be such an absurd fool as to take the place, even if it's offered to him.'

' On the contrary, Harry, I've sent in an application myself for the post this very evening.'

' My dear Hawthorn, like Paul, you are beside yourself. Much learning—of Walker on Specific Performance—has made you mad, I solemnly assure you. The place isn't worth your taking.'

' Nevertheless, if I can get it, Harry, I mean to take it.'

' If you can get it ! Fiddlesticks ! If you can get a place as crossing-sweeper ! My good friend, this is simple madness. A young man of your age, a boy, a mere child '—they were both the same age to a month, but Harry Noel always assumed the airs of a father towards his friend Hawthorn—' who has already been promoted to devil for Walker, and who knows the most influential solicitor in Chancery Lane personally—why, it's chucking up an absolute certainty ; an absolute certainty, and no mistake about it. You're the best Arabic scholar in England ; it'd be worth your while stopping here, if it comes to that, for the sake of the Arabic Professorship alone, rather than go and live in Trinidad. If you take my advice, my dear fellow, you'll have nothing more to say to the precious business.'

' Well, Harry, I have two reasons for wishing to take it. In the first place, I want to marry Marian as early as possible ; and I can't marry her until I can make myself a decent income.'

' Bleed him ! bleed him ! ' Harry Noel ejaculated parenthetically, in a gentle whisper.

' And in the second place,' Edward went on, without stopping to notice the muttered interruption, ' I want to go out as soon as I can and see my father and mother in Trinidad. If I get this district judgeship, I shall be able to write and tell them positively I'm coming, and they won't have any excuse of any sort for putting a stopper on it any longer.'

'In other words, in order to go and spy out the hidden wealth of the coiny old governor, you're going to chuck away the finest opening at the English bar, and bind yourself down to a life of exile in a remote corner of the Caribbean Sea. I believe they call the sea the Caribbean ; but anyhow, whether or not, it sounds awfully fine to end a sentence with. Well, my good friend, if you really do it, all that I can say is simply this—you'll prove yourself the most consummate ass in all Christendom.'

'Noel, I've made my mind up ; I shall really go there.'

'Then, my dear boy, allow me to tell you, as long as you live you will never cease to regret it. I believe you'll repent it, before you're done, in sackcloth and ashes.'

Edward stirred the dead fire nervously once more for a few seconds and answered nothing.

'Good-night, Hawthorn. You'll be ready to start for the boat-race at ten to-morrow ? '

'Good-night, Harry. I'll be ready to start. Good-night, my dear fellow.'

Noel turned and left the room ; but Edward Hawthorn stood still, with his bedroom candle poised reflectively in one hand, looking long and steadfastly with fixed eyes at his father's and mother's photographs before him. ' A grand-looking old man, my father, certainly,' he said to himself, scanning the fine broad brow and firm but tender mouth with curious attention—' a grand-looking old man, without a doubt, there's no denying it. But I wonder why on earth he doesn't want me to go out to Trinidad ? And a beautiful, gentle, lovable old lady, if ever there was one on this earth, my mother ! '

CHAPTER II.

You wouldn't have found two handsomer or finer young men on the day of the boat-race, in all London, than the two who started on the new dog-cart, at ten o'clock, from the door of Harry Noel's comfortable chambers in a quaint old house in Duke Street, St. James's. And yet they were very different in type indeed; as widely different as it is possible for any two young men to be, both of whom were quite unmistakable and undeniable young Englishmen.

Harry Noel was heir of one of the oldest and bluest-blooded families in all Lincolnshire; but his face and figure were by no means those of the typical Danes in that most distinctively Danish of English counties. Sir Walter, his father, was tall and fair—a bluff, honest, hard-featured Lincolnshire man; but Harry himself took rather after his mother, the famous Lady Noel, once considered the most beautiful woman of her time in London society. He was somewhat short and well knit; a very dark man, with black hair, moustache, and beard; and his face was handsome with something of a southern and fiery handsomeness, like his mother's, reminding one at times of the purest Italian or Castilian stocks. There was undeniable pride about his upper lip and his eager flashing black eye; while his customary nonchalance and coolness of air never completely hid the hot and passionate southern temperament that underlay that false exterior of Pall Mall cynicism. A man to avoid picking a quarrel with, certainly, was Harry Noel, of the Inner Temple, and of Noel Hall, near Boston, Lincolnshire, barrister-at-law.

Edward Hawthorn, on the other hand, was tall and slight, though strongly-built; a perfect model of the pure Anglo-Saxon type of manhood, with straight fair hair, nearer white almost than yellow, and deep-blue eyes, that were none the less transparently true and earnest because of their intense and unmixed blueness. His face was clear-cut and delicately moulded; and the pale and singularly straw-coloured moustache, which alone was allowed to

hide any part of its exquisite outline, did not prevent one
from seeing at a glance the almost faultless Greek regu-
larity of his perfectly calm and statuesque features. Harry
Noel's was, in short, the kind of face that women are most
likely to fall in love with: Edward Hawthorn's was the
kind that an artist would rather rejoice to paint, or that a
sculptor would still more eagerly wish to model in the perfect simplicity of pure white marble.

'Much better to go down by the road, you know,
Teddy,' Harry Noel said as they took their seats in the new
dog-cart. 'All the cads in London are going down by
rail, of course. The whole riff-raff of our fellow-man
that you're always talking about so sympathetically, with
your absurd notions, overflows to-day from its natural
reservoirs in the third class into the upper tanks of first
and second. Impossible to travel on the line this morning
without getting one's-self jammed and elbowed by all the
tinkers and tailors, soldiers and sailors, butchers and
bakers and candlestick makers in the whole of London.
Enough to cure even you, I should think, of all your nonsensical rights-of-man and ideal equality business.'

'Have you ever travelled third yourself, to see what it
was really like, Harry? I have; and, for my part, I think
the third-class people generally rather kinder and more
unselfish at bottom than the first or second.'

'My dear fellow, on your recommendation I tried it last
week; and got such a tremendous facer from a Radical
working-man as I never before got, and never expect to
get again, in the whole course of my earthly existence.
The creature opposite me was a democratic Methodist, I
think he called it, or something else equally impossible,
and he was haranguing away about the wickedness of the
aristocracy, and the toiling millions, and Lazarus and
Dives, and all the rest of it; and at last he went on
abusing me and my friends—by implication—so confoundedly, that I really couldn't stand it any longer. "My
good sir," said I, leaning over towards him very deferen-
tially—for there were half a dozen of them, all frantic
revolutionists and big hustling fellows, in the same carriage
—"my good sir," said I, "do you know, all abstract prin-

ciples must of course be finally judged, in this confessedly
imperfect world of ours, by their practical effects when
actually tested in the concrete application? Now, there
was a time in the history of the world when these liberty,
equality, fraternity notions of yours were fairly tried in
real earnest. That time was in the French Revolution.
Do you mean to tell me you think the result of the French
Revolution was of a sort to encourage further experiments
in the same direction?" And what do you suppose the
fellow answered me? He looked up in my face with the
most profound solemnity, and said he: "Well, and didn't
we beat the French at Waterloo?"'

Edward laughed heartily. 'What did you say to
that?' he asked, with a twinkle.

'Say? My dear fellow, what on earth *could* I say?
When a man gets shut up like a telescope by a regular
downright overwhelming *non sequitur* like that, any answer
or repartee at all is absolutely impossible. Besides, all the
free and independent electors in the carriage with him
were perfectly delighted to see how completely he had
bowled over the obstructive and anti-democratic scoffer.
'He ain't got nothing to say after that, anyway,' they all
whispered to one another, grinning and winking. I subsided utterly into the obscurest corner; I collapsed, morally
speaking, and was absolutely annihilated. From this day
forth, I never mean to travel any more in third-class
carriages, or to try arguing under any provocation with the
great proletariate. Their logic is too peculiarly perplexed
for me to make my way through it. And these are the
kind of fellows that you and your friends want to set up to
govern us and dance upon us! It won't hold water, my
dear boy; it won't hold water. I never can understand a
sensible sound-headed man like you being taken in by it for
a single minute.'

'Perhaps,' Edward said quietly, 'you might have found
some quite as densely illogical fellows in others beside a
third-class carriage.—But where are you going to look for
your beautiful young lady from Trinidad or Mauritius?
You made her the ostensible pretext, you know, for going
to the boat-race.'

' Oh, for that I trust entirely to the chapter of accidents. She said she was going down to see the race from somebody's lawn, facing the river; and I shall force my way along the path, as far as I can get, and simply look out for her. If we see her, I mean to push boldly for an introduction to the somebody unnamed who owns the lawn. Leave the dog-cart at some inn or other down at Putney, stroll along the river casually till you see a beatific vision of sweet nineteen or thereabout, walk in quietly as if the place belonged to you, and there you are.'

They drove on to Putney through the crowded roads, and put the dog-cart up at the *Coach and Horses*. Then Harry and Edward took to the still more crowded bank, and began to push their way among the densely packed masses of nondescript humanity in the direction of Barnes Bridge.

' Stand out of the way there, can't you,' Harry Noel cried, elbowing aside a sturdy London rough as he spoke with a dexterous application of his gold-tipped umbrella. ' Why do you get in people's way and block the road up, my good fellow ? '

' Where are you a-pushin' to ? ' the rough answered, not without reason, crowding in upon him sturdily in defence of his natural rights of standing-room, and bringing his heavy foot down plump on Harry Noel's neatly fitting walking shoe. ' An' who are you, I should like to know, a-shovin' other people aside permiscuous like, as if you was acshally the Prince of Wales or the Dook of Edingboro ? I'd like to hear you call me a fellow again, I should ! Fellow indeed ! A fellow's a sheep-stealer ! '

' Appears to be some confusion in the man's mind,' Harry Noel said, pushing past him angrily, ' between a fellow and a felon. I haven't got an etymological dictionary handy in my pocket, I regret to say, but I venture to believe, my good friend, that your philology is quite as much at fault in this matter as your English grammar.'

' My dear Noel,' Edward Hawthorn put in, ' please don't add insult to injury. The man's quite within his right in objecting to your pushing him out of a place he took up before you came here. Possession's nine points of

the law, you know—ten in the matter of occupancy, indeed
—and surely he's the prior occupant.'

' Oh, if you're going to hold a brief for the defendant,
my dear boy, why, of course I throw the case up; I
immediately enter a *nolle prosequi*.—Besides, there she is,
Teddy. By Jove, there she is. That's her. Over yonder
on the lawn there—the very pretty girl by the edge of the
wall overhanging the path here.'

' What, the one in blue ? '

' The one in blue ! Gracious Heavens, no. Is the man
mad ? The one in blue, he positively says to me ! Do you
mean to say you call her pretty ? No, no ; not her. The
other one—the very pretty girl ; the one in the pink dress,
as fresh as a daisy. Did you ever see anybody prettier ? '

' Oh, her,' Edward answered, looking across at the
lady in pink carelessly. ' Yes, yes ; I see now. Pretty
enough, as you say, Harry.'

' Pretty enough ! Is that all you've got to say about
her ! You block of ice ! you lump of marble ! Why, my
dear fellow, she's absolute perfection. That's the worst,
now, of a man's being engaged. He loses his eye entirely
for female beauty. He believes all possible human charms
are exclusively summed up in his own particular Maud or
Angelina. For my part, Ted, I go in for a judicious
eclecticism. They're all pretty alike, while you're with
them : each new one seems the prettiest you've ever seen
—till you've got tired of her.'

' What did you say her name was ? '

' Miss Dupuy. I'll introduce you in a minute.'

' But, my dear Harry, where are you going ? We
don't even know the people.'

' Nothing easier, then. We'll proceed to make their
acquaintance. See what a lot of cads climbing up and
sitting on the wall obstructing the view there ! First,
seat yourself firmly on the top the same as they do ; then,
proceed to knock off the other intruders, as if you belonged to the party by invitation ; finally, slip over quietly
inside, and mix with the lot exactly as if you really knew
them. There are such a precious crowd of people inside,
that nobody'll ever find out you weren't invited. I've long

observed that nobody ever knows who's who at a garden-party, even.   The father always thinks his son knows you; and the son always fancies indefinitely you're particular friends of his father and mother.'

As Harry spoke, he had already vaulted lightly on to the top of the wall, which was steep and high on the side towards the river, but stood only about two feet above the bank on the inner side; and Edward, seeing nothing else to do but follow his example, had taken with shame a convenient seat beside him.   In a minute more, Harry was busily engaged in clearing off the other unauthorised squatters, like an invited guest; and two minutes later, he had transferred his legs to the inner side of the wall, and was quietly identifying himself with the party of spectators on the lawn and garden.   Edward, who was not a baronet's son, and was blessed with less audacity in social matters than his easy-going friend, could only admire without wholly imitating his ready adaptiveness.

'Miss Dupuy!   How delightful!   So here you are! This is indeed lucky!   I came down on purpose to see you.   How very fortunate I should happen to have dropped down upon you so unexpectedly.'

Nora Dupuy smiled a delicious smile of frank and innocent girlish welcome, and held out her pretty little gloved hand to Harry half timidly.   'Why, Mr. Noel,' she said, blushing prettily, 'I hadn't the very slightest idea you knew our good friends the Boddingtons.'

'*Mr.* Boddington?' Harry Noel asked, with a marked emphasis on the dubious *Mr.*

'No; Colonel Boddington, of the Bengal Staff Corps. Why, how on earth do you happen not to know their name even?   Have you come here, then, with somebody?'

'Exactly,' Harry said, turning to Edward, who was speechless with surprise.   'Allow me to introduce him. My friend, Mr. Hawthorn, a shining light of the Utter Bar.—By the way, didn't you say you came from Trinidad or Mauritius or Ceylon or somewhere?   I remember distinctly you left upon me a general impression of tropical fragrance, though I can't say I recollect precisely the particular habitat.'

Nora smiled again, and blushed even more deeply than before. ' It was Trinidad,' she answered, looking down as she spoke.—' Why, Mr. Noel, what about it ? '

' Why, my friend Hawthorn here comes from Trinidad too, so you ought to be neighbours ; though, as he hasn't been there himself for a great many years, I dare say you won't know one another.'

' Oh, everybody in Trinidad knows everybody else, of course,' Nora answered, half turning to Edward. ' It's such a little pocket colony, you know, that we're all first-cousins to one another through all the island. I'm not acquainted with all the people in Trinidad myself, natur-ally, because I haven't been there since I was a baby, almost ; but my father would be perfectly sure to know him, at any rate, I'm confident.—What did you say your friend's name was, Mr. Noel ? '

' Hawthorn,' Edward answered quickly for himself— ' Edward Hawthorn.'

' Oh, Mr. Hawthorn,' Nora repeated reflectively. ' Let me see. Hawthorn, Hawthorn. No ; I don't think I ever heard the name before—connected with Trinidad, I mean ; in fact, I'm sure not. Hawthorn, Hawthorn. Do your people live out there still, Mr. Hawthorn, or have they settled over in England ? '

' My father and mother are still in the island,' Edward answered, a little uncomfortably. ' My father is Mr. James Hawthorn, of Agualta Estate, a place at the north side of Trinidad.'

' Agualta Estate,' Nora replied, turning the name over with herself once more dubiously, ' Agualta Estate. I've certainly heard the name of the place, I'm sure ; but never of your people until this minute. How very funny.'

' It's a long time since you've been in the island, you say,' Harry Noel put in suggestively, ' and no doubt you've forgotten Mr. Hawthorn's father's name. He must be pretty well known in Trinidad, I should think, for he's an Honourable, you know, and a member of the local Legislative Council.'

Nora looked decidedly puzzled. ' A member of the Legislative Council,' she said in some surprise. ' That

makes it even funnier and funnier. My papa's a member
of Council too, and he knows everybody in the place, you
know—that is to say, of course, everybody who's anybody ; and poor mamma used always to write me home
the chattiest letters, all about everybody and everybody's
wife and daughters, and all the society gossip of the
colony ; and then I see so many Trinidad people when
they come home ; and altogether, I really thought I knew,
by name at least, absolutely everyone in the whole island.'

'And this proves you must be mistaken, Miss Dupuy,'
Harry Noel put in carelessly ; for he was half jealous that
his own special and peculiar discovery in pretty girls
should take so much interest in Edward Hawthorn. 'But
anyhow, you'll know all about him before very long, I've
no doubt, for Hawthorn's going to take a judgeship in the
uttermost parts of the earth, even Trinidad. He'll be
going out there, no doubt, from what he tells me, in a
month or so from now, the silly fellow.'

'Going out there ! ' cried Nora. 'Oh, how nice. Why,
I shall be going out, too, in the end of June. How
delightful, if we should both happen to sail in the same
steamer together ! '

'Very,' Harry echoed, a little snappishly—' for Hawthorn. I should envy him the voyage immensely. But
you don't mean to say, Miss Dupuy, you're really going to
bury yourself alive in the West Indies ? '

'Oh, I don't call it burying alive, Mr. Noel ; it's
perfectly delightful, I believe, from what I remember.
Summer all the year round, and dancing, with all the doors
and windows open, from September to April.'

'Gracious Heavens, which is Colonel Boddington ? '
Harry exclaimed eagerly at this particular moment, for
he saw an old gentleman of military aspect strolling up
casually to speak to Nora. 'Point me out my host, for
mercy's sake, or else he'll be bringing a summary action
for ejectment against us both as rogues and vagabonds.'

'This is he,' Nora said, as the military gentleman
approached nearer. 'Don't you know him ? Perhaps I'd
better introduce you. Colonel Boddington—Mr. Noel, Mr.
Hawthorn.'

'And I'd better make a clean breast of it at once,'
Harry Noel continued, smiling gracefully with his pleasant
easy smile—Edward would have sunk bodily into the earth
alive, rather than make the ridiculous confession. 'The
fact is, we're intruders into your domain, sir—unauthorised
intruders. We took our seats on the top of your wall to
watch the race; and when we got there, we found a number
of roughs were obstructing the view for the ladies of your
party; and we assisted the gentlemen of your set in clearing
the ground; and then, as I saw my friend Miss Dupuy was
here, I made bold to jump over and come to speak to her,
feeling sure that a previous acquaintance with her would
be a sufficient introduction into your pleasant society here.
—What a delightful place you've got on the river here,
really.'

Colonel Boddington bowed stiffly. 'Any friend of Miss
Dupuy's is quite welcome here, I'm sure,' he said with
some chilly severity.—'Did I understand Miss Dupuy to
say your name was Rowell?'

'Noel,' Harry corrected, smiling benignly—'Noel, Noel.
You may possibly know my father, as I understand, from
Miss Dupuy, you're a Lincolnshire man' (this was a white-
lie, but it sufficiently served Harry's purpose)—Sir Walter
Noel, of Noel Hall, near Boston, Lincolnshire.'

Colonel Boddington unbent visibly. 'I'm very glad of
this opportunity, I'm sure, Mr. Noel,' he said with his most
gracious manner. 'As I remarked before, Miss Dupuy's
friends will always be welcome with us. Since you've
dropped in so unexpectedly, perhaps you and Mr.—I didn't
catch the name—will stop and take a little lunch with us.
Our friends mean to join us at lunch after the race is over.'

'Delighted, I'm sure,' Harry answered, quite truthfully.
Nothing could have pleased him better than this opportunity. 'Here they come—here they come! Round the
corner! Cambridge heads the race, by Jove. Cambridge,
Cambridge!' And for five minutes there was a fluttering
of handkerchiefs and straining of eyes and confused sound
of shouts and laughter, which left no time for Harry or
anyone else to indulge in rational conversation.

After the boats had passed out of sight, and the company had returned to the paths of sanity once more, Nora Dupuy turned round to Edward and asked curiously: 'Do you happen to know any people of the name of Ord, Mr. Hawthorn?'

Edward smiled as he answered: 'General Ord's family? Oh, yes, I know them very well indeed—quite intimately, in fact.'

Nora clapped her little hands in a sort of triumph. 'Oh, how nice!' she said gaily. 'Then you *are* the Mr. Hawthorn who is engaged to dear Marian. I felt sure you must be, the moment I heard your name. Oh, I do so hope, then, you'll get this vacant Trinidad appointment.'

'Get it! He'll get it as sure as fate,' Harry said intervening. 'But why on earth are you so anxious he should take it?'

'Why, because, then, Marian would get married, of course, and come out with him to live in Trinidad. Wouldn't that be just delightful!'

'If they do,' Harry said quietly, 'and if you're going to be there, too, Miss Dupuy, I declare I shall come out myself on purpose to visit them.'

CHAPTER III.

'Oh, Marian, do you know, I've met Mr. Hawthorn; and what a delightful man he is! I quite fell in love with him myself, I assure you! Wasn't it absurd? He came down the other morning to the boat-race; and he and a friend of his positively jumped over the wall, without an invitation, into old Colonel Boddington's front garden.'

Marian took Nora's hand warmly. 'I'm so glad you like Edward,' she said, kissing her cheek and smoothing her forehead. 'I was sure you'd like him. I've been longing for you to come to town ever since we got engaged, so that you might manage to see him.—Well, dear, and do you think him handsome?'

'Handsome! Oh, Marian, awfully handsome; and so nice, too, dear. And such a sweet voice and manner, so grave and cultivated, somehow. I always do like Oxford and Cambridge men—ever so much better than army men, Marian.'

'Who had he with him at the boat-race?' Marian asked.

'Oh, my dear, such a funny man—a Mr. Noel, whom I met last week down at the Buckleburies. Colonel Boddington says his father's one of the greatest swells in all Lincolnshire—a Sir Somebody Noel, or something. And do you know, Marian, he simply jumped over the wall, without knowing the Boddingtons one bit, just because he saw me there—wasn't it dreadful of him, after only meeting me once, too?—and then apologised to the old Colonel, who looked as if he would have sunk into the ground in horror at such an awful and unprecedented proceeding. But the moment Mr. Noel said something or other incidentally about his father Sir Somebody, the Colonel became as mild as a lamb, and asked him to lunch at once, and tried to put him sitting right between Minnie and Adela. And Mr. Noel managed to shuffle out of it somehow, and got on one side of me, with Mr. Hawthorn on the other side; and he talked so that he kept me laughing right through the whole of lunch-time.'

'He's awfully amusing,' Marian said with a slight smile.—'And I suppose you rather liked Mr. Noel, too, didn't you, Nora?'

Nora shook her head energetically. 'No, my dear; not my sort of man at all, really. I certainly wasn't in the least taken with him.'

'Not a little bit even, Nora?'

Nora pulled out the petals of the faded rose she was wearing in her bosom with a petulant gesture. 'Not even a little bit, dear,' she answered decidedly. 'He isn't at all the sort of man I should ever care for. Too dark for me, by several shades, for one thing, Marian. You know, we West Indians never can endure these very dark people.'

'But I'm dark, Nora, and you like me, you know, don't you?'

'Oh, you. Yes; that's quite another thing, Marian. That's nothing, to be dark as you are. Your hair and eyes and complexion are just absolutely perfect, darling. But Mr. Noel—well, he's a shade or two too dark for me, anyhow; and I don't mind saying so to you candidly.—Mr. Hawthorn's a great deal more my ideal of what a handsome man ought to be. I think his eyes, his hair, and his moustache are just simply lovely, Marian.'

'Why, of course, you and he ought to be friends,' Marian said, a natural thought flashing suddenly across her. 'He comes from Trinidad, just the same as you do. How funny that the two people I've liked best in all the world should both come from the very same little bit of an island. I dare say you used to know some of his people.'

'That's the very funniest part of it all, Marian. I can't recollect anything at all about his family; I don't even remember ever to have heard of them from any Trinidad people.'

Marian looked up quickly from the needlework on which she was employed, and said simply: 'I dare say they didn't happen to know your family.'

'Well, that's just what's odd about it, dear,' Nora continued, pulling out her crochet. 'Everybody in Trinidad knows my family. And Mr. Hawthorn's father's in the Legislative Council, too, just like papa; and he himself has been to Cambridge, you know, and is a barrister, and knows Arabic, and is so awfully clever, that amusing Mr. Noel tells me. I can't imagine how on earth it is I've never even heard of him before.'

'Well, at any rate, I'm so awfully glad you really like him, now that you've actually seen him, Nora. One's always so afraid that all one's friends won't like one's future husband.'

'Like him, dear; how on earth could one help liking him? Why, I think he's simply delightful. And that's so surprising, too, because generally, you know, one's friends *will* go and marry such regular horrid sticks of men, without consulting one. I think he's the nicest man I've ever met anywhere, almost.'

'And the exception is—— ?'

'Put in for propriety's sake, dear, for fear you should think I was quite too enthusiastic. And do you know, he tells me he's going in for a judgeship in Trinidad; and

won't it be splendid, Marian, if he happens to get it, and
you both go out there with me, darling ? I shall be just
too delighted. Won't you, my dearie ? '

Marian gave a little sigh.   ' I shall be very glad if he
gets it in one way,' she said, ' because then, of course,
Edward and I will be able to marry immediately; and
papa's so very much opposed to a long engagement.'

' Besides which,' Nora put in frankly, ' you'd naturally
like yourself, too, to get married as soon as possible.'

' But then, on the other hand,' Marian went on, smiling quietly, ' it would be a dreadful thing going so far
away from all one's friends and relations and so forth.
Though, of course, with dear Edward to take care of me, I
wouldn't be afraid to go anywhere.'

' Of course not,' Nora said confidently. ' And I shall
be there, too, Marian ; and we shall have such lovely times
together.   People have no end of fun in the West Indies,
you know.   Everybody says it's the most delightful place
in the world in the cool season.   All the floors are always
kept polished all the year round, without any carpets, just
like the continent, and so you can have a dance at any
moment, whenever people enough happen to drop in
together accidentally of an evening.   Mamma used to say
there was no end of gaiety ; and that she never could
endure the stiffness and unsociability of English society,
after the hospitable habits of dear old Trinidad.'

' I hope we shall like it,' Marian said, ' if Edward really
succeeds in getting this appointment.   It'll be a great
alleviation to the pain of parting, certainly, if you're going
to be there too, Nora.'

' Oh, my dear, you must get married at once, then, you
know, and we must arrange somehow to go out to Trinidad
together in the same steamer.   It'll be just too lovely.   I
mean to have no end of fun going out.   And when you get
there, of course papa'll be able to introduce you and Mr.
Hawthorn to all the society in the whole island.   I call it
just delightful.'

At that moment the servant entered and announced
Mr. Hawthorn.

Marian rose from her seat and went forward to meet
him.   Edward had a long official envelope in his hands,

with a large broken seal in red sealing-wax on the back, and the important words, ' On Her Majesty's Service,' printed in very big letters at the lower left-hand corner. Marian trembled a little with excitement, not unmixed with fear, as soon as she saw it.

' Well, dearest,' Edward cried joyously, taking her hand and kissing her once tenderly, in spite of Nora's presence, ' it's all right ; I've got the judgeship. And now, Marian, we shall be able, you see, to get married immediately.'

A woman always succeeds in doing the most incomprehensible and unexpected thing under all circumstances ; and Marian, hearing now for the first time that their hearts' desire was at last in a fair way to be accomplished, did not clap her hands or smile with joy, as Edward might have imagined she would do, but fell back upon the sofa, half faint, and burst out suddenly crying.

Edward looked at her tenderly with a mingled look of surprise and sorrow. ' Why, Marian, darling Marian,' he said, a little reproachfully, ' I thought you would be so delighted and rejoiced to hear the news, that I almost ran the whole way to tell you.'

' So I am, Edward, ever so delighted,' Marian answered sobbing ; ' but it's so sudden, so very sudden.'

' She'll be all right in a minute or two, Mr. Hawthorn,' Nora said, looking up at him with an arch smile as she held Marian's hand in hers and bent over her to kiss her forehead. ' She's only taken aback a little at the suddenness of the surprise.—It's so nice, darling, isn't it really ? And now, Marian, we shall all be able actually to go out to Trinidad together in the same steamer.'

Edward's heart smote him rather at the strange way Marian had received the news that so greatly delighted him. It was very natural, after all, no doubt. Every girl feels the wrench of having to leave her father's house and her mother and her familiar surroundings. But still, he somehow felt vaguely within himself that it seemed like an evil omen for their future happiness in the Trinidad judgeship ; and it dashed his joy not a little at the moment when his dearest hopes appeared just about to be so happily and successfully realised.

CHAPTER IV.

IT was a brilliant, cloudless, tropical day at Agualta Estate, Trinidad; and the cocoa-nut palms in front of the pretty, picturesque, low-roofed bungalow were waving gracefully in the light sea-breeze that blew fresh across the open cane-pieces from the distant horizon of the broad Atlantic. Most days, indeed, except during the rainy season, were brilliant enough in all conscience at beautiful Agualta: the sun blazed all day long in a uniform hazy-white sky, not blue, to be sure, as in a northern climate, but bluish and cloudless; and the sea shone below, hazy-white, in the dim background, beyond the waving palm-trees, and the broad-leaved bananas, and the long stretch of bright-green cane-pieces that sloped down in endless succession towards the beach and the breakers. Agualta House itself was perched, West India fashion, on the topmost summit of a tall and lonely rocky peak, a projecting spur or shoulder from the main mass of the Trinidad mountains. They chose the very highest and most beautiful situations they could find for their houses, those old matter-of-fact West Indian planters, not so much out of a taste for scenery— for their mental horizon was for the most part bounded by rum and sugar—but because a hill-top was coolest and breeziest, and coolness is the one great practical desideratum in a West Indian residence. Still, the houses that they built on these airy heights incidentally enjoyed the most exquisite prospects; and Agualta itself was no exception to the general rule in this matter. From the front piazza you looked down upon a green ravine, crowded with tree-ferns and other graceful tropical vegetation; on either side, rocky peaks broke the middle distance with their jagged tors and precipitous needles; while far away beyond the cane-grown plain that nestled snugly in the hollow below, the sky-line of the Atlantic bounded the view, with a dozen sun-smit rocky islets basking like great floating whales upon the grey horizon. No lovelier view in the whole of luxuriant beautiful Trinidad than that from the creeper-covered front piazza of the white bungalow of old Agualta.

Through the midst of the ravine, the little river from which the estate took its Spanish name—curiously corrupted upon negro lips into the form of Wagwater—tumbled in white sheets of dashing foam between the green foliage ' in cataract after cataract to the sea.' Here and there, the overarching clumps of feathery bamboo hid its course for a hundred yards or so, as seen from the piazza; but every now and again it gleamed forth, white and conspicuous once more, as it tumbled headlong down its steep course over some rocky barrier. You could trace it throughout like a long line of light among all the tangled, glossy, dark-green foliage of that wild and overgrown tropical gully.

The Honourable James Hawthorn, owner of Agualta, was sitting out in a cane arm-chair, under the broad shadow of the great mango-tree on the grassy terrace in front of the piazza. A venerable grey-haired, grey-bearded man, with a calm, clear-cut, resolute face, the very counterpart of his son Edward's, only grown some thirty years older, and sterner too, and more unbending.

'Mr. Dupuy's coming round this morning, Mary,' Mr. Hawthorn said to the placid, gentle old lady in the companion-chair beside him. ' He wants to look at some oxen I'm going to get rid of, and he thinks, perhaps, he'd like to buy them.'

'Mr. Dupuy!' Mrs. Hawthorn answered, with a slight shudder of displeasure as she spoke. ' I really wish he wasn't coming. I can't bear that man, somehow. He always seems to me the worst embodiment of the bad old days that are dead and gone, Jamie.'

The old gentleman hummed an air to himself reflectively. ' We mustn't be too hard upon him, my dear,' he said after a moment's pause, in a tone of perfect resignation. ' They were brought up in a terrible school, those old-time slavery Trinidad folk, and they can't help bearing the impress of a bad system upon them to the very last moment of their existence. I think so meanly of them for their pride and intolerance, that I take care not to

imitate it. You remember what Shelley says: "Let
scorn be not repaid with scorn." That's how I always feel,
Mary, towards Mr. Dupuy and all his fellows.'

Mrs. Hawthorn bit her lip as she answered slowly:
'All the same, Jamie, I wish he wasn't coming here this
morning ; and this the English mail-day, too ! We shall
get our letter from Edward by-and-by, you know, dear. I
hate to have these people coming breaking in upon us the
very day we want to be at home by ourselves, to have a
quiet hour alone with our dear boy over in England.'

'Here they come, at any rate, Mary,' the old gentleman said, pointing with his hand down the steep ravine to
where a couple of men on mountain ponies were slowly
toiling up the long zigzag path that climbed the shoulder.
'Here they come, Theodore Dupuy himself, and that young
Tom Dupuy as well, behind him. There's one comfort, at
any rate, in the position of Agualta—you can never possibly
be taken by surprise ; you can always see your visitors
coming half an hour before they get here. Run in, dear,
and see about having enough for lunch, will you, for Tom
Dupuy's sure to stop until he's had a glass of our old
Madeira.'

'I dislike Tom Dupuy, I think, even worse than his
old uncle, Jamie,' the bland old lady answered softly in
her pleasant voice, exactly as if she was saying that she
loved him dearly. 'He's a horrid young man, so selfish
and narrow-minded ; and I hope you won't ever ask him
again to come to Agualta. I can hardly even manage to
be decently polite to him.'

The two strangers slowly wound their way up the in-
terminable zigzags that led along the steep shoulders of the
Agualta peak, and emerged at last from under the shadow
of the green mango grove close beside the grassy terrace
in front of the piazza. The elder of the two, Nora's father,
was a jovial, round-faced, close-shaven man, with a copious
growth of flowing white hair, that fell in long patriarchal
locks around his heavy neck and shoulders ; a full-blooded,
easy-going, proud face to look at, yet not without a certain
touch of gentlemanly culture and old-fashioned courtesy.
The younger man, Tom Dupuy, his nephew, looked exactly

what he was—a born boor, awkward in gait and lubberly
in feature, with a heavy hanging lower jaw, and a pair of
sleepy boiled fish eyes, that stared vacantly out in sheepish
wonder upon a hopelessly dull and blank creation.

Mr. Hawthorn moved courteously to the gate to meet
them. 'It's a long pull and a steep pull up the hill, Mr.
Dupuy,' he said as he shook hands with him. ' Let me
take your pony round to the stables.—Here, Jo ! ' to a
negro boy who stood showing his white teeth beside the
gateway ; 'put up Mr. Dupuy's horse, do you hear, my
lad, and Mr. Tom's too, will you ?—How are you, Mr.
Tom ? So you've come over with your uncle as well, to
see this stock I want to sell, have you ? '

The elder Dupuy bowed politely as Mr. Hawthorn held
out his hand, and took it with something of the dignified
old West Indian courtesy ; he had been to school at Win-
chester forty years before, and the remote result of that
half-forgotten old English training was still plainly visible
even now in a certain outer urbanity and suavity of demeanour. But young Tom held out his hand awkwardly
like a born boor, and dropped it again snappishly as soon
as Mr. Hawthorn had taken it, merely answering, in ·a
slow, drawling West Indian voice, partly caught from his
own negro servants : 'Yes, I've come over to see the
stock ; we want some oxen. Cane's good this season ; we
shall have a capital cutting.'

'Is the English mail in ? ' Mr. Hawthorn asked
anxiously, as they took their seats in the piazza to rest
themselves for a while after their ride, before proceeding
to active business. That one solitary fortnightly channel
of communication with the outer world assumes an importance in the eyes of remote colonists which can hardly
even be comprehended by our bustling, stay-at-home
English people.

'It is,' Mr. Dupuy replied, taking the proffered glass
of Madeira from his host as he answered. Old-fashioned
wine-drinking hospitality still prevails largely in the West
Indies. 'I got my letters just as I was starting. Yours
will be here before long, I don't doubt, Mr. Hawthorn. I
had news, important news, in my budget this morning,

My daughter, sir, my daughter Nora, who has been completing her education in England, is coming out to
Trinidad by the next steamer.'

'You must be delighted at the prospect of seeing her,'
Mr. Hawthorn answered with a slight sigh. ' I only wish
I were going as soon to see my dear boy Edward.'

Mr. Dupuy's lip curled faintly as he replied in a careless manner : ' Ah, yes, to be sure. Your boy's in England,
Mr. Hawthorn, isn't he ? If I recollect right, you sent
him to Cambridge.—Ah, yes, I thought so, to Cambridge.
A very excellent thing for you to do with him. If you
take my advice, my dear sir, you'll let him stop in the old
country—a much better place for him in every way than
this island.'

' I mean to,' Mr. Hawthorn answered in a low voice.
' God forbid that I should ever be a party to bringing him
out here to Trinidad.'

' Oh, certainly not—certainly not. I quite agree with
you. Far better for him to stop where he is, and take his
chance of making a living for himself in England. Not
that he can be at any loss in that matter either. You must
be in a position to make him very comfortable too, Mr.
Hawthorn ! Fine estate, Agualta, and turns out a capital
brand of rum and sugar.'

' Best vacuum-pan and centrifugal in the whole island,'
Tom Dupuy put in parenthetically. ' Turned out four
hundred and thirty-four hogsheads of sugar and three
hundred and ninety puncheons of rum last season—largest
yield of any estate in the Windward Islands, except Mount
Arlington. You don't catch me out of it in any matter
where sugar's in question, I can tell you.'

' But my daughter, Mr. Hawthorn,' the elder Dupuy
went on, smiling, and sipping his Madeira in a leisurely
fashion—' my daughter means to come out to join me by
the next steamer ; and my nephew Tom and I are naturally looking forward to her approaching arrival with the
greatest anxiety. A young lady in Miss Dupuy's position,
I need hardly say to you, who has been finishing her
education at a good school in England, comes out to
Trinidad under exceptionally favourable circumstances,

She will have much here to interest her in society, and we hope she will enjoy herself and make herself happy.'

'For my part,' Tom Dupuy put in brusquely, 'I don't hold at all with this sending young women from Trinidad across the water to get educated in England—not a bit of it. What's the good of it ?—that's what I always want to know—what's the good of it ? What do they pick up there, I should like to hear, except a lot of trumpery Radical fal-lal, that turns their heads, and fills them brimful of all sorts of romantic topsy-turvy notions ? I've never been to England myself, thank goodness, and what's more, I don't ever want to go, that's certain. But I've known lots of fellows that have been, and have spent a deuce of a heap of money over their education too, at one place or another—I don't even know the names of 'em— and when they've come back, so far as I could see, they've never known a bit more about rum or sugar than other fellows that had never set foot for a single minute outside the island—no, nor for that matter, not so much either. Of course, it's all very well for a person in your son's position, Mr. Hawthorn ; that's quite another matter. He's gone to England, and he's going to stay there. If I were he, I should do as he does. But what on earth can be the use of sending a girl in my cousin Nora's station in life over to England, just on purpose to set her against her own flesh and blood and her own people ? Why, it really passes my comprehension.'

Mr. Dupuy's forehead puckered slightly as Tom spoke, and the corners of his mouth twitched ominously ; but he answered in a tone of affected nonchalance : 'It's a pity, Mr. Hawthorn, that my nephew Tom should take this unfavourable view of an English education, because, you see, it's our intention, as soon as my daughter, Miss Dupuy, arrives from England, to arrange a marriage at a very early date between himself and his cousin Nora. Pimento Valley, as you know, is entailed in the male line to my nephew Tom ; and Orange Grove is in my own disposal, to leave, of course, to my only daughter. But Mr. Tom Dupuy and I both think it would be a great pity that the family estates should be divided, and should in part pass out of the family ;

so we've arranged between us that Mr. Tom is to marry
my daughter Nora, and that Orange Grove and Pimento
Valley are to pass together to their children's children.'

' An excellent arrangement,' Mr. Hawthorn put in, with
a slight smile. ' But suppose—just for argument's sake—
that Miss Dupuy were not to fall in with it ? '

Mr. Dupuy's brow clouded over still more evidently.
' Not to fall in with it ! ' he cried excitedly, tossing off the
remainder of his Madeira—' not to fall in with it !—not to
fall in with it ! Why, Mr. Hawthorn, what the dickens do
you mean, sir ? Of course, if her father bids her, she'll
fall in with it immediately. If she doesn't—why, then, by
Jove, sir, I'll just simply have to make her. She shall
marry Tom Dupuy the minute I order her to. She
should marry a one-eyed man with a wooden leg if her
father commanded it. She shall do whatever I tell her.
I'll stand no refusing and shilly-shallying. By George,
sir, if there's a vice that I hate and detest, it's the vice
of obstinacy. I'll stand no obstinacy, and that I can tell
you.'

' No obstinacy in those about you,' Mr. Hawthorn put
in suggestively.

' By Jove, sir, no—not in those about me. Other
people, of course, I can't be answerable for, though I'd
like to flog every obstinate fellow I come across, just to
cure him of his confounded temper. Oh no; I'll stand
no obstinacy. Why, sir, I'll tell you what I once did with
a horse of mine which had an obstinate temper. I put
him at a cactus hedge, over in Pimento Valley, and the
brute was afraid of the spines, and wouldn't face it. Well,
I wasn't going to stand that, of course ; so I dug the spur
into his side and put him at it again ; and again he refused
it. I tried a third time, and a third time the brute hesitated. That put my blood up, and I dug the spurs in
again and again, and rode him at it full tilt till his sides
were all raw and bleeding. But still the frightened brute
was too much afraid of it ever to jump it. " By the
powers," said I, "if I stop here all day, my friend, I'll
make you jump it, or you'll never go back again alive to
your confounded stable." Well, I put him at it again and

2

again for more than two hours; and then I saw he'd made up his mind that he wouldn't do it. Of course, I wasn't going to stand any such confounded obstinacy as that; so I got off, tied him deliberately to the biggest cactus, whipped him until he'd cut his legs all to pieces, dashing up against it, and then took out my horse-pistol and shot him dead immediately on the spot. That's what I did with him, Mr. Hawthorn. Oh no, sir; I can't endure obstinacy—in man or beast, I can't endure it.'

'So it would seem,' Mr. Hawthorn replied dryly. 'I hope sincerely, Miss Dupuy will find the choice you have made for her a suitable and satisfactory one.'

'Suitable, sir ! Why, of course it's suitable ; and as to satisfactory, well, if I say she's got to take him, she'll have to be satisfied with him, willy-nilly.'

'But she won't ! ' Tom Dupuy interrupted sullenly, flicking his boot with his short riding-whip in a vicious fashion. 'She won't, you may take my word for it, Uncle Theodore. I can't imagine why it is; but these young women who've been educated in England, they'll never be satisfied with a planter for a husband. They think a gentleman and a son of gentlemen for fifty generations isn't a good enough match for such fine ladies as themselves; and they go running off after some of these red-coated military fellows down in the garrison over yonder, many of whom, to my certain knowledge, Mr. Hawthorn, are nothing more than the sons of tailors across there in England. I'll bet you a sovereign, Uncle Theodore, that Nora'll refuse to so much as look at the heir of Pimento Valley, the minute she sees him.'

'But why do you think so, Mr. Tom,' their host put in, 'before the young lady has even made your acquaintance?'

'Ah, I know well enough,' Tom Dupuy answered, with a curious leer of unintelligent cunning. 'I know the ways and the habits of the women. They go away over there to England; they get themselves crammed with French and German, and music and drawing, and all kinds of unnecessary accomplishments. They pick up a lot of nonsensical new-fangled Radical notions about Am I not a Man and a Brother ? and all that kind of Methody humbug.

They think an awful lot of themselves because they can
play and sing and gabble Italian. And they despise us
West Indians, gentlemen and planters, because we can't
parley-voo all their precious foreign lingoes, and don't
know as much as they do about who composed *Yankee
Doodle*. I know them—I know them; I know their ways
and their manners. Culture, they call it. I call it a
deuced lot of trumpery nonsense. Why, Mr. Hawthorn,
I assure you I've known some of these fine new-fangled
English-taught young women who'd sooner talk to a
coloured doctor, as black as a common nigger almost, just
because he'd been educated at Oxford, or Edinburgh, or
somewhere, than to me myself, the tenth Dupuy in lineal
succession at Pimento Valley.'

'Indeed,' Mr. Hawthorn answered innocently—no other
alternative phrase committing him, as he thought, to so
small an opinion on the merits of the question.—'But
do you know, Mr. Tom, I don't believe any person of
the Dupuy blood is very likely to take up with these
strange modern English heresies that so much surprise
you.'

'Quite true, sir,' Mr. Dupuy the elder answered with
prompt self-satisfaction, mistaking his host's delicate tone
of covert satire for the voice of hearty concurrence and
full approval. 'You're quite right there, Mr. Hawthorn,
I'm certain. No born Dupuy of Orange Grove would ever
be taken in by any of that silly clap-trap humanitarian rubbish. No foolish Exeter Hall nonsense about the fighting
Dupuys, sir, I can assure you—root and branch, not a
single ounce of it. It isn't in them, Mr. Hawthorn—it
isn't in them.'

'So I think,' Mr. Hawthorn answered quietly. 'I
quite agree with you—it isn't in them.'

As he spoke, a negro servant, neatly dressed in a cool
white linen livery, entered the piazza with a small budget
of letters on an old-fashioned Spanish silver salver. Mr.
Hawthorn took them up eagerly. 'The English mail!'
he said with an apologetic glance towards his two guests.
'You'll excuse my just glancing through them, Mr. Dupuy,
won't you? I can never rest, the moment the mail's in,

until I know that my dear boy in England is still really
well and happy.'

Mr. Dupuy nodded assent with a condescending smile :
and the master of Agualta broke open his son's envelope
with a little eager hasty flutter.   He ran his eye hurriedly
down the first page ; and then, with a sudden cry, he laid
down the letter rapidly on the table, and called out aloud :
' Mary, Mary ! '

Mrs. Hawthorn came out at once from the little boudoir
behind the piazza, whose cool Venetian blinds gave directly
upon the part where they were sitting.

' Mary, Mary ! ' Mr. Hawthorn cried, utterly regardless
of his two visitors' presence, ' what on earth do you think
has happened ?   Edward is coming out to us—coming out
immediately.   Oh, my poor boy, my poor boy, this is too
unexpected !   He's coming out to us at once, at once,
without a single moment's warning ! '

Mrs. Hawthorn took up the letter and read it through
hastily with a woman's quickness ; then she laid it down
again, and looked blankly at her trembling husband in
evident distress ; but neither of them said a single word to
one another.

The elder Dupuy was the first to break the ominous
silence. ' Not by the next steamer, I suppose ? ' he inquired
curiously.

Mr. Hawthorn nodded in reply.   ' Yes, yes ; by the
next steamer.'

As he spoke, Tom Dupuy glanced at his uncle with a
meaning glance, and then went on stolidly as ever : ' How
about these cattle, though, Mr. Hawthorn ? '

The old man looked back at him half angrily, half contemptuously.   ' Go and look at the cattle yourself, if you
like, Mr. Tom,' he said haughtily.—' Here, Jo, you take
young Mr. Dupuy round to see those Cuban bullocks in
the grass-piece, will you !   I shall meet your uncle at the
Legislative Council on Thursday, and then, if he likes, he
can talk over prices with me.   I have something else to do
at present beside haggling and debating over the sale of
bullocks ; I must go down to Port-of-Spain immediately,
immediately—this very minute.   You must please excuse

me, Mr. Dupuy, for my business is most important. Dick,
Isaac, Thomas !—some one of you there, get Pride of Barbadoes saddled at once, very fast, will you, and bring her
round here to me at the front-door the moment she's ready.'

' And Tom,' the elder Dupuy whispered to his nephew
confidentially, as soon as their host had gone back into the
house to prepare for his journey, ' I have business, too,
in Port-of-Spain, immediately. You go and look at the
bullocks if you like—that's your department. I shall ride
down the hills at once, and into town with old Hawthorn.'

Tom looked at him with a vacant stare of boorish un-
intelligence. ' Why, what do you want to go running off
like that for,' he asked, open-mouthed, ' without even
waiting to see the cattle ? What the dickens does it matter
to you, I should like to know, whether old Hawthorn's
precious son is coming to Trinidad or not, Uncle Theodore?'

The uncle looked back at him with undisguised contempt. ' Why, you fool, Tom,' he answered quietly, ' you
don't suppose I want to let Nora come out alone all the
way from England to Trinidad in the very same steamer
with that man Hawthorn's son Edward ? Impossible,
impossible !—Here, you nigger fellow you, grinning over
there at me like a chattering monkey, bring my mare out
of the stable at once, sir, will you—do you hear me,
image ?—for I'm going to ride down direct to Port-of-
Spain this very minute along with your master. Hurry
up, there, jackanapes ! '

CHAPTER V.

THE letter from Edward that had so greatly perturbed old
Mr. Hawthorn had been written, of course, some twenty
days before he received it, for the mail takes about that
time, as a rule, in going from Southampton across the
Atlantic to the port of Trinidad. Edward had already
told his father of his long-standing engagement to Marian ;
but the announcement and acceptance of the district judgeship had been so hurried, and the date fixed for his de-

parture was so extremely early, that he had only just had time by the first mail to let his father know of his approaching marriage, and his determination to proceed at once to the West Indies by the succeeding steamer. Three weeks was all the interval allowed him by the inexorable red-tape department of the Colonial Office for completing his hasty preparations for his marriage, and setting sail to undertake his newly acquired judicial functions.

'Three weeks, my dear,' Nora cried in despair to Marian ; 'why, you know, it can't possibly be done ! It's simply impracticable. Do those horrid government-office people really imagine a girl can get together a trousseau, and have all the bridesmaids' dresses made, and see about the house and the breakfast, and all that sort of thing, and get herself comfortably married, all within a single fortnight ? They're just like all men ; they think you can do things in less than no time. It's absolutely preposterous.'

'Perhaps,' Marian answered, 'the government-office people would say they engaged Edward to take a district judgeship, and didn't stipulate anything about his getting married before he went out to Trinidad to take it.'

'Oh, well, you know, if you choose to look at it in that way, of course one can't reasonably grumble at them for their absurd hurrying. But still, the horrid creatures ought to have a little consideration for a girl's convenience. Why, we shall have to make up our minds at once, without the least proper deliberation, what the bridesmaids' dresses are to be, and begin having them cut out and the trimmings settled this very morning. A wedding at a fortnight's notice ! I never in my life heard of such a thing. I wonder, for my part, your mamma consents to it.—Well, well, I shall have you to take charge of me going out, that's one comfort ; and I shall have my bridesmaid's dress made so that I can wear it a little altered, and cut square in the bodice, when I get to Trinidad, for a best dinner dress. But it's really awfully horrid having to make all one's preparations for the wedding and for going out in such a terrible unexpected hurry.'

However, in spite of Nora, the preparations for the wedding were duly made within the appointed fortnight, even that important item of the bridesmaids' dresses being quickly settled to everybody's satisfaction. Strange that when two human beings propose entering into a solemn contract together for the future governance of their entire joint existence, the thoughts of one of them, and that the one to whom the change is most infinitely important, should be largely taken up for some weeks beforehand with the particular clothes she is to wear on the morning when the contract is publicly ratified! Fancy the ambassador who signs the treaty being mainly occupied for the ten days of the preliminary negotiations with deciding what sort of uniform and how many orders he shall put on upon the eventful day of the final signature!

At the end of that short hurry-scurrying fortnight, the wedding actually took place; and an advertisement in the *Times* next morning duly announced among the list of marriages, 'At Holy Trinity, Brompton, by the Venerable Archdeacon Ord, uncle of the bride, assisted by the Rev. Augustus Savile, B.D., EDWARD BERESFORD HAWTHORN, M.A., Barrister-at-law, of the Inner Temple, late Fellow of St. Catherine's College, Cambridge, and District Judge of the Westmoreland District, Trinidad, to MARIAN ARBUTH-NOT, only daughter of General O. S. Ord, C.I.E., formerly of the H.E.I.C. Bengal Infantry.' 'The bride's toilet,' said *The Queen*, next Saturday, 'consisted of white broché satin de Lyon, draped with deep lace flounces, caught up with orange blossoms. The veil was of tulle, secured to the hair with a pearl crescent and stars. The bouquet was composed of rare exotics.' In fact, to the coarse and undiscriminating male intelligence, the whole attire, on which so much pains and thought had been hurriedly bestowed, does not appear to have differed in any respect whatsoever from that of all the other brides one has ever looked at during the entire course of a reasonably long and varied lifetime.

After the wedding, however, Marian and Edward could only afford a single week by way of a honeymoon, in that most overrun by brides and bridegrooms of all English districts, the Isle of Wight, as being nearest within call of Southampton, whence they had to start on their long ocean voyage. The aunt in charge was to send down Nora to meet them at the hotel the day before the steamer sailed; and the General and Mrs. Ord were to see them off, and say a long good-bye to them on the morning of sailing.

Harry Noel, too, who had been best-man at the wedding, for some reason most fully known to himself, professed a vast desire to ' see the last of poor Hawthorn,' before he left for parts unknown in the Caribbean; and with that intent, duly presented himself at a Southampton hotel on the day before their final departure. It was not purely by accident, however, either on his own part or on Marian Hawthorn's, that when they took a quiet walk that evening in some fields behind the battery, he found himself a little in front with Nora Dupuy, while the newly-married pair, as was only proper, brought up the rear in a conjugal *tête-à-tête.*

' Miss Dupuy,' Harry said suddenly, as they reached an open space in the fields, with a clear view uninterrupted before them, ' there's something I wish to say to you before you leave for Trinidad—something a little premature, per-haps, but under the circumstances—as you're leaving so soon—I can't delay it. I've seen very little of you, as yet, Miss Dupuy, and you've seen very little of me, so I dare say I owe you some apology for this strange precipitancy; but—— Well, you're going away at once from England; and I may not see you again for—for some months ; and if I allow you to go without having spoken to you, why——'

Nora's heart throbbed violently. She didn't care very much for Harry Noel at first sight, to be sure; but still, she had never till now had a regular offer of marriage made to her; and every woman's heart beats naturally—I be-lieve—when she finds herself within measurable distance of her first offer. Besides, Harry was the heir to a baronetcy, and a great catch, as most girls counted; and even if you don't want to marry a baronet, it's something at least to be able to say to yourself in future, ' I refused an offer to be Lady Noel.' Mind you, as women go, the heir to an old baronetcy and twelve thousand a year is not to be despised, though you may not care a single pin about his mere personal attractions. A great many girls who would refuse the man upon his own merits, would willingly say 'Yes' at once to the title and the income. So Nora Dupuy, who was, after all, quite as human as most other girls—if not rather more so—merely held her breath hard, and tried her best to still the beating of her wayward heart, as she answered back with childish innocence: 'Well, Mr. Noel, in that case, what would happen?'

'In that case, Miss Dupuy,' Harry replied, looking at her pretty little pursed-up guileless mouth with a hungry desire to kiss it incontinently then and there—'why, in that case, I'm afraid some other man—some handsome young Trinidad planter or other—might carry off the prize on his own account before I had ventured to put in my humble claim for it.—Miss Dupuy, what's the use of beating about the bush, when I see by your eyes you know what I mean? From the moment I first saw you, I said to myself, "She's the one woman I have ever seen whom I feel instinctively I could worship for a lifetime." Answer me Yes. I'm no speaker. But I love you. Will you take me?'

Nora twisted the tassel of her parasol nervously between her finger and thumb for a few seconds; then she looked back at him full in the face with her pretty girlish open eyes, and answered with charming naïveté—just as if he had merely asked her whether she would take another cup of tea: 'No, thank you, Mr. Noel; I don't think so.'

Harry Noel smiled with amusement—in spite of this curt and simple rejection—at the oddity of such a reply to such a question. 'Of course,' he said, glancing down at her pretty little feet to hide his confusion, 'I didn't expect you to answer me *Yes* at once on so very short an acquaintance as ours has been. I acknowledge it's dreadfully presumptuous in me to have dared to put you a question like that, when I know you can have seen so very little in me to make me worth the honour you'd be bestowing upon me.'

'Quite so,' Nora murmured mischievously, in a parenthetical undertone. It wasn't kind; I dare say it wasn't even lady-like; but then you see she was really, after all, only a school-girl.

Harry paused, half abashed for a second at this very literal acceptance of his conventional expression of self-

depreciation. He hardly knew whether it was worth while
continuing his suit in the face of such exceedingly outspoken
discouragement. Still, he had something to say, and he
determined to say it. He was really very much in love
with Nora, and he wasn't going to lose his chance outright
just for the sake of what might be nothing more than
a pretty girl's provoking coyness.

'Yes,' he went on quietly, without seeming to notice
her little interruption, 'though you haven't yet seen anything in me to care for, I'm going to ask you, not whether
you'll give me any definite promise—it was foolish of me
to expect one on so brief an acquaintance—but whether
you'll kindly bear in mind that I've told you I love you—
yes, I said love you'—for Nora had dashed her little hand
aside impatiently at the word. 'And remember, I shall
still hope, until I see you again, you may yet in future reconsider the question. Don't make me any promise, Miss
Dupuy; and don't repeat the answer you've already given
me; but when you go to Trinidad, and are admired and
courted as you needs must be, don't wholly forget that
someone in England once told you he loved you—loved you
passionately.'

'I'm not likely to forget it, Mr. Noel,' Nora answered
with malicious calmness; 'because nobody ever proposed
to me before, you know; and one's sure not to forget one's
first offer.'

'Miss Dupuy, you are making game of me! It isn't
right of you—it isn't generous.'

Nora paused and looked at him again. He was dark,
but very handsome. He looked handsomer still when he
bridled up a little. It was a very nice thing to look forward
to being Lady Noel. How all the other girls at school
would have just jumped at it! But no; he was too dark
by half to meet her fancy. She couldn't give him the
slightest encouragement. 'Mr. Noel,' she said, far more
seriously this time, with a little sigh of impatience, 'believe
me, I didn't really mean to offend you. I—I like you very
much; and I'm sure I'm very much flattered indeed by
what you've just been kind enough to say to me. I know
it's a great honour for you to ask me to—to ask me what

you have asked me. But, you know, I don't think of you in that light, exactly. You will understand what I mean when I say I can't even leave the question open. I—I have nothing to reconsider.'

Harry waited a moment in internal reflection. He liked her all the better because she said *No* to him. He was man of the world enough to know that ninety-nine girls out of a hundred would have jumped at once at such an eligible offer. 'In a few months,' he said quietly, in an abstracted fashion, 'I shall be paying a visit out in Trinidad.'

'Oh, don't, pray don't,' Nora cried hastily. 'It'll be no use, Mr. Noel, no use in any way. I've quite made up my mind; and I never change it. Don't come out to Trinidad, I beg of you.'

'I see,' Harry said, smiling a little bitterly. 'Someone else has been beforehand with me already. No wonder. I'm not at all surprised at him. How could he possibly see you and help it?' And he looked with unmistakable admiration at Nora's face, all the prettier now for its deep blushes.

'No, Mr. Noel,' Nora answered simply. 'There you are mistaken. There's nobody—absolutely nobody. I've only just left school, you know, and I've seen no one so far that I care for in any way.'

'In that case,' Harry Noel said, in his decided manner, 'the quest will still be worth pursuing. No matter what you say, Miss Dupuy, we shall meet again—before long—in Trinidad. A young lady who has just left school has plenty of time still to reconsider her determinations.'

'Mr. Noel! Please, don't! It'll be quite useless.'

'I must, Miss Dupuy; I can't help myself. You will draw me after you, even if I tried to prevent it. I believe I have had one real passion in my life, and that passion will act upon me like a magnet on a needle for ever after. I shall go to Trinidad.'

'At any rate, then, you'll remember that I gave you no encouragement, and that for me, at least, my answer is final.'

'I *will* remember, Miss Dupuy—and I won't believe it.'

That evening, as Marian kissed Nora good-night in her own bedroom at the Southampton hotel, she asked archly: ' Well, Nora, what did you answer him ? '

'Answer who ? what ? ' Nora repeated hastily, trying to look as if she didn't understand the suppressed antecedent of the personal pronoun.

' My dear girl, it isn't the least use your pretending you don't know what I mean by it. I saw in your face, Nora, when Edward and I caught you up, what it was Mr. Noel had been saying to you. And how did you answer him ? Tell me, Nora ! '

' I told him *No*, Marian, quite positively.'

' Oh, Nora ! '

' Yes, I did. And he said he'd follow me out to Trinidad ; and I told him he really needn't take the trouble, because in any case I could never care for him.'

' O dear, I *am* so sorry. You wicked girl ! And, Nora, he's such a nice fellow too ! and so dreadfully in love with you ! You ought to have taken him.'

' My dear Marian ! He's so awfully black, you know. I really believe he must positively be a little coloured.'

CHAPTER VI.

THE three weeks' difference in practical time between England and the West Indies, due to the mail, made the day that Edward and Marian spent at Southampton exactly coincide with the one when Mr. Dupuy and his nephew Tom went up to view old Mr. Hawthorn's cattle at Agualta Estate, Trinidad. On that very same evening, while Nora and Harry were walking together among the fields behind the battery, Mr. Tom Dupuy was strolling leisurely by himself in the cool dusk, four thousand miles away, on one of the innumerable shady bridle-paths that thread the endless tangled hills above Pimento Valley. Mr. Tom was smoking a very big Manila cheroot, and was accompanied upon his rounds by a huge and ferocious-looking Cuban bloodhound, the hungry corners of whose great greedy slobbering mouth hung down hideously on either side in loose folds of skin of the most bloodthirsty and sinister aspect. As he went along, Tom Dupuy kept patting affectionately from time to time his four-footed favourite, to whom, nevertheless, every now and again he applied, as it seemed out of pure wantonness, the knotted lash of the cruel dog-whip which he carried jauntily in his right hand. The dog, however, formidable as he was, so far from resenting this unkindly treatment, appeared to find in it something exceedingly congenial to his own proper barbarous nature ; for after each such savage cut upon his bare flanks from the knotted hide, he only cowered for a second, and then fawned the more closely and slavishly than ever upon his smiling master, looking up into his face with a strange approving glance from his dull eyes, that seemed to say : ' Exactly the sort of thing I should do myself, if you were the dog, and I were the whipholder.'

At a bend of the path, where the road turned suddenly aside to cross the dry bed of a winter torrent, Tom Dupuy came upon a clump of tall cabbage palms, hard by a low mud-built negro-hut, overshadowed in front by two or three huge flowering bushes of crimson hibiscus. A tall, spare, grey-headed negro, in a coarse sack by way of a shirt, with his bare and sinewy arms thrust loosely through the long slits which alone did duty in the place of sleeve-holes, was leaning as he passed upon a wooden post. The bloodhound, breaking away suddenly from his master, at sight and smell of the black skin, its natural prey, rushed up fiercely towards the old labourer, and leapt upon him with a savage snarl of his big teeth, and an ominous glittering in his great fishy glazed eyeball. But the negro, stronger and more muscular than he looked, instead of flinching, caught the huge brute in his long lean arms, and flung him from him by main force with an angry oath, dashing his great form heavily against the rough pathway. Quick as lightning, the dog, leaping up again at once with diabolical energy in its big flabby mouth, was just about to spring once more upon his scowling opponent, when Tom Dupuy, catching him angrily by his leather collar, threw him down and held him back, growling fiercely, and showing his huge tearing teeth in a ferocious grin, after the wonted manner of his deadly kind. ' Quiet, Slot, quiet ! ' the master said, patting his hollow forehead with affectionate admiration. ' Quiet, sir; down this minute! Down, I tell you !—He's death on niggers, Delgado—death on niggers. You should stand out of the way, you know, when you see him coming. Of course these dogs never can abide the scent of you black fellows. The *bookay d'Afreek* always drives a bloodhound frantic.'

The old negro drew himself up haughtily and sternly, and stared back in the insolent face of the slouching young white man with a proud air of native dignity. ' Buckra gentleman hab no right, den, to go about wid dem dog,' he answered angrily, fixing his piercing fiery eye on the bloodhound's face. ' Dem dog always spring at a black man wherebber dey find him. If you want to keep dem, you should keep dem tied up at de house, so as to do for watch-dog against tievin' naygur. But you doan't got no right to bring dem about de ro-ads, loose dat way, jumpin' up at people's troats, when dem standin' peaceable beside dem own hut here.'

Tom Dupuy laughed carelessly. ' It's their nature, you see, Delgado,' he answered with a pleasant smile, still holding the dog and caressing it lovingly. ' They and their fathers were trained long ago in slavery days to hunt run-away niggers up in the mountains and track them to their hiding-places, and drag them back, alive or dead, to their lawful masters; and of course that makes them run naturally after the smell of a nigger, as a terrier runs after the smell of a rat. When the rat sees the terrier coming, he scuttles off as hard as his legs can carry him into his hole ; and when you see Slot's nose turning round the corner, you ought to scuttle off into your hut as quick as light-ning, if you want to keep your black skin whole upon your infernal body. Slot never can abide the smell of a nigger. —Can you, Slot, eh, old fellow ? '

The negro looked at him with unconcealed aversion. ' I is not a rat, Mistah Dupuy,' he said haughtily. ' I is gentleman myself, same as you is, sah, when I come here over from Africa.'

Tom Dupuy sneered openly in his very face. 'That's the way with all you Africans,' he answered with a laugh, as he flipped the ash idly from his big cheroot. 'I never knew an imported nigger yet, since I was born, that wasn't a king in his own country. Seems to me they must all be kings over yonder in Congo, with never a solitary subject to divide between them.—But I say, my friend, what's going on over this way to-night, that so many niggers are going up all the time to the Methody chapel? Are you going to preach 'em a missionary sermon?'

Delgado glanced at him a trifle suspiciously. 'Dar is a prayer-meetin', sah,' he said with a cold look in his angry eye, 'up at Gilead. De bredderin gwine to meet dis ebenin'.'

'Ho, ho; so that's it! A prayer-meeting, is it? Well, if I go up there, will you let me attend it?'

Delgado's thick lip curled contemptuously, as he answered with a frown: 'When cockroach gib dance, him no ax fowl!'

'Ah, I see. The fowl would eat the cockroaches, would he? Well, then, Louis Delgado, I give you fair warning; if you don't want a white man to go and look on at your confounded Methody nigger prayer-meetings, depend upon it it's because you're brewing some mischief or other up there against the constituted authorities. I shall tell my uncle to set his police to look well after you. You're always a bad-blooded, discontented, disaffected fellow, and I believe now you're up to some of ycur African devilry or other. No obeah, mind you, Delgado—no obeah! Prayer-meetings, my good friend, as much as you like; but whatever you do, no obeah.'

'You tink I do obeah because I doan't will let you go to prayer-meetin'! Dat just like white-man argument. Him tink de naygur can nebber be in de right. Old-time folk has little proverb: "Mountain sheep always guilty when jungle tiger sit to judge him."'

Tom Dupuy laughed and nodded. 'If the sheep in Africa are black sheep,' he retorted clumsily, 'I dare say they're a beastly lot of thieving trespassers.—Good-night, my friend.—Down, Slot, down, good fellow; down, down,

down, I tell you!—Good-night, Louis Delgado, and whatever you do, no obeah!'

The negro watched him slowly round the corner, with
a suspicious eye kept well fixed upon the reluctant stealthy
retreat of the Cuban bloodhound; and as soon as Tom
had got safely beyond earshot, he sat down in the soft dust
that formed the bare platform outside his hut, and mumbled to himself, as negroes will do, a loud dramatic soliloquy, in every deep and varying tone of passion and
hatred. 'Ha, ha, Mistah Tom Dupuy,' he began quietly,
'so you go about always wid de Cuban bloodhound, an'
you laugh to see him spring at de troat ob de black man!
You tink dat frighten him from come steal your cane an'
your mangoes! You tink de black man afraid ob de dog,
yarra! yarra! Ha, dat frighten Trinidad naygur, perhaps,
but it doan't frighten salt-water naygur from Africa! I
hab charms, I hab potion, I hab draught to quiet him!
I doan't afraid ob fifty bloodhound. But it doan't good
for buckra gentleman to walk about wid dog that spring at
de black man. Black man laugh to-day, perhaps, but
press him heart tight widin him. De time come when
black man will find him heart break out, an' de hate in it
flow over an' make blood run like dry ribber in de rainy
season. Den him sweep away buckra, an' bloodhound, an'
all before him; an' seize de country, colour for colour.
De land is black, an' de land for de black man. When de
black man burst him heart like ribber burst him bank in
de rainy season, white man's house snap off before him
like bamboo hut when de flood catch it!' As he spoke,
he pushed his hands out expansively before him, and
gurgled in his throat with fierce inarticulate African gutturals, that seemed to recall in some strange fashion the
hollow eddying roar and gurgle of the mountain torrents
in the rainy season.

'Chicken doan't nebber lub jackal, yarra,' he went on
after a short pause of expectant triumph; 'an' naygur
doan't nebber lub buckra, dat certain. But ob all de
buckra in de island ob Trinidad, dem Dupuy is de very
worst an' de very contemptfullest. Some day, black man
will rise, an' get rid ob dem all for good an' ebber. If I

like, I can kill dem all to-day; but I gwine to wait. De great an' terrible day ob de Lard is not come yet. Missy Dupuy ober in England, where de buckra come from. England is de white man's Africa; de missy dar to learn him catechism. I wait till Missy Dupuy come back before I kill de whole family. When de great an' terrible day ob de Lard arrive, I doan't leave a single Dupuy a libbin soul in de island ob Trinidad. Utterly destroy de Amalekite, sait' de Lard, and spare dem not; but slay bot' man an' woman, infant an' suckling, ox an' sheep, ass an' camel. When I slay dem, I slay dem utterly. De curse ob Saul dat spared Agag shall nebber fall upon Louis Delgado. I slay dem all, an' de missy wid them, yarra, yarra!'

The last two almost inarticulate words were uttered with a horrible yell of triumph; and as Louis Delgado uttered them shrilly, he drew the fingers of his right hand with a savage joy across his bared and upturned neck, and accompanied that hideously significant action with a hissing noise of his breath, puffed out suddenly with an explosive burst between his white and closely-pressed teeth. After a minute he went on again; but this time hearing footsteps approaching, he broke out into a loud and horrible soliloquy of exultation in his own native African language. It was a deep, savage-sounding West Coast dialect, full of harsh and barbaric clicks or gutturals; for Louis Delgado, as Tom Dupuy had rightly said, was 'an imported African' —a Coromantyn, sold as a slave some thirty years before to a Cuban slave trader trying to break the blockade on the coast, and captured with all her living cargo by an English cruiser off Sombrero Island. The liberated slaves had been landed, according to custom, at the first British port where the cutter touched; and thus Louis Delgado— as he learned to call himself—a wild African born, from the Coromantyn seaboard, partially Anglicised and outwardly Christianised, was now a common West Indian plantation hand on the two estates of Orange Grove and Pimento Valley. There are dozens of such semi-civilised imported negroes still to be found under similar circumstances in every one of the West India islands.

As the steps gradually approached nearer, it became

plain, from the soft footfall in the dust of the bridle-path, that it was a shoeless black person who was coming towards him. In a minute more, the new-comer had turned the corner, and displayed herself as a young and comely negress—pretty with the round, good-humoured African prettiness of smooth black skin, plump cheeks, clear eyes, and regular, even pearl-white teeth. The girl was dressed in a loose Manchester cotton print, brightly coloured, and not unbecoming, with a tidy red bandana bound turban-wise around her shapely head, but barefooted, barelegged, and bare of arm, neck, and shoulder. Her figure was good, as the figure of most negresses usually is; and she held herself erect and upright with the peculiar lithe gracefulness said to be induced by the universal practice of carrying pails of water and other burdens on the top of the head, from the very earliest days of negro childhood. As she approached Delgado, she first smiled and showed all her pretty teeth, as she uttered the customary polite salutation of 'Marnin'! sah, marnin'!' and then dropped a profound curtsy with an unmistakable air of awe and reverence.

Louis Delgado affected not to observe the girl for a moment, and went on jabbering loudly and fiercely to himself in his swift and fluent African jargon. But it was evident that his hearer was deeply impressed at once by this rapt and prophetic inattention of the strange negro, who spoke with tongues to vacant space in such an awful and intensely realistic fashion. She paused for a while and looked at him intently; then, when he stopped for a second to take breath in the midst of one of his passionate incoherent outbursts, she came a step nearer to him and curtsied again, at the same time that she muttered in a rather injured querulous treble: 'Mistah Delgado, you no hear me, sah? You no listen to me? I tellin' you marnin'.'

The old man broke off suddenly, as if recalled to himself and common earth by some disenchanting touch, and answered dreamily: 'Marnin', Missy Rosina. Marnin', le-ady. You gwine up to Gilead now to de prayer-meetin'?

Rosina, glancing down at the Bible and hymn-book in her plump black hand, answered demurely: ' Yes, sah, I gwine dar.'

Delgado shook himself vigorously, as if in the endeavour to recover from some unearthly trance, and went on in his more natural manner: ' I gwine up too, to pray wid de bredderin. You want me for someting? You callin' to me for help you?'

Rosina dropped her voice a little as she replied in her shrill tone: ' Dem say you is African, Mistah Delgado. Naygur from Africa know plenty spell for bring back le-ady's lubber.'

Delgado nodded. ' Dem say true,' he answered. ' Creole [1] naygur doan't can make spell same as African. Coromantyn naygur hab plenty oracle, like de ephod ob de high-pries' dat de word ob de Lard command to Aaron. De oracles ob Aaron descend in right line to de chiefs ob de Coromantyn. Kwámina atinásu Koromantini marrah osráman etchwi ntwa.'

The words themselves were simple enough, being merely Fantee for, ' Here am I, Kwámina the Coromantyn, with my thunder-stones that cool the heart;' but they struck the Creole-born negress with a certain mute awe and terror, after which she hardly dared for a moment to open her mouth. As soon as she found her tongue again, she muttered softly: ' Dem say you is great chief in your own country.'

The old man drew himself up with a haughty air. ' Me fader,' he answered with evident pride, ' hab twelve wives, all princess, an' I is de eldest son ob de eldest. King Blay fight him, an' take me prisoner, an' sell me slabe, an' dat is how I come to work now ober here on Mistah Dupuy plantation. But by birt', I is prince, an' descendant ob Eleazar, de son ob Aaron, de high-pries' ob Israel.'

After a pause, he asked quickly: ' Who dis lubber dat you want spell for?'

[1] The word *Creole* is much misunderstood by most English people. In its universal West Indian sense it is applied to any person, white, black, or mulatto, born in the West Indies, as opposed to outsiders, European, American, or African.

'Isaac Pourtalès.'

'Pourtalès! Him mulatto! What for pretty naygur girl like you want to go an' lub mulatto? Mulatto bad man. Old-time folk say, mulatto always hate him fader an' despise him mudder. Him fader de white man, an' mulatto hate white; him mudder de black girl, an' mulatto despise black.'

Rosina hung her head down slightly on one side, and put the little finger of her left hand with artless coyness into the corner of her mouth. 'I doan't know, sah,' she said sheepishly after a short pause; 'but I feel somehow as if I lub Isaac Pourtalès.'

Delgado grinned a sinister grin. 'Very well, Missy Rosy,' he said shortly, 'I gain him lub for you. Wait here one, two, tree minute, le-ady, while I run in find me Bible.'

In a few seconds he came out again, dressed in his black coat for meeting, with a Bible and hymn-book in one hand, and a curious volume in the other, written in strange, twisted, twirligig characters, such as Rosina had never before in her life set eyes on. 'See here!' he cried, opening it wide before her; 'dat is book ob spells. Dat is African spell for gain lubber. I explain him to you '— and his hand turned rapidly over several of the brown and well-thumbed pages: 'Isaac Pourtalès, mulatto; Rosina Fleming, black le-ady; dat is de page. Hear what de spell say.' And he ran his finger line by line along the strange characters, as if translating them into his own negro English as he went. ' "Take toot' ob alligator," same as dis one '—and he produced a few alligators' teeth from his capacious pocket; ' " tie him up for a week in bag wid Savannah flower an' branch of calalue ; soak him well in shark's blood "—I gib de blood to you—" den write de name, Isaac Pourtalès, in big letter on slip ob white paper; drop it in de bag; an' burn it all togedder on a Friday ebenin', when it doan't no moon, wid fire ob manchineel wood." Dat will gain de lub of your lubber, as sure as de gospel.'

The girl listened carefully to the directions, and made Delgado repeat them three times over to her. When she

had learned them thoroughly, she said once more : ' How
much I got to pay you for dis, eh, sah ? '

' Nuffin.'

' Nuffin ? '

' No, nuffin. But you must do me favour. You is
house serbant at Orange Grove ; you must come see me
now an' den, an' tell me what go on ober in de house dar.'

' What far, sah ? '

' Doan't you ax what far ; but listen to me, le-ady. De
great an' terrible day ob de Lard will come before long,
when de wicked will be cut off from de face ob de eart',
an' we shall see de end ob de evil-doer. You read de
Prophets ? '

' I read dem some time.'

' You read de Prophet Jeremiah, what him say ?   Hear
de tex'. I read him to you. "Deliber up deir children to
de famine, an' pour out deir blood by de sword." Dat de
Lard's word for all de Dupuys ; an' when de missy come
from England, de word ob de prophecy comin' true.'

The girl shuddered, and opened wide her big eyes with
their great ring of white setting. ' How you know it de
Dupuys ? ' she asked hesitating. ' How you know it dem
de prophet 'ludin' to ? '

' How I know, Rosina Fleming ? How I know it ?
Because I can expound an' interpret de Scripture ; for
when de understandin' ob de man is enlightened, de mout'
speaketh forth wonderful tings. Listen here ; I tellin' you
de trut'. Before de missy lib a year in Trinidad, de Lard
will sweep away de whole house ob de Dupuys out ob de
land for ebber an' ebber.'

' But not de missy ? ' Rosina cried eagerly.

' Ah, de missy ! You tink when de black man rise like
tiger in him wrath, him spare de missy ! No, me fren'.
Him doan't gwine to spare her. Old-time folk has proverb : "Hungry jigger no respeck de white foot ob buckra
le-ady." De Dupuys is great people now ; puffed up wid
him pride ; look down on de black man. But dem will
drop dem bluster bime-by, as soon as deir pride is taken
out ob dem wid adversity. When trouble catch bull-dog,
den monkey breeches hab to fit him.'

Rosina turned away with a look of terror. ' **You comin'**
to prayer-meetin'?' she asked hastily. 'De bredderin
will all be waitin'.'

Delgado, recalled once more to his alternative character,
pushed away the strange volume through the door of his
hut, took up his Bible and hymn-book with the gravest
solemnity, drew himself up to his full height, and was soon
walking along soberly by Rosina's side, as respectable and
decorous a native Methodist class-leader as one could wish
to see in the whole green island of Trinidad. ' I was glad
when dey said unto me,' he murmured to himself audibly,
with an unctuous smile upon his lank black jaws, " Let us
go into de courts ob his house." '

Those who judge superficially of men and minds would
say at once that Delgado was a hypocrite. Those who
know what religion really means to inferior races—a strange
but sincere jumble of phrases, emotions, superstitions, and
melodies, permeating and consecrating all their acts and
all their passions, however evil, violent, or licentious—
will recognise at once that in his own mind Louis Delgado
was not conscious to himself in the faintest degree of any
hypocrisy, craft, or even inconsistency.

CHAPTER VII.

THE morning when Edward and Marian were to start on
their voyage to Trinidad, with Nora in their charge, was a
beautifully clear, calm, and sunny one. The tiny steam-
tender that took them down Southampton Water, from the
landing-stage to the moorings where the big ocean-going
Severn lay at anchor, ploughed her way merrily through
the blue ripplets that hardly broke the level surface.
Though it was a day of parting, nobody was over-sad.
General Ord had come down with Marian, his face bronzed
with twenty years of India, but straight and erect still like
a hop-pole, as he stood with his tall thin figure lithe and
steadfast on the little quarter-deck. Mrs. Ord was there
too, crying a little, of course, as is only decorous on such

occasions, yet not more so than a parting always demands
from the facile eyes of female humanity. Marian didn't
cry much either ; she felt so safe in going with Edward,
and hoped to be back so soon again on a summer visit to
her father and mother. As for Nora, Nora was always
bright as the sunshine, and could never see anything
except the bright side of things. 'We shall take such care
of dear Marian in Trinidad, Mrs. Ord!' she said gaily.
'You'll see her home again on a visit in another twelve-
month, with more roses on her cheek than she's got now,
when she's had a taste of our delicious West Indian
mountain air.'

'And if Trinidad suits Miss Ord—Mrs. Hawthorn, I
mean—dear me, how stupid of me!' Harry Noel put in
quietly, 'half as well as it seems to have suited you, Miss
Dupuy, we shall have no cause to complain of Hawthorn
for having taken her out there.'

'Oh, no fear of that,' Nora answered, smiling one of
her delicious childish smiles. 'You don't know how delightful Trinidad is, Mr. Noel ; it's really one of the most
charming places in all Christendom.'

'On your recommendation, then,' Harry answered,
bowing slightly and looking at her with eyes full of meaning, 'I shall almost be tempted to go out some day,
and see for myself how really delightful are these poetical
tropics of yours.'

Nora blushed, and her eyes fell slightly. 'You would
find them very lovely, no doubt, Mr. Noel,' she answered,
more demurely and in a half-timid fashion ; 'but I can't
recommend them, you know, with any confidence, because
I was such a very little girl when I first came home to
England. You had better not come out to Trinidad merely
on the strength of my recommendation.'

Harry bowed his head again gravely. 'As you will,'
he said. 'Your word is law. And yet, perhaps, some day,
I shouldn't be surprised either if Hawthorn and Mrs.
Hawthorn were to find me dropping in upon them unexpectedly for a scratch dinner. After all, it's a mere
nothing nowadays to run across the millpond, as the
Yankees call it.'

They reached the *Severn* about an hour before the time fixed for starting, and sat on deck talking together with that curious sense of finding nothing to say which always oppresses one on the eve of a long parting. It seems as though no subject of conversation sufficiently important for the magnitude of the occasion ever occurred to one: the mere everyday trivialities of ordinary talk sound out of place at such a serious moment. So, by way of something to do, the party soon began to institute a series of observations upon Edward and Marian's fellow-passengers, as they came on board, one after another, in successive batches on the little tender.

'Just look at that brown young man!' Nora cried, in a suppressed whisper, as a tall and gentlemanly looking mulatto walked up the gangway from the puffing tug. 'We shall be positively overwhelmed with coloured people, I declare! There are three Hottentot Venuses down in the saloon already, bound for Haiti; and a San Domingo general, as black as your hat; and a couple of walnut-coloured old gentlemen going to Dominica. And now, here's another regular brown man coming on board to us. What's his name, I wonder? Oh, there it is, painted as large as life upon his portmanteau! "Dr. Whitaker, Trinidad." Why, my dear, he's actually going the whole way with us. And a doctor too! goodness gracious. Just fancy being attended through a fever by a man of that complexion!'

'Oh, hush, Nora!' Marian cried, in genuine alarm. 'He'll overhear you, and you'll hurt his feelings. Besides, you oughtn't to talk so much about other people, whether they hear you or whether they don't.'

'Hurt his feelings, my dear! Oh dear no, not a bit of it. I know them better than you do. My dear Marian, these people haven't got any feelings; they've been too much accustomed to be laughed at from the time they were babies, ever to have had the chance of acquiring any.'

'Then the more shame,' Edward interrupted gravely, 'to those who have laughed them out of all self-respect and natural feeling. But I don't believe, for my part,

there's anybody on earth who doesn't feel hurt at being
ridiculed.'

' Ah, that's so nice of you to think and talk like that,
Mr. Hawthorn,' Nora answered frankly ; ' but you won't
think so, you know, I'm quite certain, after you've been a
month or two on shore over in Trinidad.'

' Good-morning, ladies and gentlemen,' the captain of
the *Severn* put in briskly, walking up to them as they
lounged in a group on the clean-scrubbed quarter-deck—
'good-morning, ladies and gentlemen. Fine weather to
start on a voyage. Are you all going with us ?—Why,
bless my heart, if this isn't General Ord! I sailed with
you, sir, fifteen years ago now or more, must be, when I
was a second officer in the P. and O. service.—You don't
remember me ; no, I dare say not; I was only a second
officer then, and you sat at the captain's table. But I remember you, sir—I remember you. There's more folks
know Tom Fool, the proverb says, than Tom fool knows ;
and no offence meant, General, nor none be taken. And
so you're going out with us now, are you ?—going out with
us now ? Well, you'll sit at the captain's table still, sir,
no doubt, you and your party; and as I'm the captain
now, you see, why, I shall have a better chance than I
used to have of making your acquaintance.'

The captain laughed heartily as he spoke at his own
small wit ; but General Ord drew himself up rather stiffly,
and answered in a somewhat severe tone : ' No, I'm not
going out with you this journey myself; but my daughter,
who has lately married, and her husband here, are just
setting out to their new home over in Trinidad.'

' In Trinidad,' the jolly captain echoed heartily—' in
Trinidad! Well, well, beautiful island, beautiful, beautiful! Must mind they don't take too much mainsheet, or
catch yellow Jack, or live in the marshes, that's all;
otherwise, they'll find it a delightful residence. I took out
a young sub-lieutenant, just gazetted, last voyage but two,
when they had the yellow Jack awfully bad up at canton-
ments. He was in a deadly funk of the fever all the way,
and always asking everybody questions about it. The
moment he landed, who does he go and meet but an old

Irish friend of the family, who was going home by the return steamer. The Irishman rushes up to him and shakes his hand violently, and says he—" Me dear fellow," says he, " ye've come in the very nick of time. Promotion's certain ; they're dying by thousands. Every day wan of 'em drops off the list ; and all ye've got to do is to hould yer head up, keep from drinking any brandy, and don't be frightened ; and, by George, ye'll rise in no time as fast as I have ; and I'm going home this morning a colonel." '

The General shuddered slightly. ' Not a pleasant introduction to the country certainly,' he answered in his driest manner. ' But I suppose Trinidad's fairly healthy at present ? '

' Healthy ! Well, yes, well enough as the tropics go, General.—But don't you be afraid of your young people. With health and strength they'll pull through decently, not a doubt of it.—Let me see—let me see ; I must secure 'em a place at my own table. We've got rather an odd lot of passengers this time, mostly ; a good many of 'em have got a very decided touch o' the tar-brush about 'em— a touch o' the tar-brush. There's that woolly-headed nigger fellow over there who's just come aboard ; he's going to Trinidad too ; he's a doctor, he is. We mustn't let your people get mixed up with all that lot, of course ; I'll keep 'em a place nice and snug at my own table.'

' Thank you,' the General said, rather more graciously than before.—' This is my daughter, Captain, Mrs. Hawthorn. And this is my son-in-law, Mr. Edward Hawthorn, who's going out to accept a district judgeship over yonder in Trinidad.'

' Ha ! ' the jovial captain answered in his bluff voice doffing his hat sailor-fashion to Marian and Edward. ' Going to hang up the niggers out in Trinidad, are you, sir ? Going to hang up the niggers ! Well, well, they deserve it all, every man Jack of 'em, the lazy beggars ; they all deserve hanging. A pestering set of idle, thieving, hulking vagabonds, as ever came round to coal a ship in harbour ! I'd judge 'em, I would—I'd judge 'em.' And the captain pantomimically expressed the exact nature of his judicial sentiments by pressing his own stout bull-neck, just across the windpipe, with his sturdy right hand, till his red and sunburnt face grew even redder and redder with the suggested suspension.

Edward smiled quietly, but answered nothing.

'Well, sir,' the captain went on as soon as he had recovered fully from the temporary effects of his self-inflicted strangulation, 'and have you ever been in the West Indies before, or is this your first visit?'

'I was born there,' Edward answered. 'I'm a Trinidad man by birth; but I've lived so long in England, and went there so young, that I don't really recollect very much about my native country.'

'Mr. Hawthorn's father you may know by name,' the General said, a little assertively. 'He's a son of the Honourable James Hawthorn, of Agualta Estate, Trinidad.'

The captain drew back for a moment with a curious look, and scanned Edward closely from head to foot with a remarkably frank and maritime scrutiny; then he whistled low to himself for a few seconds, and seemed to be ruminating inwardly upon some very amusing and unusual circumstance. At last he answered slowly, in a more reserved and somewhat embarrassed tone: 'Oh, yes, I know Mr. Hawthorn of Agualta—know him personally; well-known man, Mr. Hawthorn of Agualta. Member of the Legislative Council of the island. Fine estate, Agualta—very fine estate indeed, and has one of the largest out-puts of rum and sugar anywhere in the whole West Indies.'

'I told you so,' Harry Noel murmured parenthetically. 'The governor is coiny. They're all alike, the whole breed of them. Secretiveness large, acquisitiveness enormous, benevolence and generosity absolutely undeveloped. When you get to Trinidad, my dear Teddy, bleed him, bleed him!'

'Well, well, Mrs. Hawthorn,' the captain said gallantly to Marian, who stood by rather wondering what his sudden change of demeanour could possibly portend, 'you shall have a seat at my table—certainly, certainly; you shall have a seat at my table. The General's an old passenger of mine on the P. and O.; and I've known Mr. Hawthorn

of Agualta Estate ever since I first came upon the West
India liners.—And the young lady, is she going too ? '
For Captain Burford, like most others of his craft, had a
quick eye for pretty faces, and he had not been long in
picking out and noticing Nora's.

'This is Miss Dupuy, of Orange Grove,' Marian said,
drawing her young companion a little forward. ' Perhaps
you know her father too, as you've been going so long to
the island.'

'What ! a daughter of Mr. Theodore Dupuy, of Orange
Grove and Pimento Valley,' the captain replied briskly.
'Mr. Theodore Dupuy's daughter ! Lord bless my soul,
Mr. Theodore Dupuy ! Oh, yes, don't I just know him !
Why, Mr. Dupuy's one of the most respected and well-
known gentlemen in the whole island. Been settled at
Orange Grove, the Dupuys have, ever since the old
Spanish occupation.—And so you're taking out Mr.
Theodore Dupuy's daughter, are you, Mrs. Hawthorn ?
Well, well ! Taking out Mr. Theodore Dupuy's daughter.
That's a capital joke, that is.—Oh, yes, you must all sit
at the head of my table, ladies ; and I'll do everything
that lies in my power to make you comfortable.'

Meanwhile, Edward and Harry Noel had strolled off
for a minute towards the opposite end of the deck, where
the mulatto gentleman was standing quite alone, looking
down steadily into the deep-blue motionless water. As
the captain moved away, Nora Dupuy gave a little start,
and caught Marian Hawthorn's arm excitedly and suddenly. ' Look there !' she cried—'Oh, look there,
Marian ! Do you see Mr. Hawthorn ? Do you see what
he's doing ? That brown man over there, with the name
on the portmanteau, has turned round and spoken to him,
and Mr. Hawthorn actually held out his hand and is
shaking hands with him ! '

' Well,' Marian answered in some surprise, ' I see he is.
Why not ? '

' Why not ? My dear, how can you ask me such a
question ! Why, of course, because the man's a regular
mulatto—a coloured person ! '

Marian laughed. ' Really, dear,' she answered, more

amused than angry, ' you mustn't be so entirely filled up with your foolish little West Indian prejudices. The young man's a doctor, and no doubt a gentleman in education and breeding, and I can't for my part for the life of me see why one shouldn't shake hands with him as well as with any other respectable person.'

' Oh, but Marian, you know—a brown man !—his father and mother !—the associations—no, really ! '

Marian smiled again. ' They're coming this way,' she said ; ' we shall soon hear what they're talking about. Perhaps he knows something about your people, or Edward's.'

Nora looked up quite defiant. ' About my people, Marian ! ' she said almost angrily. ' Why, what can you be thinking of ? You don't suppose, do you, that *my* people are in the habit of mixing casually with woolly-headed mulattoes ?'

She had hardly uttered the harsh words, when the mulatto gentleman walked over towards them side by side with Edward Hawthorn, and lifted his hat courteously to Marian.

' My wife,' Edward said, as Marian bowed slightly in return : ' Dr. Whitaker.'

' I saw your husband's name upon his boxes, Mrs. Hawthorn,' the mulatto gentleman said with a pleasant smile, and in a soft, clear, cultivated voice ; ' and as my father has the privilege of knowing Mr. Hawthorn of Agualta, over in Trinidad, I took the liberty of introducing myself at once to him. I'm glad to hear that we're to be fellow-passengers together, and that your husband has really decided to return at last to his native island.'

' Thank you,' Marian answered simply. ' We're all looking forward much to our life in Trinidad.' Then, with a little mischievous twinkle in her eye, she turned to Nora. ' This is another of our fellow-passengers, Dr. Whitaker,' she said demurely —' my friend, Miss Dupuy, whom I'm taking out under my charge—another Trinidadian : you ought to know one another. Miss Dupuy's father lives at an estate called Orange Grove—isn't it, Nora ? '

The mulatto doctor lifted his hat again, ant bowed with marked politeness to the blushing white girl. ᵀor a second, their eyes met. Dr. Whitaker's looked at the beautiful half-childish face with unmistakable instanu·- neous admiration. Nora's flashed a little angrily, and he nostrils dilated with a proud quiver; but she said never a word; she merely gave a chilly bow, and didn't attempt even to offer her pretty little gloved hand to the brown stranger.

'I have heard of Miss Dupuy's family by name,' the mulatto answered, speaking to Marian, but looking askance at the same time towards the petulant Nora. 'Mr. Dupuy of Orange Grove is well known throughout the island. I'm glad that we're going to have so much delightful Trinidad society on our outward passage.'

'Thank him for nothing,' Nora murmured aside to Harry Noel, moving away as she spoke towards Mrs. Ord at the other end of the vessel. 'What impertinence! Marian ought to have known better than to introduce me to him.'

'It's a pity you don't like the coloured gentleman,' Harry Noel put in provokingly. 'The appreciation is un- fortunately not mutual, it seems. He appeared to me to be very much struck with you at first sight, Miss Dupuy, to judge by his manner.'

Nora turned towards him with a sudden fierceness and haughtiness that fairly surprised the easy-going young barrister. 'Mr. Noel,' she said in a tone of angry but suppressed indignation, 'how dare you speak to me so about that negro fellow, sir—how dare you? How dare you mention him and me in the same breath together? How dare you presume to joke with me on such a subject? Don't speak to me again, pray. You don't know what we West Indians are, or you'd never have ventured to utter such a speech as that to any woman with a single drop of West Indian blood in her whole body.'

Harry bowed silently and bit his lip; then, without another word, he moved back slowly towards the other group, and allowed Nora to join Mrs. Ord by the door of the companion-ladder.

In twenty minutes more, the first warning bell rang for those who were going ashore to get ready for their departure. There was the usual hurried leave-taking on every side; there was the usual amount of shedding of tears; there was the usual shouting, and bawling, and snorting, and puffing; and there was the usual calm indifference of the ship's officers, moving up and down through all the tearful valedictory groups, as through an ordinary incident of humanity, experienced regularly every six weeks of a whole lifetime. As Marian and her mother were taking their last farewells, Harry Noel ventured once more timidly to approach Nora Dupuy, and address a few parting words to her in a low undertone.

'I am sorry I offended you unintentionally just now, Miss Dupuy,' he said quietly. 'I thought the best apology I could offer at the moment was to say nothing just then in exculpation. But I really didn't mean to hurt your feelings, and I hope we still part friends.'

Nora held out her small hand to him a trifle reluctantly. 'As you have the grace to apologise,' she said, 'I shall overlook it. Yes, we part friends, Mr. Noel; I have no reason to part otherwise.'

'Then there's no chance for me?' Harry asked in a low tone, looking straight into her eyes with a searching glance.

'No chance,' Nora echoed, dropping her eyes suddenly, but speaking very decidedly. 'You must go now, Mr. Noel; the second bell's ringing.'

Harry took her hand once more, and pressed it faintly. 'Good-bye, Miss Dupuy,' he said—'good-bye—for the present. I dare say we shall meet again before long, some day—in Trinidad.'

'Oh no!' Nora cried in a low voice, as he turned to leave her. 'Don't do that, Mr. Noel; don't come out to Trinidad. I told you it'd be quite useless.'

Harry laughed one of his most teasing laughs. 'My father has property in the West Indies, Miss Dupuy,' he answered in his usual voice of light badinage, paying her out in her own coin; and I shall probably come over some day to see how the niggers are getting on upon it—that was all I meant. Good-bye—good-bye to you.'

But his eyes belied what he said, and Nora knew they did as she saw him look back a last farewell from the deck of the retreating little tender.

'Any more for the shore—any more for the shore?' cried the big sailor who rang the bell. 'No more.—Then shove off, cap'n'—to the skipper of the tug-boat.

In another minute the great anchor was heaved, and the big screw began to revolve slowly through the sluggish water. Next moment, the ship moved from her moorings and was fairly under weigh. Just as she moved, a boat with a telegraph-boy on board rowed up rapidly to her side, and a voice from the boat shouted aloud in a sailor's bass: '*Severn*, ahoy!'

'Ahoy!' answered the ship's officer.

'Passenger aboard by the name of Hawthorn? We've got a telegram for him.'

Edward rushed quickly to the ship's side, and answered in his loudest voice: 'Yes. Here I am.'

'Passenger aboard by the name of Miss Dupuy? We've got a telegram for her.'

'This is she,' Edward answered. 'How can we get them?'

'Lower a bucket,' the ship's officer shouted to a sailor. —'You can put 'em in that, boy, can't you?'

The men in the boat caught the bucket, and fastened in the letters rudely with a stone taken from the ballast at the bottom. The screw still continued to revolve as the sailors drew up the bucket hastily. A little water got over the side and wet the telegrams; but they were both still perfectly legible. Edward unfolded his in wondering silence, while Marian looked tremulously over his right shoulder. It contained just these few short words:

'*From* HAWTHORN, *Trinidad*, to HAWTHORN, R.M.S. *Severn, Southampton*.—For God's sake, don't come out. Reasons by letter.'

Marian gazed at it for a moment in speechless surprise; then she turned, pale and white, to her husband beside her. 'Oh, Edward,' she cried, looking up at him with a face of terror, 'what on earth can it mean? What on earth can they wish us not to come out for?'

Edward held the telegram open before his eyes, gazing at it blankly in inexpressible astonishment. ' My darling,' he said, ' my own darling, I haven't the remotest notion. I can't imagine why on earth they should ever wish to keep us away from them.'

At the same moment, Nora held her own telegram out to Marian with a little laugh of surprise and amusement. Marian glanced at it and read it hastily. It ran as follows.

' *From* DUPUY, *Trinidad*, to MISS DUPUY, R.M.S. *Severn, Southampton.*—Don't come out till next steamer. On no account go on board the *Severn.*'

CHAPTER VIII.

FOR a few minutes they stood looking blankly at one another in mute astonishment, turning over and comparing the two telegrams together with undecided minds ; then at last Nora broke the silence. ' I tell you what it is,' she said, with an air of profound wisdom ; ' they must have got an epidemic of yellow fever in Trinidad—they're always having it, you know, and nobody minds it, unless of course they die of it, and even then I dare say they don't think much about it. But papa and Mr. Hawthorn must be afraid that if we come out now, fresh from England, we may all of us get it.'

Edward looked once more at the telegrams very dubiously. ' I don't think that'll do, Miss Dupuy,' he said, after re-reading them with a legal scrutiny. ' You see, your father says : '' On no account go on board the *Severn.*'' Evidently, it's this particular ship he has an objection to ; and perhaps my father's objection may be exactly the same. It's very singular—very mysterious ! '

' Do you think,' Marian suggested, ' there can be anything wrong with the vessel or the machinery ? You know, they *do* say, Edward, that some ship-owners send ships to sea that aren't at all safe or seaworthy. I read such a dreadful article about it a little while ago in one of

3

the papers. Perhaps they think the *Severn* may go to the bottom.'

'Or else that there's dynamite on board,' Nora put in; 'or a clockwork thing like the one somebody was going to blow up that steamer with at Hamburg, once, you remember! Oh, my dear, the bare idea of it makes me quite shudder! Fancy being blown out of your berth, at dead of night, into the nasty cold stormy water, and having a shark bite you in two across the waist before you were really well awake, and had begun properly to realise the situation!'

'Not very likely, either of them,' Edward said. 'This is a new ship, one of the very best on the line, and perfectly safe, except of course in a hurricane, when anything on earth is liable to go down; so that can't possibly be Mr. Dupuy's objection to the *Severn*.—And as to the clockwork, you know, Nora, the people who put those things on board steamers, if there are any, don't telegraph out to give warning beforehand to the friends of passengers on the other side of the Atlantic. No; for my part, I can't at all understand it. It's a perfect mystery to me, and I give it up entirely.'

'Well, what do you mean to do, dear?' Marian asked anxiously. 'Go back at once, or go on in spite of it?'

'I don't think there's any choice left us now, darling. The ship's fairly under weigh, you see; and nothing on earth would induce them to stop her, once she's started, till we get to Trinidad, or at least to St. Thomas.'

'You don't mean to say, Mr. Hawthorn,' Nora cried piteously, 'they'll carry us on now to the end of the journey, whether we want to stop or whether we don't?'

'Yes, I do, Miss Dupuy. They will, most certainly. I suspect they've got no voice themselves in the matter. A mail-steamer is under contract to sail from a given port on a given day, and not to stop for anything on earth, except fire or stress of weather, till she lands the mails safely on the other side, according to agreement.'

'Well, that's a blessing anyhow!' Nora said resignedly; 'because, if so, it saves us the trouble of thinking anything more about the matter; and papa can't be angry

with me for having sailed, if the captain refuses to send us
back, now we've once fairly started. Indeed, for my part,
I'm very glad of it, to tell you the truth, because it would
have been such a horrid nuisance to have to go on shore
again and unpack all one's things just for a fortnight, after
all the fuss and hurry we've had already about getting
them finished. What a pity the bothering old telegrams
came at all to keep us in suspense the whole way over ! '

' But suppose there *is* some dynamite on board,' Marian
suggested timidly. ' Don't you think, Edward, you'd better
go and ask the captain ? '

' I'll go and ask the captain, by all means, if that's any
relief to you,' Edward answered; ' but I don't think it
likely he can throw any particular light of his own upon
the reason of the telegrams.'

The captain, being shortly found on the bridge, came
down at his leisure and inspected the messages ; hummed
and hawed a little dubiously ; smiled to himself with much
good-humour ; said it was a confoundedly odd coincidence;
and looked somehow as though he saw the meaning of the
two telegrams at once, but wasn't anxious to impart his
knowledge to any inquiring third party. ' Yellow fever ! '
he said, shrugging his shoulders sailor-wise, when Edward
mentioned Nora's first suggestion. ' No, no ; don't you
believe it. 'Tain't yellow fever. Why, nobody who lives
in the West Indies ever thinks anything of that, bless you.
Besides, *you* wouldn't get it ; don't you trouble your head
about it. You ain't the sort or the build to get it. Men
of your temperament never do ketch yellow fever—it don't
affect 'em. No, no ; it ain't that, you take my word for it.'

Marian gently hinted at unseaworthiness ; but at this
the good captain laughed her quite unceremoniously in the
face. ' Go down ! ' he cried—' go down, indeed ! I'd like
to see the hurricane that'd send the *Severn* spinning to the
bottom. No, no ; we may get hurricanes, of course—
though this isn't the month for them. The rhyme says :
" June—too soon ; July—stand by ; Au-gust, you must ;
September—remember ; October—all over." Still, in the
course of nature we're likely enough to have some ugly
weather—a capful of wind or so, I mean—nothing to speak

of, for a ship of her tonnage. But I'll bet you a bottle of champagne the hurricane's not alive that'll ever send the *Severn* to the bottom, and I'll pay it you (if I lose) at the first port the lifeboat puts into after the accident.—Dyna- mite! clockwork! that's all gammon, my dear ma'am, that is! The ship's as good a ship as ever sailed the Bay o' Biscay, and there's nothing aboard her more explosive than the bottle of champagne I hope you'll drink this evening for dinner.'

'Then we can't be put out?' Nora asked, with her most beseeching smile.

'My dear lady, not if I knew you were the Queen of England. Once we're off, we're off in earnest, and nothing on earth can ever stop us till we get safely across to St. Thomas—the hand of God, the perils of the sea, and the Queen's enemies alone excepted,' the captain added, quoting with a smile the stereotyped formula of the bills of lading.

'What do you think the telegram means, then?' Nora asked again, a little relieved by this confident assurance.

The captain once more hummed and hawed, and bit his nails, and looked very awkward. 'Well,' he said slowly, after a minute's internal debate, 'perhaps—perhaps the niggers over yonder may be getting troublesome, you know; and your family may think it an inopportune time for you or Mr. and Mrs. Hawthorn to visit the colony.— All right, Jones, I'm coming in a minute.—You must excuse me, ladies. In sight of land, a cap'n ought always to be at his post on the bridge. See you at dinner.—Good- morning, good-morning.'

'It seems to me, Edward,' Marian said, as he retreated opportunely, 'the captain knows a good deal more about it than he wants to tell us. He was trying to hide some- thing from us; I'm quite sure he was. Aren't you, Nora? I do hope there's nothing wrong with the steamer or the machinery!'

'I didn't notice anything peculiar about him myself,' Edward answered, with a little hesitation. 'However, it's certainly very singular. But as we've got to go on, we may as well go on as confidently as possible, and think as little as we can about it. The mystery will all be cleared up as soon as we get across to Trinidad.'

'If we ever get there!' Nora said, half jesting and half in earnest.

As she spoke, Dr. Whitaker the mulatto passed close by, pacing up and down the quarter-deck for exercise, to get his sea-legs; and as he passed her, he turned his eyes once more mutely upon her with that rapid, timid, quickly shifting glance, the exact opposite of a stare, which yet speaks more certainly than anything else can do an instinctive admiration. Nora's face flushed again, at least as much with annoyance as with self-consciousness. 'That horrid man!' she cried petulantly, with a little angry dash of her hand, almost before he was well out of earshot. 'How on earth can he have the impertinence to go and look at me in that way, I wonder!'

'Oh, don't, dear!' Marian whispered, genuinely alarmed lest the mulatto should overhear her. 'You oughtn't to speak like that, you know. Of course one feels at once a sort of natural shrinking from black people—one can't help that, I know—it seems to be innate in one. But one oughtn't to let them see it themselves, at any rate. Respect their feelings, Nora; do, dear, for my sake, I beg of you.'

'Oh, it's all very well for you, Marian,' Nora answered, quite aloud, and strumming on the deck with her parasol; 'but for my part, you know, if there's anything on earth that I can't endure, it's a brown man.'

CHAPTER IX.

ALL the way across to St. Thomas, endless speculations as to the meaning of the two mysterious telegrams afforded the three passengers chiefly concerned an unusual fund of conversation and plot-interest for an entire voyage. Still, after a while the subject palled a little; and on the second evening out, in calm and beautiful summer twilight weather, they were all sitting in their own folding chairs on the after-deck, positively free from any doubts or guesses

F

upon the important question, and solely engaged in making
the acquaintance of their fellow-passengers. By-and-by,
as the shades began to close in, there was a little sound of
persuasive language—as when one asks a young lady to
sing—at the stern end of the swiftly moving vessel ; and
then, in a few minutes, somebody in the dusk took a small
violin out of a wooden case and began to play a piece of
Spohr's. The ladies turned around their chairs to face
the musician, and listened carelessly as he went through
the preliminary scraping and twanging which seems to be
inseparable from the very nature of the violin as an instrument. Presently, having tightened the pegs to his own
perfect satisfaction, the player began to draw his bow
rapidly and surely across the strings with the unerring
confidence of a practised performer. In two minutes the
hum of conversation had ceased on deck, and all the world
of the *Severn* was bending forward its head eagerly to catch
the liquid notes that floated with such delicious clearness
upon the quiet breathless evening air. Instinctively everybody recognised at once the obvious fact that the man in
the stern to whom they were all listening was an accomplished and admirable violin-player.

Just at first, the thing that Marian and Nora noticed
most in the stranger's playing was his extraordinary bril-
liancy and certainty of execution. He was a perfect master
of the *technique* of his instrument, that was evident. But
after a few minutes more, they began to perceive that he
was something much more than merely that ; he played
not only with consummate skill, but also with infinite
grace, insight, and tenderness. As they listened, they
could feel the man outpouring his whole soul in the exquisite modulations of his passionate music : it was not
any cold, well-drilled, mechanical accuracy of touch alone ;
it was the loving hand of a born musician, wholly in harmony with the master he interpreted, the work he realised,
and the strings on which he gave it vocal utterance. As
he finished the piece, Edward whispered in a hushed voice
to Nora : 'He plays beautifully.' And Nora answered with
a sudden burst of womanly enthusiasm : ' More than beautifully—exquisitely, divinely.'

'You'll sing us something, won't you?'—'Oh, do sing us something!'—'Monsieur will not refuse us!'—'Ah, señor, it is such a great pleasure.' So a little babel of two or three languages urged at once upon the unknown figure silhouetted dark at the stern of the steamer against the paling sunset; and after a short pause, the unknown figure complied graciously, bowing its acknowledgments to the surrounding company, and burst out into a song in a glorious rich tenor voice, almost the finest Nora and Marian had ever listened to,

'English!' Nora whispered in a soft tone, as the first words fell upon their ears distinctly, uttered without any mouthing in a plain unmistakable native tone. 'I'm quite surprised at it! I made up my mind, from the intense sort of way he played the violin, that he must be a Spaniard or an Italian, or at least a South American. English people seldom play with all that depth and earnestness and fervour.'

'Hush, hush!' Marian answered under her breath. 'Don't talk while he's singing, please, Nora—it's too delicious.'

They listened till the song was quite finished, and the last echo of that magnificent voice had died away upon the surface of the still, moonlit waters; and then Nora said eagerly to Edward: 'Oh, do find out who he is, Mr. Hawthorn! Do go and get to know him! I want to be introduced to him! What a glorious singer! and what a splendid violinist! I never in my life heard anything lovelier, even at the opera.'

Edward smiled, and dived at once into the little crowd at the end of the quarter-deck, in search of the unknown and nameless musician. Nora waited impatiently in her seat to see who the mysterious personage could be. In a few seconds, Edward came back again, bringing with him the admired performer. 'Miss Dupuy was so very anxious to make your acquaintance,' he said, as he drew the supposed stranger forward, 'on the strength of your beautiful playing and singing. You see, Miss Dupuy, it's a fellow-passenger to whom we've already introduced ourselves—Dr. Whitaker.'

Nora drew back almost imperceptibly at this sudden
revelation. In the dusk and from a little distance, she
had not recognised their acquaintance of yesterday. But
it was indeed the mulatto doctor. However, now she was
fairly trapped; and having thus let herself in for the young
man's society for that particular evening, she had good
sense and good feeling enough not to let him see, at least
too obtrusively, that she did not desire the pleasure of his
further acquaintance. To be sure, she spoke as little and
as coldly as she could to him, in such ordinary phrases of
polite admiration as she felt were called for under these
painful circumstances; but she tried to temper her enthusiasm down to a proper point of chilliness for a clever and
well-taught mulatto fiddler. (He had been a 'marvellous
violinist' in her own mind five minutes before; but as
he turned out to be of brown blood, she felt now that
'clever fiddler' was quite good enough for the altered
occasion.)

Dr. Whitaker, however, remained in happy unconsciousness of Nora's sudden change of attitude. He drew over
a camp-stool from near the gunwale, and seated himself
upon it just in front of the little group in their folding
ship-chairs. 'I'm so glad you like my playing, Miss
Dupuy,' he said quietly, turning towards Nora. 'Music
always sounds at its best on the water in the evening.
And that's such a lovely piece—my pet piece—so much
feeling and pathos and delicate melody in it. Not like
most of Spohr: a very unusual work for him; he's so
often wanting, you know, in the sense of melody.'

'You play charmingly,' Nora answered, in a languid
chilly voice. 'Your song and your playing have given us a
great treat, I'm sure, Dr. Whitaker.'

'Where have you studied?' Marian asked hastily, feeling that Nora wasn't showing so deep an interest in the
subject as was naturally expected of her. 'Have you
taken lessons in Germany or Italy?'

'A few,' the mulatto doctor replied with a little sigh,
'though not so many as I could have wished. My great
ambition would have been to study regularly at the Con-
servatoire. But I never could gratify my wish in that

respect, and I learned most of my fiddling by myself at Edinburgh.'

' You're an Edinburgh University man, I suppose ? ' Edward put in.

' Yes, an Edinburgh University man. The medical course there, you know, attracts so many men who would like better, in other respects, to go to one of the English universities.—You're Cambridge yourself, I think, Mr. Hawthorn, aren't you ? '

' Yes, Cambridge.'

The mulatto sighed again. ' A lovely place ! ' he said —' a most delicious place, Cambridge. I spent a charming week there once myself. The calm repose of those grand old avenues behind John's and Trinity charmed me immensely.—A place to sit in and compose symphonies, Mrs. Hawthorn. Nothing that I have seen in England so greatly impressed me with the idea of the grand antiquity of the country—the vast historical background of civilisation, century behind century, and generation behind generation—as that beautiful mingled picture of venerable elms, and mouldering architecture, and close-cropped greensward at the backs of the colleges. The very grass had a wonderful look of antique culture. I asked the gardener in one of the courts of Trinity how they ever got such velvety carpets for their smooth quadrangles, and the answer the fellow gave me was itself redolent of the traditions of the place. "We rolls 'em and mows 'em, sir," he said, "and we mows 'em and rolls 'em, for a thousand years." '

' What a pity you couldn't have stopped there and composed symphonies, as you liked it so much ! ' Nora remarked, with hardly concealed sarcasm—' only then, of course, we shouldn't have had the pleasure of hearing you play your violin so beautifully on the *Severn* this evening.'

Dr. Whitaker looked up at her quickly with a piercing look. ' Yes,' he replied ; it *is* a pity, for I should have dearly loved it. I'm bound up in music, almost ; it's one of my two great passions. But I had more than one reason for feeling that I ought, if possible, to go back to Trinidad. The first is, that I think every West Indian, and especially every man of my colour '—he said it quite naturally, simply, and unaffectedly, without pausing or hesitating— 'who has been to Europe for his education, owes it to his country to come back again, and do his best in raising its social, intellectual, and artistic level.'

'I'm very glad to hear you say so,' Edward replied. 'I think so myself, too, and I'm pleased to find you agree with me in the matter.—And your second reason ? '

'Well, I thought my colour might stand in my way in practice in England—very naturally, I'm not surprised at it ; while in Trinidad I might be able to do a great deal of good and find a great many patients amongst my own people.'

'But I'm afraid they won't be able to pay you, you know,' Nora interposed. 'The poor black people always expect to be doctored for nothing.'

Dr. Whitaker turned upon her a puzzled pair of simple, honest, open eyes, whose curious glance of mute inquiry could be easily observed even in the dim moonlight. 'I don't think of practising for money,' he said simply, as if it were the most ordinary statement in the world. 'My father has happily means enough to enable me to live without the necessity for earning a livelihood. I want to be of some use in my generation, and to help my own people, if possible, to rise a little in the scale of humanity. I shall practise gratuitously among the poorest negroes, and do what I can to raise and better their unhappy condition.'

For a second, nobody answered a word ; this quiet declaration of an honest self-sacrifice took them all, even Nora, so utterly by surprise. Then Edward murmured musingly : 'And it was for this that you gave up the prospect of living at Cambridge, and composing symphonies in Trinity gardens ! '

The mulatto smiled a deprecating smile. 'Oh,' he cried timidly, 'you mustn't say that. I didn't want to make out I was going to do anything so very grand or so very heroic. Of course, a man *must* satisfy himself he's doing something to justify his existence in the world : and much as I love music, I hardly feel as though playing the violin were in itself a sufficient end for a man to live for.

Though I must confess I should very much like to stop in England and be a composer. I have composed one or two little pieces already for the violin, that have been played with some success at public concerts. Sarasate played a small thing of mine last winter at a festival in Vienna. But then, besides, my father and friends live in Trinidad, and I feel that that's the place where my work in life is really cut out for me.'

'And your second great passion?' Marian inquired. 'You said you had a second great passion. What is it, I wonder?—Oh, of course, I see—your profession.'

('How could she be so stupid!' Nora thought to herself. 'What a silly girl! I'm afraid of my life now, the wretched man 'll try to say something pretty.')

'Oh, no; not my profession,' Dr. Whitaker answered, smiling. 'It's a noble profession, of course—the noblest and grandest, almost, of all the professions—assuaging and alleviating human suffering; but one looks upon it, for all that, rather as a duty than as a passion. Besides, there's one thing greater even than the alleviation of human suffering, greater than art with all its allurements, greater than anything else that a man can interest himself in—though I know most people don't think so—and that's science—the knowledge of our relations with the universe, and still more of the universe's relations with its various parts.—No, Mrs. Hawthorn; my second absorbing passion, next to music, and higher than music, is one that I'm sure ladies won't sympathise with—it's only botany.'

'Goodness gracious!' Nora cried, surprised into speech. 'I thought botany was nothing but the most dreadfully hard words, all about nothing on earth that anybody cared for!'

The mulatto looked at her open-eyed with a sort of mild astonishment. 'What?' he said. 'All the glorious lilies and cactuses and palms and orchids of our beautiful Trinidad nothing but hard words that nobody cares for! All the slender lianas that trail and droop from the huge buttresses of the wild cotton trees; all the gorgeous trumpet-creepers that drape the gnarled branches of the mountain star-apples with their scarlet blossoms; all the

huge cecropias, that rise aloft with their silvery stems and
fan-shaped leaves, towering into the air like gigantic can-
delabra ; all the graceful tree-ferns and feathery bamboos,
and glossy-leaved magnolias and majestic bananas, and
luxuriant gingerworts and clustering arums, all the breadth
and depth of tropical foliage, with the rugged and knotted
creepers, festooned in veritable cables of vivid green, from
branch to branch among the dim mysterious forest shades
—stretched in tight cordage like the rigging yonder from
mast to mast, for miles together—oh, Miss Dupuy, is that
nothing ? Do you call that nothing for a man to fix his
loving regard upon ? Our own Trinidad is wonderfully
rich still in such natural glories ; and it's the hope of
doing a little in my spare hours to explore and disentomb
them, like hidden treasures, that partly urges me to go back
again where manifest destiny calls me, to the land I was
born in.'

The mulatto is always fluent, even when uneducated ;
but Dr. Whitaker, learned in all the learning of the
schools, and pouring forth his full heart enthusiastically
on the subjects nearest and dearest to him, spoke with
such a ready, easy eloquence— common enough, indeed,
among south Europeans, and among Celtic Scots and Irish
as well, but rare and almost unknown in our colder and
more phlegmatic Anglo-Saxon constitutions—that Nora
listened to him, quite taken aback by the flood of his native
rhetoric, and whispered to herself in her own soul :
' Really, he talks very well after all—for a coloured
person ! '

' Yes, of course, all those things are very lovely, Dr.
Whitaker,' Marian put in, more for the sake of drawing
him out—for he was so interesting—than because she
really wanted to disagree with him upon the subject. ' But
then that isn't botany. I always thought botany was a
mere matter of stamens and petals, and all sorts of other
dreadful technicalities.'

' Stamens and petals ! ' the mulatto echoed half contemptuously—' stamens and petals ! You might as well
say art was all a matter of pigments and perspective, or
music all a matter of crotchets and quavers, as botany

all a matter of stamens and petals. Those are only the beggarly elements: the beautiful pictures, the glorious oratorios, the lovely flowers, are the real things to which in the end they all minister. It's the trees and the plants themselves that interest me, not the mere lifeless jargon of stamens and petals.'

They sat there late into the night, discussing things musical and West Indian and otherwise, without any desire to move away or cut short the conversation; and Dr. Whitaker, his reserve now broken, talked on to them hour after hour, doing the lion's share of the conversation, and delighting them with his transparent easy talk and open-hearted simplicity. He was frankly egotistical, of course—all persons of African blood always are; but his egotism, such as it was, took the pleasing form of an enthusiasm about his own pet ideas and pursuits—a love of music, a love of flowers, a love of his profession, and a love of Trinidad. To these favourite notes he recurred fondly again and again, vigorously defending the violin as an exponent of human emotion against Edward's half-insincere expression of preference for wind instruments; going into raptures to Nora over the wonderful beauty of their common home; and describing to Marian in vivid language the grandeur of those marvellous tropical forests whose strange loveliness she had never yet with her own eyes beheld.

'Picture to yourself,' he said, looking out vaguely beyond the ship on to the starlit Atlantic, ' a great Gothic cathedral or Egyptian temple—Ely or Karnak wrought, not in freestone or marble, but in living trees—with huge cylindrical columns strengthened below by projecting buttresses, and supporting overhead, a hundred feet on high, an unbroken canopy of interlacing foliage. Dense—so dense that only an indistinct glimmer of the sky can be seen here and there through the great canopy, just as you see Orion's belt over yonder through the fringe of clouds upon the grey horizon; and even the intense tropical sunlight only reaches the ground at long intervals in little broken patches of subdued paleness. Then there's the solemn silence, weird and gloomy, that produces in one an almost painful sense of the vast, the primeval, the mystical, the infinite. Only the low hum of the insects in the forest shade, the endless multitudinous whisper of the wind among the foliage, the faint sound begotten by the tropical growth itself, breaks the immemorial stillness in our West Indian woodland. It's a world in which man seems to be a noisy intruder, and where he stands awe-struck before the intense loveliness of Nature, in the immediate presence of her unceasing forces.'

He stopped a moment, not for breath, for it seemed as if he could pour out language without an effort, in the profound enthusiasm of youth, but to take his violin once more tenderly from its case and hold it out, hesitating, before him. ' Will you let me play you just one more little piece ? ' he asked apologetically. ' It's a piece of my own, into which I've tried to put some of the feelings about these tropical ·forests that I never could possibly express in words. I call it " Souvenirs des Lianes." Will you let me play it to you ? I shan't be boring you ? Thank you—thank you.'

He stood up before them in the pale light of that summer evening, tall and erect, violin on breast and bow in hand, and began pouring forth from his responsive instrument a slow flood of low, plaintive, mysterious music. It was not difficult to see what had inspired his brain and hand in that strangely weird and expressive piece. The profound shade and gloom of the forest, the great roof of overarching foliage, the flutter of the endless leaves before the breeze, the confused murmur of the myriad wings and voices of the insects, nay, even the very stillness and silence itself of which he had spoken, all seemed to breathe forth deeply and solemnly on his quivering fiddle. It was a triumph of art over its own resources. On the organ or the flute, one would have said beforehand, such effects as these might indeed be obtained, but surely never, never on the violin. Yet in Dr. Whitaker's hand that scraping bow seemed capable of expressing even what he himself had called the sense of the vast, the primeval, and the infinite. They listened all in hushed silence, and scarcely so much as dared to breathe while the soft pensive cadences still floated out solemnly across the calm ocean. And when he had finished, they

sat for a few minutes in perfect silence, rendering the performer that instinctive homage of mute applause which is
so far more really eloquent than any mere formal and conventional expression of thanks 'for your charming playing.'

As they sat so, each musing quietly over the various
emotions aroused within them by the mulatto's forest
echoes, one of the white gentlemen in the stern, a young
English officer on his way out to join a West Indian regi-
ment, came up suddenly behind them, clapped his hand
familiarly on Edward's back, and said in a loud and cheer-
ful tone: ' Come along, Hawthorn ; we've had enough of
this music now—thank you very much, Dr. Thingummy—
let's all go down to the saloon, I say, and have a game of
nap or a quiet rubber.'

Even Nora felt in her heart as though she had suddenly been recalled by that untimely voice from some
higher world to this vulgar, commonplace little planet of
ours, the young officer had broken in so rudely on her
silent reverie. She drew her dainty white lamb's-wool
wrapper closer around her shoulders with a faint sigh,
slipped her hand gently through Marian's arm, and moved
away, slowly and thoughtfully, toward the companion-
ladder. As she reached the doorway she turned round, as
if half ashamed of her own graciousness, and said in a low
and genuine voice: ' Thank you, Dr. Whitaker—thank
you very much indeed. We've so greatly enjoyed the treat
you've given us.'

The mulatto bowed and said nothing ; but instead of
retiring to the saloon with the others, he put his violin
case quietly under his arm, and walking alone to the stern
of the vessel, leant upon the gunwale long and mutely,
looking over with all his eyes deep and far into the silent,
heaving, moonlit water. The sound of Nora's voice thanking him reverberated long through all the echoing chambers
of his memory.

CHAPTER X.

IT is a truism nowadays, in this age of travelling, that you
see a great deal more of people in a few weeks on board
ship at sea together than you would see in a few years of
that vacant calling and dining and attending crushes which
we ordinarily speak of as society. Nora Dupuy and the
two Hawthorns certainly saw a great deal more of Dr.
Whitaker during their three weeks on board the *Severn*
than they would ever have seen of him in three years of
England or of Trinidad. Nora had had the young man's
acquaintance thrust upon her by circumstances, to be sure :
but as the Hawthorns sat and talked a great deal with him,
she was compelled to do so likewise, and she had too much
good feeling to let him see very markedly her innate prejudice against his colour. Besides, she admitted even to
herself that Dr. Whitaker, for a brown man, was really a
very gentlemanly, well-informed person—quite an excep-
tional mulatto, in fact, and as such, to be admitted to the
position of a gentleman by courtesy, much as Gulliver was
excepted by the Houyhnhnms from the same category of
utter reprobation as the ordinary Yahoos of their own
country.

Most of the voyage was as decently calm as any one
can reasonably expect from the North Atlantic. There
were the usual episodes of flying-fish and Mother Carey's
chickens, and the usual excitement of a daily sweepstake
on the length of the ship's run; but, on the whole, the
only distinct landmarks of time for the entire three weeks
between Southampton and St. Thomas were breakfast,
luncheon, dinner, and bedtime. The North Atlantic, whatever novelists may say, is not a romantic stretch of ocean;
and in spite of prepossessions to the contrary, a ship at sea
is not at all a convenient place for the free exercise of the
noble art of flirting. It lacks the needful opportunities
for retirement from the full blaze of public observation to
shy corners; it is far too exposed, and on the whole too

unstable also. Altogether, the voyage was mostly a mono-
tonous one, which is equivalent to saying that it was safe
and comfortable; for the only possible break in the ordinary
routine of a sea-passage must necessarily be a fire on board
or a collision with a rival steamer. However, about two
days out from St. Thomas, there came a little relief from
the tedium of the daily situation ; and the relief assumed
the unpleasant form of a genuine West Indian hurricane.

Nora had never before seen anything like it; or, at any
rate, if she had, she had clean forgotten all about it.
Though the captain had declared it was 'too soon' for
hurricanes, this was, in fact, a very fine tropical tornado
of the very fiercest and yeastiest description. About two
o'clock in the afternoon, the passengers were all sitting
out on deck, when the sea, till then a dead calm, began to
be faintly ruffled by little whiffs and spurts of wind, which
raised here and there tiny patches of wavelets, scarcely
perceptible to the blunt vision of the unaccustomed lands-
man. But the experienced eye of a sailor could read in
it at once a malignant hint of the coming tempest. Presently, the breeze freshened with extraordinary rapidity,
and before five o'clock, the cyclone had burst upon them
in all its violence. The rush of a mighty gale was heard
through the rigging, swaying and bending the masts like
sapling willows before the autumn breezes. The waves,
lashed into fury by the fierce and fitful gusts of wind,
broke ever and anon over the side of the vessel ; and the
big *Severn* tossed about helplessly before the frantic tempest
like the veriest cockboat in an angry sea upon a northern
ocean. Of course, at the first note of serious danger, the
passengers were all ordered below to the saloon, where they
sat in mute suspense, the women pale and trembling, the
men trying to look as if they cared very little about it,
while the great ship rolled and tossed and pitched and
creaked and rattled in all her groaning timbers beneath
the mad frenzy of that terrific commotion.

Just as they were being turned off the decks to be
penned up downstairs like so many helpless sheep in the
lower cabin, Nora Dupuy, who had been standing with the
Hawthorns and Dr. Whitaker, watching the huge and ever-

increasing waves bursting madly over the side of the vessel,
happened to drop her shawl at starting on to the deck
beside the companion-ladder. At that very moment, a
bigger sea than any they had yet encountered broke with
shivering force against the broadside of the steamer, and
swept across the deck in a drowning flood as though it
would carry everything bodily before it. 'Make haste,
there!' the captain called out imperatively.—'Steward,
send 'em all down below, this minute. I shouldn't be
surprised if before night we were to have a capful of nasty
weather.'

But even as he spoke, the wave, which had caught
Nora's shawl and driven it over to the leeward side, now
in its reflux sucked it back again swiftly to windward, and
left it lying all wet and matted against the gunwale in a
mass of disorder. Dr. Whitaker jumped after it instinctively, and tried to catch it before another wave could carry
it overboard altogether. 'Oh, pray, don't trouble about it,'
Nora cried, in hasty deprecation. 'It isn't worth it. Take
care, or you'll get wet through and through yourself before
you know it!'

'The man's a fool,' the unceremonious captain called
out bluntly from his perch above. 'Get wet indeed! If
another sea like that strikes the ship, it'll wash him clean
overboard.—Come back, sir; I tell you, come back! No
one but a sailor can keep his feet properly against the force
of a sea like that one!'

Nora and the few other passengers who had still remained on deck stood trembling under shelter of the
glazed-in companion-ladder, wondering whether the rash
mulatto would really carry out his foolhardy endeavour to
recover the wrapper. The sailor stood by, ready to batten
down the hatches as soon as the deck was fairly cleared,
and waiting impatiently for the last lingerer. But Dr.
Whitaker took not the slightest notice of captain or sailor,
and merely glanced back at Nora with a quiet smile, as
if to reassure her of his perfect safety. He stood by the
gunwale, just clutching at the shawl, in the very act of
recovering it, when a second sea, still more violent than
the last, struck the ship once more full on the side, and

swept the mulatto helplessly before it right across the quarter-deck. It dashed him with terrific force against the bulwarks on the opposite side; and for a moment, Nora gave a scream of terror, imagining it would carry him overboard with its sudden flood. The next second, the ship righted itself, and they saw the young doctor rising to his feet once more, bruised and dripping, but still not seriously or visibly injured. The sea had washed the shawl once more out of his grasp, with the force of the shock; and instead of rushing back to the shelter of the ladder, he tried even now to recover it a second time from the windward side, where the recoil had again capriciously carried it. 'The shawl, the shawl!' he cried excitedly, gliding once more across the wet and slippery decks as she lurched anew, in the foolish effort to catch the worthless wrapper.

'Confound the man!' the captain roared from his place on the bridge. 'Does he think the Company's going to lose a passenger's life for nothing, just to satisfy his infernal politeness!—Go down, sir—go down, this minute, I tell you; or else, by jingo, if you don't, I shall have you put in irons at once for the rest of the voyage.'

The mulatto looked up at him with a smile and nodded cheerfully. He held up his left hand proudly above his head, with the dripping shawl now waving in his grasp like a much-bedraggled banner, while with his right he gripped a rope firmly and steadily, to hold his own against the next approaching billow. In a second, the big sea was over him once more; and till the huge wall of water had swept its way across the entire breadth of the vessel, Nora and Marian couldn't discover whether it had dashed him bodily overboard or left him still standing by the windward gunwale. There was a pause of suspense while one might count twenty; and then, as the vessel rolled once more to port, Dr. Whitaker's tall figure could be seen, still erect and grasping the cable, with the shawl triumphantly flourished, even so, in his disengaged hand. The next instant, he was over at the ladder, and had placed the wet and soaking wrapper back in the hands of its original possessor.

'Dr. Whitaker,' Nora cried to him, half laughing and half pale with terror, 'I'm very angry with you. You had no right to imperil your life like that for nothing better than a bit of a wrapper. It was awfully wrong of you; and I'll never wear the shawl again as long as I live, now that you've brought it back to me at the risk of drowning.'

The mulatto, smiling unconcernedly in spite of his wetting, bowed a little bow of quiet acquiescence. 'I'm glad to think, Miss Dupuy,' he replied in a low voice, 'that you regard my life as so well worth preserving.—But did you ever before in all your days see anything so glorious as those monstrous billows!'

Nora bit her lip tacitly, and answered nothing for a brief moment. Then she added merely : 'Thank you for your kindness,' in a constrained voice, and turned below into the crowded dining saloon. Dr. Whitaker did not rejoin them ; he went back to his own state-room, to put on some dry clothes after his foolhardy adventure, and think of Nora's eyes in the solitude of his cabin.

There is no position in life more helplessly feeble for grown-up men and women than that of people battened down in a ship at sea in the midst of a great and dangerous tempest. On deck, the captain and the officers, cut off from all communication with below, know how the storm is going and how the ship is weathering it ; but the unconscious passengers in their crowded quarters, treated like children by the rough seafaring men, can only sit below in hopeless ignorance, waiting to learn the fate in store for them when the tempest wills it. And, indeed, the hurricane that night was quite enough to make even strong men feel their own utter and abject powerlessness. From the moment they were all battened down in the big saloon, after the first fresh squall, the storm burst in upon them in real earnest with terrific and ever-increasing violence. The wind howled and whistled fiercely through the ropes and rigging. The ship bounced now on to the steep crest of a swelling billow ; now wallowed helplessly in the deep trough that intervened between each and its mad successor. The sea seemed to dash in upon the side every second with redoubled intensity, sweeping through the scupper-holes with a roar like thunder.

The waves crashed down upon the battened skylights in blinding deluges. Every now and then they could hear the cracking of a big timber—some spar or boom torn off from the masts, like rotten branches from a dead tree, by the mighty force of the irresistible cyclone. Whirling and roaring and sputtering and rattling and creaking, the storm raged on for hour after hour; and the pale and frightened women, sitting huddled together in little groups on the crimson velvet cushions of the stuffy saloon, looked at one another in silent awe, clasping each other's hands with bloodless fingers, by way of companionship in their mute terror. From time to time they could just overhear, in the lulls between the great gusts, the captain's loud voice shouting out inaudible directions to the sailors overhead; and the engineer's bell was rung over and over again, with bewildering frequency, to stop her, back her, ease her, steady her, or put her head once more bravely against the face of the ever-shifting and shattering storm.

Hour after hour went by slowly, and still nobody stirred from the hushed saloon. At eleven all lights were usually put out, with Spartan severity; but this night, in consideration of the hurricane, the stewards left them burning still: they didn't know, they said, when they might be wanted for prayers, if the ship should begin to show signs of sudden foundering. So the passengers sat on still in the saloon together, till four o'clock began to bring back the daylight again with a lurid glare away to eastward. Then the first fury of the hurricane began to abate a little—a very little; and the seas crashed a trifle less frequently against the thick and solid plate-glass of the sealed skylights. Edward at last persuaded Marian and Nora to go down to their state-rooms and try to snatch a short spell of sleep. The danger was over now, he said, and they might fairly venture to recover a bit from the long terror of that awful night.

As they went staggering feebly along the unsteady corridors below, lighted by the dim lamps as yet unextinguished, they happened to pass the door of a state-room whence, to their great surprise, in the midst of that terrible awe-inspiring hurricane, the notes of a violin could be distinctly heard.

mingling strangely in a weird harmony with the groaning
of the wind and the ominous creaking of the overstrained
and rumbling timbers. The sounds were not those of a
regular piece of studied music; they were mere fitful bars
and stray snatches of tempestuous melody, that imitated
and registered the inarticulate music of the whirlwind
itself even as it passed wildly before them. Nora paused a
moment beside the half-open door. 'Why,' she whispered
to Marian in an awe-struck undertone, clutching convulsively at the hand-rail to steady herself, 'it must be Dr.
Whitaker. He's actually playing his violin to himself in
the midst of all this awful uproar!'

'It is,' Edward Hawthorn answered confidently. 'I
know his state-room—that's the number.'

He pushed the half-open door a little farther ajar, and
peeped inside with sudden curiosity. There on the bunk
sat the mulatto doctor, unmoved amid the awful horse-play
of the careering elements, with his violin in his hands, and
a little piece of blank paper ruled with pencilled music-lines
pinned up roughly against the wall of the cabin beside him.
He started and laughed a little at the sudden apparition of
Edward Hawthorn's head within the doorway. 'Ah,' he
said, pointing to a few scratchy pencil-marks on the little
piece of ruled paper, 'you see, Mr. Hawthorn, I couldn't
sleep, and so I've been amusing myself with a fit of composing. I'm catching some fresh ideas for a piece from the
tearing wind and the hubbub of the breakers. Isn't it grand,
the music of the storm! I shall work it up by-and-by, no
doubt, into a little hurricane symphony.—Listen, here—
listen.' And he drew his bow rapidly across the strings
with skilful fingers, and brought forth from the violin some
few bars of a strangely wild and storm-like melody, that
seemed to have caught the very spirit of the terrible tornado
still raging everywhere so madly around them.

'Has the man no feelings,' Nora exclaimed with a
shudder to Marian, outside, 'that he can play his fiddle
in this storm, like Nero or somebody when Rome was
burning!'

'I think,' Marian said, with a little sigh, 'he has some
stronger overpowering feeling underneath, that makes him

think nothing of the hurricane or anything else, but keeps him wrapped up entirely in its own circle.'

Next day, when the sea had gone down somewhat, and the passengers had begun to struggle up on deck one by one with pallid faces, Dr. Whitaker made his appearance once more, clothed and in his right mind, and handed Nora a little roll of manuscript music. Nora took it and glanced carelessly at the first page. She started when she saw it was inscribed in a round and careful copper-plate hand—'To Miss Dupuy.—Hurricane Symphony. By W. Clarkson Whitaker, M.B., Mus. Bac.' Nora read hastily through the first few bars—the soughing and freshening of the wind in its earlier gusts, before the actual tempest had yet swept wildly over them—and murmured half aloud: 'It looks very pretty—very fine, I mean. I should like some day to hear you play it.'

'If you would permit me to prefix your name to the piece when it's published in London,' the mulatto doctor said with an anxious air—'just as I've prefixed it there at the head of the title-page—I should be very deeply obliged and grateful to you.'

Nora hesitated a moment. A brown man! Her name on the first page of his printed music! What would people say in Trinidad? And yet, what excuse could she give for answering no? She pretended for a while to be catching back her veil, that the wind blew about her face and hair, to gain time for consideration; then she said with a smile of apology: 'It would look so conceited of me, you know—wouldn't it, Dr. Whitaker? as if I were setting myself up to be some great one, to whom people were expected to dedicate music.'

The mulatto's face fell a little with obvious disappointment; but he answered quietly: 'As you will, Miss Dupuy. It was somewhat presumptuous of me, perhaps, to think you would accept a dedication from me on so short an acquaintance.'

Nora's cheeks coloured quickly as she replied with a hasty voice; 'O no, Dr. Whitaker; I didn't mean that—indeed, I didn't. It's very kind of you to think of putting my name to your beautiful music. If you look at it that way, I shall ask you as a personal favour to print that very dedication upon it when you get it published in London.'

Dr. Whitaker's eye lighted up with unexpected plea-sure, and he answered : ' Thank you,' slowly and softly. But Nora said to herself in her own heart : ' Goodness gracious, now, just out of politeness to this clever brown man, and because I hadn't strength of mind to say *no* to him, I've gone and put my foot in it terribly. What on earth will papa say about it when he comes to hear of it ! I must try and keep the piece away from him. That is the sort of thing that's sure to happen to one when one once begins knowing brown people !'

CHAPTER XI.

ON the morning when the *Severn* was to reach Trinidad, everybody was up betimes and eagerly looking for the expected land. Nora and Marian went up on deck before breakfast, and there found Dr. Whitaker, opera-glass in hand, scanning the horizon for the first sight of his native island. ' I haven't seen it or my dear father,' he said to Marian, ' for nearly ten years, and I can't tell you how anxious I am once more to see him. I wonder whether he'll have altered much ! But there—ten years is a long time. After ten years, one's pictures of home and friends begin to get terribly indefinite. Still, I shall know him— I'm sure I shall know him. He'll be on the wharf to wel-come us in, and I'm sure I shall recognise his dear old face again.'

' Your father's very well known in the island, the captain tells me,' Marian said, anxious to show some interest in what interested him so much. ' I believe he was very influential in helping to get slavery abolished.'

' He was,' the young doctor answered, kindling up afresh with his ever-ready enthusiasm—' he was ; very in-fluential. Mr. Wilberforce considered that my father, Robert Whitaker, was one of his most powerful coloured

supporters in any of the colonies. I'm proud of my father,
Mrs. Hawthorn—proud of the part he bore in the great
revolution which freed my race. I'm proud to think that
I'm the son of such a man as Robert Whitaker.'

'Now, then, ladies,' the captain put in dryly, coming
upon them suddenly from behind; ' breakfast's ready, and
you won't sight Trinidad, I take it, for at least another
fifty minutes. Plenty of time to get your breakfast quietly
and comfortably, and pack your traps up, before you come
in sight of the Port-o'-Spain lighthouse.'

After breakfast, they all hurried up on deck once more,
and soon the grey peaks and rocky sierras of Trinidad
began to heave in sight straight in front of them. Slowly
the land grew closer and closer, till at last the port and
town lay full in sight before them. Dr. Whitaker was
overflowing with excitement as they reached the wharf.
' In ten minutes,' he cried to Marian—' in ten minutes, I
shall see my dear father.'

It was a strange and motley scene, ever fresh and
interesting to the new-comer from Europe, that first
glimpse of tropical life from the crowded deck of an ocean
steamer. The *Severn* stood off, waiting for the gangways
to be lowered on board, but close up to the high wooden
pier of the lively, bustling little harbour. In front lay the
busy wharf, all alive with a teeming swarm of black faces
—men in light and ragged jackets, women in thin white
muslins and scarlet turbans, children barefooted and half
naked, lying sprawling idly in the very eye of the sun
Behind, white houses with green venetian blinds ; waving
palm trees ; tall hills ; a blazing pale blue sky ; a great
haze of light and shimmer and glare and fervour. All
round, boats full of noisy negroes, gesticulating, shouting
swearing, laughing, and showing their big teeth every
second anew in boisterous merriment. A general pervad
ing sense of bustle and life, all meaningless and all ineffectual ; much noise and little labour ; a ceaseless
chattering, as of monkeys in a menagerie ; a purposeless
running up and down on the pier and 'longshore with
wonderful gesticulations ; a babel of inarticulate sounds
and cries and shouting and giggling. Nothing of it all

clearly visible as an individual fact at first; only a confused mass of heads and faces and bandanas and dresses,
out of which, as the early hubbub of arrival subsided a
little, there stood forth prominently a single foremost figure
—the figure of a big, heavy, oily, fat, dark mulatto, grey-
haired and smooth-faced, dressed in a dirty white linen
suit, and waving his soiled silk pocket handkerchief ostentatiously before the eyes of the assembled passengers. A
supple, vulgar, oleaginous man altogether, with an astonishing air of conceited self-importance, and a profound consciousness of the admiring eyes of the whole surrounding
negro populace.

'How d'ye do, captain?' he shouted aloud in a clear
but thick and slightly negro voice, mouthing his words
with much volubility in the true semi-articulate African
fashion. 'Glad to see de *Severn* has come in punchshual
to her time as usual. Good ship, de *Severn*; neber minds
storms or nuffin.—Well, sah, who have you got on board?
I've come down to meet de doctor and Mr. Hawtorn.
Trinidad is proud to welcome back her children to her
shores agin. Got 'em on board, captain?—got 'em on
board, sah?'

'All right, Bobby,' the captain answered, with easy
familiarity. 'Been having a pull at the mainsheet this
morning?—Ah, I thought so. I thought you'd taken a
cargo of rum aboard. Ah, you sly dog! You've got the
look of it.'

'Massa Bobby, him don't let de rum spile in him
cellar,' a ragged fat negress standing by shouted out in a
stentorian voice. 'Him know de way to keep him from
spilin', so pour him down him own troat in time—eh, Massa
Bobby?'

'Rum,' the oily mulatto responded cheerfully, but with
great dignity, raising his fat brown hand impressively
before him—'rum is de staple produck an' chief commer-
cial commodity of de great and flourishin' island of Trinidad. To drink a moderate quantity of rum every mornin'
before brekfuss is de best way of encouragin' de principal
manufacture of dis island. I do my duty in dat respeck, I
flatter myself, as faithfully as any pusson in de whole of

Trinidad, not exceptin' His Excellency de Governor, who ought to set de best example to de entire community. As de recognised representative of de coloured people of dis colony, I feel bound to teach dem to encourage de manu- facture of rum by my own pussonal example an' earnest endeavour.' And he threw back his greasy neck playfully in a pantomimic representation of the act of drinking off a good glassful of rum-and-water.

The negroes behind laughed immoderately at this sally of the man addressed as Bobby, and cheered him on with loud vociferations. ' Evidently,' Edward said to Nora, with a face of some disgust, ' this creature is the chartered buffoon and chief jester to the whole of Trinidad. They all seem to recognise him and laugh at him, and I see even the captain himself knows him well of old, evidently.'

' Bless your soul, yes,' the captain said, overhearing the remark. ' Everybody in the island knows Bobby. Good-natured old man, but conceited as a peacock, and foolish too.—Everybody knows you here,' raising his voice, ' don't they, Bobby ? '

The grey-haired mulatto took off his broad-brimmed Panama hat and bowed profoundly. ' I flatter myself,' he said, looking round about him complacently on the crowd of negroes, ' der isn't a better known man in de whole great and flourishin' island of Trinidad dan Bobby Whitaker.'

Edward and Marian started suddenly, and even Nora gave a little shiver of surprise and disappointment. ' Whitaker,' Edward repeated slowly—' Whitaker—Bobby Whitaker !—You don't mean to tell us, surely, captain, that that man's our Dr. Whitaker's father ! '

' Yes, I do,' the captain answered, smiling grimly. ' That's his father.—Dr. Whitaker ! hi, you, sir ; where have you got to ? Don't you see ?—there's your father.'

Edward turned at once to seek for him, full of a sudden unspoken compassion. He had not far to seek. A little way off, standing irresolutely by the gunwale, with a strange terrified look in his handsome large eyes, and a painful twitching nervously evident at the trembling corners of his full mouth, Dr. Whitaker gazed intently

and speechlessly at the fat mulatto in the white linen suit.
It was clear that the old man did not yet recognise his
son ; but the son had recognised his father instantaneously
and unhesitatingly, as he stood there playing the buffoon
in broad daylight before the whole assembled ship's company. Edward locked at the poor young fellow with profound commiseration. Never in his life before had he
seen shame and humiliation more legibly written on a
man's very limbs and features. The unhappy young
mulatto, thunderstruck by the blow, had collapsed entirely.
It was too terrible for him. Coming in, fresh from his
English education, full of youthful hopes and vivid enthu-
siasms, proud of the father he had more than half forgotten, and anxious to meet once more that ideal picture
he had carried away with him of the liberator of Trinidad
—here he was met, on the very threshold of his native
island, by this horrible living contradiction of all his fervent fancies and imaginings. The Robert Whitaker he
had once known faded away as if by magic into absolute
nonentity, and that voluble, greasy, self-satisfied, buf-
foonish old brown man was the only thing left that he
could now possibly call ' my father.'

Edward pitied him far too earnestly to obtrude just
then upon his shame and sorrow. But the poor mulatto,
meeting his eyes accidentally for a single second, turned
upon him such a mutely appealing look of profound
anguish, that Edward moved over slowly toward the
grim captain and whispered to him in a low undertone:
' Don't speak to that man Whitaker again, I beg of you.
Don't you see his poor son there's dying of shame for
him ? '

The captain stared back at him with the same curious
half-sardonic look that Marian had more than once
noticed upon his impassive features. ' Dying of shame ! '
he answered, smiling carelessly. ' Ho, ho, ho ! that's a
good one ! Dying of shame is he, for poor old Bobby !
Why, sooner or later, you know, he'll have to get used to
him. Besides, I tell you, whether you talk to him or
whether you don't, old Bobby 'll go on talking about himself as long as there's anybody left anywhere about who'll

stand and listen to him.—You just hark there to what he's saying now. What's he up to next, I wonder ? '

' Yes, ladies and gentlemen,' the old mulatto was proceeding aloud, addressing now in a set speech the laughing passengers on board the *Severn*, 'I'm de Honourable Robert Whitaker, commonly called Bobby Whitaker, de leadin' member of de coloured party in dis island. Along wit my lamented friend Mr. Wilberforce, an' de British Parliament, I was de chief instrument in procurin' de abolition of slavery an' de freedom of de slaves troughout de whole English possessions. Millions of my fellow-men were moanin' an' groanin' in a painful bondage. I have a heart dat cannot witstand de appeal of misery. I laboured for dem ; I toiled for dem ; I bore de brunt of de battle ; an' in de end I conquered—I conquered. Wit de aid of my friend Mr. Wilberforce, by superhuman exertions, I succeeded in passin' de grand act of slavery emancipation. You behold in me de leadin' actor in dat famous great an' impressive drama. I'm an ole man now; but I have prospered in dis world, as de just always do, says de Psalmist, an' I shall be glad to see any of you whenever you choose at my own residence, an' to offer to you in confidence a glass of de excellent staple produck of dis island—I allude to de wine of de country, de admirable beverage known as rum ! '

There was another peal of foolish laughter from the crowd of negroes at this one ancient threadbare joke, and a faint titter from the sillier passengers on board the *Severn*. Edward looked over appealingly at the old buffoon ; but the mulatto misunderstood his look of deprecation, and bowed once more profoundly, with immense importance, straight at him, like a sovereign acknowledging the plaudits of his subjects.

' Yes,' he continued, ' I shall be happy to see any of you—you, sah, or you—at my own estate, Whitaker Hall, in dis island, whenever you find it convenient to visit me. You have on board my son, Dr. Whitaker, de future leader of de coloured party in de Council of Trinidad ; an' you have no doubt succeeded in makin' his acquaintance in de course of your voyage from de shores of England. Dr,

Whitaker, of de University of Edinburgh, after pursuin'
his studies——'

The poor young man gave an audible groan, and turned
away, in his poignant disgrace, to the very farthest end of
the vessel. It was terrible enough to have all his hopes
dashed and falsified in this awful fashion; but to be
humiliated and shamed by name before the staring eyes of
all his fellow-passengers—that last straw was more than
his poor bursting heart could possibly endure. He walked
away, broken and tottering, and leaned over the opposite
side of the vessel, letting the hot tears trickle unreproved
down his dusky cheeks into the ocean below.

At that very moment, before the man they called Bobby
Whitaker could finish his sentence, a tall white man, of
handsome and imposing presence, walked out quietly from
among the knot of people behind the negroes, and laid his
hand with a commanding air on the fat old mulatto's broad
shoulder. Bobby Whitaker turned round suddenly and
listened with attention to something that the white man
whispered gently but firmly at his astonished ear. Then
his lower jaw dropped in surprise, and he fell behind,
abashed for a second, into the confused background of
laughing negroes. Partly from his childish recollections,
but partly, too, by the aid of the photographs, Edward
immediately recognised the tall white man. 'Marian,
Marian!' he cried, waving his hand in welcome towards
the new-comer, 'it's my father, my father!'

And even as he spoke, a pang of pain ran through him
as he thought of the difference between the first two greetings. He couldn't help feeling proud in his heart of hearts
of the very look and bearing of his own father—tall, erect,
with his handsome, clear-cut face and full white beard,
the exact type of a self-respecting and respected English
gentleman; and yet, the mere reflex of his own pride and
satisfaction revealed to him at once the bitter poignancy of
Dr. Whitaker's unspeakable disappointment. As the two
men stood there on the wharf side by side, in quiet conversation, James Hawthorn with his grave, severe, earnest
expression, and Bobby Whitaker with his greasy, vulgar,
negro joviality speaking out from every crease in his fat

chin and every sparkle of his small pig's eyes, the contrast
between them was so vast and so apparent, that it seemed
to make the old mulatto's natural vulgarity and coarseness
of fibre more obvious and more unmistakable than ever to
all beholders.

In a minute more, a gangway was hastily lowered from
the wharf on to the deck; and the first man that came
down it, pushed in front of a great crowd of eager,
grinning, and elbowing negroes—mostly in search of small
jobs among the passengers—was Bobby Whitaker. The
moment he reached the deck, he seemed to take possession
of it and of all the passengers by pure instinct, as if he
were father to the whole shipload of them. The captain,
the crew, and the other authorities were effaced instantly.
Bobby Whitaker, with easy, greasy geniality, stood bowing
and waving his hand on every side, in an access of universal
graciousness towards the entire company. ' My son ! ' he
said, looking round him inquiringly—' my son, Dr.
Whitaker, of de Edinburgh University—where is he ?—
where is he ? My dear boy ! Let him come forward and
embrace his fader ! '

Dr. Whitaker, in spite of his humiliation, had all a
a mulatto's impulsive affectionateness. Ashamed and
abashed as he was, he yet rushed forward with unaffected
emotion to take his father's outstretched hand. But old
Bobby had no idea of getting over this important meeting
in such a simple and undemonstrative manner ; for him,
it was a magnificent opportunity for theatrical display, on
no account to be thrown away before the faces of so many
distinguished European strangers. Holding his son for a
second at arm's length, in the centre of a little circle that
quickly gathered around the oddly-matched pair, he surveyed the young doctor with a piercing glance from head
to foot, sticking his neck a little on one side with critical
severity, and then, bursting into a broad grin of oily delight, he exclaimed, in a loud stagey soliloquy : ' My son, my
son, my own dear son, Wilberforce Clarkson Whitaker ! De
inheritor of de tree names most intimately bound up wit de
great revolution I have had de pride and de honour of
effectin' for unborn millions of my African bredderin.

My son, my son! We receive you wit transport! Welcome to Trinidad—welcome to Trinidad!'

'Father, father,' Dr. Whitaker whispered in a low voice, 'let us go aside a little—down into my cabin or somewhere—away from this crowd here. I am so glad, so happy to be back with you again; so delighted to be home once more, dear, dear father. But don't you see, everybody is looking at us and observing us!'

The old mulatto glanced around him with an oily glance of profound self-satisfaction. Yes, undoubtedly; he was the exact centre of an admiring audience. It was just such a house as he loved to play to. He turned once more to his trembling son, whose sturdy knees were almost giving way feebly beneath him, and redoubled the ardour of his paternal demonstrativeness. 'My son, my son, my own dear boy!' he said once more; and then, stepping back two paces and opening his arms effusively, he ran forward quickly with short mincing steps, and pressed the astonished doctor with profound warmth to his swelling bosom. There was an expansiveness and a gushing effusion about the action which made the spectators titter audibly; and the titter cut the poor young mulatto keenly to the heart with a sense of his utter helplessness and ridiculousness in this absurd situation. He wondered to himself when the humiliating scene would ever be finished. But the old man was not satisfied yet. Releasing his son once more from his fat grasp, he placed his two big hands akimbo on his hips, puckered up his eyebrows as if searching for some possible flaw in a horse or in a woman's figure —he was a noted connoisseur in either—and held his head pushed jauntily forward, staring once more at his son with his small pig's eyes from top to toe. At last, satisfied apparently with his close scrutiny, and prepared to acknowledge that it was all very good, he seized the young doctor quickly by the shoulders, and kissing him with a loud smack on either cheek, proceeded to slobber him piecemeal all over the face, exactly like a nine-months-old baby. Dr. Whitaker's cheeks tingled and burned, so that even through that dusky skin, Edward, who stood a little distance off, commiserating him, could see the hot blood rushing to his face by the deepened and darkened colour in the very centre.

Presently old Bobby seemed to be sufficiently sated with this particular form of theatrical entertainment, and turned round presently to the remainder of the company. 'My son,' he said, not without a real touch of heartfelt, paternal pride, as he glanced towards the gentlemanly-looking and well-dressed young doctor, 'your fellow-passengers! Introduce me! Which is de son of my ole and valued friend, de Honourable James Hawtorn, of Wag-water?'

Dr. Whitaker, glad to divert attention from himself on any excuse, waved his hand quietly towards Edward.

'How do you do, Mr. Whitaker?' Edward said, in as low and quiet a tone as possible, anxious as he was to disappoint the little gaping crowd of amused spectators. 'We have all derived a great deal of pleasure from your son's society on our way across. His music has been the staple entertainment of the whole voyage. We have appreciated it immensely.'

But old Bobby was not to be put off with private conversation aside in a gentle undertone. He was accustomed to living his life in public, and he wasn't going to be balked of his wonted entertainment. 'Yes, Mr. Hawtorn,' he answered in a loud voice, 'you are right, sah. De taste for music, an' de taste for beauty in de ladies are two tastes dat are seldom wantin' to de sons or de grandsons of Africa, however far removed from de original negro.' (As he spoke, he glanced back with a touch of contempt and an infinite superiority of manner at the pure-blooded blacks, who were now busily engaged in picking up portmanteaus from the deck, and squabbling with one another as to which was to carry the buckras' luggage. Your mulatto, however dark, always in a good-humoured, tolerant way, utterly despises his coal-black brethren.) 'Bote dose tastes are highly developed in my own pusson. But no doubt my son, Wilberforce Clarkson Whitaker, is liable to inherit from his fader's family. In de exercise of de second, I cannot fail to perceive dat dis lady beside you must be Mrs. Hawtorn. Sah '—with a sidelong leer of his

4

fat eyes—'I congratulate you most sincerely on your own
taste in female beauty. A very nice, fresh-lookin' young
lady, Mrs. Hawtorn.'

Marian's face grew fiery red; and Edward hardly knew
whether to laugh off the awkward compliment, or to draw
himself up and stroll away, as though the conversation
had reached its natural ending.

'And de odder young lady,' Bobby went on, quite unconscious of the effect he had produced—'de odder young
lady? Your sister, now, or Mrs. Hawtorn's?'

'This is Miss Dupuy, of Orange Grove,' Edward
answered hesitatingly; for he hardly knew what remark
old Bobby might next venture upon. And, indeed, as a
matter of fact, the old mulatto's conversation, even in the
presence of ladies, was not at all times restrained by all
those artificial rules of decorum imposed on most of us
by what appeared to him a ridiculously straitlaced and
puritanical white conventionality.

But Edward's answer seemed to have an extraordinary
effect in sobering and toning down the old man's exuberant
volubility; he pulled off his hat with a respectful bow,
and said in a lower and more polite voice: 'I have de
honour of knowing Miss Dupuy's fader; I am proud to
make Miss Dupuy's acquaintance.'

'Here, Bobby!' the captain called out from a little
forward—'you come here, say. The first officer wants to
introduce you'—with a wink at Edward—'to His Excellency the Peruvian ambassador.—Look here, Mr. Hawthorn; don't you let Bobby talk too long to your ladies,
sir. He sometimes blurts out something, you know, that
ladies ain't exactly accustomed to. We seafaring men are
a bit rough on occasion ourselves, certainly; but we know
how to behave for all that before the women. Bobby
don't; you'd better be careful.'

'Thank you,' Edward said, and again felt his heart
smitten with a sort of remorse for poor Dr. Whitaker.
That quick, sensitive, enthusiastic young man to be tied
down for life to such a father! It was too terrible. In fact,
it was a tragedy.

'Splendid take-down for that stuck-up young brown

doctor,' the English officer exclaimed aside in a whisper to Edward. 'Shake a little of the confounded conceit out of him, I should say. He wanted taking down a peg.—Screaming farce, isn't he, the old father?'

'I never saw a more pitiable or pitiful scene in my whole life,' Edward answered earnestly. 'Poor fellow, I'm profoundly scrry for him; he looks absolutely broken-hearted.'

The young cfficer gazed at him in mute astonishment. 'Can't see a joke, that fellow Hawthorn,' he thought to himself. 'Had all the fun worked out of him, I suppose, over there at Cambridge. Awful prig! Quite devoid of the sense of humour. Sorry for his poor wife; she'll have a dull life of it.—Never saw such an amusing old fool in all my days as that ridiculous, fat old nigger fellow!'

Meanwhile, James Hawthorn had been standing on the wharf, waiting for the first crush of negroes and hangers-on to work itself off, and looking for an easy opportunity to ccme aboard in crder to meet his son and daughter. By-and-by the crush subsided, and the old man stepped cn to the gangway and made his way down upon the deck.

In a moment, Edward was wringing his hand fervently, and father and scn had exchanged one single kiss of recognition in that half-shamefaced, hasty fashion in which men cf our race usually get through that very un-English ceremony of greeting.

'Father, father,' Edward said, 'I am so thankful to see you once mcre; sc anxious to see my dear mother.'

There were tears standing in both their eyes as his father answered: 'My boy, my boy! I've denied myself this pleasure for years; and now—now it's ccme, it's almost too much for me.'

There was a moment's pause, and then Mr. Hawthorn turned to Marian. 'My daughter,' he said, kissing her with a fatherly kiss, 'we know you, and love you already, from Edward's letters; and we'll do our best, as far as we can, to make you happy.'

There was another pause, and then the father said again: 'You didn't get my telegram, Edward?'

'Yes, father, I got it; but not till we were on the very

point of starting. The steamer was actually under weigh, and we couldn't have stopped even if we had wished to. There was nothing for it but to come on as we were, in spite of it.'

'Oh, Mr. Hawthorn, there's papa!' Nora cried excitedly. 'There he is, coming down the gangway.' And as she spoke, Mr. Dupuy's portly form was seen advancing towards them with slow deliberateness.

For a second, he gazed about him curiously, looking for Nora; then, as he saw her, he walked over towards her in his leisurely, dawdling, West Indian fashion. Nora darted forward and flung her arms impulsively around him. 'So you've come, Nora,' the old gentleman said quietly, disembarrassing himself with elephantine gracefulness from her close embrace—'so you've come, after all, in spite of my telegram!—How was this, my dear? How was this, tell me?'

'Yes, papa,' Nora answered, a little abashed at his serene manner. 'The telegram was too late—it was thrown on board after we'd started. But we've got out all safe, you see.—And Marian—you know—Marian Ord—Mrs. Hawthorn that is now—she's taken great care of me: and, except for the hurricane, we've had such a delightful voyage!'

Mr. Dupuy drew himself up to his stateliest eminence and looked straight across at Marian Hawthorn with stiff politeness. 'I didn't know it was to Mrs. Hawthorn, I'm sure,' he said, 'that I was to be indebted for your safe arrival here in Trinidad. It was very good of Mrs. Hawthorn, I don't doubt, to bring you out to us and act as your chaperon. I am much obliged to Mrs. Hawthorn for her kind attention and care of you on the voyage. I must thank Mrs. Hawthorn very sincerely for the trouble she may have been put to on your account. Good morning, Mrs. Hawthorn.—Good morning, Mr. Hawthorn. Your son, I suppose? Ah, so I imagined. Good morning, good morning.' He raised his hat with formal courtesy to Marian, and bowed slightly to the son and father. Then he drew Nora's arm carefully in his, and was just about to walk her immediately off the steamer, when Nora burst from him in the utmost amazement and rushed up to kiss Marian.

'Papa,' she cried, 'I don't think you understand. This is Marian Ord, don't you know? General Ord's daughter, that I've written to you about so often. She's my dearest friend, and now she's married to Mr. Edward Hawthorn—this is he—and Aunt Harriet gave me in charge to her to come across with; and I *must* just say good-bye to her before I leave her.—Thank you, dear, thank you both so much for all your kindness. Not, of course, that it matters about saying good-bye to you, for you and we will be such very, very near neighbours, and of course we will see a great deal of one another.—Won't we, papa? We shall be near neighbours, and see a great deal of Marian always, now she's come here to live—won't we?'

Mr. Dupuy bowed again very stiffly. 'We shall be very near neighbours, undoubtedly,' he answered with unruffled politeness; and I shall hope to take an early opportunity of paying my respects to—to your friend, General Ord's daughter.—I am much obliged, once more, to Mrs. Hawthorn for her well-meant attentions. Good morning.—This way, Nora, my dear. This way to the Orange Grove carriage.'

'Father,' Edward exclaimed, in doubt and dismay, looking straight down into his father's eyes, 'what does it all mean? Explain it all to us. I'm utterly bewildered. Why did you telegraph to us not to come? And why did Nora Dupuy's father telegraph to her, too, an identical message?'

Mr. Hawthorn drew a deep breath and looked back at him with a face full of consternation and pity. 'He telegraphed to her, too, did he?' he muttered half to himself in slow reflection. 'He telegraphed to prevent her from coming out in the *Severn*! I might have guessed as much —it's very like him.—My boy, my boy—and my dear daughter—this is a poor welcome for you, a very poor welcome! We never wanted you to come out here; and if we could, we would have prevented it. But now that you've come, you've come, and there's no helping it. We must just try to do our best to make you both tolerably comfortable.'

Marian stood in blank astonishment and silent wonder at this strange greeting. A thousand vague possibilities floated instantaneously through her mind, to be dismissed the next second, on closer consideration, as absolutely impossible. Why on earth did this handsome, dignified, courtly old gentleman wish to keep them away from Trinidad? He wasn't poor; he wasn't uneducated; he wasn't without honour in his own country. That he was a gentleman to the backbone, she could see and feel the moment she looked at him and heard him speak. What, then, could be his objection to his son's coming out to visit him in his own surroundings? Had he committed some extraordinary crime? Was he an ex-convict, or a fraudulent bankrupt, or a defaulting trustee? Did he fear to let his son discover his shame? But no. The bare idea was absolutely impossible. You had only to gaze once upon that fine, benevolent, clear-cut, transparently truthful face —as transparently truthful as Edward's own—to see immediately that James Hawthorn was a man of honour. It was an insoluble mystery, and Marian's heart sank within her as she wondered to herself what this gloomy welcome foreboded for the future.

'Father,' Edward exclaimed, looking at him once more with appealing eyes, 'do explain to us what you mean. Why didn't you want us to come to Trinidad? The suspense is too terrible! We shall be expecting something worse than the reality. Tell us now. Whatever it is, we are strong enough to bear it. I know it can be nothing mean or dishonourable that you have to conceal from us. For Marian's sake, explain it, explain it!'

The old man turned his face away with a bitter gesture. 'My boy, my boy, my poor boy,' he answered slowly and remorsefully, 'I cannot tell you. I can never tell you. You will find it out for yourself soon enough. But I—I— I can never tell you!'

CHAPTER XII.

EDWARD and Marian spent their first week in Trinidad
with the Hawthorns senior. Mrs. Hawthorn was kindness
itself to Marian: a dear, gentle, motherly old lady, very
proud of her boy—especially of his ability to read Arabic,
which seemed to her a profundity of learning never yet
dreamt of in the annals of humanity—and immensely
pleased with her new daughter-in-law: but nothing on
earth that Marian could say to her would induce her to
unlock the mystery of that alarming telegram. 'No, no,
my dear,' she would say, shaking her head gloomily and
wiping her spectacles, whenever Marian recurred to the
subject, ' you'll find it all out only too soon. God forbid,
my darling, that ever I should break it to you. I love you
far too well for that. Marian, Marian, my dear daughter,
you should never, never, never have come here !' And
then she would burst immediately into tears. And that
was all that poor frightened Marian could ever get out of
her new mother-in-law.

All that first week, old Mr. Hawthorn was never tired
of urging upon Edward to go back again at once to England. 'I can depart in peace now, my boy,' he said; 'I
have seen you at last, and known you, and had my heart
gladdened by your presence here. Indeed, if you wish it,
I'd rather go back to England with you again, than that
you should stay in this unsuitable Trinidad. Why bury
your talents and your learning here, when you might be
rising to fame and honour over in London? What's the
use of your classical knowledge out in the West Indies?
What's the use of your Arabic? What's the use of your
law, even? We have nothing to try here but petty cases
between planter and servant; of what good to you in that
will be all your work at English tenures and English land
laws? You're hiding your light under a bushel. You're
putting a trotting horse into a hansom cab. You're wasting

your Arabic on people who don't even know the difference
between Greek and Latin.'

To all which, Edward steadily replied that he wouldn't
go back as long as this mystery still hung unsolved over
him ; and that, as he had practically made an agreement
with the Colonial Government, it would be dishonourable
in him to break it for unknown and unspecified reasons.
As soon as possible, he declared firmly, he would take up
his abode in his own district.

House-hunting is reduced to its very simplest elements
in the West Indian colonies. There is one house in each
parish or county which has been inhabited from time immemorial by one functionary for the time being. The late
Attorney-General dies of yellow fever, or drinks himself to
death, or gets promotion, or retires to England, and another
Attorney-General is duly appointed by constituted authority
in his vacant place. The new man succeeds naturally to
the house and furniture of his predecessor—as naturally,
indeed, as he succeeds to any of his other functions, offices,
and prerogatives. Not that there is the least compulsion
in the matter, only you must. As there is no other house
vacant in the community, and as nobody ever thinks of
building a new one—except when the old one tumbles
down by efflux of time or shock of earthquake—the only
thing left for one to do is to live in the place immemorially
occupied by all one's predecessors in the same office. Hence
it happened that at the beginning of their second week in
the island of Trinidad, Marian and Edward Hawthorn
found themselves ensconced with hardly any trouble in the
roomy bungalow known as Mulberry Lodge, and here-
ditarily attached to the post of District Court Judge for the
district of Westmoreland.

Marian laid herself out at once for callers, and very soon
the callers began to drop in. About the fourth day after
they had settled into their new house, she was sitting in
the big, bare, tropical-looking drawing-room—a great,
gaunt, square barn, scantily furnished with a few tables and
rocking-chairs upon the carpetless polished floor—so gaunt
that even Marian's deft fingers failed to make it at first
look home-like or habitable—when a light carriage drew

up hastily with a dash at the front door of the low bungalow.
The young bride pulled her bows straight quickly at the
heavy, old-fashioned gilt mirror, and waited anxiously to
receive the expected visitors. It was her first appearance
as mistress of her establishment. In a minute, Thomas,
the negro butler—every man-servant is a butler in Trinidad,
even if he is only a boy of twenty—ushered the new-comers
pompously into the bare drawing-room. Marian took
their cards and glanced at them hastily. Two gentlemen
—the Honourable Colonial Secretary, and the Honourable
Director of Irrigation.

The Colonial Secretary sidled into a chair, and took up
his parable at once with a very profuse and ponderous
apology. ' My wife, Mrs. Hawthorn, my wife, I'm sorry
to say, was most unfortunately unable to accompany me
here this morning.—Charmingly you've laid out this room,
really ; so very different from what it used to be in poor
old Macmurdo's time.—Isn't it, Colonel Daubeny ?—Poor
old Macmurdo died in the late yellow fever, you know, my
dear madam, and Mr. Hawthorn fills his vacancy. Excellent fellow, poor old Macmurdo—ninth judge I've known
killed off by yellow fever in this district since I've been
here.—My wife, I was saying, when your charming room
compelled me to digress, is far from well at present—a
malady of the country : this shocking climate ; or else, I'm
sure, she'd have been delighted to call upon you with
me this morning. The loss is hers, the loss is hers,
Mrs. Hawthorn. I shall certainly tell her so. Immensely
sorry.'

Colonel Daubeny, the Honourable Director of Irrigation,
was a far jauntier and more easy-spoken man. ' And Mrs.
Daubeny, my dear madam,' he said with a fluent manner
that Marian found exceedingly distasteful, ' is most unfortunately just this moment down—with toothache. Uncommon nasty thing to be down with, toothache. A
perfect martyr to it. She begged me to make her excuses.
—Mr. Hawthorn '—to Edward, who had just come in—
' Mrs. Daubeny begged me to make her excuses. She re-
grets that she can't call to-day on Mrs. Hawthorn. Beautiful view you have, upon my word, from your front piazza.'

'It's the same view, I've no doubt,' Edward answered severely, 'as it used to be in the days of my predecessor.'

'Eh! What! Ah, bless my soul! Quite so,' Colonel Daubeny answered, dropping his eye-glass from his eye in some amazement.—'Ha! Devilish good, that—devilish good, really, Mr. Hawthorn.'

Marian was a little surprised that Edward, usually so impassive, should so unmistakably snub the Colonel at first sight; and yet she felt there was something very offensive in the man's familiar manner, that made the retort perfectly justifiable, and even necessary.

They lingered a little while, talking very ordinary tropical small-talk; and then the Colonel, with an ugly smile, took up his hat, and declared, with many unnecessary asseverations, that he must really be off this very minute. Mrs. Daubeny would so much regret having lost the precious opportunity. The Honourable Colonial Secretary rose at the same moment and added that he must be going too. Mrs. Fitzmaurice would never forgive herself for that distressing local malady which had so unfortunately deprived her of the privilege and pleasure.—Good morning, good morning.

But as both gentlemen jumped into the dog-cart outside, Edward could hear the Colonial Secretary, through the open door, saying to the Colonel in a highly amused voice: 'By George, he gave you as much as he got every bit, I swear, Daubeny.'

To which the Colonel responded with a short laugh: 'Yes, my dear fellow; and didn't you see, by Jove, he twigged it?'

At this they both laughed together immoderately, and drove off at once laughing, very much pleased with one another.

Before Marian and her husband had time to exchange their surprise and wonder at such odd behaviour on the part of two apparently well-bred men, another buggy drove up to the door, from which a third gentleman promptly descended. His card showed him to be the wealthy proprietor of a large and flourishing neighbouring sugar-estate.

'Called round,' he said to Edward, with a slight bow towards Marian, 'just to pay my respects to our new judge, whom I'm glad to welcome to the district of Westmoreland. A son of Mr. Hawthorn of Agualta is sure to be popular with most of his neighbours.—Ah—hem—my wife, I'm sorry to say, Mrs. Hawthorn, is at present suffering from—extreme exhaustion, due to the heat. She hopes you'll excuse her not calling upon you. Otherwise, I'm sure, she'd have been most delighted, most delighted.— Dear me, what an exquisite prospect you have from your veranda!' The neighbouring planter stopped for perhaps ten minutes in the midst of languishing conversation, and then vanished exactly as his two predecessors had done before him.

Marian turned to her husband in blank dismay. 'O Edward, Edward!' she cried, unable to conceal her chagrin and humiliation, 'what on earth can be the meaning of it?'

'My darling,' he answered, taking her hand in his tenderly, 'I haven't the very faintest conception.'

In the course of the afternoon, three more gentlemen called, each alone, and each of them in turn apologised profusely, in almost the very selfsame words, for his wife's absence. The last was a fat old gentleman in the Customs' service, who declared with effusion many times over that Mrs. Bolitho was really prostrated by the extraordinary season. 'Most unusual weather, this, Mrs. Hawthorn. I've never known so depressing a summer in the island of Trinidad since I was a boy, ma'am.'

'So it would seem,' Edward answered dryly. 'The whole female population of the island seems to be suffering from an extraordinary complication of local disorders.'

'Bless my soul!' the fat gentleman ejaculated with a stare. 'Then you've found out that, have you?—Excuse me, excuse me. I—didn't know—— Hm, I hardly expected that you expected—or rather, that Mrs. Hawthorn expected—— Ah, quite so.—Good morning, good morning.'

Marian flung herself in a passion of tears upon the drawing-room sofa. 'If anyone else calls this afternoon,

Thomas,' she said, ' I'm not at home. I won't see them
—I can't see them; I'll endure it no longer.—O Edward,
darling, for God's sake, tell me, why on earth are they
treating us as if—as if I were some sort of moral leper?
They won't call upon me. What can be the reason of it?'

Edward Hawthorn held his head between his hands
and walked rapidly up and down the bare drawing-room.
'I can't make it out,' he cried: 'I can't understand it.
Marian—dearest—it is too terrible!'

CHAPTER XIII.

A FORTNIGHT after Nora's arrival in Trinidad, Mr. Tom
Dupuy, neatly dressed in all his best, called over one evening at Orange Grove for the express purpose of speaking
seriously with his pretty cousin. Mr. Tom had been across
to see her more than once already, to be sure, and had condescended to observe to many of his acquaintances, on his
return from his call, that Uncle Theodore's girl, just come
out from England, was really in her way a deuced elegant
and attractive creature. In Mr. Tom's opinion, she would
make a devilish fine person to sit at the head of the table
at Pimento Valley. 'A man in my position in life wants
a handsome woman, you know,' he said, ' to do the honours,
and keep up the dignity of the family, and look after the
woman-servants, and all that sort of thing; so Uncle
Theodore and I have arranged beforehand that it would be
a very convenient plan if Nora and I were just to go and
make a match of it.'

With the object of definitely broaching this precon-
certed harmony to his unconscious cousin, Mr. Tom had
decked himself in his very smartest coat and trousers,
stuck a *gloire de Dijon* rose in his top button-hole, mounted
his celebrated grey Mexican pony, ' Sambo Gal,' and ridden
across to Orange Grove in the cool of the evening.

Nora was sitting by herself with her cup of tea in the
little boudoir that opened out on to the terrace garden,
with its big bamboos and yuccas and dracæna trees, when

Mr. Tom Dupuy was announced by Rosina as waiting to see her.

'Show him in, Rosina,' Nora said with a smile: 'and ask Aunt Clemmy to send up another teacup. Good evening, Tom. I'm afraid you'll find it a little dull here, as it happens, this evening, for papa's gone down to Port-o'-Spain on business; so you'll have nobody to talk to you to-night about the prospects of the year's sugar-crop.'

Tom Dupuy seated himself on the ottoman beside her with cousinly liberty. 'Oh, it don't matter a bit, Nora,' he answered with his own peculiar gallantry. 'I don't mind. In fact, I came over on purpose this evening, Uncle Theodore was out, because I'd got something very particular I wanted to talk over with you in private.'

'In-deed,' Nora answered emphatically. 'I'm surprised to hear it. I assure you, Tom, I'm absolutely ignorant on the subject of cane-culture.'

'Girls brought up in England mostly are,' Tom Dupuy replied with the air of a man who generally makes a great concession. 'They don't appear to feel much interest in sugar, like other people. I suppose in England there's nothing much grown except corn and cattle.—But that wasn't what I came to talk about to-night, Nora. I've got something on my mind that Uncle Theodore and I have been thinking over, and I want to make a proposition to you about it.'

'Well, Tom?'

'Well, Nora, you see, it's like this. As you know, Orange Grove is Uncle Theodore's to leave; and after his time, he'll leave it to you, of course; but Pimento Valley's entailed on me; and that being so, Uncle Theodore lets me have it on lease during his lifetime, so that, of course, whatever I spend upon it in the way of permanent improvements is really spent in bettering what's practically as good as my own property.'

'I understand. Quite so.—Have a cup of tea?'

'Thank you.—Well, Pimento Valley, you know, is one of the very best sugar-producing estates in the whole island. I've introduced the patent Browning regulators for the centrifugal process; and I've imported some of these new

Indian mongooses that everybody's talking about to kill off
the cane-rats ; and I've got some splendid stock rattoons
over from Mauritius ; and altogether, a finer or more
creditable irrigated estate I don't think you'll find—though
it's me that says it—in the island of Trinidad. Why,
Nora, at our last boiling, I assure you the greater part of
the liquor turned out to be seventeen over proof ; while the
molasses stood at twenty-nine specific gravity ; giving a
yield, you know, of something like one hogshead decimal
four on the average to the acre of canes under cultivation.'

Nora held up her fan carelessly to smother a yawn.
'I dare say it did, Tom,' she answered with obvious un-
concern ; 'but, you know, I told you I didn't understand
anything on earth about sugar; and you said it wasn't
about that that you wanted to talk to me in private this
evening.'

'Yes, yes, Nora; you're quite right; it isn't. It's
about a far deeper and more interesting subject than sugar
that I'm going to speak to you.' (Nora mentally guessed
it must be rum.) 'I only mentioned these facts, you see,
just to show the sort of yield we're making now at Pimento
Valley. A man who does a return like that, of course,
must naturally be making a very tidy round little income.'

'I'm awfully glad to hear it, I'm sure, for your sake,'
Nora answered unconcernedly.

'I thought you would be, Nora; I was sure you would
be. Naturally, it's a matter that touches us both very
closely. You see, as you're to inherit Orange Grove, and
as I'm to inherit Pimento Valley, Uncle Theodore and I
think it would be a great pity that the two old estates—
the estates bound up so intimately with the name and fame
of the fighting Dupuys—should ever be divided or go out
of the family. So we've agreed together, Uncle Theodore
and I, that I should endeavour to unite them by mutual
arrangement.'

'I don't exactly understand,' Nora said, as yet quite
unsuspicious of his real meaning.

'Why, you know, Nora, a man can't live upon sugar
and rum alone.'

'Certainly not,' Nora interrupted ; 'even if he's a con-

firmed drunkard, it would be quite impossible. He must
have something solid occasionally to eat as well.'

'Ah, yes,' Tom said, in a sentimental tone, endeavouring to rise as far as he was able to the height of the occasion. 'And he must have something more than that, too,
Nora: he must have sympathy; he must have affection;
he must have a companion in life; he must have somebody,
you know, to sit at the head of his table, and to—to—
to——'

'To pour out tea for him,' Nora suggested blandly,
filling his cup a second time.

Tom reddened a little. It wasn't exactly the idea he
wanted, and he began to have a faint undercurrent of
suspicion that Nora was quietly laughing at him in her
sleeve. 'Ah, well, to pour out tea for him,' he went on,
somewhat suspiciously; 'and to share his joys and sorrows,
and his hopes and aspirations——'

'About the sugar-crop?' Nora put in once more, with
provoking calmness.

'Well, Nora, you may laugh if you like,' Tom said
warmly; 'but this is a very serious subject, I can tell you,
for both of us. What I mean to say is that Uncle Theodore
and I have settled it would be a very good thing indeed if
we two were to get up a match between us.'

'A match between you,' Nora echoed in a puzzled
manner—'a match between papa and you, Tom! What
at? Billiards? Cricket? Long jumping?'

Tom fairly lost his temper. 'Nonsense, Nora!' he said
testily. 'You know as well what I mean as I do. Not
a match between Uncle Theodore and me, but a match
between you and me—the heir and heiress of Orange Grove
and Pimento Valley.'

Nora stared at him with irrepressible laughter twinkling
suddenly out of all the corners of her merry little mouth
and puckered eyelids. 'Between you and me, Tom!' she
repeated incredulously—' between you and me, did you say?
Between you and me now? Why, Tom, do you really
mean this for a sort of an off-hand casual proposal?'

'Oh, you may laugh if you like,' Tom Dupuy replied
evasively, at once assuming the defensive, as boors always

do by instinct under similar circumstances. 'I know the ways of you girls that have been brought up at highfalutin' schools over in England. You think West Indian gentlemen aren't good enough for you, and you go running after cavalry-officer fellows, or else after some confounded upstart woolly-headed mulatto or other, who comes out from England. I know the ways of you. But you may laugh as you like. I see you don't mean to listen to me now; but you'll have to listen to me in the end, for Uncle Theodore and I have made up our minds about it; and what a Dupuy makes up his mind about, he generally sticks to, and there's no turning him. So in the end, I know, Nora, you'll have to marry me,'

'You seem to forget,' Nora said haughtily, 'that I too am a Dupuy, as much as you are.'

'Ah, but you're only a woman, and that's very different. I don't mind a bit about your answering me *no* to-day. It seems I've tapped the puncheon a bit too early; that's all: leave the liquor alone, and it 'll mature of itself in time in its own cellar. Sooner or later, Nora, you see if you don't marry me.'

'But, Tom,' Nora cried, abashed into seriousness for a moment by this sudden outburst of native vulgarity, ' this is really so unexpected and so ridiculous. We're cousins, you know; I've never thought of you at all in any way except as a cousin. I didn't mean to be rude to you; but your proposal and your way of putting it took me really so much by surprise.'

'Oh, if that's all you mean,' Tom Dupuy answered, somewhat mollified, 'I don't mind your laughing; no, not tuppence. All I mind is your saying *no* so straight outright to me. If you want time to consider——'

'Never!' Nora interrupted quickly in a sharp voice of unswerving firmness.

'Never, Nora? Never? Why never?'

'Because, Tom, I don't care for you; I can't care for you; and I never will care for you. Is that plain enough?'

Tom stroked his chin and looked at her dubiously, as a man looks at an impatient horse of doubtful temper. 'Well,' he said, 'Nora, you're a fine one, you are—a very fine one. I know what this means. I've seen it before lots of times. You want to marry some woolly-headed brown man. I heard you were awfully thick with some of those people on board the *Severn.* That's what always comes of sending West Indian girls to be educated in England. You'll have to marry me in the end, though, all the same, because of the property. But you just mark my words : if you don't marry me, as sure as fate, you'll finish with marrying a woolly-headed mulatto ! '

Nora rose to her full height with offended dignity. ' Tom Dupuy,' she said angrily, ' you insult me ! Leave the house, sir, this minute, or I shall go to my bedroom. Get back to your sugar-canes and your centrifugals until you've learned better manners.'

' Upon my word,' Tom said aloud, as if to himself, rising to go, and flicking his boot carelessly with his riding-whip, ' I admire her all the more when she's in a temper. She's one of your high-steppers, she is. She's a devilish fine girl, too—hanged if she isn't—and, sooner or later, she'll have to marry me.'

Nora swept out of the boudoir without another word, and walked with a stately tread into her own bedroom. But before she got there, the ludicrous side of the thing had once more overcome her, and she flung herself on her bed in uncontrollable fits of childish laughter. ' Oh, Aunt Clemmy,' she cried, ' bring me my tea in here, will you ? I really think I shall die of laughing at Mr. Tom there ! '

CHAPTER XIV.

FOR a few days the Hawthorns had plenty of callers—but all gentlemen. Marian did not go down to receive them. Edward saw them by himself in the drawing-room, accepting their excuses with polite incredulity, and dismissing them as soon as possible by a resolutely quiet and taciturn demeanour. Such a singularly silent man as the new judge, everybody said, had never before been known in the district of Westmoreland.

One afternoon, however, when the two Hawthorns were sitting under the spreading mango tree in the back garden, forgetting their doubts and hesitations in a quiet chat, Thomas came out to inform them duly that two gentlemen and a lady were waiting to see them in the big bare drawing-room. Marian sighed a sigh of profound relief. 'A lady at last,' she said hopefully. 'Perhaps, Edward, they've begun to find out, after all, that they've made some mistake or other. Can—can any wicked person, I wonder, have been spreading around some horrid report about me, that's now discovered to be a mere falsehood?'

'It's incomprehensible,' Edward answered moodily. 'The more I puzzle over it, the less I understand it. But as a lady's called at last, of course, darling, you'd better come in at once and see her.'

They walked together, full of curiosity, into the drawing-room. The two gentlemen rose simultaneously as they entered. To Marian's surprise, it was Dr. Whitaker and his father ; and with them had come—a brown lady.

Marian was unaffectedly glad to see their late travelling companion ; but it was certainly a shock to her, unprejudiced as she was, that the very first and only woman who had called upon her in Trinidad should be a mulatto. However, she tried to bear her disappointment bravely, and sat down to do the honours as well as she was able to her unexpected visitors.

'My daughtah!' the elder brown man said ostentatiously, with an expansive wave of his greasy left hand towards the mulatto lady—' Miss Euphemia Fowell-Buxton Duchess-of-Sutherland Whitaker.'

Marian acknowledged the introduction with a slight bow, and bit her lip. She stole a look at Dr. Whitaker, and saw at once upon his face an unwonted expression of profound dejection and disappointment.

'An' how do you like Trinidad, Mrs. Hawtorn?' Miss Euphemia asked with a society simper ; while Edward began engaging in conversation with the two men. 'You find de excessiveness of de temperature prejudicial to salubrity, after de delicious equability of de English climate?'

'Well,' Marian assented, smiling, 'I certainly do find it very hot.'

'Oh, exceedingly,' Miss Euphemia replied, as she mopped her forehead violently with a highly-scented lace-edged cambric pocket handkerchief. 'De heat is most oppressive, most unendurable. I could wring out me handkerchief, I assure you, Mrs. Hawtorn, wit de extraordinary profusion of me perspiration.'

'But this is summer, you must remember,' Dr. Whitaker put in nervously, endeavouring in vain to distract attention for the moment from Miss Euphemia's conversational peculiarities. 'In winter, you know, we shall have quite delightful English weather on the hills—quite delightful English weather.'

'Ah, yes,' the father went on with a broad smile. 'In winter, Mrs. Hawtorn, ma'am, you will be glad to drink a glass of rum-and-milk sometimes, I tell you, to warm de blood on dese chilly hilltops.'

The talk went on for a while about such ordinary casual topics; and then at last Miss Euphemia happened to remark, confidentially to Marian, that that very day her cousin, Mr. Septimius Whitaker, had been married at eleven o'clock down at the cathedral.

'Indeed,' Marian said, with some polite show of interest. 'And did you go to the wedding, Miss Whitaker?'

Miss Euphemia drew herself up with great dignity. She was a good-looking, buxom, round-faced, very negro-featured girl, about as dark in complexion as her brother the doctor, but much more decidedly thick-lipped and flat-nosed. 'Oh no,' she said, with every sign of offended prejudice. 'We didn't at all approve of de match me cousin Septimius was unhappily makin'. De lady, I regret to say, was a Sambo.'

'A what?' Marian inquired curiously.

'A Sambo, a Sambo gal,' Miss Euphemia replied in a shrill crescendo.

'Oh, indeed,' Marian assented in a tone which clearly showed she hadn't the faintest idea of Miss Euphemia's meaning.

'A Sambo,' Mr. Whitaker the elder said, smiling, and

coming to her rescue—'a Sambo, Mrs. Hawtorn, is one of de inferior degrees in de classified scale and hierarchy of colour. De offspring of an African and a white man is a mulatto—dat, madam, is my complexion. De offspring of a mulatto and a white man is a quadroon—dat is de grade immediately superior. But de offspring of a mulatto and a negress is a Sambo—dat is de class just beneat' us. De cause of complaint alleged by de family against our nephew Septimius is dis—dat bein' himself a mulatto—de very fust remove from de pure-blooded white man—he has chosen to ally himself in marriage wit a Sambo gal—de second and inferior remove in de same progression. De family feels dat in dis course Septimius has toroughly and irremediably disgraced himself.'

'And for dat reason,' added Miss Euphemia with stately coldness, 'none of de ladies in de brown society of Trinidad have been present at dis morning's ceremony. De gentlemen went, but de ladies didn't.'

'It seems to me,' Dr. Whitaker said, in a pained and humiliated tone, 'that we oughtn't to be making these absurd distinctions of minute hue between ourselves, but ought rather to be trying our best to break down the whole barrier of time-honoured prejudice by which the coloured race, as a race, is so surrounded. Don't you agree with me, Mr. Hawthorn?'

'Pho!' Miss Euphemia exclaimed, with evident disgust. 'Just listen to Wilberforce! He has no proper pride in his family or in his colour. He would go and shake hands wit any vulgar, dirty, nigger woman, I believe, as black as de poker; his ideas are so common!—Wilberforce, I declare, I's quite ashamed of you!'

Dr. Whitaker played nervously with the knob of his walking-stick. 'I feel sure, Euphemia,' he said at last, 'these petty discriminations between shade and shade are the true disgrace and ruin of our brown people. In despising one another, or boasting over one another, for our extra fraction or so of white blood, we are implicitly admitting in principle the claim of white people to look down upon all of us impartially as inferior creatures.— Don't you think so, Mr. Hawthorn?

'I quite agree with you,' Edward answered warmly
' The principle's obvious.'

Dr. Whitaker looked pleased and flattered. Edward
stole a glance at Marian, and neither could resist a faint
smile at Miss Euphemia's prejudices of colour, in spite of
their pressing doubts and preoccupations. And yet they
didn't even then begin to perceive the true meaning of the
situation. They had not long to wait, however, for before
the Whitakers rose to take their departure, Thomas came
in with a couple of cards to announce Mr. Theodore
Dupuy, and his nephew, Mr. Tom Dupuy, of Pimento
Valley.

The Whitakers went off shortly, Miss Euphemia especially in very high spirits, because Mrs. Hawthorn had
shaken hands in the most cordial manner with her, before
the face of the two white men. Edward and Marian
would fain have refused to see the Dupuys, as they hadn't
thought fit to bring even Nora with them; and at that
last mysterious insult—a dagger to her heart—the tears
came up irresistibly to poor wearied Marian's swimming
eyelids. But Thomas had brought the visitors in before
the Whitakers rose to go, and so there was nothing left
but to get through the interview somehow, with what grace
they could manage to muster.

'We had hoped to see Nora long before this,' Edward
Hawthorn said pointedly to Mr. Dupuy—after a few preliminary polite inanities—half hoping thus to bring things
at last to a positive crisis. 'My wife and she were school-
girls together, you know, and we saw so much of one
another on the way out. We have been quite looking
forward to her paying us a visit.'

Mr. Dupuy drew himself up very stiffly, and answered
in a tone of the chilliest order: 'I don't know to whom
you can be alluding, sir, when you speak of "Nora;" but
if you refer to my daughter, Miss Dupuy, I regret to say
she is suffering just at present from—ur—a severe indisposition, which unfortunately prevents her from paying a
call on Mrs. Hawthorn.'

Edward coughed an angry little cough, which Marian
saw at once meant a fixed determination to pursue the

matter to the bitter end. 'Miss Dupuy herself requested me to call her Nora,' he said, 'on our journey over, during which we naturally became very intimate, as she was put in charge of my wife at Southampton, by her aunt in England. If she had not done so, I should never have dreamt of addressing her, or speaking of her, by her Christian name. As she did do so, however, I shall take the liberty of continuing to call her by that name, until I receive a request to desist from her own lips. We have long been expecting a call, I repeat, Mr. Dupuy, from your daughter Nora.'

'Sir!' Mr. Dupuy exclaimed angrily; the blood of the fighting Dupuys was boiling up now savagely within him.

'We have been expecting her,' Edward Hawthorn repeated firmly; 'and I insist upon knowing the reason why you have not brought her with you.'

'I have already said, sir,' Mr. Dupuy answered, rising and growing purple in the face, 'that my daughter is suffering from a severe indisposition.'

'And I refuse,' Edward replied, in his sternest tone, rising also, 'to accept that flimsy excuse—in short, to call it by its proper name, that transparent falsehood. If you do not tell me the true reason at once, much as I respect and like Miss Dupuy, I shall have to ask you, sir, to leave my house immediately.'

A light seemed to burst suddenly upon the passionate planter, which altered his face curiously, by gradual changes from livid blue to bright scarlet. The corners of his mouth began to go up sideways in a solemnly ludicrous fashion: the crow's-feet about his eyes first relaxed and then tightened deeply; his whole big body seemed to be inwardly shaken by a kind of suppressed impalpable laughter. 'Why, Tom,' he exclaimed, turning with a curious half-comical look to his wondering nephew, 'do you know—upon my word—I really believe—no, it can't be possible—but I really believe—they don't even now know anything at all about it.'

'Explain yourself,' Edward said sternly, placing himself between Mr. Dupuy and the door, as if on purpose to bar the passage outward.

'If you really don't know about it,' Mr. Dupuy said
slowly, with an unusual burst of generosity for him,
'why, then, I admit, the insult to Miss Dupuy is—is—is
less deliberately intentional than I at first sight imagined.
But no, no : you *must* know all about it already. You
can't still remain in ignorance. It's impossible, quite
impossible.'

'Explain,' Edward reiterated inexorably.

'You compel me ? '

'I compel you.'

'You'd better not; you won't like it.'

'I insist upon it.'

'Well, really, since you make a point of it—but there,
you've been brought up like a gentleman, Mr. Hawthorn,
and you've married a wife who, as I learn from my daughter,
is well connected, and has been brought up like a lady ; and
I don't want to hurt your feelings needlessly. I can understand that under such circumstances——'

'Explain. Say what you have to say; I can endure
it.'

'Tom ! ' Mr. Dupuy murmured imploringly, turning to
his nephew. After all, the elder man was something of
a gentleman ; he shrank from speaking out that horrid
secret.

'Well, you see, Mr. Hawthorn,' Tom Dupuy went on,
taking up the parable with a sardonic smile—for he had
no such scruples—'my uncle naturally felt that with a man
of *your colour*——' He paused significantly.

Edward Hawthorn's colour at that particular moment
was vivid crimson. The next instant it was marble white.
'A man of my colour ! ' he exclaimed, drawing back in astonishment, not unmingled with horror, and flinging up his
arms wildly—'a man of my colour ! For Heaven's sake,
sir, what, in the name of goodness, do you mean by a man
of my colour ? '

'Why, of course,' Tom Dupuy replied maliciously and
coolly, ' seeing that you're a brown man yourself, and that
your father and mother were brown people before you
naturally, my uncle——'

Marian burst forth into a little cry of intense excitement.

It wasn't horror; it wasn't anger; it wasn't disappointment: it was simply relief from the long agony of that endless, horrible suspense.

'We can bear it all, Edward,' she cried aloud cheerfully, almost joyously—'we can bear it all! My darling, my darling, it is nothing, nothing, nothing!'

And regardless of the two men, who waited yet, cynical and silent, watching the effect of their unexpected thunderbolt, the poor young wife flung her arms wildly around her newly wedded husband, and smothered him in a perfect torrent of passionate kisses.

But as for Edward, he stood there still, as white, as cold, and as motionless as a statue.

CHAPTER XV.

'WE'D better go, Tom,' Mr. Dupuy said, almost pitying them. 'Upon my soul, it's perfectly true; they neither of them knew a word about it.'

'No, by Jove, they didn't,' Tom Dupuy answered with a sneer, as he walked out into the piazza.—'What a splendid facer, though, it was, Uncle Theodore, for a confounded upstart nigger of a brown man.—But, I say,' as they passed out of the piazza and mounted their horses once more by the steps—for they were riding—'did you ever see anything more disgusting in your life than that woman there—a real white woman, and a born lady, Nora tells me—slobbering over and hugging that great, ugly, hulking coloured fellow!'

'He's white enough to look at,' Mr. Dupuy said reflectively. 'Poor soul, she married him without knowing anything about it. It'll be a terrible blow for her, I expect, finding out, now she's tied to him irrevocably, that he's nothing more than a common brown man.'

'She ought to be allowed to get a divorce,' Tom Dupuy exclaimed warmly. 'By George, it's preposterous to think that a born lady, and the daughter of a General Somebody over in England, should be tethered for life to a creature of

that sort, whom she's married under what's as good as
false pretences ! '

Meanwhile the unhappy woman who had thus secured
the high prize of Mr. Tom Dupuy's distinguished compassion was sitting on the sofa in the big bare drawing-room,
holding her husband's hand tenderly in hers, and soothing
him gently by murmuring every now and then in a soft
undertone : ' My darling, my darling, I shall love you for
ever. How glad we are to know that, after all, it's nothing,
nothing ! '

Edward's stupor lasted for many minutes ; not so
much because he was deeply hurt or horrified, for there
wasn't much at bottom to horrify him, but simply because
he was stunned by the pure novelty and strangeness of
that curious situation. A brown man—a brown man ! It
was too extraordinary ! He could hardly awake himself
from the one pervading thought that absorbed and possessed
for the moment his whole nature. At last, however, he
awoke himself slowly. After all, how little it was, compared with their worst fears and anticipations ! ' Thomas,'
he cried to the negro butler, ' bring round our horses as
quick as you can saddle them. Darling, darling, we must
ride up to Agualta this moment, and speak about it all to
my father and mother.'

In Trinidad, everybody rides. Indeed, there is no other
way of getting about from place to place among the moun·
tains, for carriage-roads are there unknown, and only
narrow winding horse-paths climb slowly round the inter-
minable peaks and gullies. The Hawthorns' own house
was on the plains just at the foot of the hills ; but Agualta
and most of the other surrounding houses were up high
among the cooler mountains. So the very first thing
Marian and Edward had had to do on reaching the island
was to provide themselves with a couple of saddle-horses,
which they did during their first week's stay at Agualta.
In five minutes the horses were at the door ; and Marian,
having rapidly slipped on her habit, mounted her pony and
proceeded to follow her agitated husband up the slender
thread of mountain-road that led tortuously to his father's
house. They rode along in single file, as one always must

on these narrow, ledge-like West Indian bridle-paths, and
in perfect silence. At first, indeed, Marian tried to throw
out a few casual remarks about the scenery and the tree-
ferns, to look as if the disclosure was to her less than
nothing—as, indeed, but for Edward's sake, was actually
the case—but her husband was too much wrapped up in
his own bitter thoughts to answer her by more than single
monosyllables. Not that he spoke unkindly or angrily;
on the contrary, his tenderness was profounder than ever,
for he knew now to what sort of life he had exposed Marian;
but he had no heart just then for talking of any sort; and
he felt that until he understood the whole matter more
perfectly, words were useless to explain the situation.

As for Marian, one thought mainly possessed her : had
even Nora, too, turned against them and forsaken them ?

Old Mr. Hawthorn met them anxiously on the terrace
of Agualta. He saw at once, by their pale and troubled
faces, that they now knew at least part of the truth.
'Well, my boy,' he said, taking Edward's hand in his
with regretful gentleness, 'so you have found out the curse
that hangs over us ? '

'In part, at least,' Edward answered, dismounting;
and he proceeded to pour forth into his father's pitying
and sympathetic ear the whole story of their stormy interview with the two Dupuys. 'What can they mean,' he
asked at last, drawing himself up proudly, 'by calling
such people as you and me " brown men," father ? '

The question, as he asked it that moment, in the full
sunshine of Agualta Terrace, did indeed seem a very absurd
one. Two more perfect specimens of the fair-haired, blue-
eyed, pinky-white-skinned Anglo-Saxon type it would have
been extremely difficult to discover even in the very heart
of England itself, than the father and son who thus faced
one another. But old Mr. Hawthorn shook his handsome
grey old head solemnly and mournfully. 'It's quite true,
my boy,' he answered with a painful sigh—'quite true,
every word of it. In the eyes of all Trinidad, of all the
West Indies, you and I are in fact coloured people.'

'But, father, dear father,' Marian said pleadingly, 'just
look at Edward ! There isn't a sign or a mark on him

anywhere of anything but the purest English blood! Just
look at him, father; how can it be possible?'—and she
took up, half unconsciously, his hand—that usual last
tell-tale of African descent, but in Edward Hawthorn's case
stainless and white as pure wax. 'Surely you don't mean
to tell me,' she said, kissing it with wifely tenderness,
'there is negro blood—the least, the tiniest fraction, in
dear Edward!'

'Listen to me, dearest,' the old man said, drawing
Marian closer to his side with a fatherly gesture. 'My
father was a white man. Mary's father was a white man.
Our grandfathers on both sides were pure white, and our
grandmothers on one side were white also. All our ancestors in the fourth degree were white, save only one—
fifteen whites to one coloured out of sixteen quarters—and
that one was a mulatto in either line—Mary's and my
great-great-grandmother. In England, or any other
country of Europe, we should be white—as white as you
are. But such external and apparent whiteness isn't
enough by any means for our West Indian prejudices. As
long as you have the remotest taint or reminiscence of
black blood about you in any way—as long as it can be
shown, by tracing your pedigree pitilessly to its fountain-
head, that any one of your ancestors was of African origin
—then, by all established West Indian reckoning, you are
a coloured man, an outcast, a pariah.—You have married
a coloured man, Marian; and your children and your
grandchildren to the latest generations will all of them for
ever be coloured also.

'How cruel—how wicked—how abominable!' Marian
cried, flushed and red with sudden indignation. 'How
unjust so to follow the merest shadow or suspicion of
negro blood age after age to one's children's children!'

'And how far more unjust still,' Edward exclaimed
with passionate fervour, 'ever so to judge of any man not
by what he is in himself, but by the mere accident of the
race or blood from which he is descended!'

Marian blushed again with still deeper colour; she felt
in her heart that Edward's indignation went further than
hers, down to the very root and ground of the whole matter.

'But, O father,' she began again after a slight pause, clinging passionately both to her husband and to Mr. Hawthorn, ' are they going to visit this crime of birth even on a man of Edward's character and Edward's position ? '

' Not on him only,' the old man whispered with infinite tenderness—' not on him only, my daughter, my dear daughter—not on him only, but on you—on you, who are one of themselves, an English lady, a true white woman of pure and spotless lineage. You have broken their utmost and sacredest law of race; you have married a coloured man ! They will punish you for it cruelly and relentlessly. Though you did it, as he did it, in utter ignorance, they will punish you for it cruelly ; and that's the very bitterest drop in all our bitter cup of ignominy and humiliation.'

There was a moment's silence, and then Edward cried to him aloud : ' Father, father, you ought to have told me of this earlier ! '

His father drew back at the word as though one had stung him. ' My boy,' he answered tremulously, ' how can you ever reproach me with that ? You at least should be the last to reproach me. I sent you to England, and I meant to keep you there. In England, this disgrace would have been nothing—less than nothing. Nobody would ever have known of it, or if they knew of it, minded it in any way. Why should I trouble you with a mere foolish fact of family history utterly unimportant to you over in England ? I tried my hardest to prevent you from coming here ; I tried to send you back at once when you first came. But do you wonder, now, I shrank from telling you the ban that lies upon all of us here ? And do you blame me for trying to spare you the misery I myself and your dear mother have endured without complaining for our whole lifetime ? '

' Father, father,' Edward cried again, ' I was wrong; I was ungrateful. You have done it all in kindness. Forgive me—forgive me ! '

' There is nothing to forgive, my boy—nothing to forgive, Edward. And now, of course, you will go back to England ? '

Edward answered quickly, ' Yes, yes, father; they have conquered—they have conquered—I shall go back to England; and you, too, shall come with me. If it were for my own sake alone, I would stop here even so, and fight it out with them to the end till I gained the victory. But I can't expose Marian—dear, gently nurtured, tender Marian —to the gibes and scorn of these ill-mannered planter people. She shall never again submit to the insult and contumely she has had to endure this morning.—No, no, Marian, darling, we shall go back to England—back to England—back to England ! '

' And why, father,' Marian asked, looking up at him suddenly, ' didn't you yourself leave the country long ago ? Why didn't you go where you could mix on equal terms with your natural equals ? Why have you stood so long this horrible, wicked, abominable injustice ? '

The old man straightened himself up, and fire flashed from his eyes like an old lion's as he answered proudly : ' For Edward—for Edward ! First of all, I stopped here and worked to enable me to bring up my boy where his talents would have the fullest scope—in free England. Next, when I had grown rich and prosperous here at Agualta, I stopped on because I wouldn't be beaten in the battle and driven out of the country by the party of injustice and social intolerance. I wouldn't yield to them ; I wouldn't give way to them ; I wouldn't turn my back upon the baffled and defeated clique of slave-owners, because, though my father was an English officer, my mother was a slave, Marian ! '

He looked so grand and noble an old man as he uttered simply and unaffectedly those last few words—the pathetic epitaph of a terrible dead and buried wrong, still surviving in its remote effects—that Marian threw her arms around his neck passionately, and kissed him with one fervent kiss of love and admiration, almost as tenderly as she had kissed Edward himself in the heat of the first strange discovery.

' Edward,' she cried, with resolute enthusiasm, ' we will not go home ! We will not return to England. We, too, will stay and fight out the cruel battle against this wicked prejudice. We will do as your father has done. I love him for it—I honour him for it! To me it's less than nothing, my darling, my darling, that you should seem to have some small taint by birth in the eyes of these miserable, little, outlying islanders. To me, it's less than nothing that they should dare to look down upon you, and to set themselves up against you—you, so great, so learned, so good, so infinitely nobler than them, and better than them in every way! Who are they, the wretched, ignorant, out-of-the-way creatures, that they venture to set themselves up as our superiors? I will not yield, either. I'm my father's daughter, and I won't give way to them. Edward, Edward, darling Edward, we will stop here still, we will stop here and defeat them!'

'My darling,' Edward answered, kissing her forehead tenderly, 'you don't know what you say; you don't realise what it would be like for us to live here. I can't expose you to so much misery and awkwardness. It would be wrong of me—unmanly of me—cowardly of me—to let my wife be constantly met with such abominable, undeserved insult!'

'Cowardly! Edward,' Marian cried, stamping her pretty little foot upon the ground impatiently with womanly emphasis, 'cowardly—cowardly! The cowardice is all the other way, I fancy. I'm not ashamed of my husband, here or anywhere. I love you; I adore you; I admire you; I respect you. But I can never again respect you so much if you run away, even for my sake, from this unworthy prejudice. I don't want to live here always, for ever: God forbid! I hate and detest it. But I shall stop here a year —two years—three years, if I like, just to show the hateful creatures I love you and admire you, and I'm not afraid of them!'

'No, no, my child,' old Mr. Hawthorn murmured tenderly, smoothing her forehead; 'this is no home for you, Marian. Go back to England—go back to England!' Marian turned to him with feverish energy. 'Father,' she cried, 'dear, good, kind, gentle, loving father! You've taught me better yourself; your own words have taught me better. I won't give way to them; I'll stop in the land where you have stopped, and I'll show them I'm not ashamed of you or of Edward either! Ashamed! I'm only ashamed to say the word. What is there in either of you for a woman not to be proud of with all the deepest and holiest pride in her whole nature?'

'My darling, my darling,' Edward answered thoughtfully, 'we shall have to think and talk more with one another about this wretched, miserable business.'

CHAPTER XVI.

THE very next morning, as Edward and Marian were still loitering over the mangoes and bananas at eleven o'clock breakfast—the West Indies keep Continental hours—they were surprised and pleased by hearing a pony's tramp cease suddenly at the front door, and Nora Dupuy's well-known voice calling out as cheerily and childishly as ever: 'Marian, Marian! you dear old thing, please send somebody out here at once, to hold my horse for a minute, will you?'

The words fell upon both their ears just then as an oasis in the desert of isolation from women's society, to which they had been condemned for the last ten days. The tears rose quickly into Marian's eyes at those familiar accents, and she ran out hastily, with arms outstretched, to meet her one remaining girl-acquaintance. 'O Nora, Nora, darling Nora!' she cried, catching the bright little figure lovingly in her arms, as Nora leaped with easy grace from her mountain pony, 'why didn't you come before, my darling? Why did you leave me so long alone, and make us think you had forgotten all about us?'

Nora flung herself passionately upon her friend's neck, and between laughing and crying, kissed her over and over again so many times without speaking, that Marian knew at once in her heart it was all right there at least, and that Nora, for one, wasn't going to desert them. Then the poor girl, still uncertain whether to cry or laugh, rushed up to Edward and seized his hand with such warmth of friendliness, that Marian half imagined she was going to kiss him fervently on the spot, in her access of emotion. And indeed, in the violence of her feeling, Nora very nearly did fling her arms around Edward Hawthorn, whom she had learned to regard on the way out almost in the light of an adopted brother.

'My darling,' Nora cried vehemently, as soon as she could find space for utterance, 'my pet, my own sweet Marian, you dear old thing, you darling, you sweetheart!— I didn't know about it; they never told me. Papa and Tom have been deceiving me disgracefully: they said you were away up at Agualta, and that you particularly wished to receive no visitors until you'd got comfortably settled in at your new quarters here at Mulberry. And I said to papa, nonsense! that that didn't apply to me, and that you'd be delighted to see me wherever and whenever I chose to call upon you. And papa said—O Marian, I can't bear to tell you what he said: it's so wicked, so dreadful—papa said that he'd met Mr. Hawthorn—Edward, I mean—and that Edward had told him you didn't wish at present to see me, because—well, because, he said, you thought our circles would be so very different. And I couldn't imagine what he meant, so I asked him. And then he told me—he told me that horrid, wicked, abominable, disgraceful calumny. And I jumped up and said it was a lie—yes, I said a lie, Marian—I didn't say a story; I said it was a lie, and I didn't believe it. But if it was true—and I don't care myself a bit whether it's true or whether it isn't—I said it was a mean, cowardly, nasty thing to go and rake it up now about two such people as you and Edward, darling. And whether it's true or whether it isn't, Marian, I love you both dearly with all my heart, and I shall always love you; and I don't care a pin who on earth hears me say so.' And then Nora broke down at once into a flood of tears, and flung herself once more with passionate energy on Marian's shoulder.

'Nora darling,' Marian whispered, crying too, 'I'm so glad you've come at last, dearest. I didn't mind any of the rest a bit, because they're nothing to me; it doesn't matter; but when I thought *you* had forgotten us and given us up, it made my heart bleed, darling, darling ! '

Nora's tears began afresh. ' Why, pet,' she said, ' I've been trying to get away to come and see you every day for the last week ; and papa wouldn't let me have the horses ; and I didn't know the way ; and it was too far to walk : and I didn't know what on earth to do, or how to get to you. But last night papa and Tom came home '—here Nora's face burned violently, and she buried it in her hands to hide her vicarious shame,—' and I heard them talking in the piazza : and I couldn't understand it all ; but, O Marian, I understood enough to know that they had called upon you here without me, and that they had behaved most abominably, most cruelly, to you and Edward. And I went out to the piazza, as white as a sheet, Rosina says, and I said : " Papa, you have acted as no gentleman would act ; and as for you, Tom Dupuy, I'm heartily ashamed to think you're my own cousin ! " and then I went straight up to my bedroom that minute, and haven't said a word to either of them ever since ! '

Marian kissed her once more, and pressed the tearful girl tight against her bosom—that sisterly embrace seemed to her now such an unspeakable consolation and comfort. ' And how did you get away this morning, dear ? ' she asked softly.

' Oh,' Nora exclaimed, with a childish smile and a little cry of triumph, ' I was determined to come, Marian, and so I came here. I got Rosina—that's my maid, such a nice black girl—to get her lover, Isaac Pourtalès, who isn't one of our servants, you know, to saddle the pony for me ; because papa had told our groom I wasn't to have the horses without his orders, or to go to your house if the groom was with me, or else he'd dismiss him. So Isaac Pourtalès, he saddled it for me ; and Rosina ran all the way here to show me the road till she got nearly to the last corner ; but she wouldn't come on and hold the pony for me, for if she did, she said, de massa would knock de very breff out of her body ; and I really believe he would too, Marian, for papa's a dreadful man to deal with when he's in a passion.'

5

'But won't he be awfully angry with you, darling,' Marian asked, 'for coming here when he told you not to?'

'Of course he will,' Nora replied, drawing herself up and laughing quietly. 'But I don't care a bit, you know, for all his anger. I'm not going to keep away from a dear old darling like you, and a dear, good, kind fellow like Edward, all for nothing, just to please him. He may storm away as long as he has a mind to; but I tell you what, my dear, he won't prevent me.'

'I don't mind a bit about it now, Nora, since you're come at last to me.'

'Mind it, darling! I should think not! Why on earth should you mind it? It's too preposterous! Why, Marian, whenever I think of it—though I'm a West Indian born myself, and dreadfully prejudiced, and all that wicked sort of thing, you know—it seems to me the most ridiculous nonsense I ever heard of. Just consider what kind of people these are out here in Trinidad, and what kind of people you and Edward are, and all your friends over in England! There's my cousin, Tom Dupuy, now, for example; what a pretty sort of fellow he is, really! Even if I didn't care a pin for you, I couldn't give way to it; and as it is, I'm going to come here just as often as ever I please, and nobody shall stop me. Papa and Tom are always talking about the fighting Dupuys; but I can tell you they'll find I'm one of the fighting Dupuys too, if they want to fight me about it.—Now, tell me, Marian, doesn't it seem to you yourself the most ridiculous reversal of the natural order of things you ever heard of in all your life, that these people here should pretend to set themselves up as—as being in any way your equals, darling?' And Nora laughed a merry little laugh of pure amusement, so contagious that Edward and Marian joined in it too, for the first time almost since they came to that dreadful Trinidad.

Companionship and a fresh point of view lighten most things. Nora stopped with the two Hawthorns all that day till nearly dinner-time, talking and laughing with them much as usual after the first necessary explanations; and **by five o'clock Marian and Edward were positively**

ashamed themselves that they had ever made so much of
what grew with thinking on it into so absurdly small and
unimportant a matter. ' Upon my word, Marian,' Edward
said, as Nora rode away gaily unprotected—she positively
wouldn't allow him to accompany her homeward—' I really
begin to believe it would be better, after all, to stop in
Trinidad and fight it out bravely as well as we're able for
just a year or two.'

' I thought so from the first,' Marian answered courage-
ously ; ' and now that Nora has cheered us up a little, I
think so a great deal more than ever.'

When Nora reached Orange Grove, Mr. Dupuy stood,
black as thunder, waiting to receive her in the piazza.
Two negro man-servants were loitering about casually in
the doorway.

' Nora,' he said, in a voice of stern displeasure, ' have
you been to visit these new nigger people ? '

Nora glanced back at him defiantly and haughtily. ' I
have not,' she answered with a steady stare. ' I have been
calling upon my very dear friends, the District Court Judge
and Mrs. Hawthorn, who are both our equals. I am not
in the habit of associating with what you choose to call
nigger people.'

Mr. Dupuy's face grew purple once more. He glanced
round quickly at the two men-servants. ' Go to your
room, miss,' he said with suppressed rage—' go to your
room, and stop there till I send for you ! '

' I was going there myself,' Nora answered calmly,
without moving a muscle. ' I mean to remain there, and
hold no communication with the rest of the family, as long
as you choose to apply such unjust and untrue names to
my dearest friends and oldest companions.—Rosina, come
here, please ! Have the kindness to bring me up some
dinner to my own boudoir ; will you, Rosina ? '

CHAPTER XVII.

IT was the very next day when the Governor's wife came to call. In any case, Lady Modyford would have had to call on Marian: for etiquette demands, from the head of the colony at least, a strict disregard for distinctions of cuticle, real or imaginary. But Nora Dupuy had seen Lady Modyford that very morning, and had told her all the absurd story of the Hawthorns' social disqualifications. Now, the Governor's wife was a woman of the world, accustomed to many colonial societies, big and small, as well as to the infinitely greater world of London; and she was naturally moved, at first hearing, rather to amusement than to indignation at the idea of Tom Dupuy setting himself up as the social superior of a fellow of Catherine's and barrister of the Inner Temple. This point of view itself certainly lost nothing from Nora's emphatic way of putting it; for, though Nora had herself a bountiful supply of fine old crusted West Indian prejudices, producible on occasion, and looked down upon ' brown people ' of every shade with that peculiarly profound contempt possible only to a descendant of the old vanquished slave-owning oligarchy, yet her personal affection for Marian and Edward was quite strong enough to override all such abstract considerations of invisible colour; and her sense of humour was quite keen enough to make her feel the full ridiculousness of comparing such a man as Edward Hawthorn with her own loutish sugar-growing cousin. She had lived so long in England, as Tom Dupuy himself would have said, that she had begun to pick up at least some faint tincture of these new-fangled, radical, Exeter Hall opinions; in other words, she had acquired a little ballast of common sense and knowledge of life at large to weigh down in part her tolerably large original cargo of colonial prejudices.

But when Nora came to tell Lady Modyford, as far as she knew them, the indignities to which the Hawthorns had already been subjected by the pure blue blood of

Trinidad, the Governor's wife began to perceive there was
more in it than matter for mere laughter; and she bridled
up a little haughtily at the mention of Mr. Tom Dupuy's
free-spoken comments, as overheard by Nora on the Orange
Grove piazza. 'Nigger people!' the fat, good-natured,
motherly little body echoed angrily. 'Did he say nigger
people, my dear?—What! a daughter of General Ord of
the Bengal infantry—why, I came home from Singapore in
the same steamer with her mother, the year my father
went away from the Straits Settlements to South Australia!
Do you mean to say, my dear, they won't call upon her,
because she's married a son of that nice old Mr. Hawthorn
with the white beard up at Agualta! A perfect gentleman,
too! Dear me, how very abominable! You must excuse
my saying it, my child, but really you West Indian people
do mistake your own little hole and corner for the great
world, in a most extraordinary sort of a fashion. Now,
confess to me, don't you?'

So the same afternoon, Lady Modyford had powdered
her round, fat little face, and put on her pretty coquettish
French bonnet, and driven round in full state from Government House to Edward Hawthorn's new bungalow in the
Westmoreland valleys.

As the carriage with its red-liveried black footmen
drove up to the door, Marian's heart sank once more
within her: she knew it was the Governor's wife come to
call; and she had a vague presentiment in her own mind
that the fat little woman inside the carriage would send in
her card out of formal politeness, and drive away at once
without waiting to see her. But instead of that, Lady
Modyford came up the steps with great demureness, and
walked into the bare drawing-room, after Marian's rather
untidy and quite raw black waiting-maid; and the moment
she saw Marian, she stepped up to her very impulsively,
and held out both her hands, and kissed the poor young
bride on either cheek with genuine tenderness. 'My dear,'
she said, with a motherly tremor in her kind old voice,
'you must forgive me for making myself quite at home
with you at once, and not standing upon ceremony in any
way; but I knew your mother years ago—she was just

K

like you then—and I know what a lonely thing it is for a
newly-married girl to come out to a country like this, quite
away from her own people ; and I shall be so glad if you'll
take Sir Adalbert and me just as we are. We're homely
people, and we don't live far away from you ; and if you'll
run round and see me any time you feel lonely or are in
want of anything, why, you know, of course, my dear, we
shall be delighted to see you.'

And then, before Marian could wipe away the tears that
rose quickly to her eyes, fat little Lady Modyford had gone
off into reminiscences of Singapore and Bombay, and that
dear Mrs. Ord, and the baby that died—' Your sister, you
know, my dear—the one that was born at Calcutta, and
died soon after your dear mamma reached England.—No,
of course, my dear ; your mamma couldn't know that I was
here, because, you see, when she and I came home together
—why, that was twenty-two years ago—no, twenty-four, I
declare, because Sir Adalbert—he was plain Mr. Modyford
then, on three hundred a year, in the Straits Settlements
colonial service—didn't propose to me till the next summer,
when he came home on leave, you know, just before he
was removed to Hong-kong by that horrid Lord Modbury,
who was Colonial Secretary in those days, and afterwards
died of suppressed gout, the doctors said, which I call D. T.,
at his own villa at that delightful Spezzia. So you see I
was Kitty Fitzroy at that time, my child ; and I dare say
your mamma, who's older than me a good bit, of course,
never heard about my marrying Sir Adalbert, for we were
married very quietly down in Devonshire, where Sir
Adalbert's father was rector in a very small parish, on a
tiny income ; and we started at once for Hong-kong, and
spent our honeymoon at Venice—a nasty, damp, uncom-
fortable place for a wedding tour, I call it, but not nearly
so bad as you coming out here straight from the church
door almost, Miss Dupuy told me ; and Trinidad too, well
known to be an unsociable, dead-alive sort of an island.
But whenever you like, dear, you must just jump on your
horse—you've got horses, of course ?—yes, I thought so—
and ride over to Government House, and have a good chat
with me and Emily ; for, indeed, Mrs. Hawthorn—what's

your Christian name ?—Marian—ah, **very pretty**—we should like to see you as often as you choose; and next week, after you've settled down a little, you must really come up and stop some time with us; for I assure you I've quite taken a fancy to you, my dear; and Sir Adalbert, when he saw Mr. Hawthorn, the other day, at the Island Secretary's office, came home quite delighted, and said to me : " Kitty, the young man they've sent out for the new District judge is the very man to keep that something old fool Dupuy in order in future." '

Lady Modyford waited a good deal longer than is usual with a first call, and got very friendly indeed with poor Marian before the end of her visit; for, coarse-grained woman of the world as she was, her heart warmed not a little towards the friendless young bride who had come out to Trinidad—dull hole, Trinidad, not at all like Singapore, or Mauritius, or Cape Town—to find herself so utterly deserted by all society. And next day, all female Trinidad was talking over five o'clock tea about the re-markable fact, learnt indirectly through those unrecognised purveyors of fashionable intelligence, the servants, that that horrid proud Lady Modyford—'who treats you and me, my dear, as if we were the dirt beneath her feet, don't you know, and must call with two footmen and so much grandeur and formality '—had actually kissed that brown man's wife, that's to be the new District judge in West-moreland, on both cheeks, the very first moment she saw her. Female Trinidad was so inexpressibly shocked at this disgraceful behaviour in a person officially charged with the maintenance of a high standard of decorum, that it was really half inclined to think it ought to cut Lady Modyford direct on next meeting her. It was restrained from this extreme measure, however, by a wholesome consideration of the fact that Lady Modyford would undoubtedly take the rebuff with unruffled amusement; so it contented itself by merely showing a little coldness to the Governor's wife when it happened to meet her, and refusing to enter into conversation with her on the subject of Marian and Edward Hawthorn.

As for Marian herself, she had a good cry, as soon as

Lady Modyford was gone, over this interview also. Kind as the Governor's wife had wished to show herself, and genuinely sympathetic as she had actually been, Marian couldn't help recognising that there was a certain profound undercurrent of degradation in having to accept the ready sympathy of such a woman at all on such a matter. Anywhere else, Marian would have felt that Lady Modyford, motherly as she was, stood just a grade or two by nature below her; in fact, she felt so there too; but still she was compelled by circumstances to take the good fat body's consolation and condolence as a sort of favour; while anywhere else she would rather have repelled it as a disagreeable impertinence, or at least as a distasteful interference with her own individuality. It was impossible not to be dimly conscious that coming to Trinidad had made a real difference in her own social position. At home, she had no need for anybody's condescension or anybody's affability; here, she was forced to recognise the fact that even Lady Modyford was making generous concessions on purpose in her favour. It was galling, but it was inevitable. There is nothing more painful to persons who have always mixed in society on terms of perfect and undoubted equality, than thus to put themselves into false positions, where it is possible for equals, or even for natural inferiors, to seem to patronise them.

Nevertheless, that evening Marian said to Edward very firmly : ' Edward, you must make up your mind to stop in Trinidad. I shall never feel so much confidence again in your real courage if you turn and run from Nora's father. Besides, now Lady Modyford has called, and Nora has been here, I dare say we shall get a little society of our own—people who know too much about the outer world to be wholly governed by the fads and fancies of Trinidad planters.'

And Edward answered in a somewhat faltering voice : ' Very well, my darling. One's duty lies that way, I know; and if you're strong enough to stand up and face it, why, I must try to face it also.'

And they did face it, with less difficulty even than they at first imagined. Presently, Mrs. Castello came to call, the wife of the Governor's aide-de-camp ; a pretty, pleasant, sisterly little woman, who struck up a mutual attachment with Marian almost at first sight, and often dropped in to see them afterwards. Then one or two others of the English officials brought their wives ; and before long, when Marian went to stay at Government House, it was clear that in the imported official society at any rate the Hawthorns were to be at least tolerated. Toleration is a miserable sort of standing for people to submit to ; but in the last resort, it is better than isolation. And as time went on, the toleration grew into friendliness and intimacy in many quarters, though never among the native planter aristocracy. Those noble people, intensely proud of their pure white blood, held themselves entirely aloof with profound dignity. ' Poor souls ! ' Sir Adalbert Modyford said contemptuously to Captain Castello, ' they forget how little it is to be proud of, and that every small street Arab in London could consider himself a gentleman in Trinidad on the very selfsame grounds of birth as they do.'

CHAPTER XVIII.

THERE was great excitement in the District Court at Westmoreland one sunny morning, a few days later, for the new judge was to sit and hear an appeal, West Indian fashion, from a magistrate's decision in the case of Delgado *versus* Dupuy. The little court-house in the low parochial buildings of Westmoreland was crowded with an eager throng of excited negroes. Much buzzing and humming of voices filled the room, for it was noised abroad among the blacks that Mistah Hawtorn, being a brown man born, was likely to curry favour with the buckras—as brown men will—by giving unjust decisions in their favour against the black men ; and this was a very important case for the agricultural negroes, as it affected a question of paying wages for work performed in the Pimento Valley canepieces.

Rosina Fleming was there among the crowd ; and as

Louis Delgado, the appellant in the case, came into court, he paused for a moment to whisper hurriedly a few words to her. ' De med'cine hab effeck like I tell you, Missy Rosina ? ' he asked in an undertone.

Rosina laughed and showed her white teeth. 'Yes, Mistah Delgado, him hab effeck, sah, same like you tell me. Isaac Pourtalès, him lub me well for true, nowadays.'

' Him gwine to marry you, missy ? '

Rosina shook her head. ' No ; him can't done dat,' she answered carelessly, as though it were the most natural thing in the world. ' Him got anudder wife already.'

' Ha ! Him got wife ober in Barbadoes ? ' Delgado muttered. ' Him doan't nebber tell me dat.—Well, Missy Rosy, I want you bring Isaac Pourtalès to me hut dis one day. I want Isaac to help me wit de great an' terrible day ob de Lard. De cup ob de Dupuys is full dis day ; an' if de new judge gib decision wrongfully agin me, de Lard will arise soon in all him glory, like him tell de prophets, an' make de victory for him own people.'

' But not hurt de missy ? ' Rosina inquired anxiously.

' Yah, yah ! You is too chupid, Miss Rosy, I tellin' you. You tink when de Lard bare him arm in him wrat, him gwine to turn aside in de day ob vengeance for your missy ? De Dupuys is de Lard's enemy, le-ady, an' he will destroy dem utterly, men and women.'

Before Rosina could find time to reply, there was a sudden stir in the body of the court, and Edward Hawthorn, entering from the private door behind, took his seat upon the judge's bench in hushed silence.

' Delgado *versus* Dupuy, an appeal from a magistrate's order, referred to this court as being under twenty shillings in value.—Who heard the case in the first instance ? ' Edward inquired.

' Mr. Dupuy of Orange Grove and Mr. Henley,' Tom Dupuy, the defendant, answered quietly.

Edward's forehead puckered up a little. ' You are the detendant, I believe, Mr. Thomas Dupuy ? ' he said to the young planter with a curious look.

Tom Dupuy nodded acquiescence.

' And the case was heard in the first instance by Mr.

Theodore Dupuy of Orange Grove, who, if I am rightly
informed, happens to be your own uncle?'

'Rightly informed!' Tom Dupuy sneered half angrily
—'rightly informed, indeed! Why, you know he is, of
course, as well as I do. Didn't we both call upon you
together the other day? I should say, considering what
sort of interview we had, you can't already have quite forgotten it!'

Edward winced a little, but answered nothing. He
merely allowed the plaintiff to be put in the box, and proceeded to listen carefully to his rambling evidence. It
wasn't very easy, even for the sharp, half-Jewish brown
barrister who was counsel for the plaintiff, to get anything
very clear or definite out of Louis Delgado with his vague
rhetoric. Still, by dint of patient listening, Edward
Hawthorn was enabled at last to make out the pith and
kernel of the old African's excited story. He worked, it
seemed, at times on Orange Grove estate, and at times,
alternately, at Pimento Valley. The wages on both estates,
as frequently happens in such cases, were habitually far in
arrears; and Delgado claimed for many days, on which,
he asserted, he had been working at Tom Dupuy's cane-
pieces; while Tom Dupuy had entered a plea of never indebted, on the ground that no entry appeared in his own
book-keeper's account for those dates of Delgado's presence.
Mr. Theodore Dupuy had heard the case, and he and a
brother magistrate had at once decided it against Delgado.
'But I know, sah,' Delgado said vehemently, looking up
to the new judge with a certain defiant air, as of a man who
comes prepared for injustice, 'I know I work dem days at
Pimento Valley, because I keep book meself, an' put down
in him in me own hand all de days I work anywhere.'

'Can you produce the book?' Edward inquired of the
excited negro.

'It isn't any use,' Tom Dupuy interrupted angrily.
'I've seen the book myself, and you can't read it. It's all
kept in some heathenish African language or other.'

'I must request you, Mr. Dupuy, not to interrupt,'
Edward Hawthorn said in his sternest voice. 'Please to
remember, I beg of you, that this room is a court of justice.'

'Not much justice here for white men, I expect,' Tom Dupuy muttered to himself in a half-audible undertone. 'The niggers 'll have it all their own way in future, of course, now they've got one of themselves to sit upon the bench for them.'

'Produce the book,' Edward said, turning to Delgado, and restraining his natural anger with some difficulty.

'It doan't no good, sah,' the African answered, with a sigh of despondency, pulling out a greasy account-book from his open bosom, and turning over the pages slowly in moody silence. 'It me own book, dat I hab for me own reference, an' I keep him all in me own hand-writing.'

Edward held out his hand commandingly, and took the greasy small volume that the African passed over to him, with some little amusement and surprise. He didn't expect, of course, that he would be able to read it, but he thought at least he ought to see what sort of accounts the man kept; they would at any rate be interesting, as throwing light upon negro ideas and modes of reckoning. He opened the book the negro gave him and turned it over hastily with a languid curiosity. In a second, a curious change came visibly over his startled face, and he uttered sharply a little sudden cry of unaffected surprise and astonishment. 'Why,' he said in a strangely altered voice, turning once more to the dogged African, who stood there staring at him in stolid indifference, 'what on earth is the meaning of this? This is Arabic—excellent Arabic!'

Rosina Fleming, looking eagerly from in front at the curious characters, saw at once they were the same in type as the writing in the obeah book Delgado had showed her the evening she went to consult him at his hut about Isaac Pourtalès.

Delgado glanced back at the young judge with a face full of rising distrust and latent incredulity. 'You doan't can read it, sah?' he asked suspiciously. 'It African talk. You doan't can read it?'

'Certainly I can,' Edward answered with a smile. 'It's very beautifully and clearly written, and it's all exceedingly good and accurate Arabic entries.' And he read a word or two of the entries aloud, in proof of his ability to decipher at sight the mysterious characters.

Delgado in turn gave a sudden start; and drawing himself up to his full height, with new-born pride and dignity, he burst forth at once into a few sentences in some strange foreign tongue, deep and guttural, addressed apparently, as Tom Dupuy thought, to the new judge in passionate entreaty. But in reality the African was asking Edward Hawthorn, earnestly and in the utmost astonishment, whether it was a fact that he could really and truly speak Arabic.

Edward answered him back in a few words, rapidly spoken, in the fluent colloquial Egyptian dialect which he had learnt in London from his Mohammedan teacher, Sheikh Abdullah. It was but a short sentence, but it was quite enough to convince Delgado that he did positively understand the entries in the account-book. 'De Lard be praise!' the African shouted aloud excitedly. 'De new judge, him can read de book I keep for me own reckonin'! De Lard be praise! Him gwine to delibber me.'

'Did ever you see such a farce in your life?' Tom Dupuy whispered in a stage aside to his Uncle Theodore. 'I don't believe the fellow understands a single word of it; and I'm sure the gibberish they were talking to one another can't possibly be part of any kind of human language even in Africa. And yet, after all, I don't know. The fellow's a nigger himself, and perhaps he may really have learnt from his own people some of their confounded African lingoes. But who on earth would ever have believed, Uncle Theodore, we'd have lived to hear such trash as that talked openly from the very Bench in a Queen's court in the island of Trinidad?'

Edward coloured up again at the few words which he caught accidentally of this ugly monologue; but he only said to the eager African: 'I cannot speak with you here in Arabic, Delgado; here we must use English only.'

'Certainly,' Tom Dupuy suggested aloud—colonial courts are even laxer than English ones. 'We mustn't forget, of course, Mr. Hawthorn, as you said just now, that this room is a court of justice.'

The young judge turned over the book to conceal his chagrin, and examined it carefully. ' What are the dates in dispute ? ' he asked, turning to the counsel.

Delgado and Tom Dupuy in one breath gave a full list of them. Counsel handed up a little written slip with the various doubtful days entered carefully upon it in ordinary English numbers. Edward ticked them off one by one in Delgado's note-book, quietly to himself, smiling as he did so at the quaint Arabic translations of the Grove of Oranges and the Valley of Pimento. Every one of Delgado's dates was quite accurately and carefully entered in his own account-book.

When they came to examine Tom Dupuy and his Scotch book-keeper, their account of the whole transaction was far less definite, clear, and consistent. Tom Dupuy, with a certain airy lordly indifference, admitted that his payments were often in arrears, and that his modes of book-keeping were often somewhat rough and ready. He didn't pretend to keep an account personally of every man's labour on his whole estate, he said ; he was a gentleman himself, and he left that sort of thing, of course, to his book-keeper's memory. The book-keeper didn't remember that Louis Delgado had worked at Pimento Valley on those particular disputed mornings ; though, to be sure, one naturally couldn't be quite certain about it. But if you were going to begin taking a nigger's word on such a matter against a white man's, why, what possible security against false charges could you give in future to the white planter ?

' How often do you post up the entries in that book ? ' Delgado's counsel asked the book-keeper in cross-examination.

The book-keeper was quite as airy and easy as his master in this matter. ' Weel, whiles I do it at the time,' he answered quietly, ' an' whiles I do it a wee bit later.'

' An' I put him down ebbery evening, de minute I home, sah, in dis note-book,' Delgado shouted eagerly with a fierce gesticulation.

' You must be quiet, please,' Edward said, turning to him. ' You mustn't interrupt the witness or your counsel.'

'Did Delgado work at Pimento Valley yesterday?' the brown barrister asked, looking up from the books which Tom Dupuy had been forced to produce and hand in, in evidence.

The book-keeper hesitated and smiled a sinister smile. 'He did,' he answered after a moment's brief internal conflict.

'How is it, then, that the day's work isn't entered here already?' the brown barrister went on pitilessly.

The book-keeper shuffled with an uneasy shuffle. 'Ah, weel, I should have entered it on Saturday evening,' he answered evasively.

Edward turned to Delgado's note-book. The last day's work was entered properly in an evidently fresh ink, that of the previous two days looking proportionately blacker and older. There could be very little doubt, indeed, which of the two posted his books daily with the greater care and accuracy.

He heard the case out patiently and temperately, in spite of Delgado's occasional wild outbursts and Tom Dupuy's constant sneers, and at the end he proceeded to deliver judgment as calmly as he was able, without prejudice. It was a pity that the first case he heard should have been one which common justice compelled him to give against Tom Dupuy, but there was no helping it. 'The court enters judgment for the plaintiff,' he said in a loud clear voice. 'Delgado's books, though unfortunately kept only in Arabic for his own reference, have been very carefully and neatly posted.—Yours, Mr. Dupuy, I regret to say, are extremely careless, inadequate, and inaccurate; and I am also sorry to see that the case was heard in the first instance by one of your own near relations. Under such circumstances, it would have been far wiser, as well as far more seemly, to avoid all appearance of evil.'

Tom Dupuy grew red and pale by turns as he listened in blank surprise and dismay to this amazing and unprecedented judgment. A black man's word taken in evidence in open court against a white gentleman's! It was too appalling! 'Well, well, Uncle Theodore,' he said bitterly, rising to go, 'I expected as much, though it's hard to believe it. I knew we should never get any decent justice in this court any longer!'

But Delgado stood there, dazed and motionless, gazing with mute wonder at the pale face of the new judge, and debating within himself whether it could be really true or not that he had gained his case against the powerful Dupuy faction. Not that he understood for a moment the exact meaning of the legal words, 'judgment for the plaintiff;' but he saw at once on Tom Dupuy's face that the white man was positively livid with anger, and had been severely reprimanded. 'De Lard be praise!' he ejaculated again, at last. 'De judge is righteous judge, an' lub de black man!' Then he added in a lower and more solemn tone to Rosina Fleming, who stood once more now beside him: 'In de great an' terrible day ob de Lard, missy, de sword ob de Lard an' ob his people will pass ober all de house ob de Hawtorn, as de angel pass ober de children ob Israel in de day when him slay de firstborn ob de Egyptian, from de son ob Pharaoh dat sit upon de trone to de son ob de captive dat languish in de dungeon!'

Edward would have given a great deal just then if Delgado in the moment of his triumph had not used those awkward words, 'Him lub de black man!' But there was no use brooding over it now; so he merely signed with his finger to Delgado, and whispered hastily in his ear as he dismissed the case: 'Come to me this evening in my own room as soon as court is all over; I want to hear from you how and where you learnt Arabic.'

CHAPTER XIX.

WHEN all the other cases had been gradually dismissed—the petty larceny of growing yams; the charge of stealing a pair of young turkeys; the disputed question as to the three-halfpence balance on the account for sweet-potatoes, and so forth *ad infinitum*—Edward made his way, wearied and anxious, into his own room behind the court-house. Delgado was waiting for him there, and as the judge

entered, he rose quickly and uttered a few words of customary salutation in excellent Arabic. Edward Hawthorn
observed at once that a strange change seemed to have
come over the ragged old negro in the course of those few
hours. He had lost his slouching, half-savage manner,
and stood more erect, or bowed in self-respecting obeisance,
with a certain obvious consciousness of personal dignity
which at once reminded him of Sheikh Abdullah. He
noticed, too, that while the man's English was the mere
broken Creole language he had learned from the other
negroes around him, his Arabic was the pure colloquial
classical Arabic of the Cairo ulemas. It was astonishing
what a difference this change of tongue made in the
tattered old black field-labourer : when he spoke English,
he was the mere ordinary plantation negro ; when he spoke
Arabic, he was the decently educated and perfectly cour-
teous African Moslem.

'You have quite surprised me, Delgado,' Edward said,
still in colloquial Arabic. 'I had no idea there were any
Africans in Trinidad who understood the language of the
Koran. How did you ever come to learn it ? '

The old African bowed graciously, and expanded his
hands with a friendly gesture. 'Effendi,' he answered,
'Allah is not wholly without his true followers in any
country. Is it not written in your own book that when
Elijah, the forerunner of the Prophet, cried in the cave,
saying : " I alone am left of the worshippers of Allah,"
the Lord answered and said unto him in his mercy :
" I have left me seven thousand souls in Israel which
have not bowed the knee to Baal " ? Even so, Allah
has his followers left even here among the infidels in
Trinidad.'

'Then you are still a Mussulman ? ' Edward cried in
surprise.

The old African rose again from the seat into which
Edward had politely motioned him, and folding both his
hands reverently in front of him, answered in a profoundly
solemn voice : 'There is no God but Allah, and Mohammed
is his prophet.'

'But I thought—I understood—I was told that you

were a teacher and preacher up yonder in the Methodist chapel.'

Delgado shrugged his shoulders with African expressiveness. 'What can I do?' he said, throwing open his hands sideways. 'They have brought me here all the way from the Gold Coast. There is no mosque here, no ulema, no other Moslems. What can I do? I have to do as the other negroes do.—But see!' and he drew something carefully from the folds of his dirty cotton shirt: 'I have brought a Book with me. I have kept it sacredly all these years. Have you seen it? Do you know it?'

Edward opened the soiled and dog's-eared but carefully treasured volume that the negro handed him. He knew it at once. It was a hand-copied Koran. He turned the pages over lightly till he came to the famous chapter of the Seven Treasures; then he began to read aloud a few verses in a clear, easy, Arabic intonation.

Delgado started when he heard the young judge actually reading the sacred volume. 'So you, too, are a Moslem!' he cried excitedly.

Edward smiled. 'No,' he answered; 'I am no Mussulman. But I have learnt Arabic, and I have read the Koran.'

'Mussulman or Christian,' Delgado answered fervently, throwing up his head, 'you are a servant of Allah. You have given judgment to-day like Daniel the Hebrew, or like Othman Calif, the successor of the Prophet. When the great and terrible day of the Lord arrives, Allah will surely not forget the least among his servants.'

Edward did not understand the hidden meaning of that seemingly conventional pious tag, so he merely answered: 'But you haven't yet told me, remnant of the faithful, how you ever came to learn Arabic.'

Thus encouraged, Delgado loosed the strings of his tongue, and poured forth rapidly with African volubility the whole marvellous story of his life. The son of a petty chieftain on the Guinea coast, he had been sent in his boyhood by his father, a Mohammedan convert, to the native schools for the negroes at Cairo, where he had remained till he was over seventeen years old, and had then

returned to his father's principality. There, he had gone
out to fight in some small war between two neighbouring
negro chieftains, whose events he insisted on detailing to
Edward at great length; and having been taken prisoner
by the hostile party, he had at last been sold in the bad
old days, when a contraband 'ebony trade' still existed, to
a Cuban slaver. The slaver had been captured off Sombrero
Rock by an English cruiser, and all the negroes landed at
Trinidad. That was the sum and substance of the strangely
romantic story told by the old African to the young English
barrister in the Westmoreland court-house. Couched in
his childish and ignorant negro English, it would no doubt
have sounded ludicrous and puerile; but poured forth in
classical Arabic almost as pure and fluent as Sheikh
Abdullah's own, it was brimful of pathos, eloquence, interest, and weirdness. Yet strange and almost incredible as
it seemed to Edward's mind, the old African himself apparently regarded it as the most natural and simple con-
catenation of events that could easily happen to anybody
anywhere.

'And how is it,' Edward asked at last, in profound
astonishment, lapsing once more into English, 'that you
have never tried to get back to Africa?'

Delgado smiled an ugly smile, that showed all his
teeth, not pleasantly, but like the teeth of a bull-dog
snarling. 'Do you tink, sah,' he said sarcastically, 'dat
dem fightin' Dupuy is gwine to help a poor black naygur
to go back to him own country? Ole-time folk has proverb: "Mongoose no help cane-rat find de way back to
him burrow."'

Edward could hardly believe the sudden transforma-
tion. In a single moment, with the change of language,
the educated African had vanished utterly, and the plantation negro stood once more undisguised before him. And
yet, Edward thought curiously to himself, which, after all,
was the truest and most genuine of those two contrasted
but united personalities—the free Mussulman, or the cowed
and hopeless Trinidad field-labourer? Strange, too, that
while this born African could play as he liked at fetichism
or Christianity, could do obeah or sing psalms from his

English hymn-book, the profoundly penetrating **and ab-**
sorbing creed of Islam was the only one that had **sunk**
deep into the very inmost marrow of his negro nature.
About that fact, Edward could not for a moment have the
faintest hesitation. Delgado—Coromantyn or West Indian
—was an undoubting Mussulman. Christianity was but
a cloak with which he covered himself outwardly, to himself and others ; obeah was but an art that he practised in
secret for unlawful profit ; Islam, the faith most profoundly
and intimately adapted to the negro idiosyncrasy, was the
creed that had burnt itself into his very being, in spite
of all changes of outer circumstance. Not that Delgado
believed his Bible the less ; with the frank inconsistency
of early minds, he held the two incompatible beliefs without
the faintest tinge of conscious hypocrisy ; just as many of
ourselves, though Christian enough in all externals, hold
lingering relics of pagan superstitions about horseshoes,
and crooked sixpences, and unlucky days, and the mystic
virtues of a carnelian amulet. Every morning he spelt
over religiously a chapter in the New Testament; and
every night, in the gloom of his hut, he read to himself
in hushed awe a few versicles of the holy Koran.

When story and comment were fully finished, the old
African rose to go. As he opened the door, Edward held
out his hand for the negro to shake. Delgado, now once
more the plantation labourer, hesitated for a second, fearing
to take it ; then at last, drawing himself up to his full height,
and instinctively clutching at his loose cotton trousers,
as though they had been the flowing white robes of his old
half-forgotten Egyptian school days, he compromised the
matter by making a profound salaam, and crying in his clear
Arabic gutturals : ' May the blessing of Allah, the all-wise,
the merciful, rest for ever on the effendi, his servant, who
has delivered a just judgment ! '

In another moment he had glided through the door ;
and Edward, hardly yet able to realise the strangeness of
the situation, was left alone with his own astonishment.

CHAPTER XX.

THREE or four months rolled rapidly away, and the Hawthorns began to feel themselves settling down quietly to their new, strange, and anomalous position in the island of Trinidad. In spite of her father's prohibition, Nora often came around to visit them ; and though Mr. Dupuy fought hard against her continuing ' that undesirable acquaintance' he soon found that Nora, too, had a will of her own, and that she was not to be restrained from anything on which she had once set her mind, by such very simple and easy means as mere prohibition. ' The girl's a Dupuy to the backbone,' her cousin Tom said to her father more than once, in evident admiration. ' Though she does take up with a lot of coloured trash—which, of course, is very unladylike—by George, sir, when once she sets her heart upon a thing, she does it too, and no mistake about it either.'

Dr. Whitaker was another not infrequent visitor at the Hawthorns' bungalow. He had picked up, as he desired, a gratuitous practice among the poorer negroes ; and though it often sorely tried his patience and enthusiasm, he found in it at least some relief and respite from the perpetual annoyance and degradation of his uncongenial home life with his father and Miss Euphemia. His botany, too, gave him another anodyne—something to do to take his mind off the endless incongruity of his settled position. He had decided in his own mind, almost from the very first day of landing, to undertake a Flora of Trinidad—a new work on all the flowering plants in the rich vegetation of that most luxuriant among tropical islands ; and in every minute of leisure time that he could spare from the thankless care of his poor negro patients, he was hard at work among the tangled woods and jungle undergrowth, or else in his own little study at home, in his father's house, collecting, arranging, and comparing the materials for this his great work on the exquisite flowers of his native country. The faithful violin afforde him his third great resource and alle-

viation. Though Miss Euphemia and her lively friends were
scarcely of a sort to appreciate the young doctor's touching
and delicate execution, he practised by himself for an hour
or two in his own rooms every evening ; and as he did so, he
felt that the strings seemed ever to re-echo with one sweet
and oft-recurring name—the name of Nora. To be sure,
he was a brown man, but even brown men are more or less
human. How could he ever dream of falling in love with
one of Miss Euphemia's like-minded companions ?

He met Nora from time to time in the Hawthorns'
drawing-room ; there was no other place under the circumstances of Trinidad where he was at all likely ever to meet
her. Nora was more frankly kind to him now than
formerly ; she felt that to be cool or indifferent towards
him before Edward and Marian might seem remotely like
an indirect slight upon their own position. One afternoon
he met her there accidentally, and she asked him, with
polite interest, how his work on the flowers of Trinidad
was getting on.

The young doctor cast down his eyes and answered
timidly that he had collected an immense number of specimens, and was arranging them slowly in systematic order.

'And your music, Dr. Whitaker ? '

The mulatto stammered for a moment. 'Miss Dupuy,'
he said with a slight hesitation, 'I have—I have published
the little piece—the Hurricane Symphony, you know—that
I showed you once on board the *Severn*. I have published
it in London. If you will allow me—I—I—I will present
you, as I promised, with a copy of the music.'

'Thank you,' Nora said. 'How very good of you !
Will you send it to me to Orange Grove, or—will you
leave it here some day with Mrs. Hawthorn ? '

The mulatto felt his face grow hot and burning as he
answered with as much carelessness as he could readily
command : ' I have a copy here with me—it's with my hat
in the piazza. If you will permit me, Mrs. Hawthorn,
I'll just step out and fetch it. I—I brought it with me,
Miss Dupuy, thinking it just possible I might happen to
meet you here this morning.' He didn't add that he had
brought it out with him day after day for the last fortnight,

in the vain hope of chancing to meet her ; and had carried
it back again with a heavy heart night after night, when
he had failed to see her in that one solitary possible meet-
ing-place.

Nora took the piece that he handed her, fresh and white
from the press of a famous London firm of music-sellers,
and glanced hastily at the top of the title-page for the promised dedication. There was none visible anywhere. The
title-page ran simply : ' Op. 14. Hurricane Symphony.
Souvenir des Indes. By W. Clarkson Whitaker.'

' But, Dr. Whitaker,' Nora said, pouting a little in her
pretty fashion, ' this isn't fair, you know. You promised
to dedicate the piece to me. I was quite looking forward
to seeing my name in big letters, printed in real type, on
the top of the title-page ! '

The mulatto doctor's heart beat fast that moment with
a very unwonted and irregular pulsation. Then she really
wished him to dedicate it to her ! Why on earth had he
been so timorous as to strike out her name at the last
moment on the fair copy he had sent to London for publi-
cation ? ' I thought, Miss Dupuy,' he answered slowly,
' our positions were so very different in Trinidad, that when
I came here and felt how things actually stood, I—I judged
it better not to put your name in conjunction with mine on
the same title-page.'

' Then you did quite wrong ! ' Nora retorted warmly ;
' and I'm very angry with you—I am really, I assure you.
You ought to have kept your promise when you gave it me.
I wanted to see my own name in print, and on a piece of
music too. I expect, now, I've lost the chance of seeing
myself in black and white for ever and ever.'

The mulatto smiled a smile of genuine pleasure. ' It's
easily remedied, Miss Dupuy,' he answered quickly. ' If
you really mean it, I shall dedicate my very next compo-
sition to you. You're extremely kind to take such a friendly
interest in my poor music.'

' I hope I'm not overdoing it,' Nora thought to herself.
' But the poor fellow really has so much to put up with,
that one can't help behaving a little kindly to him when
one happens to get the opportunity.'

When **Dr.** Whitaker rose to leave, he shook hands with Nora very warmly, and said as he did so : ' Good-bye, Miss Dupuy. I shan't forget next time that the dedication is to be fairly printed in good earnest.'

' Mind you don't, Dr. Whitaker,' Nora responded gaily. ' Good-bye. I suppose I shan't see you again, as usual, for another week of Sundays ! '

The mulatto smiled once more, a satisfied smile, as he answered quickly : ' Oh yes, Miss Dupuy. We shall meet on Monday next. Of course, you're going to the Governor's ball at Banana Garden ? '

Nora started. ' The Governor's ball ! ' she repeated— ' the Governor's ball ! Oh yes, of course I'm going there, Dr. Whitaker.—But are you invited ? '

She said it thoughtlessly, on the spur of the moment, for it had never occurred to her that the brown doctor would have an invitation also ; but the tone of surprise in which she spoke cut the poor young mulatto to the very quick in that moment of triumph. He drew himself up proudly as he answered in a hasty tone : ' Oh yes ; even I am invited to Banana Garden, you know, Miss Dupuy. The Governor of the colony at least can recognise no distinction of class or colour in his official capacity.'

Nora's face flushed crimson. ' I shall hope to see you there,' she answered quickly. ' I'm glad you're going.— Marian dear, we shall be quite a party. I only wish I was going with you, instead of being trotted off in proper style by that horrid old Mrs. Pereira.'

Dr. Whitaker said no more, but raised his hat upon the piazza steps, jumped upon his horse, and took his way along the dusty road that led from the Hawthorns' cottage to the residence of the Honourable Robert Whitaker. As he reached the house, Miss Euphemia was laughing loudly in the drawing-room with her bosom friend, Miss Seraphina M'Culloch. ' Wilberforce ! ' Miss Euphemia cried, the moment her brother made his appearance on the outer piazza, ' jest you come straight in here, I tellin' you. Here's Pheenie come around to hab a talk wit you. You is too unsocial altogedder. You always want to go an' bury yourself in your own study. Oh my, oh my ! Young man dat come from England, dey hasn't got no conversation at all for to talk wit de ladies.'

Dr. Whitaker was not in the humour just that moment to indulge in pleasantries with Miss Seraphina M'Culloch, a brown young lady of buxom figure and remarkably free-and-easy conversation; so he sighed impatiently as he answered with a hasty wave of his hand : ' No, Euphemia ; I can't come in and see your friend just this minute. I must go into my own room to make up some medicines—some very urgent medicines—wanted immediately—for some of my poor sick patients.'—Heaven help his soul for that transparent little prevarication, for all the medicine had been sent out in charge of a ragged negro boy more than two hours ago ; and it was Dr. Whitaker's own heart that was sick and ill at ease, beyond the power of any medicine ever to remedy.

Miss Euphemia pouted her already sufficiently protruding lips. ' Always dem stoopid niggers,' she answered contemptuously. ' How on eart a man like you, Wilberforce, dat has always been brought up respectable an' proper, in a decent fam'ly, can bear to go an' trow away his time in attendin' to a parcel of low nigger people, is more dan I can ever understan'.—Can you, Seraphina ? '

Miss Seraphina responded immediately, that, in her opinion, niggers was a disgraceful set of dat low, disreputable people, dat how a man like Dr. Wilberforce Whitaker could so much demean hisself as ever to touch dem, really surpassed her limited comprehension.

Dr. Whitaker strode angrily away into his own room, muttering to himself as he went, that one couldn't blame the white people for looking down upon the browns, when the browns themselves, in their foolish travesty of white prejudice, looked down so much upon their brother blacks beneath them. In a minute more, he reappeared with a face of puzzled bewilderment at the drawing-room door, and cried to his sister angrily : ' Euphemia, Euphemia ! what have you done, I'd like to know, with all those specimens I brought in this morning, and left, when I went out, upon my study table ? '

' Wilberforce,' Miss Euphemia answered with stately

dignity, rising to confront him, ' I tink I can't stand dis mess an' rubbish dat you make about de house a minute longer.—Pheenie! I tell you how dat man treat de fam'ly. Every day, he goes out into de woods an' he cuts bush—common bush, all sort of weed an' trash an' rubbish ; an' he brings dem home, an' puts dem in de study, so dat de house don't never tidy, however much you try for to tidy him. Well, dis mornin' I say to myself : "I don't goin' to stand dis lumber-room in a respectable fam'ly any longer." So I take de bush dat Wilberforce bring in ; I carry him out to de kitchen altogedder ; I open de stove, an' I trow him in all in a lump into de very middle of de kitchen fire. Ha, ha, ha! him burn an' crackle all de same as if he was chock-full of blazin' gunpowder ! '

Dr. Whitaker's eyes flashed angrily as he cried in surprise : ' What! all my specimens, Euphemia! all my specimens! all the ferns and orchids and curious club-mosses I brought in from Pimento Valley Scrubs early this morning ? '

Miss Euphemia tossed her head contemptuously in the air. ' Yes, Wilberforce,' she answered with a placid smile ; ' every one of dem. I burn de whole nasty lot of bush an' trash togedder. An' den, when I finished, I burn de dry ones—de nasty dry tings you put in de cupboards all around de study.'

Dr. Whitaker started in horror. ' My herbarium ! ' he cried—' my whole herbarium ! You don't mean to say, Euphemia, you've actually gone and wantonly destroyed my entire collection ? '

' Yes,' Miss Euphemia responded cheerfully, nodding acquiescence several times over ; ' I burn de whole lot of dem—paper an' everyting. De nasty tings, dey bring in de cockroach an' de red ants into de study cupboards.'

The mulatto rushed back eagerly and hastily into his own study ; he flung open the cupboard doors, and looked with a sinking heart into the vacant spaces. It was too true, all too true ! Miss Euphemia had destroyed in a moment of annoyance the entire result of his years of European collection and his five months' botanical work since he had arrived in Trinidad. The poor young man

sat down distracted in his easy chair, and flinging himself
back on the padded cushions, ruefully surveyed the bare
and empty shelves of his rifled cupboards. It was not so
much the mere loss of the pile of specimens—five months'
collection only, as well as the European herbarium he had
brought with him for purposes of comparison—the one
could be easily replaced in a second year; the other could
be bought again almost as good as ever from a London
dealer—it was the utter sense of loneliness and isolation,
the feeling of being so absolutely misunderstood, the entire
want of any reasonable and intelligent sympathy. He sat
there idly for many minutes, staring with blank resignation at the empty cases, and whistling to himself a low
plaintive tune, as he gazed and gazed at the bare walls in
helpless despondency. At last, his eye fell casually upon
his beloved violin. He rose up, slowly and mournfully,
and took the precious instrument with reverent care from
its silk-lined case. Drawing his bow across the familiar
strings, he let the music come forth as it would; and the
particular music that happened to frame itself upon the
trembling catgut on the humour of the moment was his
own luckless Hurricane Symphony. For half an hour he
sat there still, varying that well-known theme with un-
studied impromptus, and playing more for the sake of forgetting everything earthly, than of producing any very
particular musical effect. By-and-by, when his hand had
warmed to its work, and he was beginning really to feel
what it was he was playing, the door opened suddenly, and
a bland voice interrupted his solitude with an easy flow
of colloquial English.

'Wilberforce, my dear son,' the voice said in its most
sonorous accents, 'dere is company come; you will excuse
my interruptin' you. De ladies an' gentlemen dat we
expec' to dinner has begun to arrive. Dey is waitin' to
be introduced to de inheritor of de tree names most intimately connected wit de great revolution which I have
had de pleasure an' honour of bringin' about for my en-
slaved bredderin. De ladies especially is most anxious to
make your acquaintance. He, he, he! de ladies is most
anxious. An', my dear son, whatever you do, don't go on

playin' any longer dat loogoobrious melancholy fiddle-
toon. If you *must* play someting, play us someting lively
—*Pretty little yaller Gal*, or someting of dat sort !—
Ladies an' gentlemen, I have de pleasure of introducin' to
you my dear son, Dr. Wilberforce Clarkson Whitaker, of
de Edinburgh University.'

Dr. Whitaker almost flung down his beloved violin in
his shame and disgrace at this untimely interruption.
'Father,' he said, as kindly as he was able, 'I am not
well to-night—I am indisposed—I am suffering somewhat
—you must excuse me, please ; I'm afraid I shan't be able
to meet your friends at dinner this evening.' And taking
down his soft hat from the peg in the piazza, he crushed it
despairingly upon his aching head, and stalked out, alone
and sick at heart, into the dusty, dreary, cactus-bordered
lanes of that transformed and desolate Trinidad.

CHAPTER XXI.

THE Governor's dance was the great event of the Trinidad
season—the occasion to which every girl in the whole
island looked forward for months with the intensest interest. And it was also a great event to Dr. Whitaker ; for
it was the one time and place, except the Hawthorns'
drawing-room, where he could now meet Nora Dupuy on
momentary terms of seeming equality. In the eye of the
law, even in Trinidad, white men, black men, and brown
men are all equal ; and under the Governor's roof, as
became the representative of law and order in the little
island, there were no invidious distinctions of persons
between European and negro. Every well-to-do inhabit-
ant, irrespective of cuticular peculiarities, was duly bidden
to the Governor's table : ebony and ivory mingled freely
together once in a moon at the Governor's At Homes and
dances. And Dr. Whitaker had made up his mind that
on that one solitary possible occasion he would venture on
his sole despairing appeal to Nora Dupuy, and stand or
fall by her final answer.

It was not without serious misgivings that the mulatto doctor had at last decided upon thus tempting Providence. He was weary of the terrible disillusion that had come upon him on his return to the home of his fathers; weary of the painfully vulgar and narrow world into which he had been cast by unrelenting circumstances. He could not live any longer in Trinidad. Let him fight it out as he would for the sake of his youthful ideals, the battle had clearly gone against him, and there was nothing left for him now but to give it up in despair and fly to England. He had talked the matter over with Edward Hawthorn—not, indeed, the question of proposing to Nora Dupuy, for that he held too sacred for any other ear, but the question of stopping in the island and fighting down the unconquerable prejudice—and even Edward had counselled him to go; for he felt how vastly different were the circumstances of the struggle in his own case and in those of the poor young mulatto doctor. He himself had only to fight against the social prejudices of men his real inferiors in intellect and culture and moral standing. Dr. Whitaker had to face as well the utterly uncongenial brown society into which he had been rudely pitchforked by fate, like a gentleman into the midst of a pothouse company. It was best for them all that Dr. Whitaker should take himself away to a more fitting environment; and Edward had himself warmly advised him to return once more to free England.

The Governor's dance was given, not at Government House in the Plains, but at Banana Garden, the country bungalow, perched high up on a solitary summit of the Westmoreland mountains. The big ball-room was very crowded; and Nora Dupuy, in a pale maize-coloured evening dress, was universally recognised by black, brown, and white alike as the belle of the evening. She danced almost every round with one partner after another; and it was not till almost half the evening had passed away that Dr. Whitaker got the desired chance of even addressing her. The chance came at last just before the fifth waltz, a dance that Nora had purposely left vacant, in case she should happen to pick up in the earlier part of the evening an

exceptionally agreeable and promising partner. She was
sitting down to rest beside her chaperon of the night, on a
bench placed just outside the window in the tropical garden,
when the young mulatto, looking every inch a gentleman
in his evening dress—the first time Nora had ever seen
him so attired—strolled anxiously up to her, with ill-
affected carelessness, and bowed a timid bow to his former
travelling companion. Pure opposition to Mr. Dupuy, and
affection for the two ·Hawthorns, had made Nora exceptionally gracious just that moment to all brown people;
and, on purpose to scandalise her chaperon—an amusement always dear to every girl—she returned the doctor's
hesitating salute with a pleasant smile of perfect cordiality.
' Dr. Whitaker ! ' she cried, leaning over towards him in a
kindly way, which made the poor mulatto's heart flutter
terribly; ' so here you are, as you promised ! I'm so glad
you've come this evening. And have you brought Miss
Whitaker with you ? '

The mulatto hesitated and stammered. If he had been
a white man, he would have blushed as well; indeed, he
did blush internally, though, of course, Nora did not perceive it through his dusky skin. She could not possibly
have asked him a more *mal à propos* question. The poor
young man looked about him feebly, and then answered in
a low voice: ' Yes ; my father and sister are here somewhere.'

' Nora, my dear,' her chaperon said in a tone of subdued
feminine thunder, ' I didn't know you had the pleasure of
Miss Whitaker's acquaintance.'

' Neither have I, Mrs. Pereira ; but perhaps Dr.
Whitaker will be good enough to introduce me.—Not now,
thank you, Dr. Whitaker ; I don't want you to run away
this minute and fetch your sister. Some other time will
do as well. It's so seldom, you know, we have the chance
of a good talk now together.'

Dr. Whitaker smiled and stammered. It was possible,
of course, to accept Nora's reluctance in either of two
senses : she might be anxious that he should stop and talk
to her ; or she might merely wish indefinitely to postpone
the pleasure of making Miss Euphemia's personal acquaint-

ance; but she flooded him so with the light of her eyes
as she spoke, that he chose to put the most flattering of
the two alternative interpretations upon her ambiguous
sentence.

'You are very good to say so,' he answered, still
timidly; and Nora noticed how very different was his
manner of speaking now from the self-confident Dr.
Whitaker of the old *Severn* days. Trinidad had clearly
crushed all the confidence as well as all the enthusiasm
clean out of him. 'You are very good indeed, Miss Dupuy;
I wish the opportunities for our meeting occurred oftener.'

He stood talking beside her for a minute or two longer,
uttering the mere polite commonplaces of ball-room conversation—the heat of the evening, the shortcomings of
the band, the beauty of the flowers—when suddenly Nora
gave a little jump and seized her programme with singular
discomposure. Dr. Whitaker looked up at once, and
divined by instinct the cause of her hasty movement. Tom
Dupuy, just fresh from the cane-cutting, was looking about
for her down the long corridor at the opposite end of the
inner garden. 'Where's my cousin? Have you seen my
cousin?' he was asking everybody; for the seat where
Nora was sitting with Mrs. Pereira stood under the shade
of a big papaw tree, and so it was impossible for him to
discern her face, though she could see his features quite
distinctly.

'I won't dance with that horrid man, my cousin Tom!'
Nora said in her most decided voice. 'I'm quite sure he's
coming here this minute on purpose to ask me.'

'Is your programme full?' Dr. Whitaker inquired with
a palpitating heart.

'No, not quite,' she answered, and handed it to him
encouragingly. There was just one dance still left vacant
—the next waltz. 'I'm too tired to dance it out,' Nora
cried pettishly. 'The horrid man! I hope he won't see me.'

'He's coming this way, dear,' Mrs. Pereira put in with
placid composure. 'You'll have to sit it out with him
now; there's no help for it.'

'Sit it out with him!—sit it out with Tom Dupuy! O
no, Mrs. Pereira; I wouldn't do it for a thousand guineas.'

'What will you do, then?' Dr. Whitaker asked tremulously, still holding the programme and pencil in his undecided hand. Dare he—dare he ask her to dance just once with him?

'What shall I do? Why, nothing simpler. Have an engagement already, of course, Dr. Whitaker.'

She looked at him significantly. Tom Dupuy was just coming up. If Dr. Whitaker meant to ask her, there was no time to be lost. His knees gave way beneath him, but he faltered out at last in some feeble fashion : 'Then, Miss Dupuy, may I—may I—may I have the pleasure?'

To Mrs. Pereira's immense dismay, Nora immediately smiled and nodded. 'I can't dance it with you,' she said with a hasty gesture—she shrank, naturally, from that open confession of faith before the whole assembled company— 'but if you'll allow me, I'll sit it out with you here in the garden. You may put your name down for it if you like. Quickly, please—write it quickly ; here's Tom Dupuy just coming.'

The mulatto had hardly scratched his own name with shaky pencilled letters on the little card, when Tom Dupuy swaggered up in his awkward, loutish, confident manner, and with a contemptuous nod of condescending half-recognition to the overjoyed mulatto, asked, in his insular West Indian drawl, whether Nora could spare him a couple of dances.

'Your canes seem to have delayed you too late, Tom Dupuy,' Nora answered coldly. 'Dr. Whitaker has just asked me for my last vacancy. You should come earlier to a dance, you know, if you want to find a good partner.'

Tom Dupuy stared hard at her face in puzzled astonishment. 'Your last vacancy!' he cried incredulously. 'Dr. Whitaker! No more dances to spare, Nora! No, no, I say ; this won't do, you know! You've done this on purpose. Let me have a squint at your programme, will you?'

'If you don't choose to take my word for the facts,' Nora answered haughtily, 'you can see the names and numbers of my engagements for yourself on my programme, Tom.—Dr. Whitaker, have the kindness to hand my cousin my programme, if you please.—Thank you.'

Tom Dupuy took the programme ungraciously, and glanced down it with an angry eye. He read every name out aloud till he came to number eleven, ' Dr. Whitaker.' As he reached that name, his lip curled with an ugly suddenness, and he handed the bit of cardboard back coldly to his defiant cousin. ' Very well, Miss Nora,' he answered with a sneer. ' You're quite at liberty, of course, to choose your own company however it pleases you. I see your programme's quite full; but your list of names is rather comprehensive than select, I fancy. The last name was written down as I was coming towards you. This is a plot to insult me.—Dr. Whitaker, we shall settle this little difference elsewhere, probably—with the proper weapon—a horse-whip. Though your ancestors, to be sure, were better accustomed, I believe, sir, to a good raw cowhide.— Good evening, Miss Nora.—Good evening, Dr. Whitaker.'

The mulatto's eyes flashed fire, but he replied with a low and stately bow, in suppressed accents: 'I shall be ready to answer you in this matter whenever you wish, Mr. Dupuy—and with your own weapon. Good evening.' And he held out his arm quietly to Nora.

Nora rose and took the mulatto's proffered arm at once with a sweeping air of utter indifference. ' Shall we take a turn around the gardens, Dr. Whitaker?' she asked calmly, reassuring herself at the same time with a rapid glance that nobody except poor frightened Mrs. Pereira had overheard this short altercation. ' How lovely the moon looks to-night! What an exquisite undertone of green in the long shadows of those columns in the portico!'

' Undertone of green!' Tom Dupuy exclaimed aloud in vulgar derision (he was too much of a clod to see that his cue in the scene was fairly past, and that dignity demanded of him now to keep perfectly silent). ' Undertone of green, indeed, with her precious nigger!—Mrs. Pereira, this is your fault! A pretty sort of chaperon *you* make, upon my word, to let her go and engage herself to sit out a dance with a common mulatto!—Where's Uncle Theodore? Where is he, I tell you? I shall run and fetch him this very minute. I always said that in the end that girl Nora would go and marry a woolly-headed brown man.'

CHAPTER XXII.

Nora and the mulatto walked across the garden in unbroken silence; past the fountain in the centre of the courtyard; past the corridor by the open supper-room; past the hanging lanterns on the outer shrubbery; and down the big flight of stone steps to the gravelled Italian terrace that overlooked the deep tropical gully. When they reached the foot of the staircase, Nora said in as unconcerned a tone as she could muster up: 'Let us walk down here, away from the house, Dr. Whitaker. Tom may perhaps send papa out to look for me, and I'd rather not meet him till the next dance is well over. Please take me along the terrace.'

Dr. Whitaker turned with her silently along the path, and uttered not a word till they reached the marble seat at the end of the creeper-covered balustrade. Then he sat down moodily beside her, and said in what seemed a perfectly unruffled voice: 'Miss Dupuy, I am not altogether sorry that this little incident has turned out just as it has happened. It enables you to judge for yourself the sort of insult that men of my colour are liable to meet with here in Trinidad.'

Nora fingered her fan nervously. 'Tom Dupuy's always an unendurably rude fellow,' she said, with affected carelessness. 'He's rude by nature, you know, that's the fact of it. He's rude to me. He's rude to everybody. He's a boor, Dr. Whitaker; a boor at heart. You mustn't take any notice of what he says to you.'

'Yes, he's a boor, Miss Dupuy—and I shall venture to say so, although he's your own cousin—but in what other country in the world would such a boor venture to believe himself able to look down upon other men, his equals in everything except an accident of colour?'

'Oh, Dr. Whitaker, you make too much altogether of his rudeness. It isn't personal to you; it's part of his nature.'

'Miss Dupuy,' the young mulatto burst out suddenly,

after a moment's pause and internal struggle, 'I'm not
sorry for it, as I said before; for it gives me the opportunity of saying something to you that I have long been
waiting to tell you.'

'Well?' frigidly.

'Well, it is this: I mean at once to leave Trinidad.'

Nora started. It was not quite what she was expecting.
'To leave Trinidad, Dr. Whitaker? And where to go?
Back to England?'

'Yes, back to England.—Miss Dupuy, for Heaven's
sake, listen to me for a moment. This dance won't be very
long. As soon as it's over, I must take you back to the
ball-room. I have only these few short minutes to speak
to you. I have been waiting long for them—looking forward to them; hoping for them; dreading them; foreseeing
them. Don't disappoint me of my one chance of a hearing. Sit here and hear me out: I beg of you—I implore
you.'

Nora's fingers trembled terribly, and she felt half inclined to rise at once and go back to Mrs. Pereira; but she
could not find it in her heart utterly to refuse that pleading
tone of profound emotion, even though it came from only
a brown man. 'Well, Dr. Whitaker,' she answered tremulously, 'say on whatever you have to say to me.'

'I'm going to England, Miss Dupuy,' the poor young
mulatto went on in broken accents; 'I can stand no longer
the shame and misery of my own surroundings in this
island. You know what they are. Picture them to yourself for a moment. Forget you are a white woman, a
member of this old proud unforgiving aristocracy—"for
they ne'er pardon who have done the wrong:" forget it
for once, and try to think how it would feel to you, after
your English up-bringing, with your tastes and ideas and
habits and sentiments, to be suddenly set down in the midst
of a society like that of the ignorant coloured class here in
Trinidad. On the one side, contempt and contumely from
the most boorish and unlettered whites; on the other side,
utter uncongeniality with one's own poor miserable people.
Picture it to yourself—how absolutely unendurable!'

Nora bethought her silently of Tom Dupuy from both

points of view, and answered in a low tone : ' Dr. Whitaker,
I recognise the truth of what you say. I—I am sorry for
you ; I sympathise with you.'

It was a great deal for a daughter of the old slave-
owning oligarchy to say—how much, people in England
can hardly realise ; and Dr. Whitaker accepted it grate-
fully. ' It's very kind of you, Miss Dupuy,' he went on
again, the tears rising quickly to his eyes, ' very, very kind
of you. But the struggle is over ; I can't stand it any
longer ; I mean at once to return to England.'

' You will do wisely, I think,' Nora answered, looking
at him steadily.

' I will do wisely,' he repeated in a wandering tone.
' Yes, I will do wisely. But, Miss Dupuy, strange to say,
there is one thing that still binds me down to Trinidad.—
Oh, for Heaven's sake, listen to me, and don't condemn me
unheard.—No, no, I beg of you, don't rise yet ! I will be
brief. Hear me out, I implore of you, I implore of you !
I'm only a mulatto, I know ; but mulattoes have a heart
as well as white men—better than some, I do honestly
believe. Miss Dupuy, from the very first moment I saw
you, I—I loved you ! yes, I *will* say it—I loved you !—I
loved you ! '

Nora rose, and stood erect before him, proud but tremulous, in her girlish beauty. ' Dr. Whitaker,' she
said, in a very calm tone, ' I knew it ; I saw it. From
the first moment you ever spoke to me, I knew it perfectly.'

He drew a long breath to still the violent throbbing of
his heart. ' You knew it,' he said, almost joyously—' you
knew it ! And you did not repel me ! Oh, Miss Dupuy,
for one of your blood and birth, that was indeed a great
condescension ! '

Nora hesitated. ' I liked you, Dr. Whitaker,' she answered slowly—' I liked you, and I was sorry for you.'

' Thank you, thank you. Whatever else you say, for
that one word I thank you earnestly. But oh, what more
can I say to you ? I love you ; I have always loved you.
I shall always love you in future. Take me or reject me,
I shall always love you. And yet, how can I ask you ?

But in England—in England, Miss Dupuy, the barrier would be less absolute.—Yes, yes ; I know how hopeless it is : but this once—this once only ! I *must* ask you ! Oh, for Heaven's sake, in England—far away from it all—in London, where nobody thinks of these things ! Why, I know a Hindu barrister—— But there ! it's not a matter for reasoning ; it lies between heart and heart ! Oh, Miss Dupuy, tell me—tell me, for God's sake, tell me, is there—is there any chance for me ? '

Nora's heart relented within her. ' Dr. Whitaker,' she said slowly and remorsefully, ' you can't tell how much I feel for you. I can see at once what a dreadful position you are placed in. I can see, of course, how impossible it is for you ever to think of marrying any—any lady of your own colour—at least as they are brought up here in Trinidad. I can see that you could only fall in love with—with a white lady—a person fitted by education and manners to be a companion to you. I know how clever you are, and I think I can see how good you are too. I know how far all your tastes and ideas are above those of the people you must mix with here, or, for that matter, above Tom Dupuy's —or my own either. I see it all ; I know it all. And, in-deed, I like you. I admire you and I like you. I don't want you to think me unkind and unappreciative.—Dr. Whitaker, I feel truly flattered that you should speak so to me this even-ing—but——' And she hesitated. The young mulatto felt that that ' but ' was the very death-blow to his last faint hope and aspiration. ' But—— Well, you know these things are something more than a mere matter of liking and admiring. Let us still be friends, Dr. Whitaker—let us still be friends. —And there's the band striking up the next waltz. Will you kindly take me back to the ball-room ? I—I am en-gaged to dance it with Captain Castello.'

' One second, Miss Dupuy—for God's sake, one second ! Is that final ? Is that irrevocable ? '

' Final, Dr. Whitaker—quite final. I like you ; I ad-mire you ; but I can never, never, never—never accept you ! '

The mulatto clapped his hand wildly for one moment to his forehead, and uttered a little low sharp piercing cry. ' My God, my God,' he exclaimed in an accent of terrible

despair, 'then it is all over—all, all over!' Next instant
he had drawn himself together with an effort again, and
offering Nora his arm with constrained calmness, he began
to lead her back towards the crowded ball-room. As he
neared the steps, he paused once more for a second, and
almost whispered in her ear in a hollow voice : 'Thank
you, thank you for ever for at least your sympathy.'

CHAPTER XXIII.

THEY had reached the top of the stone steps, when two
voices were borne upon them from the two ends of the
corridor opposite. The first was Mr. Dupuy's. ' Where is
she ? ' it said.—' Mrs. Pereira, where's Nora ? You don't
mean to say this is true that Tom tells me—that you've
actually gone and let her sit out a dance with that conceited
nigger fellow, Dr. Whitaker ? Upon my word, my dear
madam, what this island is coming to nowadays is really
more than I can imagine.'

The second voice was a louder and blander one. ' My
son, my son,' it said, in somewhat thick accents, ' my dear
son, Wilberforce Clarkson Whitaker ! Where is he ? Is
he in de garden ? I want to introduce him to de Governor's
lady. De Governor's lady has been graciously pleased to
express an interes in de inheritor of de tree names most closely
bound up wit de great social revolution, in which I have
had de honour to be de chief actor, for de benefit of millions
of my fellow-subjecks.—Walkin' in de garden, is he, wit de
daughter of my respected friend, de Honourable Teodore
Dupuy of Orange Grove ? Ha, ha ! Dat's de way wit de
young dogs—dat's de way wit dem. Always off walkin' in
de garden wit de pretty ladies. Ha, ha, ha ! I don't blame
dem ! '

Dr. Whitaker, his face on fire and his ears tingling,
pushed on rapidly down the very centre of the garden,
taking no heed of either voice in outward seeming, but
going straight on, with Nora on his arm, till he reached
the open window-doors that led directly into the big ball-

room. There, seething in soul, but outwardly calm and polite, he handed over his partner with a conventional smile to Captain Castello, and turning on his heel, strode away bitterly across the ball-room to the outer doorway. Not a few people noticed him as he strode off in his angry dignity, for Tom Dupuy had already been blustering—with his usual taste—in the corridors and refreshment-room about his valiant threat of soundly horsewhipping the woolly-headed mulatto. In the vestibule, the doctor paused and asked for his dust-coat. A negro servant, in red livery, grinning with delight at what he thought the brown man's discomfiture, held it up for him to put his arms into. Dr. Whitaker noticed the fellow's malevolent grin, and making an ineffectual effort to push his left arm down the right arm sleeve, seized the coat angrily in his hand, doubled it up in a loose fold over his elbow, and then, changing his mind, as an angry man will do, flung it down again with a hasty gesture upon the hall table. 'Never mind the coat,' he said fiercely. 'Bring round my horse! Do you hear, fellow? My horse, my horse! This minute, I tell you!'

The red-liveried servant called to an invisible negro outside, who soon returned with the doctor's mountain pony.

'Better take de coat, sah,' the man in livery said with a sarcastic guffaw. 'Him help to proteck your back an' sides from Mistah Dupuy, him horsewhip!'

Dr. Whitaker leaped upon his horse, and turned to the man with a face livid and distorted with irrepressible anger. 'You black devil, you!' he cried passionately, using the words of reproach that even a mulatto will hurl in his wrath at his still darker brother, 'do you think I'm running away from Tom Dupuy's miserable horsewhip? I'm not afraid of a hundred fighting Dupuys and all their horse-whips. Let him dare to touch me, and, by Heaven, he'll find he'd better far have touched the devil.—You black image, you! how dare you speak to me? How dare you—how dare you?' And he cut at him viciously in impotent rage with the little riding-whip he held in his fingers.

The negro laughed again, a loud hoarse laugh, and flung both his hands up with open fingers in African

derision. Dr. Whitaker dug his spurless heel deep into
his horse's side, sitting there wildly in his evening dress,
and turned his head in mad despair out towards the outer
darkness. The moon was still shining brightly overhead,
but by contrast with the lights in the gaily illuminated
ball-room, the path beneath the bamboo clumps in the
shrubbery looked very gloomy, dark, and sombre.

Two or three of the younger men, anxious to see
whether Tom Dupuy would get up ' a scene ' then and there,
crowded out hastily to the doorway, to watch the nigger
fellow ride away for his life for fear of a horsewhipping.
As they stood in the doorway, peering into the darkness
after the retreating upright figure, there came all at once,
with appalling suddenness, a solitary vivid flash of lightning,
such as one never sees outside the tropics, illuminating with
its awful light the whole length of the gardens and the
gully beneath them. At the same second, a terrific clap
of thunder seemed to burst, like innumerable volleys of the
heaviest artillery, right above the roof of the Governor's
bungalow. It was ghastly in its suddenness and in its
strength. No one could say where the lightning struck,
for it seemed to have struck on every side at once : all that
they saw was a single sheet of all-pervading fire, in whose
midst the mulatto and his horse stood silhouetted out in
solid black, a statuesque group of living sculpture, against
the brilliant fiery background. The horse was rearing,
erect on his hind legs ; and Dr. Whitaker was reining him
in and patting his neck soothingly with hand half lifted.
So instantaneous was the flash, indeed, that no motion or
change of any sort was visible in the figures. The horse
looked like a horse of bronze, poised in the air on solid
metal legs, and merely simulating the action of rearing.

For a minute or two, not a soul spoke a word, or broke
in any way the deathless silence that succeeded that awful
and unexpected outburst. The band had ceased playing as
if by instinct, and every person in the ball-room stood still
and looked one at another with mute amazement. Then,
by a common impulse, they pressed all out slowly together,
and gazed forth with wondering eyes upon the serene moonlight. The stars were shining brightly overhead : the clap

had broken from an absolutely clear sky. Only to northward,
on the very summits of the highest mountains, a gathering
of deep black clouds rolled slowly onward, and threatened
to pass across the intervening valley. Through the profound silence, the ring of Dr. Whitaker's horse's hoofs
could be heard distinctly down below upon the solid floor
of the mountain pathway.

' Who has left already ? ' the Governor asked anxiously
of the negro servants.

' Dr. Whitaker, your Excellency, sah,' the man in red
livery answered, grinning respectfully.

' Call him back ! ' the Governor said in a tone of command. ' There's an awful thunderstorm coming. No man
will ever get down alive to the bottom of the valley until
it's over.'

' It doan't no use, sah,' the negro answered. ' His
horse's canterin' down de hill-side de same as if him starin'
mad, sah ! ' And as he spoke, Dr. Whitaker's white shirt-
front gleamed for a second in the moonlight far below, at a
turn of the path beside the threatening gully.

Almost before any one could start to recall him, the rain
and thunder were upon them with tropical violence. The
clouds had drifted rapidly across the sky ; the light of the
moon was completely effaced ; black darkness reigned over
the mountains ; not a star, not a tree, not an object of any
sort could now be discerned through the pitchy atmosphere.
Rain ! it was hardly rain, but rather a continuous torrent
outpoured as from some vast aërial fountain. Every minute
or two a terrific flash lighted up momentarily the gloomy
darkness ; and almost simultaneously, loud peals of thunder
bellowed and re-echoed from peak to peak. The dance was
interrupted for the time at least, and everybody crowded
out silently to the veranda and the corridors, where the
lightning and the rain could be more easily seen, mingling
with the thunder in one hideous din, and forming torrents
that rushed down the dry gullies in roaring cataracts to
the plains below.

And Dr. Whitaker ? On he rode, the lightning terrify-
ing his little mountain pony at every flash, the rain beating
down upon him mercilessly with equatorial fierceness, the

darkness stretching in front of him and below him, save when, every now and then, the awful forks of flame illumined for a second the gulfs and precipices that yawned beneath in profoundest gloom. Yet still he rode on, erect and heedless, his hat now lost, bareheaded to the pitiless storm, cold without and fiery hot at heart within. He cared for nothing now—for nothing—for nothing. Nora had put the final coping-stone on that grim growth of black despair within his soul, that palace of nethermost darkness which alone he was henceforth to inhabit. Nay, in the heat and bitterness of the moment, had he not even sealed his own doom ? Had he not sunk down actually to the level of those who despised and contemned him ? Had he not used words of contemptuous insolence to his own colour, in the ' black devil' he had flung so wildly at the head of the negro in livery ? What did it matter now whatever happened to him ? All, all was lost ; and he rode on recklessly, madly, despairingly, down that wild and precipitous mountain pathway, he knew not and he cared not whither.

It was a narrow track, a mere thread of bridle-path, dangerous enough even in the best of seasons, hung halfway up the steep hill-side, with the peak rising sheer above on one hand, and the precipice yawning black beneath on the other. Stones and creepers cumbered the ground ; pebbles and earth, washed down at once by the violence of the storm, blocked and obliterated the track in many places ; here, a headlong torrent tore across it with resistless vehemence ; there, a little chasm marked the spot where a small landslip had rendered it impassable. The horse floundered and reared and backed up again and again in startled terror ; Dr. Whitaker, too reckless at last even to pat and encourage him, let him go whatever way his fancy led him among the deep brake of cactuses and tree-ferns. And still the rain descended in vast sheets and flakes of water, and still the lightning flashed and quivered among the ravines and gullies of those torn and crumpled mountain sides. The mulatto took no notice any longer ; he only sang aloud in a wild, defiant, half-crazy voice the groaning notes of his own terrible Hurricane Symphony.

So they went, on and down, on and down, on and

down always, through fire and water, the horse plunging and kicking and backing; the rider flinging his arms carelessly around him, till they reached the bend in the road beside Louis Delgado's mud cottage. The old African was sitting cross-legged by himself at the door of his hut, watching the rain grimly by the intermittent light of the frequent flashes. Suddenly, a vivider flash than any burst in upon him, with a fearful clap; and by its light, he saw a great gap in the midst of the path, twenty yards wide, close by the cottage; and at its upper end, a horse and rider, trembling on the very brink of the freshly cut abyss.

Next instant the flash was gone, and when the next came Louis Delgado saw nothing but the gap itself and the wild torrent that had so instantly cut it.

The old man smiled an awful smile of gratified male-volence. ' Ha, ha ! ' he said to himself aloud, hugging his withered old breast in malicious joy; ' I guess dat buckra lyin' dead by now, down, down, down, at de bottom ob de gully. Ha, ha! ha, ha, ha ! him lyin' dead at de bottom ob de gully; an' it one buckra de less left alive to bodder us here in de island ob Trinidad.' He had not seen the mulatto's face; but he took him at once to be a white man because, in spite of rain and spattered mud, his white shirt front still showed out distinctly in the red glare of the vivid lightning.

CHAPTER XXIV.

No human eye ever again beheld Wilberforce Whitaker, alive or dead. The torrent that had washed down the gap in the narrow horsepath tore away with it in the course of that evening's rain a great mass of tottering earth that had long trembled on the edge of the precipice; and when next day the Governor's servants went down in awed silence to hunt among the débris for the mangled body, they found nothing but a soaked hat on the road behind, and a broken riding-whip close to the huge rent that yawned across the path by the crumbling ledge of newly fallen clay. Louis Delgado alone could tell of what had happened; and in Louis Delgado's opinion, Dr. Whitaker's crushed and shapeless body must be lying below under ten thousand tons of landslip rubbish. 'I see de gentleman haltin' on de brink ob de hole,' he said a hundred times over to his gossips next day, 'and I tink I hear him call aloud someting as him go ober de tip ob de big precipice. But it doan't sound to me ezackly as if him scared and shoutin'; 'pears more as if him singing to hisself a kind ob mournful miserable psalm tune.'

In tropical countries, people are accustomed to hurricanes and thunderstorms and landslips and sudden death in every form—does not the Church service even contain that weirdly suggestive additional clause among the petitions of the Litany, ' From earthquake, tempest, and violent commotion, good Lord, deliver us '?—and so nobody ever tried to dig up Wilberforce Whitaker's buried body; and if they had tried, they would never have succeeded in the vain attempt, for a thousand tons of broken fragments lay on top of it, and crushed it to atoms beneath them. Poor old Bobby felt the loss acutely, after his childish fashion, for nearly a fortnight, and then straightway proceeded to make love as usual to Miss Seraphina and the other ladies, and soon forgot his whole trouble in that one congenial lifelong occupation.

Nora Dupuy did not so quickly recover the shock that the mulatto's sudden and almost supernatural death had given her system. It was many weeks before she began to feel like herself again, or to trust herself in a room alone for more than a very few minutes together. Born West Indian as she was, and therefore superstitious, she almost feared that Dr. Whitaker's ghost would come to plead his cause with her once more, as he himself had pleaded with her that last unhappy evening on the Italian terrace. It wasn.'t her fault, to be sure, that she had been the unwitting cause of his death; and yet in her own heart she felt to herself almost as if she had deliberately and intentionally killed him. That insuperable barrier of race that had stood so effectually in his way while he was still alive was partly removed now that she could no longer see him in person; and more than once, Nora found herself in her own room with tears standing in both her eyes for the poor mulatto she could never possibly or conceivably have married.

As for Tom Dupuy, he couldn't understand such delicate shades and undertones of feeling as those which came so naturally to Nora; and he had, therefore, a short and easy explanation of his own for his lively little cousin's altered demeanour. 'Nora was in love with that infernal nigger fellow,' he said confidently over and over again to his Uncle Theodore. 'You take my word for it, she was head over ears in love with him; that's about the size of it. And that evening when she behaved so disgracefully with him on the terrace at the Governor's, he proposed to her, and she accepted him, as sure as gospel. If I hadn't threatened him with a good sound horsewhipping, and driven him away from the house in a deuce of a funk, so that he went off with his tail between his legs, and broke his damned neck over a precipice in that terrible thunderstorm—you mark my words, Uncle Theodore—she'd have gone off, as I always said she would, and she'd have ended by marrying a woolly-headed brown man.'

Mr. Theodore Dupuy, for his part, considered that even to mention the bare possibility of such a disgrace within the bosom of the family was an insult to the pure blood of the Dupuys that his nephew Tom ought to have been the last man on earth to dream of perpetrating.

Time rolled on, however, month after month, and gradually Nora began to recover something of her natural gaiety. Even deep impressions last a comparatively short time with bright young girls; and before six months more had fairly rolled by, Nora was again the same gay, light, merry, dancing little thing that she had always been, in England or in Trinidad.

One morning, about twelve months after Nora's first arrival in the island, the English mail brought a letter for her father, which he read with evident satisfaction, and then handed it contentedly to Nora across the breakfast-table. Nora recognised the crest and monogram in a moment with a faint flutter: she had seen them once before, a year ago, in England. They were Harry Noel's,

But the postmark was Barbadoes. She read the letter eagerly and hastily.

'DEAR SIR '—it ran—' I have had the pleasure already of meeting some members of your family on the other side of the Atlantic '—that was an overstatement, Nora thought to herself quietly ; the plural for the singular—' and as I have come out to look after some property of my father's here in Barbadoes, I propose to run across to Trinidad also, by the next steamer, and gain a little further insight into the habits and manners of the West Indies. My intention is to stop during my stay with my friend Mr. Hawthorn, who—as you doubtless know—holds a District judgeship or something of the sort somewhere in Trinidad. But I think it best at the same time to inclose a letter of intro- duction to yourself from General Sir Henry Laboutillière, whom I dare say you remember as formerly commandant of Port-of-Spain when the Hundred and Fiftieth were in your island. I shall do myself the honour of calling upon you very shortly after my arrival, and am meanwhile, very faithfully yours,   HARRY NOEL.'

The letter of introduction which accompanied this very formal note briefly set forth that Sir Walter Noel, Mr. Noel's father, was an exceedingly old and intimate friend of the writer's, and that he would feel much obliged if Mr. Dupuy would pay young Mr. Noel any attentions in his power during his short stay in the island of Trinidad.

It would be absurd to deny that Nora felt flattered. She blushed, and blushed, and blushed again, with un- mistakable pleasure. To be sure, she had refused Harry Noel ; and if he were to ask her again, even now, she would refuse him a second time. But no girl on earth is wholly proof in her own heart against resolute persistence. Even if she doesn't care a pin for the man from the matri- monial point of view, yet provided only he is ' nice ' and ' eligible,' she feels naturally flattered by the mere fact that he pays her attention. If the attention is marked and often renewed, the flattery is all the deeper, subtler, and more effective. But here was Harry Noel, pursuant of his threat (or should we rather say his promise ?), following

her up right across the Atlantic, and coming to lay siege
to her heart with due formalities once more, in the very
centre of her own stronghold! Yes, Nora was undeniably
pleased. Of course, she didn't care for him; oh dear no,
not the least little bit in the world, really; but still, even
if you don't want to accept a lover, you know, it is at any
rate pleasant to have the opportunity of a second time
cruelly rejecting him. So Nora blushed, and smiled to
herself, and blushed over again, and felt by no means out
of humour at Harry Noel's evident persistence.

'Well, Nora?' her father said to her, eyeing her inter-
rogatively. 'What do you think of it?'

'I think, papa, Mr. Noel's a very gentlemanly, nice
young man, of a very good old English family.'

'Yes, yes, Nora: I know that, of course. I see as
much from Sir Henry Laboutillière's letter of introduction.
But what I mean is, we must have him here, at Orange
Grove, naturally, mustn't we? It would never do, you
see, to let a member of the English aristocracy'—Mr.
Dupuy dwelt lovingly upon these latter words with some
unction, as preachers dwell with lingering cadence upon
the special shibboleths of their own particular sect or per-
suasion—'go to stop with such people as your coloured
friends over yonder at Mulberry, the Hawthorns.'

Nora was silent.

'Why don't you answer me, miss?' Mr. Dupuy asked
testily, after waiting for a moment in silent expectation.

'Because I will never speak to you about my own
friends, papa, when you choose to talk of them in such
untrue and undeserved language.'

Mr. Dupuy smiled urbanely. He was in a good humour.
It flattered him, too, to think that when members of the
English aristocracy came out to Trinidad they should
naturally select him, Theodore Dupuy, Esquire, of Orange
Grove, as the proper person towards whom to look for
hospitality. The fame of the fighting Dupuys was probably
not unknown to the fashionable world even in London. They
were recognised and talked about. So Mr. Dupuy merely
smiled a bland smile of utter obliviousness, and observed
in the air (as men do when they are addressing nobody in

particular) : ' Coloured people are always coloured people, I suppose, whether they're much or little coloured ; just as a dog's always a dog, whether he's a great big heavy St. Bernard or a little snarling snapper of a Skye terrier.   But anyhow, it's quite clear to me individually that we can't let this young Mr. Noel—a person of distinction, Nora, a person of distinction —go and stop at any other house in this island except here at Orange Grove, I assure you, my dear.   Tom or I must certainly go down to meet the steamer, and bring him up here bodily in the buggy, before your friend Mr. Hawthorn—about whose personal complexion I prefer to say absolutely nothing, for good or for evil—has time to fasten on him and drag him away by main force to his own dwelling-place.' (Mr. Dupuy avoided calling Mulberry Lodge a house on principle ; for in the West Indies it is an understood fact that only white people live in houses.)

' But, papa,' Nora cried, ' you really mustn't.   I don't think you ought to bring him up here.   Wouldn't it—well, you know, wouldn't it look just a little pointed, considering there's nobody else at all living in the house except you and me, you know, papa ? '

' My dear,' Mr. Dupuy said, not unkindly, ' a member of the English aristocracy, when he comes to Trinidad, ought to be received in the house of one of the recognised gentry of the island, and not in that—well, not in the dwelling-place of any person not belonging to the aristocracy of Trinidad.   *Noblesse oblige*, Nora ; *noblesse oblige*, remember.   Besides, when you consider the relation in which you already stand to your cousin Tom, my dear— why, an engaged young lady, of course, an engaged young lady occupies nearly the same position in that respect as if she were already actually married.'

' But I'm not engaged, papa,' Nora answered earnestly. ' And I never will be to Tom Dupuy, if I die unmarried, either.'

' That, my dear,' Mr. Dupuy responded blandly, looking at her with parental fondness, ' is a question on which I venture to think myself far better qualified to form an opinion than a mere girl of barely twenty.   Tom and I have arranged between us, as I have often already pointed

out to you, that the family estates ought on all accounts to
be reunited in your persons. As soon as you are twenty-
two, my dear, we propose that you should marry. Meanwhile, it can only arouse unseemly differences within the
family to discuss the details of the question prematurely.
I have made up my mind, and I will not go back upon it.
A Dupuy never does. As to this young Mr. Noel who's
coming from Barbadoes, I shall go down myself to the
next steamer, and look out to offer him our hospitality immediately on his arrival, before any coloured people—I
mention no names—can seize upon the opportunity of
intercepting him, and carrying him off forcibly against his
will, bag and baggage, to their own dwelling-places.'

CHAPTER XXV.

On the morning when Harry Noel was to arrive in Trinidad,
Mr. Dupuy and Edward Hawthorn both came down early
to the landing-stage to await the steamer. Mr. Dupuy
condescended to nod in a distant manner to the young
judge—he had never forgiven him that monstrous decision
in the case of Delgado *versus* Dupuy—and to ask chillily
whether he was expecting friends from England.

' No,' Edward Hawthorn answered with a bow as cold
as Mr. Dupuy's own. ' I have come down to meet an old
English friend of mine, a Mr. Noel, whom I knew very
well at Cambridge and in London, but who's coming at
present only from Barbadoes.'

Mr. Dupuy astutely held his tongue. *Noblesse* did not
so far impose upon him as to oblige him to confess that it
was Harry Noel he, too, had come down in search of. But
as soon as the steamer was well alongside, Mr. Dupuy, in
his stately, slow, West Indian manner, sailed ponderously
down the special gangway, and asked a steward at once to
point out to him which of the passengers was Mr. Noel.

Harry Noel, when he received Mr. Dupuy's pressing
invitation, was naturally charmed at the prospect of thus
being quartered under the same roof with pretty little

Nora. Had he known the whole circumstances of the case,
indeed, his native good feeling would, of course, have
prompted him to go to the Hawthorns'; but Edward had
been restrained by a certain sense of false shame from
writing the whole truth about this petty local race prejudice
to his friend in England; and so Harry jumped at once at
the idea of being so comfortably received into the very
house of which he so greatly desired to become an inmate.
' You're very good, I'm sure,' he answered in his off-hand
manner to the old planter. ' Upon my word, I never met
anything in my life to equal your open-hearted West
Indian hospitality. Wherever one goes, one's uniformly
met with open arms. I shall be delighted, Mr. Dupuy, to
put up at your place—Orange Grove, I think you call it—
ah, exactly—if you'll kindly permit me.—Here, you fellow,
go down below, will you, and ask for my luggage.'

Edward Hawthorn was a minute or two too late.
Harry came forward eagerly in the old friendly fashion, to
grasp his hand with a hard grip, but explained to him
with a look, which Edward immediately understood, that
Orange Grove succeeded in offering him superior attractions even to Mulberry. So the very next morning found
Nora and Harry Noel seated together at lunch at Mr.
Dupuy's well-loaded table; while Tom Dupuy, who had
actually stolen an hour or two from his beloved canes,
dropped in casually to take stock of this new possible rival,
as he half suspected the gay young Englishman would
turn out to be. From the first moment that their eyes
met, Tom Dupuy conceived an immediate dislike and distrust for Harry Noel. What did he want coming here to
Trinidad? Tom wondered: a fine-spoken, stuck-up, easy-
going, haw-haw Londoner, of the sort that your true-born
colonist hates and detests with all the force of his good-
hater's nature. Harry irritated him immensely by his natural
superiority: a man of Tom Dupuy's type can forgive anything in any other man except higher intelligence and
better breeding. Those are qualities for which he feels a
profound contempt, not unmingled with hatred, envy,
malice, and all uncharitableness. So, as soon as Nora
had risen from the table and the men were left alone,

West Indian fashion, to their afternoon cigar and cup of coffee, Tom Dupuy began to open fire at once on Harry about his precious coloured friends the Hawthorns at Mulberry.

' So you've come across partly to see that new man at the Westmoreland District Court, have you?' he said sneeringly. ' Well, I dare say he was considered fit company for gentlemen over in England, Mr. Noel—people seem to have very queer ideas about what's a gentleman and what's not, over in England—but though I didn't like to speak about it before Nora, seeing that they're friends of hers, I think I ought to warn you beforehand that you mustn't have too much to say to them if you want to get on out here in Trinidad. People here are a trifle particular about their company.'

Harry looked across curiously at the young planter, leaning back in awkward fashion with legs outstretched and half turned away from the table, as he sipped his coffee, and answered quietly, with some little surprise: ' Why, yes, Mr. Dupuy, I think our English idea of what constitutes a gentleman does differ slightly in some respects from the one I find current out here in the West Indies. I knew Hawthorn intimately for several years at Cambridge and in London, and the more I knew of him the better I liked him and the more I respected him. He's a little bit too radical for me, I confess, and a little bit too learned as well; but in every other way, I can't imagine what possible objection you can bring against him.'

Tom Dupuy smiled an ugly smile, and gazed hard at Harry Noel's dark and handsome face and features. ' Well,' he said slowly, a malevolent light gleaming hastily from his heavy eyes, ' we West Indians may be prejudiced; they say we are; but still, we're not fond somehow of making too free with a pack of niggers. Now, I don't say your friend Hawthorn's exactly a nigger outside, to look at: he isn't: he's managed to hide the outer show of his colour finely. I've seen a good many regular white people, or what passed for white people '—and here he glanced significantly at the fine-spoken Londoner's dark fingers, toying easily with the amber mouthpiece of his dainty cigar-holder—'who were a good many shades darker in the skin than this fellow Hawthorn, for all they thought themselves such very grand gentlemen. Some of 'em may be coloured, and some of 'em mayn't: there's no knowing, when once you get across to England; for people there have no proper pride of race, I understand, and would marry a coloured girl, if she happened to have money, as soon as look at her. But this fellow Hawthorn, though he seems externally as white as you do—and a great deal whiter too, by Jove—is well known out here to be nothing but a coloured person, as his father and his mother were before him.'

Harry Noel puffed out a long stream of white smoke as he answered carelessly: 'Ah, I dare say he is, if what you mean is just that he's got some remote sort of negro tinge somewhere about him—though he doesn't look it; but I expect almost all the old West Indian families, you know, must have intermarried long ago, when English ladies were rare in the colonies, with pretty half-castes.'

Quite unwittingly, the young Englishman had trodden at once on the very tenderest and dearest corn of his proud and unbending West Indian entertainers. Pride of blood is the one form of pride that they thoroughly understand and sympathise with; and this remote hint of a possible (and probable) distant past when the purity of the white race was not quite so efficiently guaranteed as it is nowadays, roused both the fiery Dupuys immediately to a white-heat of indignation.

'Sir,' Mr. Theodore Dupuy said stiffly, 'you evidently don't understand the way in which we regard these questions out here in the colonies, and especially in Trinidad. There is one thing which your English Parliament has not taken from us, and can never take from us; and that is the pure European blood which flows unsullied in all our veins, nowhere polluted by the faintest taint of a vile African intermixture.'

'Certainly,' Mr. Tom Dupuy echoed angrily, 'if you want to call us niggers, you'd better call us niggers outright, and not be afraid of it.'

'Upon my soul,' Harry Noel answered with an

apologetic smile, ' I hadn't the least intention, my dear sir,
of seeming to hint anything against the purity of blood in
West Indians generally; I only meant, that if my friend
Hawthorn—who is really a very good fellow and a perfect
gentleman—does happen to have a little distant infusion
of negro blood in him, it doesn't seem to me to matter
much to any of us nowadays. It must be awfully little—a
mere nothing, you know; just the amount one would
naturally expect if his people had intermarried once with
half-castes a great many generations ago.   I was only
standing up for my friend, you see.   Surely,' turning to
Tom, who still glared at him like a wild beast aroused, ' a
man ought to stand up for his friends when he hears them
ill spoken of.'

' Oh, quite so,' Mr. Theodore Dupuy replied, in a mollified voice. ' Of course, if Mr. Hawthorn's a friend of
yours, and you choose to stand by him here, in spite of his
natural disabilities, on the ground that you happened to
know him over in England—where, I believe, he concealed
the fact of his being coloured—and you don't like now to
turn your back upon him, why, naturally, that's very
honourable of you, very honourable.—Tom, my dear boy,
we must both admit that Mr. Noel is acting very honour-
ably.   And, indeed, we can't expect people brought up
wholly in England '—Mr. Dupuy dwelt softly upon this
fatal disqualification, as though aware that Harry must be
rather ashamed of it—' to feel upon these points exactly as
we do, who have a better knowledge and insight into the
negro blood and the negro character.'

' Certainly not,' Tom Dupuy continued maliciously.
' People in England don't understand these things at all
as we do.—Why, Mr. Noel, you mayn't be aware of it, but
even among the highest English aristocracy there are an
awful lot of regular coloured people, out-and-out mulattoes.
West Indian heiresses in the old days used to go home—
brown girls, or at any rate young women with a touch of
the tar-brush—daughters of governors and so forth, on
the wrong side of the house—you understand '—Mr. Tom
Dupuy accompanied these last words with an upward and
backward jerk of his left thumb, supplemented by a pecu-

liarly ugly grimace, intended to be facetious—'the sort of trash no decent young fellow over here would have so much as touched with a pair of tongs (in the way of marrying 'em, I mean) ; and when they got across to England, hanged if they weren't snapped up at once by dukes and marquises, whose descendants, after all, though they may be lords, are really nothing better, you see, than common brown people ! '

He spoke snappishly, but Harry only looked across at him in mild wonder.   On the calm and unquestioning pride of a Lincolnshire Noel, remarks such as these fell flat and pointless.   If a Noel had chosen to marry a kitchenmaid, according to their simple old-fashioned faith, he would have ennobled her at once, and lifted her up into his own exalted sphere of life and action.   Her children after her would have been Lincolnshire Noels, the equals of any duke or marquis in the United Kingdom.   So Harry only smiled benignly, and answered in his easy off-hand manner : ' By Jove, I shouldn't wonder at all if that were really the case now.   One reads in Thackeray, you know, so much about the wealthy West Indian heiresses, with suspiciously curly hair, who used to swarm in London in the old slavery days. But of course, Mr. Dupuy, it's a well-known fact that all our good families have been awfully recruited by actresses and so forth.   I believe some statistical fellow or other has written a book to show that if it weren't for the actresses, the peerage and baronetage would all have died out long ago, of pure inanition.   I dare say the West Indian heiresses, with the frizzy hair, helped to fulfil the same good and useful purpose, by bringing an infusion of fresh blood every now and then into our old families.'   And Harry ran his hand carelessly through his own copious curling black locks, in perfect unconsciousness of the absurdly malàpropos nature of that instinctive action at that par-ticular moment.   His calm sense of utter superiority—that innate belief so difficult to shake, even on the most rational grounds, in most well-born and well-bred Englishmen—kept him even from suspecting the real drift of Tom Dupuy's reiterated innuendoes.

' You came out to Barbadoes to look after some property

of your father's, I believe ? ' Mr. Dupuy put in, anxious to
turn the current of the conversation from this very dangerous
and fitful channel.

'I did,' Harry Noel answered unconcernedly. ' My
father's, or rather my mother's. Her people have property
there. We're connected with Barbadoes, indeed. My
mother's family were Barbadian planters.'

At the word, Tom Dupuy almost jumped from his seat
and brought his fist down heavily upon the groaning table.
' They were ? ' he cried inquiringly. ' Barbadian planters ?
By Jove, that's devilish funny ! You don't mean to say,
then, Mr. Noel, that some of your own people were really
and truly born West Indians ? '

' Why the dickens should he want to get so very excited
about it ? ' Harry Noel thought to himself hastily. ' What
on earth can it matter to him whether my people were
Barbadian planters or Billingsgate fishmongers ? '—' Yes,
certainly, they were,' he went on to Tom Dupuy with a
placid smile of quiet amusement. ' Though my mother
was never in the island herself from the time she was
a baby, I believe, still all her family were born and bred
there, for some generations.—But why do you ask me ?
Did you know anything of her people—the Budleighs of
the Wilderness ? '

' No, no ; I didn't know anything of them,' Tom Dupuy
replied hurriedly, with a curious glance sideways at his
uncle.—' But, by George ! Uncle Theodore, it's really a very
singular thing, now one comes to think of it, that Mr. Noel
should happen to come himself, too, from a West Indian
family.'

As Harry Noel happened that moment to be lifting his
cup of coffee to his lips, he didn't notice that Tom Dupuy
was pointing most significantly to his own knuckles, and
signalling to his uncle, with eyes and fingers, to observe
Harry's. And if he had, it isn't probable that Lincolnshire
Noel would even have suspected the hidden meaning of
those strange and odd-looking monkey-like antics.

By-and-by, Harry rose from the table carelessly, and
asked in a casual way whether Mr. Dupuy would kindly
excuse him ; he wanted to go and pay a call which he felt

he really mustn't defer beyond the second day from his arrival in Trinidad.

' You'll take a mount ? ' Mr. Dupuy inquired hospitably. ' You know, we never dream of walking out in these regions. All the horses in my stable are entirely at your disposal. How far did you propose going, Mr. Noel ? A letter of introduction you wish to deliver, I suppose, to the Governor or somebody ? '

Harry paused and hesitated for a second. Then he answered as politely as he was able : ' No, not exactly a letter of introduction. I feel I mustn't let the day pass without having paid my respects as early as possible to Mrs. Hawthorn.'

Tom Dupuy nudged his uncle; but the elder planter had too much good manners to make any reply save to remark that one of his niggers would be ready to show Mr. Noel the way to the District judge's—ah—dwelling-place at Mulberry.

As soon as Harry's back was turned, however, Mr. Tom Dupuy sank back incontinently on the dining-room sofa and exploded in a loud and hearty burst of boisterous laughter.

' My dear Tom,' Mr. Theodore Dupuy interposed nervously, ' what on earth are you doing? Young Noel will certainly overhear you. Upon my word, though I can't say I agree with all the young fellow's English sentiments, I really don't see that there's anything in particular to laugh at in him. He seems to me a very nice, gentlemanly, well-bred, intelligent—— Why, goodness gracious, Tom, what the deuce has come over you so suddenly ? You look for all the world as if you were positively going to kill yourself outright with laughing about nothing ! '

Mr. Tom Dupuy removed his handkerchief hastily from his mouth, and with an immense effort to restrain his merriment, exclaimed in a low suppressed voice : ' Good heavens, Uncle Theodore, do you mean to tell me you don't see the whole joke ! you don't understand the full absurdity of the situation ? '

Mr. Dupuy gazed back at him blankly. ' No more than I understand why on earth you are making such a confounded fool of yourself now,' he answered contemptuously.

Tom Dupuy calmed himself slowly with a terrific effort, and blurted out at last in a mysterious undertone : ' Why, the point of it is, don't you see, Uncle Theodore, the fellow's a coloured man himself, as sure as ever you and I are standing here this minute ! '

A light burst in upon Mr. Dupuy's benighted understanding with extraordinary rapidity. ' He is ! ' he cried, clapping his hand to his forehead hurriedly in the intense excitement of a profoundly important discovery. ' He is, he is ! There can't be a doubt about it ! Baronet or no baronet, as sure as fate, Tom my boy, that man's a regular brown man ! '

' I knew he was,' Tom Dupuy replied exultantly, ' the very moment I first set eyes upon that ugly head of his ! I was sure he was a nigger as soon as I looked at him ! I suspected it at once from his eyes and his knuckles. But when he told me his mother was a Barbadian woman—why, then, I knew, as sure as fate, it was all up with him.'

' You're quite right, quite right, Tom ; I haven't a doubt about it,' Mr. Theodore Dupuy continued helplessly, wringing his hands before him in bewilderment and horror. ' And the worst of it is I've asked him to stop here as long as he's in Trinidad ! What a terrible thing if it were to get about all over the whole island that I've asked a brown man to come and stop for an indefinite period under the same roof with your cousin Nora ! '

Tom Dupuy was not wanting in chivalrous magnanimity. He leaned back on the sofa and screwed his mouth up for a moment with a comical expression ; then he answered slowly : ' It's a very serious thing, of course, to accuse a man off-hand of being a nigger. We mustn't condemn him unheard or without evidence. We must try to find out all we can about his family. Luckily, he's given us the clue himself. He said his mother was a Barbadian woman— a Budleigh of the Wilderness. We'll track him down. I've made a mental note of it ! '

Just at that moment, Nora walked quietly into the dining-room to ask the gentlemen whether they meant to go for a ride by-and-by in the cool of the evening. 'For if you do, papa,' she said in explanation, 'you know you must send for Nita to the pasture, for Mr. Noel will want a horse, and you're too heavy for any but the cob, so you'll have to get up Nita for Mr. Noel.'

Tom Dupuy glanced at her suspiciously. 'I suppose since your last particular friend fell over the gully that night at Banana Garden,' he said hastily, 'you'll be picking up next with a new favourite in this fine-spoken, new-fangled, haw-haw, English fellow ! '

Nora looked back at him haughtily and defiantly. 'Tom Dupuy,' she answered with a curl of her lip (she always addressed him by both names together), 'you are quite mistaken—utterly mistaken. I don't feel in the least pre-possessed by Mr. Noel's personal appearance.'

'Why not ? Why not ? ' Tom inquired eagerly.

'I don't know by what right you venture to cross-question me about such a matter ; but as you ask me, I don't mind answering you. Mr. Noel is a shade or two too dark by far ever to take my own fancy.'

Tom whistled low to himself and gave a little start. 'By Jove,' he said half aloud and half to himself, 'that was a Dupuy that spoke that time, certainly. After all, the girl's got some proper pride still left in her. She doesn't want to marry him, *although* he's a brown man. I always thought myself, as a mere matter of taste, she positively preferred these woolly-headed mulattoes ! '

CHAPTER XXVI.

MEANWHILE, Harry Noel himself was quite unconsciously riding round to the Hawthorns' cottage, to perform the whole social duty of man by Edward and Marian.

'So you've come out to look after your father's estates in Barbadoes, have you, Mr. Noel ? ' Marian inquired with a quiet smile, after the first greetings and talk about the voyage were well over.

Harry laughed. 'Well, Mrs. Hawthorn,' he said con-

fidentially, ' my father's estates there seem to have looked
after themselves pretty comfortably for the last twenty
years, or at least been looked after vicariously by a rascally
local Scotch attorney; and I've no doubt they'd have continued to look after themselves for the next twenty years
without my intervention, if nothing particular had occurred
otherwise to bring me out here.'

' But something particular did occur—eh, Mr. Noel ? '

' No, nothing occurred,' Harry Noel answered with a
distinct stress upon the significant verb. ' But I had
reasons of my own which made me anxious to visit Trinidad ; and I thought Barbadoes would be an excellent
excuse to supply to Sir Walter for the expenses of the
journey. The old gentleman jumped at it—positively
jumped at it. There's nothing loosens Sir Walter's purse-
strings like a devotion to business ; and he declared to me
on leaving, with tears in his eyes almost, that it was the
first time he ever remembered to have seen me show any
proper interest whatsoever in the family property.'

' And what were the reasons that made you so very
anxious then to visit Trinidad ? '

' Why, Mrs. Hawthorn, how can you ask me ? Wasn't
I naturally desirous of seeing you and Edward once more
after a year's absence ? '

Marian coughed a little dry cough. ' Friendship is a
very powerfully attractive magnet, isn't it, Edward ? ' she
said with an arch smile to her husband. ' It was very good
of Mr. Noel to have thought of coming four thousand
miles across the Atlantic just to visit you and me, dear—
now wasn't it ? '

' So very good,' Edward answered, laughing, ' that I
should almost be inclined myself (as a lawyer) to suspect
some other underlying motive.'

' Well, she *is* a very dear little girl,' Marian went on
reflectively.

' She is, certainly,' her husband echoed.

Harry laughed. ' I see you've found me out,' he answered, not altogether unpleased. ' Well, yes, I may as
well make a clean breast of it, Mrs. Hawthorn. I've come
across on purpose to ask her ; and I won't go back either

till I can take her with me. I've waited for twelve months,
to make quite sure I knew my own heart and wasn't mistaken about it. Every day, her image has remained there
clearer and clearer than before, and I *will* win her, or else
stop here for ever.'

' When a man says that and really means it,' Marian
replied encouragingly, ' I believe in the end he can always
win the girl he has set his heart upon.'

' But I suppose you know,' Edward interrupted, ' that
her father has already made up his mind that she's to
marry a cousin of hers at Pimento Valley, a planter in the
island, and has announced the fact publicly to half Trinidad ? '

' Not Mr. Tom Dupuy ? ' Harry cried in amazement.

' Yes, Tom Dupuy—the very man. Then you've met
him already ? '

' He lunched with us to-day at Orange Grove ! ' Harry
answered, puckering his brow a little. ' And her father
actually wants her to marry that fellow ! By Jove, what a
desecration ! '

' Then you don't like what you've seen so far of Mr.
Tom ? ' Marian asked with a smile.

Harry rose and leaned against the piazza pillar with his
hands behind him. ' The man's a cad,' he answered
briefly.

' If we were in Piccadilly again,' Edward Hawthorn
said quietly, ' I should say that was probably a piece of
pure class prejudice, Noel ; but as we are in Trinidad, and
as I happen to know Mr. Tom Dupuy by two or three
pieces of personal adventure, I don't mind telling you, in
strict confidence, I cordially agree with you.'

' Ah ! ' Harry Noel cried with much amusement, clapping him heartily on his broad shoulder. ' So coming
to Trinidad has knocked some of that radical humbug
and nonsense clean out of you, has it, Teddy ? I
knew it would, my dear fellow ; I knew you'd get rid
of it ! '

' On the contrary, Mr. Noel,' Marian answered with
quiet dignity, ' I think it has really made us a great deal
more confirmed in our own opinions than we were to begin

with. We have suffered a great deal ourselves, you know, since we came to Trinidad.'

Harry flushed in the face a little. 'You needn't tell me all about it, Mrs. Hawthorn,' he said uneasily. 'I've heard something about the matter already from the two Dupuys, and all I can say is, I never heard such a foolish, ridiculous, nonsensical, cock-and-bull prejudice as the one they told me about, in the whole course of my precious existence. If it hadn't been for Nora's sake—I mean for Miss Dupuy's'—and he checked himself suddenly—'upon my word, I really think I should have knocked the fellow down in his uncle's dining-room the very first moment he began to speak about it.'

'Mr. Noel,' Marian said, 'I know how absurd it appears to you, but you can't imagine how much Edward and I have suffered about it since we've been in this island.'

'I can,' Harry answered. 'I can understand it easily. I had a specimen of it myself from those fellows at lunch this morning. I kept as calm as I could outwardly; but, by Jove, Mrs. Hawthorn, it made my blood boil over within me to hear the way they spoke of your husband.— Upon my soul, if it weren't for—for Miss Dupuy,' he added thoughtfully, 'I wouldn't stop now a single night to accept that man's hospitality another minute after the way he spoke about you.'

'No, no; do stop,' Marian answered simply. 'We want you so much to marry Nora ; and we want to save her from that horrid man her father has chosen for her.'

And then they began unburdening their hearts to Harry Noel with the long arrears of twelve months' continuous confidences. It was such a relief to get a little fresh external sympathy, to be able to talk about it all to somebody just come from England, and entirely free from the merest taint of West Indian prejudice. They told Harry everything, without reserve ; and Harry listened, growing more and more indignant every minute, to the long story of petty slights and undeserved insults. At last he could restrain his wrath no longer. 'It's preposterous,' he cried, walking up and down the piazza angrily, by way of giving

vent to his suppressed emotion; it's abominable! it's outrageous! it's not to be borne with! The idea of these
people, these hole-and-corner nobodies, these miserable,
stupid, ignorant noodles, with no more education or
manners than an English ploughboy—oh yes, my dear
fellow, I know what they are—I've seen them in Barbadoes
—setting themselves up to be better than you are—there,
upon my word I've really no patience with it. I shall
kick some of them soundly, some day, before I've done
with them; I know I shall. I can't avoid it. But what
on earth can have induced you to stop here, my dear
Teddy, when you might have gone back again comfortably
to England, and have mixed properly in the sort of society
you're naturally fitted for?'

'I did,' Marian answered firmly; I induced him, Mr.
Noel. I wouldn't let him run away from these miserable
people. And besides, you know, he's been able to do such
a lot of good here. All the negroes love him dearly,
because he's protected them from so much injustice. He's
the most popular man in the island with the black people;
he's been so good to them, and so useful to them, and such
a help against the planters, who are always trying their
hardest to oppress them. And isn't that something worth
staying for, in spite of everything?'

Harry Noel paused and hesitated. 'Tastes differ, Mrs.
Hawthorn,' he answered more soberly. 'For my part, I
can't say I feel myself very profoundly interested in the
eternal nigger question; though, if a man feels it's his
duty to stop and see the thing out to the bitter end, why,
of course he ought in that case to stop and see it. But
what does rile me is the idea that these wretched Dupuy
people should venture to talk in the way they do about
such a fellow as your husband—confound them!'

Tea interrupted his flow of indignation.

But when Harry Noel had ridden away again towards
Orange Grove on Mr. Dupuy's pony, Edward Hawthorn and
his wife stood looking at one another in dubious silence for
a few minutes. Neither of them liked to utter the thought
that had been uppermost in both their minds at once from
the first moment they saw him in Trinidad.

At last Edward broke the ominous stillness. 'Harry Noel's awfully dark, isn't he, Marian?' he said uneasily.

'Very,' Marian answered in as unconcerned a voice as she could well summon up. 'And so extremely handsome, too, Edward,' she added after a moment's faint pause, as if to turn the current of the conversation.

Neither of them had ever observed in England how exceedingly olive-coloured Harry Noel's complexion really was—in England, to be as dark as a gipsy is of no importance; but now in Trinidad, girt round by all that curiously suspicious and genealogically inquiring society, they couldn't help noticing to themselves what a very dark skin and what curly hair he happened to have inherited.

'And his mother's a Barbadian lady,' Edward went on uncomfortably, pretending to play with a book and a paper-knife.

'She is,' Marian answered, hardly daring to look up at her husband's face in her natural confusion. 'He—he always seems so very fond of his mother, Edward, darling.'

Edward went on cutting the pages of his newly arrived magazine in grim silence for a few minutes longer; then he said: 'I wish to goodness he could get engaged and married off-hand to Nora Dupuy very soon, Marian, and then clear out at once and for ever from this detestable island as quickly as possible.'

'It would be better if he could, perhaps,' Marian answered, sighing deeply. 'Poor dear Nora! I wish she'd take him. She could never be happy with that horrid Dupuy man.'

They didn't dare to speak, one to the other, the doubt that was agitating them; but they both agreed in that half-unspoken fashion that it would be well if Harry pressed his suit soon, before any sudden thunderbolt had time to fall unexpectedly upon his head and mar his chance with poor little Nora.

As Harry Noel rode back to Orange Grove alone, along the level bridle-path, he chanced to drop his short riding-whip at a turn of the road by a broad cane-piece. A tall negro was hoeing vigorously among the luxuriant rows of cane close by. Harry Noel called out to him carelessly, as

he would have done to a labourer at home : ' Here you, hi,
sir, come and pick up my whip, will you ? '

The tall negro turned and stared at him. ' Who you
callin' to come an' pick up your whip, me fren' ? ' he
answered somewhat savagely.

Harry Noel glanced back at the man with an angry
glare. ' You ! ' he said, pointing with an imperious gesture
to the whip on the ground. ' I called you to pick it up
for me. Don't you understand English ? Eh ! Tell me ? '

' You is rude gentleman for true,' the old negro responded quietly, continuing his task of hoeing in the cane-
piece, without any attempt to pick up the whip for the
unrecognised stranger. ' If you want de whip picked up,
what for you doan't speak to naygur decently ? Ole-time
folk has proverb, " Please am a good dog, an' him keep
doan't cost nuffin'." Get down yourself, sah, an' pick up
your own whip for you-self if you want him.'

Harry was just on the point of dismounting and following the old negro's advice, with some remote idea of apply-
ing the whip immediately after to the back of his adviser,
when a younger black man, stepping out hastily from
behind a row of canes that had hitherto concealed him,
took up the whip and handed it back to him with a respectful
salutation. The old man looked on disdainfully while Harry
took it ; then, as the rider went on with a parting angry
glance, he muttered sulkily : ' Who dat man dat you gib de
whip to ? An' what for you want to gib it him dere, Peter ? '

The younger man answered apologetically : ' Dat Mr.
Noel, buckra from Englan' ; him come to stop at Orange
Grove along ob de massa.'

' Buckra from Englan' ! ' Louis Delgado cried incredulously. ' Him doan't no buckra from Englan', I tellin'
you, me brudder ; him Trinidad brown man as sure as de
gospel. You doan't see him is brown man, Peter, de
minnet you look at him ? '

Peter shook his head and grinned solemnly. ' No,
Mistah Delgado, him doan't no brown man,' he answered,
laughing. ' Him is dark for true, but still him real buckra.
Him stoppin' up at house along ob de massa ! '

Delgado turned to his work once more, doggedly. ' If

him buckra, an' if him stoppin' up wit dem cursed Dupuy,'
he said half aloud, but so that the wondering Peter could
easily overhear it, 'when de great an' terrible day ob de
Lard come, he will be cut off wit all de household, as de
Lard spake in de times ob old by de mout of him holy
prophet. An' de day ob de Lard doan't gwine to be delayed
long now, neider.' A mumbled Arabic sentence, which
Peter of course could not understand, gave point and terror
to this last horribly mouthed prediction. Peter turned
away, thinking to himself that Louis Delgado was a terrible
obeah man and sorcerer for certain, and that whoever
crossed his path had better think twice before he offended
so powerful an antagonist.

Meanwhile, Harry Noel was still riding on to Orange
Grove. As he reached the garden gate, Tom Dupuy met
him, out for a walk in the cool of the evening with big Slot,
his great Cuban bloodhound. As Harry drew near, Slot
burst away suddenly with a leap from his master, and before
Harry could foresee what was going to happen, the huge
brute had sprung up at him fiercely, and was attacking him
with his mighty teeth and paws, as though about to drag
him from his seat forcibly with his slobbering canines.
Harry hit out at the beast a vicious blow from the butt-
end of his riding-whip, and at the same moment Tom
Dupuy, sauntering up somewhat more lazily than politeness
or even common humanity perhaps demanded, caught the
dog steadily by the neck and held him back by main force,
still struggling vehemently and pulling at the collar. His
great slobbering jaws opened hungrily towards the angry
Englishman, and his eyes gleamed with the fierce light of
a starving carnivore in sight and smell of his natural prey.

'Precious vicious dog you keep, Mr. Dupuy,' Harry exclaimed, not over-good-humouredly, for the brute had
made its teeth meet through the flap of his coat lappets:
'you oughtn't to let him go at large, I fancy.'

Tom Dupuy stooped and patted his huge favourite
lovingly on the head with little hypocritical show of
penitence or apology. 'He don't often go off this way,'
he answered coolly. 'He's a Cuban bloodhound, Slot
is ; pure-blooded—the same kind we used to train in

7

the good old days to hunt up the runaway niggers; and they often go at a black man or a brown man—that's what they're meant for. The moment they smell African blood, they're after it like a greyhound after a hare, as quick as lightning. But I never knew Slot before go for a white man! It's very singular—excessively singular. I never before knew him go for a real white man.'

' If he was my dog,' Harry Noel answered, walking his pony up to the door with a sharp look-out on the ugly mouth of the straining and quivering bloodhound, ' he'd never have the chance again, I can tell you, to go for another. The brute's most dangerous—a most blood-thirsty creature. And, indeed, I'm not sentimental myself on the matter of niggers; but I don't know that in a country where there are so many niggers knocking about casually everywhere, any man has got a right to keep a dog that darts straight at them as a greyhound darts at a hare, according to your very own confession. It doesn't seem to me exactly right or proper somehow.'

Tom Dupuy glanced carlesssly at the struggling brute, and answered with a coarse laugh : ' I see, Mr. Noel, you've been taking counsel already with your friend Hawthorn. Well, well, in my opinion, I expect there's just about a pair of you ! '

CHAPTER XXVII.

In spite of his vigorous dislike for Tom Dupuy, Harry Noel continued to stop on at Orange Grove for some weeks to-gether, retained there irresistibly by the potent spell of Nora's presence. He could not tear himself away from Nora. And Nora, too, though she could never conquer her instinctive prejudice against the dark young Englishman—a prejudice that seemed to be almost ingrained in her very nature—couldn't help feeling on her side, also, that it was very pleasant to have Harry Noel stopping in the house with her; he was such a relief and change after Tom Dupuy and the other sugar-growing young gentlemen of Trinidad. He had some other ideas in his head beside vacuum pans and saccharometers and centrifugals; he could talk about something else besides the crop and the cutting and the boiling. Harry was careful not to recur for the present to the subject of their last conversation at Southampton ; he left that important issue aside for a while, till Nora had time to make his acquaintance for herself afresh. A year had passed since she came to Trinidad ; she might have changed her mind meanwhile. At nineteen or twenty, one's views often undergo a rapid expansion. In any case, it would be best to let her have a little time to get to know him better. In his own heart, Harry Noel had inklings of a certain not wholly unbecoming consciousness that he cut a very decent figure indeed in Nora's eyes, by the side of the awkward, sugar-growing young men of Trinidad.

One afternoon, a week or two later, he was out riding among the plains with Nora, attended behind by the negro groom, when they happened to pass the same corner where he had already met Louis Delgado. The old man was standing there again, cutlass in hand—the cutlass is the common agricultural implement and rural jack-of-all-trades of the West Indies, answering to plough, harrow, hoe, spade, reaping-hook, rake, and pruning-knife in England—and as Nora passed he dropped her a grudging, half-satirical salutation, something between a bow and a courtesy, as is the primitive custom of the country.

'A very murderous-looking weapon, the thing that fellow's got in his hand,' Harry Noel said, in passing, to his pretty companion as they turned the corner. 'What on earth does he want to do with it, I wonder ?'

'Oh, that ! ' Nora exclaimed carelessly, glancing back in an unconcerned fashion. 'That's only a cutlass. All our people work with cutlasses, you know. He's merely going to hoe up the canes with it.'

'Nasty things for the niggers to have in their hands, in case there should ever be any row in the island,' Harry murmured half aloud ; for the sight of the wild-looking old man ran strangely in his head, and he couldn't help thinking to himself how much damage could easily be done by a sturdy negro with one of those rude and formidable weapons.

'Yes,' Nora answered with a childish laugh, 'those are just what they always hack us to pieces with, you know, whenever there comes a negro rising. Mr. Hawthorn says there's very likely to be one soon. He thinks the negroes are ripe for rebellion. He knows more about them than any one else, you see ; and he's thoroughly in the confidence of a great many of them, and he says they're almost all fearfully disaffected. That old man Delgado there, in particular—he's a shocking old man altogether. He hates papa and Tom Dupuy ; and I believe if ever he got the chance, he'd cut every one of our throats in cold blood as soon as look at us.'

'I hope to Heaven he won't get the chance, then,' Harry ejaculated earnestly. 'He seems a most uncivil, ill-conditioned, independent sort of a fellow altogether. I dropped my whip on the road by chance the very first afternoon I came here, and I asked this same man to pick it up for me ; and, would you believe it ? the old wretch wouldn't stoop to hand the thing to me ; he told me I might just jump off my horse and pick it up for myself, if I wanted to get it ! Now, you know, a labourer in England, though he's a white man like one's self, would never have dared to answer me that way. He'd have stooped down and picked it up instinctively, the moment he was asked to by any gentleman.'

'Mr. Hawthorn says,' Nora answered, smiling, 'that our negroes here are a great deal more independent, and have a great deal more sense of freedom than English country people, because they were emancipated straight off all in one day, and were told at once : " Now, from this time forth you're every bit as free as your masters ; " whereas the English peasants, he says, were never regularly emancipated at all, but only slowly and unconsciously came out of serfdom, so that there never was any one day when they felt to themselves that they had become freemen. I'm not quite sure whether that's exactly how he puts it, but I think it is. Anyhow, I know it's a fact that all one's negro women-servants out here are a great deal more independent and saucy than the white maids used to be over in England.'

'Independence,' Harry remarked, cracking his short whip with a sharp snap, ' is a very noble quality, considered in the abstract ; but when it comes to taking it in the concrete, I should much prefer for my part not to have it in my own servants.'

(A sentiment, it may be observed in passing, by no means uncommon, even when not expressed, among people who make far more pretensions to democratic feeling than did Harry Noel.)

Louis Delgado, standing behind, and gazing with a malevolent gleam in his cold dark eyes after the retreating buckra figures, beckoned in silence with his skinny hand to the black groom, who came back immediately and unhesitatingly, as if in prompt obedience to some superior officer.

'You is number forty-tree, I tink,' the old man said, looking at the groom closely. ' Yes, yes, dat's your number. Tell me ; you know who is dis buckra from Englan' ? '

' Dem callin' him Mistah Noel, sah,' the black groom answered, touching the brim of his hat respectfully.

'Yes, yes, I know him name; I know dat already,' Delgado answered with an impatient gesture. ' But what I want to know is jest dis—can you find out for me from de house-serbants, or anybody up at Orange Grove, where him fader an' mudder come from ? I want to know all about him.'

' Missy Rosina find dat out for me,' the groom answered, grinning broadly. ' Missy Rosina is de young le-ady's waiting-maid ; an' de young le-ady, him tell Rosina pretty well eberyting. Rosina, she is Isaac Pourtalès' new sweetheart.'

Delgado nodded in instantaneous acquiescence. ' All right, number forty-tree,' he answered, cutting him short carelessly. ' Ride after buckra, an' say no more about it. I get it all out ob him now, surely. I know Missy Rosina well, for true. I gib him de lub of Isaac Pourtalès wit me obeah, I tellin' you. Send Missy Rosina to me dis ebenin'. I has plenty ting I want to talk about wit her.'

CHAPTER XXVIII.

THAT evening, Rosina Fleming went as she was bid to the old African's tent about half-past eleven, groping her way along the black moonless roads in fear and trembling, with infinite terror of the all-pervading and utterly ghastly West Indian ghosts or duppies. It was a fearful thing to go at that time of night to the hut of an obeah man; Heaven knows what grinning, gibbering ghouls and phantoms one might chance to come across in such a place at such an hour. But it would have been more fearful still to stop away; for Delgado, who could so easily bring her Isaac Pourtalès for a lover by his powerful spells, could just as easily burn her to powder with his thunder and lightning, or send the awful duppies to torment her in her bed, as she lay awake trembling through the night-watches. So poor Rosina groped her way fearfully round to Delgado's hut with wild misgivings, and lifted the latch with quivering fingers, when she heard its owner's gruff 'Come in den, missy,' echoing grimly from the inner recesses.

When she opened the door, however, she was somewhat relieved to find within a paraffin lamp burning brightly; and in the place of ghouls or ghosts or duppies, Isaac Pourtalès himself, jauntily seated smoking a fresh tobacco-leaf cigarette of his own manufacture, in the corner of the hut where Louis Delgado was sitting cross-legged on the mud floor,

'Ebenin', missy,' Delgado said, rising with African politeness to greet her; while the brown Barbadian, without moving from his seat, allowed his lady-love to stoop down of herself to kiss him affectionately. 'I send for you dis ebenin' becase we want to know suffin' about dis pusson dat callin' himself buckra, an' stoppin' now at Orange Grobe wit you. What you know about him, tell us dat, missy. You is Missy Dupuy own serbin'-le-ady: him gwine to tell you all him secret. What you know about dis pusson Noel?'

Thus adjured, Rosina Fleming, sitting down awkwardly on the side of the rude wooden settee, and with her big white eyes fixed abstractedly upon the grinning skull that decorated the bare mud wall just opposite her, pulled her turban straight upon her woolly locks with coquettish precision, and sticking one finger up to her mouth like a country child, began to pour forth all she could remember of the Orange Grove servants' gossip about Harry Noel. Delgado listened impatiently to the long recital without ever for a moment trying to interrupt her; for long experience had taught him the lesson that little was to be got out of his fellow-countrywomen by deliberate cross-questioning, but a great deal by allowing them quietly to tell their own stories at full length in their own rambling, childish fashion.

At last, when Rosina, with eyes kept always timidly askance, half the time upon the frightful skull, and half the time on Isaac Pourtalès, had fairly come to the end of her tether, the old African ventured, with tentative cunning, to put a leading question : ' You ebber hear dem say at de table, missy, who him mudder and fader is, and where dem come from ? '

' Him fader is very great gentleman ober in Englan',' Rosina answered confidently—' very grand gentleman, wit house an' serbant, an' coach an' horses, an' plenty cane-piece, an' rum an' sugar, an' yam garden an' plantain, becase I 'member Aunt Clemmy say so; an' de missy him say so himself too, sah. An' de missy say dat de pusson dat marry him will be real le-ady—same like de gubbernor le-ady; real le-ady, like dem hab in Englan'. De missy tellin' me all about him dis berry ebenin'.

Delgado smiled. ' Den de missy in lub wit him him self, for certain,' he answered with true African shrewdness and cynicism. ' Ole-time folk has proverb, " When naygur woman say, ' Dat fowl fat,' him gwine to steal him same ebenin' for him pickany dinner." An' when le-ady tell you what happen to gal dat marry gentleman, him want to hab de gentleman himself for him own husband.'

' Oh no, sah ; dat doan't so,' Rosina cried with sudden energy. ' De missy doan't lubbin' de buckra gentleman at all. She tell me him look altogedder too much like naygur.'

Delgado and Pourtalès exchanged meaning looks with one another, but neither of them answered a word to Rosina.

' An' him mudder ? ' Delgado inquired curiously after a moment's pause, taking a lazy puff at a cigarette which Isaac handed him.

' Him mudder ! ' Rosina said. ' Ah, dere now, I forgettin' clean what Uncle 'Zekiel, him what is butler up to de house dar, an' hear dem talk wit one anodder at dinner —I forgettin' clean what it was him tell me about him mudder.'

Delgado did not urge her to rack her feeble little memory on this important question, but waited silently, with consummate prudence, till she should think of it herself and come out with it spontaneously.

' Ha, dere now,' Rosina cried at last, after a minute or two of vacant and steady staring at the orbless eyeholes of the skull opposite ; ' I is too chupid—too chupid altogedder. Mistah 'Zekiel, him tellin' me de odder marnin dat Mistah Noel's mudder is le-ady from Barbadoes.—Dat whar you come from yourself, Isaac, me fren'. You must be memberin' de family ober in Barbadoes.'

' How dem call de family ? ' Isaac asked cautiously. ' You ebber hear, Rosie, how dem call de family ? Tell me, dar is good girl, an' I gwine to lub you better'n ebber.'

Rosina hesitated, and cudgelled her poor brains eagerly a few minutes longer ; then another happy flash of recollection came across her suddenly like an inspiration, and she cried out in a joyous tone : ' Yes, yes : I got him now, I got him now, Isaac ! Him mudder family, deir name is Budleigh, an' dem lib at place dem call de Wilderness. Mistah 'Zekiel tell me all about dem. Him say dat dis le-ady, what him name Missy Budleigh, marry de buckra gentleman fader, what him name Sir-waltah Noel.'

It was an enormous and unprecedented fetch of memory for a pure-blooded black woman, and Rosina Fleming was justly proud of it. She stood there grinning and smiling

from ear to ear, so that even the skull upon the wall opposite was simply nowhere in the competition.

Delgado turned breathlessly to Isaac Pourtalès. ' You know dis fam'ly ? ' he asked with eager anticipation. ' You ebber hear ob dem ? You larn at all whedder dem is buckra or only brown people ? '

Isaac Pourtalès laughed hoarsely. Brown man as he was himself, he chuckled and hugged himself with sardonic delight over the anticipated humiliation of a fellow brown man who thought himself a genuine buckra. ' Know dem, sah ! ' he cried in a perfect ecstasy of malicious humour— ' know de Budleighs ob de Wilderness ! I tink for true I know dem ! *Hé !* Mistah Delgado, me fren', I tellin' you de trut, sah ; me own mudder an' Mrs. Budleigh ob de Wilderness is first cousin, first cousin to one anudder.'

It was perfectly true. Strange as such a relationship sounds to English ears, in the West Indies cases of the sort are as common as earthquakes. In many a cultivated light-brown family, where the young ladies of the household, pretty and well educated, expect and hope to marry an English officer of good connections, the visitor knows that, in some small room or other of the back premises, there still lingers on feebly an old black hag, wrinkled and toothless, full of strange oaths and incomprehensible African jargons, who is nevertheless the grandmother of the proud and handsome girls, busy over Mendelssohn's sonatas and the ' Saturday Review,' in the front drawing-room. Into such a family it was that Sir Walter Noel, head of the great Lincolnshire house, had actually married. The Budleighs of the Wilderness had migrated to England before the abolition of slavery, when the future Lady Noel was still a baby ; and getting easily into good society in London, had only been known as West Indian proprietors in those old days when to be a West Indian proprietor was still equivalent to wealth and prosperity, not, as now, to poverty and bankruptcy.

Strange to say, too, Lady Noel herself was not by any means so dark as her son Harry. The Lincolnshire Noels belonged themselves to the black-haired type so common in their county ; and the union of the two strains had pro-

duced in Harry a complexion several degrees **more swarthy**
than that of either of his handsome parents. In England,
nobody would ever have noticed this little peculiarity;
they merely said that Harry was the very image of the old
Noel family portraits; but in Trinidad, where the abiding
traces of negro blood are so familiarly known and so carefully looked for, it was almost impossible for him to pass a
single day without his partially black descent being
immediately suspected. He had 'thrown back,' as the
colonists coarsely phrase it, to the dusky complexion of
his quadroon ancestors.

Louis Delgado hugged himself and grinned at this
glorious discovery. 'Ha, ha!' he cried, rocking himself
rapidly to and fro in a perfect frenzy of gratified vindictiveness; 'him doan't buckra, den!—him doan't buckra! He
hold himself so proud, an' look down on naygur; an' after
all, him doan't buckra, him only brown man! De Lard
be praise, I gwine to humble him! I gwine to let him
know him doan't buckra!'

'You will tell him?' Rosina Fleming asked curiously.

Delgado danced about the hut in a wild ecstasy, with
his fingers snapping about in every direction, like the half-
tamed African savage that he really was. 'Tell *him*,
Missy Rosie!' he echoed contemptuously—'tell *him*, you
sayin' to me! Yah, yah! you hab no sense, missy. I
doan't gwine to tell *him*, for certain; I gwine to tell dat
cheatin' scoundrel, Tom Dupuy, missy, so humble him in
de end de wuss for all dat.'

Rosina gazed at him in puzzled bewilderment. 'Tom
Dupuy!' she repeated slowly. 'You gwine to tell Tom
Dupuy, you say, Mistah Delgado? What de debbel de
use, I wonder, sah, ob tell Tom Dupuy dat de buckra
gentleman an' Isaac is own cousin?'

Delgado executed another frantic *pas de seul* across the
floor of the hut, to work off his mad excitement, and then
answered gleefully: 'Ha, ha, Missy Rosie, you is woman,
you is creole naygur gal—you doan't understand de depth
an' de wisdom ob African naygur. Look you here, me
fren', I explain you all about it. De missy up at house,
him fall in lub wid dis brown man, Noel. Tom Dupuy,

him want for go an' marry de missy. Dat make Tom Dupuy hate de brown man. I tell him, Noel doan't no buckra—him common brown man, own cousin to Isaac Pourtalès. Den Tom Dupuy laugh at Noel! Ha, ha! I turn de hand ob one proud buckra to bring down de pride ob de odder!'

Isaac Pourtalès laughed too. 'Ha, ha!' he cried, 'him is proud buckra, an' him is me own cousin! Ha, ha, I hate him! When de great an' terrible day ob de Lard come, I gwine to hack him into little bit, same like one hack de pinguin in de hedge when we breakin' fence down to grub up de boundaries!'

Rosina gazed at her mulatto lover in rueful silence. She liked the English stranger—he had given her a shilling one day to post a letter for him—but still, she daren't go back upon Isaac and Louis Delgado. 'Him is fren' ob Mistah Hawtorn,' she murmured apologetically at last after a minute's severe reflection—'great fren' ob Mistah Hawtorn. Dem is old-time fren' in Englan' togedder; and when Mistah Tom Dupuy speak bad 'bout Mistah Hawtorn, Mistah Noel him flare up like angry naygur, an' him gib him de lie, an' him speak out well for him!'

Delgado checked himself, and looked closely at the hesitating negress with more deliberation. 'Him is fren' ob Mistah Hawtorn,' he said in a meditative voice—'him is fren' ob Mistah Hawtorn! De fren' ob de Lard's fren' shall come to no harm when de great an' terrible day ob de Lard comin'. I gwine to tell Tom Dupuy. I must humble de buckra. But in de great an' terrible day, dem shall not hurt a hair of him head, if de Lard wills it.' And then he added somewhat louder, in his own sonorous and mystic Arabic: 'The effendi's brother is dear to Allah even as the good effendi himself is.'

Isaac Pourtalès made a wry face aside to himself. Evidently he had settled in his own mind that whatever might be Delgado's private opinion about the friends of the Lord's friend, he himself was not going to be bound, when the moment for action actually arrived, by anybody else's ideas or promises.

By-and-by, Rosina rose to go. 'You is comin' wit me, Isaac?' she asked coquettishly, with her finger stuck once more in coy reserve at the corner of her mouth, and her head a little on one side, bewitching negress fashion.

Isaac hesitated; it does not do for a brown man to be too condescending and familiar with a nigger girl, even if she does happen to be his sweetheart. Besides, Delgado signed to him with his withered finger that he wanted him to stop a few minutes longer. 'No, Missy Rosie,' the mulatto answered, yawning quietly; 'I doan't gwine yet. You know de road to house, I tink. Ebenin', le-ady.'

Rosina gave a sighing, sidelong look of disappointed affection, took her lover's hand a little coldly in her own black fingers, and sidled out of the hut with much reluctance, half frightened still at the horrid prospect of once more facing alone the irrepressible and ubiquitous duppies.

As soon as she was fairly out of earshot, Louis Delgado approached at once close to the mulatto's ear and murmured in a mysterious hollow undertone: 'Next Wednesday!'

The mulatto started. 'So soon as dat!' he cried. 'Den you has got de pistols?'

Delgado, with his wrinkled finger placed upon his lip, moved stealthily to a corner of his hut, and slowly opened a chest, occupied on the top by his mouldy obeah mummery of loose alligators' teeth and well-cleaned little human knuckle-bones. Carefully removing this superstitious rubbish from the top of the box with an undisguised sneer—for Isaac as a brown man was *ex officio* superior to obeah—he took from beneath it a couple of dozen old navy pistols, of a disused pattern, bought cheap from a marine store-dealer of doubtful honesty down at the harbour. Isaac's eyes gleamed brightly as soon as he saw the goodly array of real firearms. '*Hé, hé!*' he cried joyously, fingering the triggers with a loving touch, 'dat de ting to bring down de pride ob de proud buckra. Ha, ha! Next Wednesday, next Wednesday! We waited long, Mistah Delgado, for de Lard's delibberance; but de time come now, de time come at last, sah, an' we gwine to hab de island ob Trinidad all to ourselves for de Lard's inheritance.'

The old African bowed majestically. 'Slay ebbery male among dem,' he answered aloud in his deepest accents, with a not wholly unimpressive mouthing of his hollow

vowels—'slay ebbery male, sait' de Lard by de mout' ob
de holy prophet, an' take de women captive, an' de maidens,
an' de little ones; an' divide among you de spoil ob all
deir cattle, an' all deir flocks, an' all deir goods, an' deir
cities wherein dey dwell, and all deir vineyards, an' deir
goodly castles.'

Isaac Pourtalès' eyes gleamed hideously as he listened
in delight to that awful quotation from the Book of
Numbers. ' Ha, ha,' he cried, ' " take de women captive ! " '
De Lard say dat ? De Lard say dat, now ? Ha, ha,
Mistah Delgado ! dat is good prophecy, dat is fine pro-
phecy ; de prophet say well, " Take de women captive."

CHAPTER XXIX.

DELGADO had fixed the great and terrible day of the Lord
for Wednesday evening. On Monday afternoon, Harry and
Nora, accompanied by Mr. Dupuy, went for a ride in the
cool of dusk among the hills together. Trinidad that day
was looking its very best. The tall and feathery bamboos
that overhung the serpentine pathways stood out in exquisite
clearness of outline, like Japanese designs, against the tender background of pearl-grey sky. The tree-ferns rose lush
and green among the bracken after yesterday's brief and
refreshing thunder-shower. The scarlet hibiscus trees
beside the negro huts were in the full blush of their first
flowering season. The poinsettias, not, as in England, mere
stiff standard plants from florists' cuttings, but rising proudly
into graceful trees of free and rounded growth, with long
drooping branches, spread all about their great rosettes of
crimson leaflets to the gorgeous dying sunlight. The broad
green foliage of the ribbed bananas in the negro gardens put
to shame the flimsy tropical make-believes of Kew or Monte
Carlo. For the first time, it seemed to Harry Noel, he was
riding through the true and beautiful tropics of poets and
painters; and the reason was not difficult to guess, for Nora
—Nora really seemed to be more kindly disposed to him.
After all, she was not made of stone, and they had an in-

terest in common which the rest of the house of Dupuy did
not share with Nora—the interest in Edward and Marian
Hawthorn. You can't have a better introduction to any
girl's heart—though I dare say it may be very wicked indeed
to acknowledge it—than a common attachment to somebody
or something tabooed or opposed by the parental authorities.

Mr. Dupuy rode first in the little single-file calvacade,
as became the senior; and Mr. Dupuy's cob had somehow
a strange habit of keeping fifty yards ahead of the other
horses, which gave its owner on this particular occasion no
little trouble. Harry and Nora followed behind at a respectful distance; and Harry, who had bought a new horse
of his own the day before, and who brought up the rear on
his fresh mount, seemed curiously undesirous of putting his
latest purchase through its paces, as one might naturally
have expected him to do under the circumstances. On the
contrary, he hung about behind most unconscionably, de-
laying Nora by every means in his power; and Mr. Dupuy,
looking back from his cob every now and again, grew almost
weary of calling out a dozen times over : ' Now then, Nora,
you can canter up over this little bit of level, and catch me
up, can't you, surely ? '

' If it weren't for the old gentleman,' Harry thought to
himself more than once, ' I really think I should take this
opportunity of speaking again to Nora '—he always called
her ' Nora ' in his own heart—a well-known symptom of
the advanced stages of the disease—though she was of
course ' Miss Dupuy ' alone in conversation. ' Or even if
we were on a decent English road, now, where you can ride
two abreast, and have a *tête-à-tête* quite as comfortably as
in an ordinary drawing-room ! But it's clearly impossible
to propose to a girl when she's riding a whole horse's length
in front of you on a one-horse pathway. You can't shout
out to her : " My beloved, I adore you," at the top of your
voice, as they do at the opera, especially with her own
father—presumably devoted to the rival interest—hanging
a hundred yards ahead within moderate earshot.' So
Harry was compelled to repress for the present his ardent
declaration, and continue talking to Nora Dupuy about
Edward and Marian, a subject which, as he acutely per-

ceived, was more likely to bring them into sympathy with one another than any alternative theme he could possibly have hit upon.

Presently, they descended again upon the plain, and Mr. Dupuy was just about to rejoin them in a narrow lane, almost wide enough for three abreast, and bordered by a prickly hedge of cactus and pinguin, when, to Nora's great surprise, Tom Dupuy, on his celebrated chestnut mare Sambo Gal, came cantering up in the opposite direction, as if on purpose to catch and meet them. Tom wasn't often to be found away from his canes at that time of day, and Nora had very little doubt indeed that he had caught a glimpse of Harry and herself from Pimento Valley, on the zigzag mountain path, without noticing her father on in front of them, and had ridden out with the express intention of breaking in upon their supposed *tête-à-tête.*

Mr. Dupuy unconsciously prevented him from carrying out this natural design. Meeting his nephew first in the narrow pathway, he was just going to make him turn round and ride alongside with him, when Nora, seized with a sudden fancy, half whispered to Harry Noel : ' I'm not going to ride with Tom Dupuy; I can't endure him ; I shall turn and ride back in the opposite direction.'

' We must tell your father,' Harry said, hesitating.

' Of course,' Nora answered decidedly.—' Papa,' she continued, raising her voice, ' we're going to ride back again and round by Delgado's hut, you know—the mountain cabbage palm-tree way is so much prettier, and I want to show it to Mr. Noel. You and Tom Dupuy can turn round and follow us.—The cob always goes ahead, you see, Mr. Noel, if once he's allowed to get in front of the other horses.'

They turned back once more in this reversed order, Nora and Harry Noel leading the way, and Mr. Dupuy, abreast with Tom, following behind somewhat angrily, till they came to a point in the narrow lane where a gap in the hedge led into a patch of jungle on the right-hand side. An old negro had crept out of it just before them, carrying on his head, poised quite evenly, a big fagot of sticks for his outdoor fireplace. The old man kept the middle of the lane, just in front of them, and made not the slightest movement to right or left, as if he had no particular intention of allowing them to pass. Harry had just given his new horse a tap with the whip, and they were trotting along to get well in front of the two followers, so he didn't greatly relish this untoward obstacle thrown so unexpectedly in his way. 'Get out of the road, will you, you there?' he shouted angrily. 'Don't you see a lady's coming? Stand aside this minute, my good fellow, and let her pass, I tell you.'

Delgado turned around, almost as the horse's nose was upon him, and looking the young man defiantly in the face, answered with an obvious sneer : 'Who is you, sah, dat you speak to me like-a dat ? Dis is de Queen high-road, for naygur an' for buckra. You doan't got no right at all to turn me off it.'

Harry recognised his man at once, and the hot temper of the Lincolnshire Noels boiled up within him. He hit out at the fellow with his riding-whip viciously. Delgado didn't attempt to dodge the blow—a negro never does— but merely turned his head haughtily, so that the bundle of sticks pushed hard against the horse's nose, and set it bleeding with the force of the sudden turn. Delgado knew it would : the sticks, in fact, were prickly acacia. The horse plunged and reared a little, and backed up in fright against the cactus hedge. The sharp cactus spines and the long aloe-like needles of the pinguin leaves in the hedgerow goaded his flank severely as he backed against them. He gave another plunge, and hit up wildly against Nora's mount. Nora kept her seat bravely, but with some difficulty. Harry was furious. Forgetting himself entirely, he knocked the bundle of sticks off the old man's head with a sudden swish of his thick riding-crop, and then proceeded to lay the whip twice or three times about Delgado's ears with angry vehemence. To his great surprise, Delgado stood, erect and motionless, as if he didn't even notice the blows. Appeased by what he took to be the man's submissiveness, Harry dug his heel into his horse's side and hurried forward to rejoin Nora, who had ridden ahead hastily to avoid the turmoil.

'He's an ill-conditioned, rude, bad-blooded fellow, that nigger there,' he said apologetically to his pretty companion. 'I know him before. He's the very same man I told you of the other evening, that wouldn't pick my whip up for me the first day I came to Trinidad. I'm glad he's had a taste of it to-day for his continual impudence.'

'He'll have you up for assault, you may be sure, Mr. Noel,' Nora answered earnestly. 'And if Mr. Hawthorn tries the case, he'll give it against you, for he'll never allow any white man to strike a negro. The man's name is Delgado; he's an African, you know—an imported African—and a regular savage; and he had a fearful quarrel once with papa and Tom Dupuy about the wages, which papa has never forgiven. But Mr. Hawthorn *does* say'—and Nora dropped her voice a little—'that he's really had a great deal of provocation, and that Tom Dupuy behaved abominably, which of course is very probable, for what can you expect from Tom Dupuy, Mr. Noel?—But still'—and this she said very loudly—'all the negroes themselves will tell you that Louis Delgado's a regular rattlesnake, and you must put your foot firmly down upon him if you want to crush him.'

'If you put your foot on rattlesnake,' Louis Delgado cried aloud from behind, in angry accents, 'you crush rattlesnake; but rattlesnake sting you, so you die.' And then he muttered to himself in lower tones: 'An' de rattlesnake has got sting in him tail dat will hurt dat mulatto man from Englan', still, dat tink himself proper buckra.'

Tom Dupuy and his uncle had just reached the spot when Louis Delgado said angrily to himself, in negro soliloquy, this damning sentence. Tom reined in and looked smilingly at his uncle as Delgado said it. 'So you know something, too, about this confounded Englishman, you damned nigger you!' he said condescendingly. 'You've found out that our friend Noel's a woolly-headed mulatto, have you, Delgado?'

Louis Delgado's eyes sparkled with gratified malevolence as he answered with a cunning smile: 'Aha, Mistah Tom Dupuy, you glad to hear dat, sah! You want to get some

information from de poor naygur dis ebenin', do you? No,
no, sah; de Dupuys an' me, we is not fren'; we is at
variance one wit de odder. I doan't gwine to tell you
nuffin' at all, sah, about de buckra from Englan'. But
when mule kick too much, I say to him often : " Ha, ha,
me fren', you is too proud. You tink you is horse. I
s'pose you doan't rightly remember dat your own fader
wasn't nuffin' but a common jackass ! " '

He loved to play with both his intended victims at once,
as a cat plays with a captured mouse before she kills it.
Keep him in suspense as long as you can—that's the point
of the game. Dandle him, and torture him, and hold him
off; but never tell him the truth outright, for good or for
evil, as long as you can possibly help it.

' Do you really know anything,' Tom Dupuy asked
eagerly, ' or are you only guessing like all the rest of us?
Do you mean to tell me you've got any proof that the fellow's a nigger?—Come, come, Delgado, we may have
quarrelled, but you needn't be nasty about it. I've got a
grudge against this man Noel, and I don't mind paying
you liberally for anything you can tell me against him.'

But Delgado shook his head doggedly. ' I doan't want
your money, sah,' he answered with a slow drawl ; ' I want
more dan your money, if I want anyting. But I doan't
gwine to help you agin me own colour. Buckra for buckra,
an' colour for colour ! If you want to find out about him,
why don't you write to de buckra gentlemen over in
Barbadoes ? '

He kept the pair of white men there, dawdling and
parleying for twenty minutes nearly, while Harry and
Nora went riding away alone towards the mountain cabbage-
palms. It pleased Delgado thus to be able to hold the two
together on the tenter-hooks of suspense—to exercise his
power before the two buckras. At last, Tom Dupuy condescended to direct entreaty. ' Delgado,' he said with much
magnanimity, ' you know I don't often ask a favour of a
nigger, it ain't the way with us Dupuys ; it don't run in
the family—but still, I ask you as a personal favour to tell
me whatever you know about this matter : I have reasons
of my own which make me ask you as a personal favour.'

Delgado's eyes glistened horribly. 'Buckra,' he answered with a hideous grin, dropping all the usual polite formulas, 'I will tell you for true, der ; I will tell you all about it. Dat man Noel is son ob brown gal from ole Barbadoes. Her name is Budleigh, 'an her fam'ly is brown folks dat lib at place dem call de Wilderness. I hear all about dem from Isaac Pourtalès. Pourtalès an' dis man Noel, dem is bot' cousin. De man is brown just same like Isaac Pourtalès !'

'By George, Uncle Tom ! ' Tom Dupuy cried exultantly, 'Delgado's right—right to the letter. Pourtalès is a Barbadoes man : his father was one of the Pourtalèses of this island who settled in Barbadoes, and his mother must have been one of these brown Budleighs. Noel told us himself the other day his mother was a Budleigh—a Budleigh of the Wilderness. He's been over in Barbadoes looking after their property.—By Jove, Delgado, I'd rather have a piece of news like that than a hundred pounds !—We shall stick a pin, after all, Uncle Theodore, in that confounded, stuck-up, fal-lal mulatto man.'

'It's too late to follow them up by the mountain cabbages,' Mr. Theodore Dupuy exclaimed with an anxious sigh—how did he know but that at that very moment this undoubted brown man might be proposing (hang his impudence !) to his daughter Nora ?—' it's too late to follow them, if we mean to dress for dinner. We must go home straight by the road, and even then we won't overtake them before they're back at Orange Grove, I'm afraid, Tom.'

Delgado stood in the middle of the lane and watched them retreating at an easy canter ; then he solemnly replaced the bundle of sticks on the top of his head, spread out his hands and fingers in the most expressively derisive African attitudes, and began to dance with wild glee a sort of imaginary triumphal war-dance over his intended slaughter. ' Ha, ha ! ' he cried aloud, ' Wednesday ebenin' —Wednesday ebenin' ! De great and terrible day ob de Lard comin' for true on Wednesday ebenin' ! Slay, slay, slay, sait' de Lard, an' leave not one libbin' soul behind in de land ob de Amalekites. Dat is de first an' de last good

turn I ever gwine to do for Tom Dupuy, for certain. I
doan't want his money, I tell him, but I want de blood ob
him.　On Wednesday night I gwine to get it.　Ha, ha, de
Lard is wit us!　We gwine to slay de remnant ob de ac-
cursed Amalekites.'　He paused a moment, and poised the
bundle more evenly on his head ; then he went on walking
homewards more quietly, but talking to himself aloud, in a
clear, angry, guttural voice, as negroes will do under the
influence of powerful excitement.　'What for I doan't tell
dat man Noel himself dat he is mulatto when him hit me?'
he asked himself with rhetorical earnestness.　'Becase I
doan't want to go an' spoil de fun ob de whole discovery.
If *I* tell him, dat doan't nuffin'—even before de missy.
Tom Dupuy is proper buckra : he hate Noel, an' Noel hate
him!　He gwine to tell it so it sting Noel.　He gwine to
disgrace dat proud man before de buckras an' before de
missy!'

He paused again, and chewed violently for a minute or
two at a piece of cane he pulled out of his pocket ; then he
spat out the dry refuse with a fierce explosion of laughter,
and went on again : 'But I doan't gwine to punish Noel
like I gwine to punish de Dupuys an' de missy.　Noel is
fren' ob Mistah Hawtorn, de fren' ob de naygur : dat gwine
to be imputed to him for righteousness, when de Lard's
time comin'.　In de great an' terrible day ob de Lard, de
angel gwine to pass ober Noel, same as him pass ober de
house ob Israel ; but de house ob Dupuy shall perish
utterly, like de house ob Pharaoh, an' like de house ob Saul
king ob Israel, whose seed was destroyed out ob de land, so
dat not one ob dem left libbin'.'

CHAPTER XXX.

'This is awkward, Tom, awfully awkward,' Mr. Theodore
Dupuy said to his nephew as they rode homeward.　'We
must manage somehow to get rid of this man as early as
possible.　Of course, we can't keep him in the house any
longer with your cousin Nora, now that we know he's really

nothing more—baronet or no baronet—than a common
mulatto. But at the same time, you see, we can't get
rid of him anyhow by any possibility before the dinner
to-morrow evening. I've asked several of the best
people in Trinidad especially to meet him, and I don't
want to go and stultify myself openly before the eyes
of the whole island. What the dickens can we do about
it ? '

'If you'd taken my advice, Uncle Theodore,' Tom
Dupuy answered sullenly, in spite of his triumph, ' you'd
have got rid of him long ago. As it is, you'll have to keep
him on now till after Tuesday, and then we must manage
somehow to dismiss him politely.'

They rode on without another word till they reached
the house ; there, they found Nora and Harry had arrived
before them, and had gone in to dress for dinner. Mr.
Dupuy followed their example ; but Tom, who had made
up his mind suddenly to stop, loitered about on the lawn
under the big star-apple tree, waiting in the cool till the
young Englishman should make his appearance.

Meanwhile, Nora, in her own dressing-room, attended
by Rosina Fleming and Aunt Clemmy, was thinking over
the afternoon's ride very much to her own satisfaction.
Mr. Noel was really after all a very nice fellow—if he
hadn't been so dreadfully dark ; but there, he was really
just one shade too dusky in the face ever to please a West
Indian fancy. And yet he was certainly very much in
love with her ! The very persistence with which he avoided
reopening the subject, while he went on paying her such
very marked attention, showed in itself how thoroughly in
earnest he was. ' He'll propose to me again to-morrow—
I'm quite sure he will,' Nora thought to herself, as Rosina
fastened up her hair with a sprig of plumbago and a little
delicate spray of wild maidenhair. ' He was almost going
to propose to me as we came along by the mountain cabbages this afternoon, only I saw him hesitating, and I
turned the current of the conversation. I wonder why I
turned it ? I'm sure I don't know why. I wonder whether
it was because I didn't know whether I should answer
" Yes " or " No," if he were really to ask me ? I think

one ought to decide in one's own mind beforehand what one's going to say in such a case, especially when a man has asked one already. He's awfully nice. I wish he was just a shade or two lighter. I believe Tom really fancies— he's so dark—it isn't quite right with him.'

Isaac Pourtalès, lounging about that minute, watching for Rosina, whom he had come to talk with, saw Nora flit for a second past the open window of the passage, in her light and gauze-like evening dress, with open neck in front, and the flowers twined in her pretty hair ; and he said to himself as he glanced up at her : ' De word ob de Lard say right, " Take captive de women ! " '

At the same moment, Tom Dupuy, strolling idly on the lawn in the thickening twilight, caught sight of Pourtalès, and beckoned him towards him with an imperious finger. ' Come here,' he said ; ' I want to talk with you, you nigger there.—You're Isaac Pourtalès, aren't you ?—I thought so. Then come and tell me all you know about this confounded cousin of yours—this man Noel.'

Isaac Pourtalès, nothing loth, poured forth at once in Tom Dupuy's listening ear the whole story, so far as he knew it, of Lady Noel's antecedents in Barbadoes. While the two men, the white and the brown, were still conversing under the shade of the star-apple tree, Nora, who had come down to the drawing-room meanwhile, strolled out for a minute, beguiled by the cool air, on to the smoothly kept lawn in front of the drawing-room window. Tom saw her, and beckoned her to him with his finger, exactly as he had beckoned the tall mulatto. Nora gazed at the beckoning hand with the intensest disdain, and then turned away, as if perfectly unconscious of his ungainly gesture, to examine the tuberoses and great bell-shaped brugmansias of the garden border.

Tom walked up to her angrily and rudely. ' Didn't you see me calling you, miss ? ' he said in his harsh drawl, with no pretence of unnecessary politeness. ' Didn't you see I wanted to speak to you ? '

' I saw you making signs to somebody with your hand, as if you took me for a servant,' Nora answered coldly ; ' and not having been accustomed in England to be called

in that way, I thought you must have made a mistake as to
whom you were dealing with.'

Tom started and muttered an ugly oath. 'In England,' he repeated. 'Oh, ah, in England. West Indian
gentlemen, it seems, aren't good enough for you, miss,
since this fellow Noel has come out to make up to you. I
suppose you don't happen to know that he's a West Indian
too, and a precious rum sort of one into the bargain? I
know you mean to marry him, miss; but all I can tell you
is, your father and I are not going to permit it.'

'I don't wish to marry him,' Nora answered, flushing
fiery red all over ('Him is pretty for true when him blush
like dat,' Isaac Pourtalès said to himself from the shade of
the star-apple tree). 'But if I did, I wouldn't listen to
anything *you* might choose to say against him, Tom Dupuy;
so that's plain speaking enough for you.'

Tom sneered. 'O no,' he said; 'I always knew you'd
end by marrying a woolly-headed mulatto; and this man's
one, I don't mind telling you. He's a brown man born;
his mother, though she *is* Lady Noel—fine sort of a Lady,
indeed—is nothing better than a Barbadoes brown girl;
and he's own cousin to Isaac Pourtalès over yonder! He
is, I swear to you.—Isaac, come here, sir!'

Nora gave a little suppressed scream of surprise and
horror as the tall mulatto, in his ragged shirt, leering horribly, emerged unexpectedly, like a black spectre, from the
shadows opposite.

'Isaac,' the young planter said with a malicious smile,
'who is this young man, I want to know, that calls himself
Mister Noel?'

Isaac Pourtalès touched his slouching hat awkwardly
as he answered, under his breath, with an ugly scowl:
'Him me own cousin, sah, an' me mudder cousin. Him
an' me mudder is fam'ly long ago in ole Barbadoes.'

'There you are, Nora!' Tom Dupuy cried out to her
triumphantly. 'You see what sort of . person your fine
English friend has turned out to be.'

'Tom Dupuy,' Nora cried in her wrath—but in her own
heart she knew it wasn't true—'if you tell me this, trying
to set me against Mr. Noel, you've failed in your purpose,

sir: what you say has no effect upon me. I do not care
for him; you are quite mistaken about that; but if I did,
I don't mind telling you, your wicked scheming would only
make me like him all the better. Tom Dupuy, no real
gentleman would ever try so to undermine another man's
position.'

At that moment, Harry Noel, just descending to the
drawing-room, strolled out to meet them on the lawn,
quite unconscious of this little family altercation. Nora
glanced hastily from Tom Dupuy, in his planter coat and
high riding-boots, to Harry Noel, looking so tall and handsome in his evening dress, and couldn't help noticing in
her own mind which of the two was the truest gentleman.
' Mr. Noel,' she said, accepting his half-proffered arm with
a natural and instinctive gracious movement, ' will you
take me in to dinner? I see it's ready.'

Tom Dupuy, crestfallen and astonished, followed after,
and muttered to himself with deeper conviction than ever
that he always knew that girl Nora would end in the long
run by marrying a confounded woolly-headed mulatto.

CHAPTER XXXI.

NEXT day was Tuesday; and to Louis Delgado and his
friends at least, the days were now well worth counting;
for was not the hour of the Lord's deliverance fixed for
eight o'clock on Wednesday evening?

Nora, too, had some reason to count the days for her
own purposes, for on Tuesday night they were to have a
big dinner-party—the biggest undertaken at Orange Grove
since Nora had first returned to her father's house in the
capacity of hostess. Mr. Dupuy, while still uncertain
about Harry Noel's precise colour, had thought it well—
giving him the benefit of the doubt—to invite all the
neighbouring planters to meet the distinguished member
of the English aristocracy; it reminded him, he said, of
those bygone days when Port-of-Spain was crowded with
carriages, and Trinidad was still one of the brightest jewels

in the British crown (a period perfectly historical in every
English colony all the world over, and usually placed
about the date when the particular speaker for the time
being was just five-and-twenty).

That Tuesday morning, as fate would have it, Mr.
Dupuy had gone with the buggy into Port-of-Spain for the
very prosaic purpose—let us fain confess it—of laying in
provisions for the night's entertainment. In a country
where the fish for your evening's dinner must all have
been swimming about merrily in the depths of the sea at
eight o'clock the same morning, where your leg of mutton
must have been careering joyously in guileless innocence
across the grassy plain, and your chicken cutlets must
have borne their part in investigating the merits of the
juicy caterpillar while you were still loitering over late
breakfast, the question of commissariat is of course a far
less simple one than in our own well-supplied and market-
stocked England. To arrange beforehand that a particular
dusky fisherman shall stake his life on the due catching
and killing of a turtle for the soup on that identical
morning and no other ; that a particular oyster-woman
shall cut the bivalves for the oyster sauce from the tidal
branches of the mangrove swamp not earlier than three or
later than five in the afternoon, on her honour as a pur-
veyor ; and that a particular lounging negro coffee-planter
somewhere on the hills shall guarantee a sufficient supply
of black land-crabs for not less than fourteen persons—
turtle and oyster and crab being all as yet in the legitimate
enjoyment of their perfect natural freedom—all this, I say,
involves the possession of strategical faculties of a high
order, which would render a man who has once kept house
in the West Indies perfectly capable of undertaking the
res frumentaria for an English army on one of its innumerable slaughtering picnics, for the extension of the
blessings of British rule among a totally new set of black,
benighted, and hitherto happy heathen. Now Mr. Dupuy
was a model entertainer, of the West Indian pattern ; and
having schemed and devised all these his plans beforehand
with profound wisdom, he had now gone into Port-of-Spain
with the buggy, on hospitable thoughts intent, to bring

out whatever he could get, and make arrangements, by
means of tinned provisions from England, for the inevitable
deficiencies which always turn up under such circumstances
at the last moment.　So Harry and Nora were left alone
quite to themselves for the whole morning.

The veranda of the house—it fronted on the back
garden at Orange Grove—is always the pleasantest place
in which to sit during the heat of the day in a West
Indian household.　The air comes so delightfully fresh
through the open spaces of the creeper-covered trellis-
work, and the humming-birds buzz about so merrily among
the crimson passion-flowers under your very eyes, and the
banana bushes whisper so gently before the delicate fan-
ning of the cool sea breezes in the leafy courtyard, that
you lie back dreamily in your folding chair and half believe
yourself, for once in your life, in the poet's Paradise.　On
such a veranda Harry Noel and Nora Dupuy sat together
that Tuesday morning ; Harry pretending to read a paper,
which lay, however, unfolded on his knees—what does one
want with newspapers in Paradise?—and Nora almost
equally pretending to busy herself, Penelope-like, with a
wee square of dainty crewel-work, concerning which it
need only be said that one small flower appeared to take
a most unconscionable and incredible time for its proper
shaping.　They were talking together as young man and
maiden will talk to one another idly under such circumstances—circling half unconsciously round and round the
object of both their thoughts, she avoiding it, and he per-
petually converging towards it, till at last, like a pair of
silly, fluttering moths around the flame of the candle, they
find themselves finally landed, by a sudden side-flight, in
the very centre at an actual declaration.

'Really,' Harry said at length, at a pause in the conversation, 'this is positively too delicious, Miss Dupuy, this
sunshine and breeziness.　How the light glances on the
little green lizards on the wall over yonder !　How beautiful the bougainvillea looks, as it clambers with its great
purple masses over that big bare trunk there !　We have a
splendid bougainvillea in the greenhouse at our place in
Lincolnshire ; but oh, what a difference, when one sees it

clambering in its native wildness like that, from the poor
little stunted things we trail and crucify on our artificial
supports over yonder in England! I almost feel inclined
to take up my abode here altogether, it all looks so green
and sunny and bright and beautiful.'

'And yet,' Nora said, 'Mr. Hawthorn told me your
father's place in Lincolnshire is so very lovely. He thinks
it's the finest country seat he's ever seen anywhere in
England.'

'Yes, it *is* pretty, certainly,' Harry Noel admitted with
a depreciating wave of his delicate right hand—'very
pretty, and very well kept up, one must allow, as places go
nowadays. I took Hawthorn down there one summer vac.,
when we two were at Cambridge together, and he was quite
delighted with it; and really it *is* a very nice place too,
though it *is* in Lincolnshire. The house is old, you know,
really old—not Elizabethan, but early Tudor, Henry the
Seventh, or something thereabouts: all battlements and
corner turrets, and roses and portcullises on all the shields,
and a fine old portico, added by Inigo Jones, I believe, and
out of keeping, of course, with the rest of the front, but
still very fine and dignified in its own way, for all that, in
spite of what the architects (awful prigs) say to the contrary. And then there's a splendid avenue of Spanish
chestnuts, considered to be the oldest in all England, you
know (though, to be sure, they've got the oldest Spanish
chestnuts in the whole country at every house in all
Lincolnshire that I've ever been to). And the lawn's pretty,
very pretty; a fine stretch of sward, with good parterres of
these ugly, modern, jam-tart flowers, leading down to
about the best sheet of water in the whole county, with
lots of swans on it.—Yes,' he added reflectively, contrast-
ing the picture in his own mind with the one then actually
before him, 'the Hall's not a bad sort of place in its own
way—far from it.'

'And Mr. Hawthorn told me,' Nora put in, 'that you'd
got such splendid conservatories and gardens, too.'

'Well, we have: there's no denying it. They're certainly good in their way, too, very good conservatories.
You see, my dear mother's very fond of flowers: it's a

perfect passion with her; brought it over from Barbadoes,
I fancy. She was one of the very first people who went
in for growing orchids on the large scale in England. Her
orchid-houses are really awfully beautiful. We never have
anything but orchids on the table for dinner—in the way
of flowers, I mean—we don't dine off a lily, of course, as
they say the æsthetes do. And my mother's never so
proud as when anybody praises and admires her masde-
vallias or her thingumbobianas—I'm sorry to say I don't
myself know the names of half of them. She's a dear,
sweet old lady, my mother, Miss Dupuy; I'm sure you
couldn't fail to like my dear mother.'

' She's a Barbadian too, you told us,' Nora said reflectively. ' How curious that she, too, should be a West
Indian ! '

Harry half sighed. He misunderstood entirely the train
of thought that was passing that moment through Nora's
mind. He believed she saw in it a certain *rapprochement* between them two, a natural fitness of things to bring them
together. ' Yes,' he said with more tenderness in his tone
than was often his wont, ' my mother's a Barbadian, Miss
Dupuy; such a grand, noble-looking, commanding woman
—not old yet; she never *will* be old, in fact; she's too
handsome for that; but so graceful and beautiful, and
wonderfully winning as well, in all her pretty, dainty, old
coffee-coloured laces.' And he pulled from his pocket a
little miniature, which he always wore next to his heart. He
wore another one beside it too, but that one he didn't show
her just then; it was her own face, done on ivory by a
well-known artist, from a photograph which he had begged
or borrowed from Marian Hawthorn's album twelve months
before in London.

' She's a beautiful old lady, certainly,' Nora answered,
gazing in some surprise at Lady Noel's clear-cut and
haughty, high born looking features. She couldn't for the
moment exactly remember where she had seen some others
so very like them; and then, as Harry's evil genius would
unluckily have it, she suddenly recollected with a start of
recognition; she had seen them just the evening before on
the lawn in front of her; they answered precisely, in a

lighter tint, to the features and expression of Isaac Pourtalès!

'How proud she must be to be the mistress of such a place as Noel Hall!' she said musingly, after a short pause, pursuing in her own mind to herself her own private line of reflection. It seemed to her as if the heiress of the Barbadian brown people must needs find herself immensely lifted up in the world by becoming the lady of such a splendid mansion as Harry had just half unconsciously described to her.

But Harry himself, to whom, of course, Lady Noel had been Lady Noel, and nothing else, as long as ever he could remember her, again misunderstood entirely the course of Nora's thoughts, and took her naïve expression of surprise as a happy omen for his own suit. 'She thinks,' he thought to himself quietly, 'that it must be not such a very bad position after all to be mistress of the finest estate in Lincolnshire! But I don't want her to marry me for that. O no, not for that! that would be miserable! I want her to marry me for my very self, or else for nothing.' So he merely added aloud, in an unconcerned tone : 'Yes; she's very fond of the place and of the gardens ; and as she's a West Indian by birth, I'm sure you'd like her very much, Miss Dupuy, if you were ever to meet her.'

Nora coloured. 'I should like to see some of these fine English places very much,' she said, half timidly, trying with awkward abruptness to break the current of the conversation. 'I never had the chance when I was last in England. My aunt, you know, knew only very quiet people in London, and we never visited at any of the great country houses.'

Harry determined that instant to throw his last die at once on this evident chance that opened up so temptingly before him, and said with fervour, bending forward towards her : 'I hope, Miss Dupuy, when you are next in England, you'll have the opportunity of seeing many, and some day of becoming the mistress of the finest in Lincolnshire. I told you at Southampton, you know, that I would follow you to Trinidad, and I've kept my promise.—Oh, Miss Dupuy, I hope you don't mean to say *no* to me this time

again ! We have each had twelve months more to make
up our minds in. During all those twelve months, I have
only learned every day, whether in England or in Trinidad,
to love you better. I have felt compelled to come out here
and ask you to accept me. And you—haven't you found
your heart growing any softer meanwhile towards me ?
Will you unsay now the refusal you gave me a year ago
over in England ? '

He spoke in a soft persuasive voice, which thrilled
through Nora's very inmost being ; and as she looked at
him, so handsome, so fluent, so well-born, so noble-looking,
she could hardly refrain from whispering low a timid ' Yes,'
on the impulse of the moment. But something that was
to her almost as the prick of conscience arose at once
irresistibly within her, and she motioned away quickly,
with a little gesture of positive horror, the hand with which
Harry strove half forcibly to take her own. The image of
scowling Isaac Pourtalès as he emerged, all unexpectedly,
from the shadow the night before, rose up now in strange
vividness before her eyes and blinded her vision ; next
moment, for the first time in her life, she perceived
hurriedly that Isaac not only resembled Lady Noel, but
quite as closely resembled in face and feature Harry also.
That unhappy resemblance was absolutely fatal to poor
Harry's doubtful chance of final acceptance. Nora shrank
back, half frightened and wholly disenchanted, as far as she
could go, in her own chair, and answered in a suddenly
altered voice : ' Oh, Mr. Noel, I didn't know you were
going to begin that subject again ; I thought we met on
neutral ground, merely as friends now. I—I gave you my
answer definitely long ago at Southampton. There has
been nothing—nothing of any sort—to make me alter it
since I spoke to you then. I like you—I like you very
much indeed ; and I'm so grateful to you for standing up
as you have stood up for Mr. Hawthorn and for poor dear
Marian—but I can never, never, never—never marry
you ! '

Harry drew back hastily with sudden surprise and
great astonishment. He had felt almost sure she was
going this time really to accept him ; everything she said

had sounded so exactly as if she meant at last to take him.
The disappointment took away his power of fluent speech.
He could only ask, in a suddenly checked undertone:
'Why, Miss Dupuy? You will at least tell me, before
you dismiss me for ever, why your answer is so absolutely
final.'

Nora took up the little patch of crewel-work she had
momentarily dropped, and pretended, with rigid, trembling
fingers, to be stitching away at it most industriously. 'I
cannot tell you,' she answered very slowly, after a moment's long hesitation: 'don't ask me. I can never tell
you.'

Harry rose and gazed at her anxiously. 'You cannot
mean to say,' he whispered, bending down towards her
till their two faces almost touched one another, 'that you
are going willingly to marry your cousin, for whom your
father intends you? Miss Dupuy, that would be most
unworthy of you! You do not love him! You cannot
love him!'

'I hate him!' Nora answered with sudden vehemence;
and at the words the blood rushed hot again into Harry's
cheek, and he whispered once more: 'Then, why do you
say—why do you say, Nora, you will never marry me?'

At the sound of her name, so uttered by Harry Noel's
lips, Nora rose and stood confronting him with crimson
face and trembling fingers. 'Because, Mr. Noel,' she
answered slowly and with emphasis, 'an impassable barrier
stands for ever fixed and immovable between us!'

'Can she mean,' Harry thought to himself hastily,
'that she considers my position in life too far above her
own to allow of her marrying me?—O no; impossible,
impossible! A lady's a lady wherever she may be; and
nobody could ever be more of a lady, in every action and
every movement, than Nora, my Nora. She *shall* be my
Nora. I *must* win her over. But I can't say it to her; I
can't answer her little doubt as to her perfect equality
with me; it would be far too great presumption even to
suggest it.'

Well it was, indeed, for Harry Noel that he didn't hint
aloud in the mildest form this unlucky thought, that flashed

for one indivisible second of time across the mirror of his inner consciousness; if he had, Heaven only knows whether Nora would have darted away angrily like a wounded tigress from the polluted veranda, or would have stood there petrified and chained to the spot, like a Gorgon-struck Greek figure in pure white marble, at the bare idea that any creature upon God's earth should even for a passing moment appear to consider himself superior in position to a single daughter of the fighting Dupuys of Orange Grove, Trinidad!

' Then you dismiss me for ever ? ' Harry asked, quivering.

Nora cast her eyes irresolutely down upon the ground and faltered for a second ; then, with a sudden burst of firmness, she answered tremulously : ' Yes, for ever.'

At the word, Harry bounded away like a wounded man from her side, and rushed wildly with tempestuous heart into his own bedroom. As for Nora, she walked quietly back, white, but erect, to her little boudoir, and when she reached it, astonished Aunt Clemmy by flinging herself with passionate force down at full length upon the big old sofa, and bursting at once into uncontrollable floods of silent, hot, and burning tears.

CHAPTER XXXII.

THAT same afternoon, Rosina Fleming met Isaac Pourtalès, hanging about idly below the shrubbery, and waiting to talk with her, by appointment, about some important business she had to discuss with him of urgent necessity.

' Isaac, me fren',' Rosina began in her dawdling tone, as soon as they had interchanged the first endearments of negro lovers, ' I send for you to-day to ax you what all dis talk mean about de naygur risin' ? I want to know when dem gwine to rise, an' what de debbil dem gwine to do when dem done gone risen ? '

Isaac smiled a sardonic smile of superior intelligence. ' Missy Rosie, sweetheart,' he answered evasively, ' le-ady doan't understand dem ting same as men does. Dis is political business, I tell you. Le-ady doan't nebber hab no call to go an' mix himself up along wit politic an' political business.'

'But I tellin' you, Isaac, what I want for to know is about de missy. Mistah Delgado, him tell me de odder ebenin', when de great an' terrible day ob de Lard come, de missy an' all gwine to be murdered. So I come for to ax you, me fren', what for dem want to go an' kill de poor little missy? Him doan't nebber do no harm to nobody. Him is good little le-ady, kind little le-ady. Why for you doan't can keep him alive an' let him go witout hurtin' him, Isaac?'

Pourtalès smiled again, this time a more diabolical and sinister smile, as though he were concealing something from Rosina. 'We doan't gwine to kill her,' he answered hastily, with that horrid light illumining once more his cold grey eyes. 'We gwine to keep de women alive, accordin' to de word ob de Lard dat he spake by de mout' ob de holy prophet. "Have dey not divided de prey? To ebbery man a damsel or two: to Sisera, a prey ob divers colours." What dat mean, de divers colours, Rosie? Dat no mean you an' de missy? Ha, ha, ha! you an' de missy!'

Rosina started back a little surprised at this naïve personal effort of exegetical research. 'How dat, Isaac?' she screamed out angrily. 'You lub de missy! You doan't satisfied wit your fren' Rosie?'

Isaac laughed again. 'Ho, ho!' he said; 'dat make you jealous, Missy Rosie? Ha, ha, dat good now! Pretty little gal for true, de missy! Him white troat so soft and smoove! Him red cheek so plump an' even! What you want now we do wit him, Missy Rosie? You tink me gwine to kill him when him so pretty?'

Rosina gazed at him open-eyed in blank astonishment. 'You doan't must kill him,' she answered stoutly. 'I lub de missy well meself for true, Isaac. If you kill de missy, I doan't nebber gwine to speak wit you any more. I gwine to tell de missy all about dis ting ob Delgado's, I tink, to-morrow.'

Isaac stared her hard in the face. 'You doan't dare, Rosie,' he said doggedly.

8

The girl trembled and shuddered slightly before his steady gaze. A negro, like an animal, can never bear to be stared at straight in the eyes. After a moment's restless shrinking, she withdrew her glance uneasily from his, but still muttered to herself slowly: 'I tell de missy—I tell de missy!'

'If you tell de missy,' Pourtalès answered with rough emphasis, seizing her by the shoulder with his savage grasp, 'you know what happen to you? Delgado send debbil an' duppy to walk about you an' creep ober you in de dead ob night ebbery ebenin', an' chatter obeah to you, an' tear de heart out ob you when you lyin' sleepin'. If you tell de missy, you know what happen to me? Dem will take me down to de big court-house in Wes'moreland village, sit on me so try me for rebel, cut me up into little pieces, burn me dead, an' trow de ashes for rubbish into de harbour. Den I come, when I is duppy, sit at de head ob your pillow ebbery ebenin', grin at you, jabber at you, ho, ho, ho; ha, ha, ha: show you de holes where dem cut my body up, show you de blood where de wounds is bleedin', make you scream an' cry an' wish youself dead, till you dribben to trow youself down de well wit horror, or poison youself for fright wit berry ob machineel bush!'

This short recital of penalties to come was simple and ludicrous enough in its own matter, but duly enforced by Isaac's horrid shrugs and hideous grimaces, as well as by the iron clutch with which he dug his firm-gripped fingers, nails and all, deep into her flesh, to emphasise his prediction, it affected the superstitious negro girl a thousand times more than the most deliberately awful civilised imprecation could possibly have done. 'You doan't would do dat, Isaac,' she cried all breathless, struggling in vain to free her arm from the fierce grip that held it resistlessly—'you doan't would do dat, me fren'? You doan't would come when you is duppy to haunt me an' to frighten me?'

'I would!' Isaac answered firmly, with close-pressed lips, inhuman mulatto fashion (for when there is a devil in the mulatto nature, it is a devil more utterly diabolical than any known to either white or black men: it combines the dispassionate intellectual power of the one with the

low cunning and savage moral code of the other). ' I
would hound you to deat', Rosie, an' kill you witout pity.
For if you tell de missy about dis, dem will cut your fren'
all up into little pieces, I tellin' you, le-ady.'

'Doan't call me le-ady,' Rosina said, melting at the
formal address and seizing his hand penitently: 'call me
Rosie, call me Rosie. O Isaac, I doan't will tell de missy,
if you doan't like ; but you promise me for true you nebber
gwine to take him an' kill him.'

Isaac smiled again the sinister smile. ' I promise,' he
said, with a curious emphasis ; 'I doan't gwine to *kill* him,
Rosie ! When I take him, I no will *kill* him ! '

Rosina hesitated a moment, then she asked shortly :
'What day you tink Delgado gwine at last to hab him
risin' ? '

The mulatto laughed a scornful little laugh of supreme
mockery. 'Delgado's risin' ! ' he cried, with a sneer—
'Delgado's risin' ! You tink, den, Rosie, dis is Delgado's
risin' ! You tink we gwine to risk our own life, black men
an' brown men, so make Delgado de king ob Trinidad ! Ha,
ha, ha ! dat is too good, now. No, no, me fren'; dis doan't
at all Delgado's risin' ! You tink we gwine to hand ober
de whole island to a pack ob dam common contemptful
naygur fellow ! Ha, ha, ha ! Le-ady doan't nebber understand politic an' political business. *Hé*, Rosie, I tell you
de trut' : when we kill de buckra clean out ob de island, I
gwine meself to be de chief man in all Trinidad ! ' And as
he spoke, he drew himself up proudly to his full height,
and put one hand behind his back in his most distinguished
and magnificent attitude.

Rosina looked up at him with profound admiration.
'You is clebber gentleman for certain, Isaac,' she cried in
unfeigned reverence for his mental superiority. 'You
let Delgado make de naygur rise ; den, when dem done
gone risen, you gwine to eat de chestnut yourself him pull
out ob de fire witout burn your fingers ! '

Isaac nodded sagaciously. 'Le-ady begin to understand politic a little,' he said condescendingly. 'Dat what
for dem begin to ax dis time for de female suffrage.'

Grotesque, all of it, if you forget that each of these

childish creatures is the possessor of a sharp cutlass and a pair of stout sinewy arms, as hard as iron, wherewith to wield it: terrible and horrible beyond belief if only you remember that one awful element of possible tragedy enclosed within it. The recklessness, the folly, the infantile misapprehension of mischievous children, incongruously combined with the strength, the passions, the firm purpose of fierce and powerful full-grown men. An infant Hercules, with superadded malevolence—the muscles of a gorilla, with the brain of a cruel schoolboy—that is what the negro is in his worst and ugliest moments of vindictive anger.

'You doan't tell me yet,' Rosina said again, pouting, after a short pause, 'what day you gwine to begin your war ob de delibberance ? '

Isaac pondered. If he told her the whole truth, she would probably reveal it. On the other hand, if he didn't mention Wednesday at all, she would probably hear some vague buzzing rumour about some Wednesday unfixed, from the other conspirators. So he temporised and conciliated. ' Well, Rosie,' he said in a hesitating voice, ' if I tell you de trut', you will not betray me ? ' Rosie nodded. ' Den de great an' terrible day ob de Lard is comin' true on Wednesday week, Rosie ! '

' Wednesday week,' Rosina echoed. ' Den, on Wednesday week, I gwine to make de missy go across to Mistah Hawtorn's ! '

Isaac smiled. His precautions, then, had clearly not been unheeded. You can't trust le-ady with high political secrets. He smiled again, and muttered complacently: ' Quite right, quite right, Rosie.'

' When can I see you again, me darlin'? ' Rosie inquired anxiously.

Isaac bethought him in haste of a capital scheme for removing Rosina to-morrow evening from the scene of operations. ' You can get away to-morrow ? ' he asked with a cunning leer. ' About eight o'clock at me house, Rosie ? '

Rosie reflected a moment, and then nodded. ' Aunt Clemmy will do the missy hair,' she answered slowly. ' I come down at de time, Isaac.

Isaac laughed again. 'Perhaps,' he said, 'I doan't can get away so early, me fren', from de political meetin' —dar is political meetin' to-morrow ebenin' down at Delgado's; but anyhow, you wait till ten o'clock. Sooner or later, I is sure to come dar.'

Rosina gave him her hand reluctantly, and glided away back to the house in a stealthy fashion. As soon as she was gone, Pourtalès flung his head back in a wild paroxysm of savage laughter. 'Ho, ho, ho!' he cried. 'De missy, de missy! Ha, ha, I get Rosina out ob de road anyhow. Him doan't gwine to tell nuffin' now, an' him clean off de scent ob de fun altogedder to-morrow ebenin'! Pretty little gal, dat white missy! Him sweet little troat, so soft and shinin'!'

CHAPTER XXXIII.

AT the dinner that evening, Macfarlane, the Scotch doctor, took in Nora; while Harry Noel had handed over to his care a dowager planteress from a neighbouring estate; so Harry had no need to talk any further to his pretty little hostess during that memorable Tuesday. On Wednesday morning he had made up his mind he would find some excuse to get away from this awkward position in Mr. Dupuy's household; for it was clearly impossible for him to remain there any longer, after he had again asked and been rejected by Nora; but of course he couldn't go so suddenly before the dinner to be given in his honour; and he waited on, impatiently and sullenly.

Tom Dupuy was there too; and even Mr. Theodore Dupuy himself, who knew the whole secret of Harry's black blood, and therefore regarded him now as almost beyond the pale of human sympathy, couldn't help noticing to himself that his nephew Tom really seemed quite unnecessarily anxious to drag this unfortunate young man Noel into some sort of open rupture. 'Very ill-advised of Tom,' Mr. Dupuy thought to himself; 'and very bad manners, too, for a Dupuy of Trinidad. He ought to know well enough that whatever the young man's undesirable antecedents may happen to be, as long as he's here in the position of a guest, he ought at least to be treated with common decency and common politeness. To-morrow, we shall manage to hunt up some excuse, or give him some effectual hint, which will have the result of clearing him bodily off the premises. Till then, Tom ought to endeavour to treat him, as far as possible, in every way like a perfect equal.

Even during the time while the ladies still remained in the dining-room, Tom Dupuy couldn't avoid making several severe hits, as he considered them, at Harry Noel from the opposite side of the hospitable table. Harry had happened once to venture on some fairly sympathetic commonplace remark to his dowager planteress about the planters having been quite ruined by emancipation, when Tom Dupuy fell upon him bodily, and called out with an unconcealed sneer: 'Ruined by emancipation—ruined by emancipation! That just shows how much you know about the matter, to talk of the planters being ruined by emancipation! If you knew anything at all of what you're talking about, you'd know that it wasn't emancipation in the least that ruined us, but your plaguy parliament doing away with the differential duties.'

Harry bit his lip, and glanced across the table at the young planter with a quiet smile of superiority; but the only word he permitted himself to utter was the one harmless and neutral word 'Indeed!'

'O yes, you may say "Indeed" if you like,' Tom Dupuy retorted warmly. 'That's just the way of all you conceited English people. You think you know such a precious lot about the whole subject, and you really and truly know in the end just less than absolutely nothing.'

'Pardon me,' Harry answered carelessly, with his wine-glass poised for a moment half lifted in his hand. 'I admit most unreservedly that you know a great deal more than I do about the differential duties, whatever they may be, for I never so much as heard their very name in all my life until the present moment.'

Tom Dupuy smiled a satisfied smile of complete triumph. 'I thought as much,' he said exultantly; 'I

knew you hadn't. That's just the way of all English
people. They know nothing at all about the most important and essential matters, and yet they venture to talk
about them for all the world as if they knew as much as
we do about the whole subject.'

' Really,' Harry answered with a good-humoured smile,
' I fancied a man might be fairly well informed about things
in general, and yet never have heard in his pristine innocence of the differential duties. I haven't the very faintest
idea myself, to tell you the truth, of what they are.
Perhaps you will be good enough to lighten my darkness.'

' What they are ! ' Tom Dupuy ejaculated in pious
horror. ' They aren't anything. They're done away with.
They've ceased to exist long ago. You and the other
plaguy English people took them off, and ruined the
colonies; and now you don't as much as know what you've
done, or whether they're existing still or done away with ! '

' Tom, my boy,' Mr. Theodore Dupuy interposed
blandly, ' you really mustn't hold Mr. Noel personally
responsible for all the undoubted shortcomings of the
English nation ! You must remember that his father is,
like ourselves, a West Indian proprietor, and that the
iniquitous proceedings with reference to the differential
duties—which nobody can for a moment pretend to justify
—injured him every bit as much as they injured ourselves.'

' But what *are* the differential duties ? ' Harry whispered
to his next neighbour but one, the Scotch doctor. ' I
never heard of them in my life, I assure you, till this very
minute.'

' Well, ye ken,' Dr. Macfarlane responded slowly,
' there was a time when shoogar from the British colonies
was admeetted into Britain at a less duty than shoogar
from Cuba or other foreign possessions ; and at last, the
British consumer tuke the tax off the foreign shoogar,
and cheapened them all alike in the British market.
Vera guid, of course, for the British consumer, but clean
ruination and nothing else for the Treenidad planter.'

For the moment the conversation changed, but not the
smouldering war between the two belligerents. Whatever
subject Harry Noel happened to start during that unlucky

dinner, **Tom** Dupuy, watching him closely, pounced down upon him at once like an owl on the hover, and tore him to pieces with prompt activity. Harry bore it all as good-naturedly as he could, though his temper was by no means naturally a forbearing one ; but he didn't wish to come to an open rupture with Tom Dupuy at his uncle's table, especially after that morning's occurrences.

As soon as the ladies had left the room, however, Tom Dupuy drew up his chair so as exactly to face Harry, and began to pour out for himself in quick succession glass after glass of his uncle's very fiery sherry, which he tossed off with noisy hilarity. The more he drank, the louder his voice became, and the hotter his pursuit of Harry Noel. At last, when Mr. Theodore Dupuy, now really alarmed as to what his nephew was going to say next, ordered in the coffee prematurely, to prevent an open outbreak by rejoining the ladies, Tom walked deliberately over to the sideboard and took out a large square decanter, from which he poured a good-sized liqueur-glassful of some pale liquid for himself and another for Harry.

'There ! ' he cried boisterously. 'Just you try that, Noel, will you ? There's liquor for you ! That's the real old Pimento Valley rum, the best in the island, double distilled, and thirty years in bottle. You don't taste any *hogo* about that, Mr. Englishman, eh, do you ? '

' Any what ? ' Harry inquired politely, lifting up the glass and sipping a little of the contents out of pure courtesy, for neat rum is not in itself a very enticing beverage to any other than West Indian palates.

' Any *hogo*,' Tom Dupuy repeated loudly and insolently —' *hogo, hogo*. I suppose, now, you mean to say you don't even know what *hogo* is, do you ? Never heard of *hogo* ? Precious affectation ! Don't understand plain language ! Yah, rubbish ! '

' Why, no, certainly,' Harry assented as calmly as he was able ; ' I never before did hear of *hogo*, I assure you. I haven't the slightest idea what it is, or whether I ought rather to admire or to deplore its supposed absence in this very excellent old rum of yours.'

' *Hogo's* French,' Tom Dupuy asserted doggedly,

' *hogo*'s French, and I should have thought you ought to have known it. Everybody in Trinidad knows what *hogo* is. It's French, I tell you. Didn't you ever learn any French at the school you went to, Noel ? '

' Excuse me,' Harry said, flushing up a little, for Tom Dupuy had asked the question very offensively. ' It is *not* French. I know enough of French at least to say that such a word as *hogo*, whatever it may mean, couldn't possibly be French for anything.'

' As my nephew pronounces it,' Mr. Dupuy put in diplomatically, ' you may perhaps have some difficulty in recognising its meaning ; but it's our common West Indian corruption, Mr. Noel, of *haut goût—haut goût*, you understand me—precisely so ; *haut goût*, or *hogo*, being the strong and somewhat offensive molasses-like flavour of new rum, before it has been mellowed, as this of ours has been, by being kept for years in the wood and in bottle.'

' Oh, ah, that's all very well ! I suppose *you*'re going to turn against me now, Uncle Theodore,' Tom Dupuy exclaimed angrily—he was reaching the quarrelsome stage of incipient drunkenness. ' I suppose *you* must go and make fun of me, too, for my French pronunciation as well as this fine-spoken Mr. Noel here. But I don't care a pin about it, or about either of you, either. Who's Mr. Noel, I should like to know, that he should come here, with his fine new-fangled English ways, setting himself up to be better than we are, and teaching us to improve our French pronunciation ?—Oh yes, it's all very fine ; but what does he want to go stopping in our houses for, with our own ladies, and all that, and then going and visiting with coloured rubbish, that I wouldn't touch with a pair of tongs—the woolly-headed niggers !—that's what I want to know, Uncle Theodore ? '

Mr. Dupuy and Harry rose together. ' Tom, Tom ! ' Mr. Dupuy cried warningly, ' you are quite forgetting yourself. Remember that this gentleman is my guest, and is here to-day by my invitation. How dare you say such things as that to my own guest, sir, at my own table ? You insult me, sir, you insult me ! '

' I think,' Harry interrupted, white with anger, ' I had

better withdraw at once, Mr. Dupuy, before things go any further, from a room where I am evidently, quite without any intention on my own part, a cause of turmoil and disagreement.'

He moved hastily towards the open window, which gave upon the lawn, where the ladies were strolling, after the fashion of the country, in the silvery moonlight, among the tropical shrubbery. But Tom Dupuy jumped up before him and stood in his way, now drunk with wine and rum and insolence and temper, and blocked his road to the open window.

'No, no,' he cried, 'you shan't go yet;—I'll tell you all the reason why, gentlemen. He shall hear the truth. I'll take the vanity and nonsense out of him! He's a brown man himself, nothing but a brown man!—Do you know, you fine fellow you, that you're only, after all, a confounded woolly-headed brown mulatto? You are, sir! you are, I tell you! Look at your hands, you damned nigger, look at your hands, I say, if ever you doubt it.'

Harry Noel's proud lip curled contemptuously as he pushed the half-tipsy planter aside with his elbow, and began to stride angrily away towards the moonlit shrubbery. 'I dare say I am,' he answered coolly, for he was always truthful, and it flashed across his mind in the space of a second that Tom Dupuy was very possibly right enough. 'But if I am, my good fellow, I will no longer inflict my company, I tell you, upon persons who, I see, are evidently so little desirous of sharing it any further.'

'Yes, yes,' Tom Dupuy exclaimed madly, planting himself once more like a fool in front of the angry and retreating Englishman, 'he's a brown man, a mulatto, a coloured fellow, gentlemen, own cousin of that infernal nigger scamp, Isaac Pourtalès, whose woolly head I'd like to knock this minute against his own woolly head, the insolent upstart! Why, gentlemen, do you know who his mother was? Do you know who this fine Lady Noel was that he wants to come over us with? She was nothing better, I swear to you solemnly, than a common brown wench over in Barbadoes!'

Harry Noel's face grew livid purple with that foul

insult, as he leaped like a wild beast at the roaring West
Indian, and with one fierce blow in the centre of his chest,
sent him reeling backward upon the floor at his feet like a
senseless lump of dead matter. ' Hound and cur! how
dare you ? ' he hissed out hoarsely, placing the tip of his
foot contemptuously on the fallen planter's crumpled shirt-
front. ' How dare you ?—how dare you ? Say what you
will of me, myself, you miserable blackguard—but my
mother! my mother ! ' And then suddenly recollecting
himself, with a profound bow to the astonished company, he
hurried out, hatless and hot, on to the darkling shrubbery,
casting the dust of Orange Grove off his feet half instinctively behind him as he went.

Next moment a soft voice sounded low beside him, to
his intense astonishment. As he strode alone across the
dark lawn, Nora Dupuy, who had seen the whole incident
from the neighbouring shrubbery, glided out to his side
from the shadow of the star-apple tree and whispered a
few words earnestly in his ear. Harry Noel, still white
with passion and trembling in every muscle like a hunted
animal, could not but stop and listen to them eagerly even
in that supreme moment of righteous indignation. ' Thank
you, Mr. Noel,' she said simply—' thank you, thank you ! '

CHAPTER XXXIV.

THE gentlemen in the dining-room stood looking at one
another in blank dismay for a few seconds, and then Dr.
Macfarlane broke the breathless silence by saying out loud,
with his broad Scotch bluntness : ' Ye're a fool, Tom Dupuy
—a vera fine fool, ye are, of the first watter ; and I'm not
sorry the young Englishman knocked ye doon and gave ye
a lesson, for speaking ill against his own mother.'

' Where has he gone ? ' Dick Castello, the Governor's
aide-de-camp, asked quickly, as Tom picked himself up with
a sheepish, awkward, drunken look. ' He can't sleep here
to-night now, you know, and he'll have to sleep somewhere or other, Macfarlane, won't he ? '

'Run after him,' the doctor said, 'and tak' him to
your own house, I tell ye. Not one of these precious
Treenidad folk'll stir hand or fute to befriend him anyhow, now they've once been told he's a puir brown body.'

Dick Castello took up his hat and ran as fast as he
could go after Harry Noel. He caught him up, breathless,
half-way down to the gate of the estate ; for Harry, though
he had gone off hurriedly without hat or coat, was walking
alone down the main road coolly enough now, trying to
look and feel within himself as though nothing at all unusual in any way had happened.

'Where are you going to, Noel ? ' Dick Castello asked,
in a friendly voice.—' By Jove! I'm jolly glad you knocked
that fellow down, and tried to teach him a little manners,
though he *is* old Dupuy's nephew. But of course you
can't stop there to-night. What do you mean now to do
with yourself ? '

'I shall go to Hawthorn's,' Harry answered, quietly.

'Better not go there,' Dick Castello urged, taking him
gently by the shoulder. 'If you do, you know, it 'll look
as if you wanted to give a handle to Tom Dupuy and break
openly with the whole lot of them. Tom Dupuy insulted
you abominably, and you couldn't have done anything else
but knock him down, of course, my dear fellow, and he
needed it jolly well too, we all know perfectly. But don't
let it seem as if you were going to quarrel with the whole
lot of us. Come home to my house now at Savannah
Garden. I'll walk straight over there with you and have
a room got ready for you at once ; and then I'll go back to
Orange Grove for Mrs. Castello, and bring across as much
of your luggage as I can in my carriage—at least, as much
as you'll need for the present.'

'Very well, Captain Castello,' Harry Noel answered
submissively. 'It's very kind of you to take me in. I'll
go with you ; you know best about it. But hang it all,
you know, upon my word I expect the fellow may have
been telling the truth after all, and I dare say I really am
what these fools of Trinidad people call a brown man.
Did ever you hear such infernal nonsense? Calling me a
brown man! As if it ever mattered twopence to any

sensible person whether a man was black, brown, white, or yellow, as long as he's not such a confounded cad and boor as that roaring tipsy lout of a young Dupuy fellow ! '

So Harry Noel went that Tuesday night to Captain Castello's at Savannah Garden, and slept, or rather lay awake, there till Wednesday morning—the morning of the day set aside by Louis Delgado and Isaac Pourtalès for their great rising and general massacre.

As for Nora, she went up to her own boudoir as soon as the guests had gone—they didn't stay long after this awkward occurrence—and threw herself down once more on the big sofa, and cried as if her heart would burst for very anguish and humiliation.

He had knocked down Tom Dupuy. That was a good thing as far as it went ! For that at least, if for nothing else, Nora was duly grateful to him. But had she gone too far in thanking him ? Would he accept it as a proof that she meant him to reopen the closed question between them ? Nora hoped not, for that—that at any rate was now finally settled. She could never, never, never marry a brown man ! And yet, how much nicer and bolder he was than all the other men she saw around her ! Nora liked him even for his faults. That proud, frank, passionate Noel temperament of his, which many girls would have regarded with some fear and no little misgiving, exactly suited her West Indian prejudices and her West Indian ideal. His faults were the faults of a proud aristocracy, and it was entirely as a member of a proud aristocracy herself that Nora Dupuy lived and moved and had her being. A man like Edward Hawthorn she could like and respect ; but a man like Harry Noel she could admire and love—if he were only not a brown man ! What a terrible cross-arrangement of fate that the one man who seemed otherwise exactly to suit her girlish ideal, should happen to belong remotely to the one race between which and her own there existed in her mind for ever and ever an absolutely fixed and irremovable barrier !

So Nora, too, lay awake all night ; and all night long she thought but of one thing and one person—the solitary man she could never, never, never, conceivably marry.

And Harry, for his part, thinking to himself, on his tumbled pillow, at Savannah Garden, said to his own heart over and over and over again: 'I shall love her for ever; I can never while I live leave off loving her. But after what occurred yesterday and last night, I mustn't dream for worlds of asking her a third time. I know now what it was she meant when she spoke about the barrier between us. Poor girl! how very wild of her! How strange that she should think in her own soul a Dupuy of Trinidad superior in position to one of the ancient Lincolnshire Noels!'

For pride always sees everything from its own point of view alone, and never for a moment succeeds in envisaging to itself the pride of others as being equally reasonable and natural with its own.

CHAPTER XXXV.

TWILIGHT, the beautiful serene tropical twilight, was just gathering on Wednesday evening, when the negroes of all the surrounding country, fresh from their daily work in the cane-pieces, with cutlasses and sticks and cudgels in their hands, began to assemble silently around Louis Delgado's hut, in the bend of the mountains beside the great clump of feathery cabbage-palms. A terrible motley crowd they looked, bareheaded and bare of foot, many of them with their powerful black arms wholly naked, and thrust loosely through the wide sleeve-holes of the coarse sack-like shirt which, with a pair of ragged trousers, formed their sole bodily covering. Most of the malcontents were men, young and old, sturdy and feeble; but among them there were not a few fierce-looking girls and women, plantation hands of the wildest and most unkempt sort, carelessly dressed in short ragged filthy kirtles, that reached only to the knee, and with their woolly hair tangled and matted with dust and dirt, instead of being covered with the comely and becoming bandana turban of the more civilised and decent household negresses. These women carried cutlasses too, the ordinary agricultural implement of all sugar-growing

tropical countries; and one had but to glance at their stal-
wart black arms or their powerful naked legs and feet, as
well as at their cruel laughing faces, to see in a moment
that, if need were, they could wield their blunt but heavy
weapons fully as effectively and as ruthlessly in their own
way as the resolute vengeful men themselves. So wholly
unsexed were they, indeed, by brutal field-labour and brutal
affections, that it was hard to look upon them closely for a
minute and believe them to be really and truly women.

The conspirators assembled silently, it is true, so far as
silence under such circumstances is ever possible to the
noisy demonstrative negro nature; but in spite of the evident effort which every man made at self-restraint, there
was a low under-current of whispered talk, accompanied by
the usual running commentary of grimaces and gesticulations, which made a buzz or murmur hum ceaselessly
through the whole crowd of five or six hundred armed
semi-savages. Now and again, the women especially,
looking down with delightful anticipation at their newly
whetted cutlasses, would break out into hoarse ungovernable laughter, as they thought to themselves of the proud
white throats they were going to cut that memorable
evening, and the dying cries of the little white pickanies
they were going to massacre in their flounced and embroi-
dered lace bassinettes.

'It warm me heart, Mistah Delgado, sah,' one white-
haired, tottering, venerable old negro mumbled out slowly
with a pleasant smile, 'to see so many good neighbour all
come togedder again for kill de buckra. It long since I see
fine gadering like dis. I mind de time, sah, in slavery day,
when I was young man, just begin for to make lub to de
le-adies, how we rise all togedder under John Trelawney
down at Star-Apple Bottom, go hunt the white folk in the
great insurrection. Ha, dem was times, sah—dem was
times, I tellin' you de trut,' me fr̯en', in de great insurrection. We beat de goomba drum, we go up to Mistah
Pourtalès—same what flog me mudder so unmerciful dat
the buckra judges even fine him—an' we catch de massa
himself, an' we beat him dead wit stick an' cutlass. Ha,
ha, dem was times, sah. Den we catch de young le-adies,

an' we hack dem all to pieces, an' we burn de bodies. Den we go on to odder house, take all de buckra we find, shoot some, roast some same we roast pig, an' burn some in deir own houses. Dem was times, sah—dem was times. I doan't s'pose naygur now will do like we do when I is young man. But dis is good meeting, fine meeting: we cry " Colour for colour." " Buckra country for us," an' de Lard prosper us in de work we hab in hand! Hallelujah! '

One of the women stood listening eagerly to this thrilling recital of early exploits, and asked him in a hushed voice of the intensest interest: ' An' what de end ob it all, Mistah Corella ? What come ob it ? How you no get buckra house, den, for yourself lib in ? '

The old man shook his head mournfully as he answered with a meditative sigh: ' Ah, buckra too strong for us, too strong for us altogedder ! come upon us too many. Colonel Macgregor, him come wit plenty big army, gun an' bay'net, an' shoot us down, an'charge us ridin' ; so we all frightened, an' run away hide in de' bush right up in de mountains. Den dem bring Cuban bloodhound, hunt us out ; an' dem hab court-martial, an' dem sit on Trelawney, an' dem hang him, hang him dead, de buckra. An' dem hang plenty. We kill twenty—twenty-two—twenty-four buckra ; an' buckra kill hundred an' eighty poor naygur, so make tings even. For one buckra, dem kill ten, fifteen, twenty naygur. But my master hide me till martial law blow ober, because I is strong, hearty young naygur, an' can work well for him down in cane-piece. Him say: " Doan't must kill valuable property ! " An' I get off dat way. So dat de end ob John Trelawney him rebellion.'

If the poor soul could only have known it, he might have added with perfect truth that it was the end of every other negro rebellion too ; the white oppressor is always too strong for them. But hope springs eternal in the black breast as in all others, and it was with a placid smile of utter oblivion that he added next minute: ' But we doan't gwine to be beaten dis time. We too strong ourselbes now for de soldier an' de buckra. Delgado make tings all snug ; buy pistol, drill naygur, plan battle, till we sure ob de victory. De Lard wit us, an' Delgado him serbant.'

At that moment Louis Delgado himself stepped forward, erect and firm, with the unmistakable air of a born commander, and said a few words in a clear low earnest voice to the eager mob of armed rioters. 'Me fren's,' he said, 'you must obey orders. Go quiet, an' make no noise till you get to de buckra houses. Doan't turn aside for de rum or de trash-houses; we get plenty rum for ourselves, I tellin' you, when we done killed all de buckra. Doan't set fire to de house anywhere; only kill de male white folk; we want house to lib in ourselves, when de war ober. Doan't burn de factories; we want factory for make sugar ourselves when de buckra dribben altogether clean out ob the country. Doan't light fire at all; if you light fire, de soldiers in Port-ob-Spain see de blaze directly, and come up an' fight us hard, before we get togedder enough black men to make sure ob de glorious victory. Nebber mind de buckra le-ady; we can get dem when we want dem. Kill, kill, kill! dat is de watchword. Kill, kill, kill de buckra, an' de Lard delibber de rest into the hands ob his chosen people.' As he spoke, he raised his two black hands, palm upwards, in the attitude of earnest supplication, towards the darkening heaven, and flung his head fervently backward, with the whites of his big eyes rolling horribly, in his unspoken prayer to the God of battles.

The negroes around, caught with the contagious enthusiasm of Delgado's voice and mutely eloquent gesture, flung up their own dusky hands, cutlasses and all, with the selfsame wild and expressive pantomime, and cried aloud, in a scarcely stifled undertone : 'De Lard delibber dem, de Lard delibber dem to Louis Delgado.'

The old African gazed around him complacently for a second at the goodly muster of armed followers, to the picked men among whom Isaac Pourtalès was already busily distributing the pistols and the cartridges. 'Are you ready, me fren's?' he asked again, after a short pause. And, like a deep murmur, the answer rang unanimously from the great tumultuous black mass : 'Praise de Lard, sah, we ready, we ready!'

'Den march!' Delgado cried, in the loud tone of a commanding officer; and suiting the action to the word,

the whole mob turned after him silently, along the winding
path that led down by tortuous twists from the clump of
cabbage-palms to the big barn-like Orange Grove trash-
houses.

With their naked feet and their cat-like tread, the
negroes marched along far more silently than white men
could ever have done, towards the faint lights that gleamed
fitfully beyond the gully. If possible, Delgado would have
preferred to lead them straight to Orange Grove House,
for his resentment burnt fiercest of all against the Dupuy
family, and he wished at least, whatever else happened, to
make sure of massacring that one single obnoxious household. But it was absolutely necessary to turn first to the
trash-houses and the factory, for rumours of some impend-
ing trouble had already vaguely reached the local authorities.
The two constables of the district stood there on guard, and
the few faithful and trustworthy plantation hands were
with them there, in spite of Mr. Dupuy's undisguised ridicule, half expecting an insurgent attack that very evening.
It would never do to leave the enemy thus in the rear,
ready either to attack them from behind, or to bear down
the news and seek for aid at Port-of-Spain. Delgado's
plan was therefore to carry each plantation entire as he
went, without allowing time to the well-affected negroes to
give the alarm to the whites in the next one. But he
feared greatly the perils and temptations of the factory for
his unruly army. ' Whatebber else you do, me fren's,' the
old African muttered more than once, turning round be-
seechingly to his ragged black followers, ' doan't drink de
new rum, and doan't set fire to de buckra trash-houses.'

At the foot of the little knoll under whose base the
trash-houses lay, they came suddenly upon one of the
faithful field-hands, Napoleon Floreal, whose fidelity
Delgado had already in vain attempted with his rude
persuasions. The negroes singled him out at once for their
first vengeance. Before the man could raise so much as a
sharp shout, Isaac Pourtalès had seized him from behind
and gagged his mouth with a loose bandana. Two of the
other men, quick as lightning, snatched his arms, and held
them bent back in a very painful attitude behind his

shoulders. ' If you is wit us,' Delgado said, in a hoarse whisper, ' lift your right foot, fellah.' Floreal kept both feet pressed doggedly down with negro courage upon the ground. ' Him is traitor, traitor ! ' Pourtalès muttered, between his clenched teeth. ' Him hab black skin but white heart. Kill him, kill him ! '

In a second, a dozen angry negroes had darted forward, with their savage cutlasses brandished aloft in the air, ready to hack their offending fellow-countrymen into a thousand pieces. ' Cut out him heart,' cried one fiercely, ' an' let me eat it ! ' But Delgado, his black hands held up with a warning air before them, thundered out in a tone of bitter indignation : ' Doan't kill him !—doan't kill him ! My children, kill in good order. Dar is plenty buckra for you to kill, witout want to kill your own brudder. Tie de han'kercher around him mout', bind rope around him arm an' leg, an' trow him down de gully yonder among de cactus jungle ! '

Even as he spoke, one of the men produced a piece of stout rope from his pocket, brought for the very purpose of tying the ' prisoners,' and proceeded to wind it tightly around Floreal's body. They fastened it well round arms and legs ; stuffed the bandana firmly down his throat, so as to check all his futile attempts at shouting, and rolled him over the slight bank of earth, down among the thick scrub of prickly cactus. Then, as the blood spurted out of the small wounds made by the sharp thorns, they gave a sudden low yell, and burst in a body upon the guardians of the trash-houses.

Before the two black policemen had time to know what was actually happening, they found themselves similarly gagged and bound, and tossed down beside Napoleon Floreal on the prickly cactus bed. In a minute, the insurgents had surrounded the trash-houses, cut down and taken prisoners the few faithful negroes, and marched them along unwillingly in their own body as hostages for the better behaviour of the Orange Grove house-servants.

' Now, me fren's,' Delgado shouted, with fierce energy, ' down wit de Dupuys ! We gwine to humble de proud white man ! We must hab blood ! De Lard is wit us !

He hat' put down de mighty from deir seats, an' hat'
exalted de lowly an' meek ! '

But as he spoke, one or two of the heaviest-looking
among the rioters began to cast their longing eyes upon the
unbroached hogsheads. ' De rum, de rum ! ' one of them
cried hoarsely. ' We want suffin for keep our courage up.
Little drop o' rum help naygur man well to humble de
buckra.'

Delgado rushed forward and placed himself resolutely,
pistol in hand, before the seductive hogsheads. ' Whoebber drink a drop ob dat rum dis blessed ebenin',' he
hissed out angrily, ' before all de Dupuys is lyin' cold in
deir own houses, as sure as de gospel I shoot him dead here
wit dis very pistol ! '

But the foremost rioters only laughed louder than before, and one of them even wrenched the pistol suddenly
from his leader's grasp with an unexpected side movement.
' Look hyar, Mistah Delgado,' the man said quietly : ' dis
risin' is all our risin', an' we has got to hab voice ourselbes
in de partickler way we gwine to manage him. We doan't
gwine away witout de rum, an' we gwine to break just one
little pickanie hogshead.' At the word, he raised his
cutlass above his head, and lunging forward with it like a
sword, with all his force, stove in one of the thick cross-
pieces at the top of the barrel, and let the precious liquor
dribble out slowly from the chink in a small but continuous
trickling stream. Next moment a dozen black hands were
held down to the silent rill like little cups, and a dozen
dusky mouths were drinking down the hot new rum, neat
and unalloyed, with fierce grimaces of the highest gusto.
' Ha, dat good ! ' ran round the chorus in thirsty appro-
bation : ' dat warm de naygur's heart. Us gwine now to
kill de buckra in true earnes'.'

Delgado stood by, mad with rage and disappointment,
as he saw his followers, one after another, scrambling for
handful after handful of the fiery liquor, and watched some
of them, the women especially, reeling about foolishly
almost at once from the poisonous fumes of the unrefined
spirit. He felt in his heart that his chances were slipping
rapidly from him, even before the insurrection was well

begun, and that it would be impossible for a crowd of half-
drunken negroes to preserve the order and discipline which
alone would enable them to cope with the all-puissant and
regularly drilled white men. But the more he stormed
and swore and raved at them, the more did the greedy
and uncontrolled negroes, now revelling in the unstinted
supply, hold their hands to the undiminished stream, and
drink it off by palmfuls with still deeper grunts and groans
of internal satisfaction. ' If it doan't no hope ob conquer
de island,' the African muttered at last with a wild Guinea
oath to Isaac Pourtalès, ' at any rate we has time to kill
de Dupuys—an' dat always some satisfaction.'

The men were now thoroughly inflamed with the hot
new rum, and more than one of them began to cry aloud :
' It time to get to de reg'lar business.' But a few still
lingered lovingly around the dripping hogshead, catching
double handfuls of the fresh spirit in their capacious palms.
Presently, one of the women, mad with drink, drew out a
short pipe from her filthy pocket and began to fill it to the
top with raw tobacco. As she did so, she turned tipsily to
a man by her side and asked him for a light. The fellow
took a match in his unsteady fingers and struck it on a
wooden post, flinging it away when done with among a few
small scraps of dry trash that lay by accident upon the
ground close by. Trash is the desiccated refuse of cane
from which the juice has been already extracted, and it is
ordinarily used as a convenient fuel to feed the crushing-
mills and boil the molasses. Dry as tinder it lighted up
with a flare instantaneously, and raised a crackling blaze,
whose ruddy glow pleased and delighted the childish minds
of the half-drunken negroes. ' How him burn ! ' the woman
with the pipe cried excitedly. ' Sposin' we set fire to de
trash-house ! My heart, how him blaze den ! Him light
up all de mountains ! Burn de trash-house ! Burn de
trash-house ! Dat pretty for true ! Burn de trash-house !

Quick as lightning, the tipsiest rioters had idly kicked
the burning ends of loose trash among the great stacked
heaps of dry cane under the big sheds ; and in one second,
before Delgado could even strive in vain to exert his feeble
authority, the whole mass had flashed into a single huge

sheet of flame, rising fiercely into the evening sky, and reddening with its glow the peaks around, like the lurid glare of a huge volcano. As the flames darted higher and ever higher, licking up the leaves and stalks as they went, the negroes, now fairly loosed from all restraint, leaped and shrieked wildly around them—some of them half-drunk, others absolutely reeling, and all laughing loud with hideous, wild, unearthly laughter, in their devilish, murderous merriment. Delgado alone saw with horror that his great scheme of liberation was being fast rendered ultimately hopeless, and could only now concentrate his attention upon his minor plan of personal vengeance against the Dupuy family. Port-of-Spain would be fairly roused by the blaze in half an hour, but at least there was time to murder outright the one offending Orange Grove household.

For a few minutes, helpless and resourceless, he allowed the half-tipsy excited creatures to dance madly around the flaring fire, and to leap and gesticulate with African ferocity in the red glare of the rapidly burning trash-house. ' Let dem wear out de rum,' he cried bitterly to Pourtalès : ' de heat help to sweat it out ob dem. But in a minute, de Dupuys gwine to be down upon us wit de constables an' de soldiers, if dem doan't make haste to kill dem beforehand.'

Soon the drunken rioters themselves began to remember that burning trash-houses and stealing rum was not the only form of amusement they had proposed to themselves for that evening's entertainment. 'Kill de buckra!—kill de buckra!' more than one of them now yelled out fiercely at the top of his voice, brandishing his cutlass. ' Buckra country for us ! Colour for colour ! Kill dem all ! Kill de buckra !'

Delgado seized at once upon the slender opportunity. ' Me fren's,' he shrieked aloud, raising his palms once more imploringly to heaven, ' kill dem, kill dem ! Follow me ! Hallelujah ! I gwine to lead you to kill de buckra !'

Most of the negroes, recalled to duty by the old African's angry voice, now fell once more into their rude marching order ; but one or two of them, and those the tipsiest, began to turn back wistfully in the direction of the little pool of new rum that lay sparkling in the glare like molten gold in front of the still running hogshead. Louis Delgado looked at them with the fierce contempt of a strong mind for such incomprehensible vacillating weakness. Wrenching his pistol once more from the tipsy grasp of the man who had first seized it, he pointed it in a threatening attitude at the head of the foremost negro among the recalcitrant drunkards. 'Dis time I tellin' you true,' he cried fiercely, in a tone of unmistakable wrath and firmness. 'De first man dat take a single step nearer dat infernal liquor, so help me God, I blow his brains out ! '

Reckless with drink, and unable to believe in his leader's firmness, the foremost man took a step or two, laughing a drunken laugh meanwhile, in the forbidden direction, and then turned round again, grinning like a baboon, towards Louis Delgado.

He had better have trifled with an angry tiger. The fierce old African did not hesitate or palter for a single second ; pulling the trigger, he fired straight at the grinning face of the drunken renegade. The shot rang sharp and clear against the fellow's teeth, and passed downward through the back of his head, killing him instantaneously. He fell like a log in the pool of new rum, and reddened the stream even as they looked with the quick flow of crimson blood from the mangled arteries.

Delgado himself hardly paused a second to glance contemptuously at the fallen recalcitrant. 'Now, me fren's,' he cried firmly, kicking the corpse in his wrath, and with his eyes twitching in a terrible fashion, 'whoebber else disobeys orders, I gwine to shoot him dead dat very minute, same as I shoot dat good-for-nuffin disobedient naygur dar ! We has got to kill de buckra to-night, an' ebbery man ob you must follow me now to kill dem 'mediately. De Lard delibber dem into our hand ! Follow me, an' colour for colour ! '

At the word, the last recalcitrants, awed into sobriety for the moment by the sudden and ghastly death of their companion, turned trembling to their place in the rude ranks, and began once more to march on in serried order

after Louis Delgado.   And with one voice, the tumultuous
rabble, putting itself again in rapid motion towards Orange
Grove, shrieked aloud once more the terrible watchword :
' Colour for colour !   Kill de buckra ! '

CHAPTER XXXVI.

MR. DUPUY was seated quietly at dinner in his own dining-
room, with Nora at the opposite end of the table, and
Uncle Zekiel, the butler, in red plush waistcoat as usual,
standing solemnly behind his chair.   Mr. Dupuy was in
excellent spirits that evening, in spite of the little affair
last night, for the cane had cut very heavy, and the boiling
was progressing in the most admirable manner.   He sipped
his glass of St. Emilion (as imported) with the slow, easy
air of a person at peace with himself and with all creation.
The world at large seemed just that moment to suit him
excellently.   ' Nora, my dear,' he drawled out lazily, with
the unctuous deliberateness of the full-blooded man well
fed, 'this is a capital pine-apple certainly—a Ripley, I
perceive ; far superior in flavour, Ripleys, to the cheap
common black sugar-pines : always insist upon getting
Ripleys—I think, if you please, I'll take another piece of
that pine-apple.'
Nora cut him a good thick slice from the centre of the
fruit—it is only in England that people commit the vul-
garian atrocity of cutting pine in thin layers—and laid
down the knife with a stifled yawn upon the tall dessert
dish.   She was evidently bored—very deeply bored indeed.
Orange Grove without Harry Noel began to seem a trifle
dull ; and it must be confessed that to live for months
together with an old gentleman of Mr. Dupuy's sluggish
temperament was scarcely a lively mode of life for a pretty,
volatile, laughter-loving girl of twenty, like little Nora.
' What's this, papa,' she asked languidly, just by way of
keeping up the conversation, ' about the negroes here in
Westmoreland being so dreadfully discontented?   Somebody was telling me '—Nora prudently suppressed Marian

Hawthorn's name, for fear of an explosion—'that there's a great deal of stir and ferment among the plantation hands. What are they bothering and worrying about now, I wonder?'

Mr. Dupuy rolled the remainder of his glassful of claret on his discriminative palate, very reflectively, for half a minute or so, and then answered in his most leisurely fashion: 'Lies, lies—a pack of lies, the whole lot of it, Nora. I know who you heard that from, though you won't tell me so. You heard it from some of your fine coloured friends there, over at Mulberry.—Now, don't deny it, for I won't believe you. When I say a thing, you know I mean it. You heard it, I say, from some of these wretched, disaffected coloured people. And there isn't a word of truth in the whole story—not a syllable—not a shadow—not a grain—not a penumbra. Absolute false-hood, the entire lot of it, got up by these designing radical coloured people, on purpose to serve their own private purposes. I assure you, Nora, there isn't in the whole world a finer, better paid, better fed, better treated, or more happy and contented peasantry than our own com-fortable West Indian negroes. For my part, I can't conceive what on earth they've ever got to be discontented about.'

'But, papa, they *do* say there's a great chance of a regular rising.'

'Rising, my dear!—rising! Did you say a rising? Ho, ho! that's really too ridiculous! What, these niggers rise in revolt against the white people! Why, my dear child, they'd never dare to do it. A pack of cowardly, miserable, quaking and quavering nigger blackguards. Rise, indeed! I'd like to see them try it! O no; nothing of the sort. Somebody's been imposing on you. They're a precious sight too afraid of us, ever to think of venturing upon a regular rising. Show me a nigger, I always say to anybody who talks that sort of precious nonsense to me, and I'll show you an infernal coward, and a thief too, and a liar, and a vagabond.—'Zekiel, you rascal, pour me out another glass of claret, sir, this minute, will you!'

Uncle 'Zekiel poured out the claret for his red-faced

master with a countenance wholly unclouded by this violent denunciation of his own race; to say the truth, the old butler was too much accustomed to similar sentiments from Mr. Dupuy's lips even to notice particularly what his master was saying. He smiled and grinned, and showed his own white teeth good-humouredly as he laid down the claret jug, exactly as though Mr. Dupuy had been ascribing to the African race in general, and to himself in particular, all the virtues and excellences ever observed in the most abstractly perfect human character.

'No,' Mr. Dupuy went on dogmatically, 'they won't rise : a pack of mean-spirited, cowardly, ignorant vagabonds as ever were born, the niggers, the whole lot of them. I never knew a nigger yet who had a single ounce of courage in him. You might walk over them, and trample them down in heavy riding-boots, and they wouldn't so much as dare to raise a finger against you. And besides, what the dickens have they got to rise for? Haven't they got everything they can ever expect to have? Haven't they got their freedom and their cottages? But they're always grumbling, always grumbling about something or other—a set of idle, lazy, discontented vagabonds as ever I set eyes on!'

'I thought you said just now,' Nora put in with a provoking smile, 'they were the finest, happiest, and most contented peasantry to be found anywhere.'

There was nothing more annoying to Mr. Dupuy than to have one of his frequent conversational inconsistencies ruthlessly brought home to him by his own daughter—the only person in the whole world who would ever have ventured upon taking such an unwarrantable liberty. So he laid down his glass of claret with a forced smile, and by way of changing the subject, said unconcernedly : 'Bless my soul, what on earth can all that glare be over yonder? Upon my word, now I look at it, I fancy, Nora, it seems to come from the direction of the trash-houses.'

Uncle 'Zekiel, standing up behind his master's chair, and gazing outward, could see more easily over the dining-table, and out through the open doorway of the room to the hillside beyond, where the glare came from. In a moment, he realised the full meaning of the unwonted blaze, and cried out sharply, in his shrill old tones : 'O sah, O sah ! de naygurs hab risen, an' dem burning' de trash-houses, dem burnin' de trash-houses ! '

Mr. Dupuy, aghast with righteous anger and astonishment, could hardly believe his own ears at this unparalleled piece of nigger impertinence coming from so old a servant as Uncle 'Zekiel. He turned round upon his trusty butler slowly and solemnly, chair and all, and with his two hands planted firmly on his capacious knees, he said in his most awful voice : ' 'Zekiel, I'm quite at a loss to understand what you can mean by such conduct. Didn't you hear me distinctly say to Miss Nora this very minute that the niggers don't rise, won't rise, can't rise, and never have risen ? How dare you, sir, how dare you contradict me to my very face in this disgraceful, unaccountable manner ? '

But Uncle 'Zekiel, quite convinced in his own mind of the correctness of his own hasty inference, could only repeat, more and more energetically every minute : ' It de trut' I telling you, sah ; it de trut' I tellin' you. Naygur hab risen, runnin' an' shoutin', kickin' fire about, an' burnin' de trash-houses ! '

Mr. Dupuy rose from the table, pale but incredulous. Nora jumped up, white and terrified, but with a mute look of horror-struck appeal to Uncle 'Zekiel. ' Doan't you be afraid, missy,' the old man whispered to her in a loud undertone ; ' we fight all de naygur in all Trinidad before we let dem hurt a single hair ob your sweet, pretty, white little head, dearie.'

At that moment, for the first time, a loud shout burst suddenly upon their astonished ears, a mingled tumultuous yell of ' Kill de buckra—kill de buckra ! ' broken by deep African guttural mumblings, and the crackling noise of the wild flames among the dry cane-refuse. It was the shout that the negroes raised as Delgado called them back from the untimely fire to their proper work of bloodshed and massacre.

In her speechless terror, Nora flung herself upon her father's arms, and gazed out upon the ever-reddening glare beyond with unspeakable alarm.

Next minute, the cry from without rose again louder and louder : ' Buckra country for us ! Kill de buckra ! Colour for colour ! Kill dem—kill dem ! ' And then, another deep negro voice, clearer and shriller far than all of them, broke the deathly stillness that succeeded for a second, with the perfectly audible and awful words : ' Follow me ! I gwine to lead you to kill de Dupuys an' all de buckra ! '

' 'Zekiel ! ' Mr. Dupuy said, coming to himself, and taking down his walking-stick with that calm unshaken courage in which the white West Indian has never been found lacking in the hour of danger—' 'Zekiel, come with me ! I must go out at once and quell these rioters.'

Nora gazed at him in blank dismay. ' Papa, papa ! she cried breathlessly, ' you're not going out to them just with your stick, are you ? You're not going out alone to all these wretches without even so much as a gun or a pistol ! '

' My dear,' Mr. Dupuy answered, coolly and collectedly, disengaging himself from her arms not without some quiet natural tenderness, ' don't be alarmed. You don't under-stand these people as well as I do. I'm a magistrate for the county : they'll respect my position. The moment I come near, they'll all disperse and grow as mild as babies.'

And even as he spoke, the confused shrieks of the women surged closer and closer upon their ears : ' Kill dem—kill dem ! De liquor—de liquor ! '

' Ah ! I told you so,' Mr. Dupuy murmured, half to himself, very complacently, with a deep breath. ' Only a foolish set of tipsy negresses, waking and rum-drinking, and kicking about firebrands.'

For another second there was a slight pause again, while one might count twenty ; and then the report of a pistol rang out clear and definite upon the startled air from the direction of the flaring trash-houses. It was Delgado's pistol, shooting down the tipsy recalcitrant.

' This means business ! ' Mr. Dupuy ejaculated, raising his voice, with a sidelong glance at poor trembling Nora. —' Come along, 'Zekiel ; come along all of you. We must go out at once and quiet them or disperse them.—Dick,

Thomas, Emilius, Robert, Jo, Mark Antony; every one of you! come along with me, come along with me, and see to the trash-houses before these tipsy wretches have utterly destroyed them!'

CHAPTER XXXVII.

HALF-WAY down to the blazing trash-houses, Mr. Dupuy and his little band of black allies, all armed only with the sticks they had hastily seized from the stand in the piazza, came on a sudden face to face with the wild and frantic mob of half-tipsy rioters. ' Halt!' Mr. Dupuy cried out in a cool and unmoved tone of command to the reckless insurgents, as they marched on in irregular order, brandishing their cutlasses wildly in the flickering firelight. ' You infernal blackguards, what the devil are you doing here, and what do you mean by firing and burning my trash-houses?'

By the ruddy light of the lurid blaze behind him, Louis Delgado recognised at once the familiar face of his dearest enemy. ' Me fren's,' he shrieked, in a loud outburst of gratified vindictiveness, ' dis is him—dis is him— dis de buckra Dupuy we come to kill now! De Lard has delibbered him into our hands without so much as gib us de trouble ob go an' attack him.'

But before even Delgado could bring down with savage joy his uplifted weapon on his hated enemy's bare head, Mr. Dupuy had stepped boldly and energetically forward, and catching the wiry African by his outstretched arm, had cried aloud in his coolest and most deliberate accents : ' Louis Delgado, put down your cutlass. As a magistrate for this island, I arrest you for riot.'

His resolute boldness was not without its due effect. For just the swing of a pendulum there was a profound silence, and that great mob of strangely beraged and rum-maddened negroes held its breath irresolutely, doubting in its own six hundred vacillating souls which of the two things rather to do—whether to yield as usual to the accustomed authority of that one bold and solitary white man, the accredited mouthpiece of law and order, or else to rush forward madly and hack him then and there into a thousand pieces with African ferocity. So instinctive in the West Indian negro's nature is the hereditary respect for European blood, that even though they had come there for the very purpose of massacring and mutilating the defenceless buckra, they stood appalled, now the actual crisis had fairly arrived, at the bare idea of venturing to dispute the question openly with the one lone and unarmed white man.

But Louis Delgado, African born as he was, had no such lingering West Indian prejudices. Disengaging his sinewy captive arm from Mr. Dupuy's flabby grasp with a sudden jerk, he lifted his cutlass once more high into the air, and held it, glittering, for the twinkling of an eye, above the old man's defenceless head. One moment, Uncle 'Zekiel saw it gleam fearfully in the red glare of the burning trash-houses; the next, it had fallen on Mr. Dupuy's shoulder, and the blood was spurting out in crimson splashes over his white tie and open shirt-front, in which he had risen but three minutes before so unsuspectingly from his own dinner-table.

The old planter reeled terribly before the violent force of that staggering blow, but kept his face turned bravely with undiminished courage towards the exultant enemy. At the sight of the gushing blood, however—the proud buckra blood, that shows so visibly on the delicate white European skin—the negroes behind set up a loud and horrid peal of unearthly laughter, and rushed forward, all their hesitation flung away at once, closing round him in a thickly packed body—like a bully at football—each eager not to lose his own share in the delightful excitement of hacking him to pieces. A dozen cutlasses gleamed aloft at once in the bare black arms, and a dozen more blows were aimed at the wounded man fiercely by as many hideous grinning rioters.

Uncle 'Zekiel and the household negroes, oblivious and almost unconscious of themselves, as domestic servants of their race always are in the presence of danger for their

master or his family, pressed around the reeling white man
in a serried ring, and with their sticks and arms, a frail
barrier, strove manfully to resist the fierce onslaught of
the yelling and leaping plantation negroes. In spite of
what Mr. Dupuy had just been saying about the negroes
being all alike cowards, the petty handful of faithful blacks,
forming a close and firm semicircle in front of their
wounded master, fought like wild beasts at bay before
their helpless whelps, with hands, and arms, and legs, and
teeth, and sticks, and elbows, opposing stoutly, by fair
means and foul, the ever-pressing sea of wild rioters. As
they fought, they kept yielding slowly but cautiously before
the steady pressure ; and Mr. Dupuy, reeling and staggering he knew not how, but with his face kept ever, like a
fighting Dupuy, turned dauntlessly towards the surging
enemy, retreated slowly backward step by step in the
direction of his own piazza. Just as he reached the
bottom of the steps, Uncle 'Zekiel meanwhile shielding
and protecting him manfully with his portly person, a
woman rushed forth from the mass of the rioters, and with
hideous shrieks of ' Hallelujah, hallelujah ! ' hacked him
once more with her blunt cutlass upon the ribs and body.

Mr. Dupuy, faint and feeble from loss of blood, but still
cool and collected as ever, groped his way ever backward
up the steps, in a blind, reeling, failing fashion, and stood
at last at bay in the doorway of the piazza, with his faithful bodyguard, wounded and bleeding freely like himself,
still closing resolutely around him.

' This will do, 'Zekiel,' he gasped out incoherently, as
he reached the top landing. ' In the pass of the doorway.
Stop them easily. Fire rouse the military. Hold the
house for half an hour—help from the Governor. Quick,
quick ! give me the pistol.'

Even as he spoke, a small white hand, delicate and
bloodless, appearing suddenly from the room behind him,
placed his little revolver, cocked and loaded, between the
trembling fingers of his left hand, for the right lay already
hacked and useless, hanging idly by his side in limp
helplessness.

' Nora, my dear,' the old man sobbed out in a half-

articulate gurgling voice, ' go back—go back this moment
to the boudoir. Back garden; slip away quietly—no place
for you, Orange Grove, this evening. Slight trouble with
the plantation blacks. Quell the rioters.—Close up,
'Zekiel.—Close up, Dick, Thomas, Jo, Robert, Emilius,
Mark, Antony!' And with a quivering hand, standing
there alone in the narrow doorway, while the mob below
swarmed and pressed up the piazza steps in wild confusion,
the wounded planter fired the revolver, with no definite
aim, blank into the surging midst of the mob, and let his
left hand drop as he did so, white and fainting by his side,
with his vain endeavour.

The bullet had hit one of the negro women full in the
thigh, and it only served still further to madden and enrage
the clamouring mob, now frantically thirsty for the buckra
blood.

' Him wounded Hannah—him wounded Hannah!' the
negroes yelled in their buzzing indignation; and at the
word, they rushed forward once more with mad gesticulations, those behind pushing those in front against the
weak yielding wall of Orange Grove servants, and all
menacing horribly with their blood-reddened cutlasses, as
they shrieked aloud frantically : ' Kill him—kill him!'

The servants still held firm with undaunted courage,
and rallied bravely round their tottering master ; but the
onslaught was now far too fierce for them, and one by one
they were thrust back helpless by the raging mob, who
nevertheless abstained so far as possible from hurting any
one of them, aiming all their blows directly at the detested
white man himself alone. If by chance at any moment a
cutlass came down unintentionally upon the broad backs
of the negro defenders, a cry arose at once from the women
in the rear of ' Doan't hit him—doan't hit him. Him me
brudder. Colour for colour! Kill de buckra! Hallelujah !'

And all this time, Nora Dupuy looked on from behind,
holding her bloodless hands clasped downward in mute
agony, not so much afraid as expectant, with Aunt Clemmy
and the women-servants holding her and comforting her

with well-meant negro consolation, under the heavy mahogany arch of the dining-room doorway.

At last, Delgado, standing now on the topmost step, and half within the area of the piazza, aimed one terrible slashing cut at the old planter, as he stood supporting himself feebly by a piece of the woodwork, and hacked him down, a heavy mass, upon the ground before them with a wild African cry of vengeance. The poor old man fell, insensible, in a little pool of his own blood; and the Orange Grove negroes, giving way finally before the irresistible press of their overwhelming opponents, left him there alone, surrounded on every side by the frantic mob of enraged insurgents.

Nora, clasping her hands tighter than ever, and immovable as a statue, stood there still, without uttering a cry or speaking a word—as cold and white and motionless as marble.

'Hack him to pieces!' 'Cut out his heart!' 'Him doan't dead yet!' 'Him only faintin'!' 'Burn him—burn him!' A chorus of cries rose incoherently from the six hundred lips of the victorious negroes. And as they shouted, they mangled and mutilated the old man's body with their blunt cutlasses in a way perfectly hideous to look at; the women especially crowding round to do their best at kicking and insulting their fallen enemy.

'Tank de Lard—tank de Lard!' Delgado, now drunk with blood, shouting out fiercely to his frenzied followers. 'We done killed de ole man. Now we gwine to kill de missy!'

CHAPTER XXXVIII.

EVEN as Delgado stood there still on the steps of the piazza, waving his blood-stained cutlass fiercely about his head, and setting his foot contemptuously on Mr. Dupuy's prostrate and bleeding body, Harry Noel tore up the path that led from Dick Castello's house at Savannah Garden, and halted suddenly in blank amazement in front of the doorway—Harry Noel in evening dress, hatless and spurless;

9

just as he had risen in horror from his dinner, and riding his new mare without even a saddle, in his hot haste to see the cause of the unexpected tumult at the Dupuy's estate. The fierce red glare of the burning cane-houses had roused him unawares at Savannah Garden in the midst of his coffee ; and the cries of the negroes and the sound of pistol-shots had cast him into a frantic fever of anxiety for Nora's safety. ' The niggers have risen, by Jove ! ' Dick Castello cried aloud, as the flames rose higher and higher above the blazing cane-houses. ' They must be attacking old Dupuy ; and if once their blood's up, you may take your oath upon it, Noel, they won't leave him until they've fairly murdered him.'

Harry Noel didn't wait a moment to hear any further conjectures of his host's on the subject, but darting round to the stables bareheaded, clapped a bit forthwith into his mare's mouth, jumped on her back just as she stood, in a perfect frenzy of fear and excitement, and tore along the narrow winding road that led by tortuous stretches to Orange Grove, as fast as his frightened horse's legs could possibly carry him.

As he leaped eagerly from his mount to the ground in the midst of all that hideous din and uproar and mingled confusion, Delgado was just calling on his fellow-blacks to follow him boldly into the house and to ' Kill de missy ; ' and the Orange Grove negroes, cowed and terrified now that their master had fallen bodily before them, were beginning to drop back, trembling, into the rooms behind, and to allow the frantic and triumphant rioters to have their own way unmolested. In a moment, Harry took in the full terror of the scene—saw Mr. Dupuy's body lying, a mass of hacked and bleeding wounds, upon the wooden floor of the front piazza ; saw the infuriated negroes pressing on eagerly with their cutlasses lifted aloft, now fairly drunk with the first taste of buckra blood ; and Delgado in front of them all, leaping wildly, and gesticulating in frantic rage with all his arms and hands and fingers, as he drove back the terrified servants through the heavy old mahogany doorway of the great drawing-room into the room that opened out behind towards Nora's own little sacred boudoir.

Harry had no weapon of any sort with him except the frail riding-whip he carried in his hand; but without waiting for a second, without thinking for one instant of the surrounding danger, he rushed frantically up the piazza steps, pushed the astonished rioters to right and left with his powerful arms, jumped over the senseless planter's prostrate body, swept past Delgado into the narrow doorway, and there stood confronting the savage ringleader boldly, his little riding-whip raised high above his proud head with a fierce and threatening angry gesture. ' Stop there ! ' he cried, in a voice of stern command, that even in that supreme moment of passion and triumph had its full effect upon the enraged negroes. ' Stop there, you mean-spirited villains and murderers ! Not a step farther—not a step farther, I tell you ! Cowards, cowards, cowards, every one of you, to kill a poor old man like that upon his own staircase, and to threaten a helpless innocent lady.'

As he spoke, he laid his hand heavily upon Louis Delgado's bony shoulder, and pushed the old negro steadily backward, out of the doorway and through the piazza, to the front steps, where Mr. Dupuy's body was still lying untended and bleeding profusely. ' Stand back, you old devil ! ' he cried out fiercely and authoritatively. ' Stand back this minute, and put down your infernal cutlass ! You shall not hurt another hair of their heads, I tell you. Cowards, cowards, cowards, every man of you. If you want to fight the whites, you cowardly scoundrels you, why don't you fight the men like yourselves, openly and straightforward, instead of coming by night, without note or warning, burning and hacking and killing and destroying, and waging war against defenceless old men and women and children ? '

The negroes fell back a little grudgingly as he spoke, and answered him only by the loud and deep guttural cry —an inarticulate, horribly inhuman gurgle—which is their sole possible form of speech in the very paroxysm of African passion. Louis Delgado held his cutlass half doubtfully in his uplifted hand : he had tasted blood once now ; he had laid himself open to the fierce vengeance of the English law ; he was sorely tempted in the whirlwind of the moment to cut down Harry Noel too, as he had cut down the white-headed old planter the minute before. But the innate respect of the essentially fighting negro for a resolute opponent held him back deliberating for a moment; and he drew down his cutlass as quickly as he had raised it, divided in mind whether to strike or permit a parley.

Harry Noel seized the occasion with intuitive strategy. 'Here you, my friends,' he cried boldly, turning round towards the cowering Orange Grove servants—'is this the way you defend your master? Pick him up, some of you —pick him up this minute, I tell you, and lay him out decently on the sofa over yonder.—There, there; don't be afraid. Not one of these confounded rogues and cowards dares to touch you or come one pace nearer you as long as you're doing it. If he does, by George! cutlass or no cutlass, I'll break this riding-whip to pieces, I tell you, across his damned black back as soon as look at him.' And he brandished the whip angrily in front of him, towards the mad and howling group of angry rioters, held at bay for the moment on the piazza steps by that solitary undis-mayed young Englishman with his one frail and ridiculous weapon.

The rioters howled all the louder at his words, and leaped and grinned and chattered and gesticulated like wild beasts behind an iron railing; but not one of them ven-tured to be the first in aiming a blow with his deadly imple-ment at Harry Noel. They only yelled once more incom-prehensibly in their deep gutturals, and made hideous wild grimaces, and waved their cutlasses frantically around them with horrible inarticulate negro imprecations.

But Harry stood there firm and unyielding, facing the maddened crowd with his imperious manner, and overawing them in spite of themselves with that strange power of a superior race over the inferior in such critical moments of intense passion.

The Orange Grove servants, having fresh courage put into their failing breasts once more, by the inspiring presence of a white man at their sides, and being true at heart to their poor master, as negro house-servants always are and always have been in the worst extremities, took

advantage of the momentary lull in the storm to do as
Harry told them, and lift Mr. Dupuy's body up from the
ground, laying it carefully on the piazza sofa. ' That's
better,' Harry said, as they finished their task.—' Now, we
must go on and drive away these murderous rascals. If we
don't drive them away, my good friends, they'll kill Miss
Nora—they'll kill Miss Nora. Would you have it said of
you that you let a parcel of murderous plantation rioters
kill your own dead master's daughter right before your
very faces ? '

As he spoke, he saw a pale face, pale, not with fear, but
with terrible anger, standing mute and immovable beside
him ; and next moment he heard Nora Dupuy's voice
crying out deeply, in the very echo of his own angry
words : ' Cowards, cowards ! '

At the sight of the hated Dupuy features, the frenzied
plantation hands seemed to work themselves up into a
fresh access of ungovernable fury. With indescribable
writhings and mouthings and grimaces, their hatred and
vengeance found articulate voice for a moment at least, and
they cried aloud like one man : ' Kill her—kill her ! Kill
de missy ! Kill her—kill her ! '

' Give me a pistol,' Harry Noel exclaimed wildly to the
friendly negroes close behind his back : ' a gun—a knife—
a cutlass—anything ! '

' We got nuffin, sah,' Uncle 'Zekiel answered, blankly
and whiningly, now helpless as a child before the sudden
inundation of armed rioters, for without his master he
could do nothing.

Harry looked around him desperately for a moment,
then, advancing a step with hasty premeditation, he
wrenched a cutlass suddenly by an unexpected snatch
from one of the foremost batch of rioters, and stepped
back with it once more unhurt, as if by miracle, into the
narrow pass of the mahogany doorway.

' Stand away, Miss Dupuy ! ' he cried to her earnestly.
' If you value your life, stand back, stand back, I beg of you.
This is no place for you to-night. Run, run ! If you don't
escape, there'll be more murder done presently.'

' I shall not go,' Nora answered, clenching her fist hard

and knitting her brows sternly, 'as long as one of these abominable wretches dares to stop without permission upon my father's piazza.'

'Then stand away, you there!' Harry shouted aloud to the surging mob; 'stand away this moment, every one of you! Whoever steps one single step nearer this lady behind me, by Heaven, I'll hack him down without pity that minute, as you'd hack down a stinging cactus tree!'

Delgado stood still and hesitated once more, with strange irresolution—he didn't like to hit the brown man—but Isaac Pourtalès, lifting his cutlass wildly above his head, took a step in front and brought it down with a fierce swish towards Harry's skull, in spite of kinship. Harry parried it dexterously with his own cutlass, like a man who has learned what fencing means; and then, rushing, mad with rage, at the astonished Isaac before he knew what to look for, brought down a heavy blow upon his right shoulder, that disabled his opponent outright, and made him drop at once his useless weapon idly by his side. 'Take that, you damned nigger dog!' Harry hissed out fiercely through his close-set teeth; 'and if any other confounded nigger among you all dares to take a single step nearer in the same direction, he'll get as much and more, too, than this insolent fellow here has got for his trouble.'

The contemptuous phrase once more roused all the negroes' anger. 'Who you call nigger, den?' they cried out fiercely, leaping in a body like wild beasts upon him. 'Kill him—kill him! Him doan't fit to live. Kill him— kill him, dis minute—kill him!'

But Delgado, some strange element of compassion for the remote blood of his own race still rising up instinctively and mysteriously within him, held back the two or three foremost among the pressing mass with his sinewy arm. 'No, no, me fren's,' he shouted angrily, 'doan't kill him, doan't kill him. Tiger no eat tiger, ole-time folk say; tiger no eat tiger. Him is nigger himself. Him is Isaac Pourtalès' own cousin.—Doan't kill him. His mudder doan't nobody, I tell you, me fren's, but coloured gal, de same as yours is —coloured gal from ole Barbadoes. I sayin' to you, me fren's, ole-time folk has true proverb, tiger no eat tiger.'

The sea of angry black faces swelled up and down wildly and dubiously for a moment, and then, with the sudden fitful changefulness of negro emotion, two or three voices, the women's especially, called aloud, with sobs and shrieks : ' Doan't kill him—doan't kill him ! Him me brudder—him me brudder. Doan't kill him ! Hallelujah ! '

Harry looked at them savagely, with knit brows and firm-set teeth, his cutlass poised ready to strike in one hand, and his whole attitude that of a forlorn hope at bay against overwhelming and irresistible numbers.

' You black devils ! ' he cried out fiercely flinging the words in their faces, as it were, with a concentrated power of insult and hatred, ' I won't owe my life to that shameful plea, you infernal cowards. Perhaps I may have a drop or two of your damned black blood flowing somewhere in my veins somehow, and perhaps I mayn't again ; but whether I have or whether I haven't, I wouldn't for dear life itself acknowledge kindred with such a pack of cowardly vagabonds and murderers as you, who would hack an old man brutally to death like that, before his own poor daughter's face, helplessly, upon his own staircase.'

' Mr. Noel,' Nora echoed, in a clear defiant tone, nothing trembling, from close behind him, ' that was well said—that was bravely spoken ! Let them come on and kill us if they will, the wretches. We're not afraid of them, we're not afraid of them.'

' Miss Dupuy,' Harry cried earnestly, looking back towards her with a face of eager entreaty, ' save yourself ! for God's sake, save yourself. There's still time even now to escape—by the garden gate—to Hawthorn's—while these wretches here are busy murdering me.'

At the word, Louis Delgado sprang forward once more, cutlass in hand, no longer undecided, and with one blow on the top of the head felled Harry Noel heavily to the ground.

Nora shrieked, and fainted instantly.

' Him doan't dead yet,' Delgado yelled aloud in devilish exultation, lifting his cutlass again with savage persistence. ' Hack him to pieces, dar—hack him to pieces ! Him doan't dead yet, I tellin' you, me fren's. Hack him to pieces! An' when him dead, we gwine to carry him an' de missy an' Massa Dupuy out behind dar, and burn dem all in a pile togedder on de hot ashes ob de smokin' cane-house!'

CHAPTER XXXIX.

BEFORE the yelling mob could close again round Harry Noel's fallen body, with their wild onslaught of upraised cutlasses, more dangerous to one another in the thick press than to the prostrate Englishman or to poor fainting and unconscious Nora, another hasty clatter of horses' hoofs burst upon them from behind, up the hilly pathway, and a loud, clear, commanding voice called out in resonant tones that overtopped and stilled for a moment the tumultuous murmur of negro shrieks : ' In the Queen's name— in the Queen's name, hold ; disperse there!'

That familiar adjuration, so comparatively powerless upon an English mob at home in England, acted like magic on the fierce and half-naked throng of ignorant and superstitious plantation negroes. It was indeed to them a mighty word to conjure with, that loud challenge in the name of the great distant Queen, whose reality seemed as far away from them and as utterly removed from their little sphere as heaven itself. They dropped their cutlasses instantaneously, for a brief moment of doubt and hesitation ; a few voices still shouted fiercely, ' Kill him—kill him!' and then a unanimous cry arose among all the surging mass of wild and scowling black humanity : ' Mr. Hawtorn, Mr. Hawtorn! Him come in Missis Queen name, so gib us warnin'. Now us gwine to get justice. Mr. Hawtorn, Mr. Hawtorn!'

But while the creole-born plantation hands thus welcomed eagerly what they looked upon, in their simplicity, as the Queen's direct mouthpiece and representative, Louis Delgado, his face distorted with rage, and his arms plying his cutlass desperately, frowned and gnashed his teeth more fiercely than ever with rage and disappointment; for his wild African passion was now fully aroused, and,

like the tiger that has once tasted blood, he didn't want
to be balked of the final vengeful delight of hacking his
helpless victim slowly to pieces in a long-drawn torture.
' Missis Queen ! ' he cried contemptuously, turning round
and brandishing his cutlass with savage joy once more
before the eyes of his half-sobered companions—' Missis
Queen, him say dar ! Ha, ha, what him say dat for ?
What de Queen to me, I want you tell me ? I doan't
care for Queen, or judge, or magistrate, or nuffin ! I
gwine to kill all de white men togedder, in all Trinidad,
de Lard helpin' me ! '

As he spoke, Edward Hawthorn jumped hastily from
his saddle, and advanced with long strides towards the
fiercely gesticulating and mumbling African. The plantation negroes, cowed and tamed for the moment by
Edward's bold and resolute presence, and overawed by
the great name of that mysterious, unknown, half-mythi-
cal Queen Victoria, beyond the vast illimitable ocean, fell
back sullenly to right and left, and made a little lane
through the middle of the crowd for the Queen's representative to mount the staircase. Edward strode up, without
casting a single glance on either side, to where Delgado
stood savagely beside Harry Noel's fallen body, and put
his right hand with an air of indisputable authority upon
the frantic African's uplifted arm. Delgado tried to shake
him off suddenly with a quick, adroit, convulsive movement ; but Edward's grip was tight and vice-like, and he
held the black arm powerless in his grasp, as he spoke
aloud a few words in some unknown language, which
sounded to the group of wondering negroes like utter
gibberish—or perhaps some strange spell with which the
representative of Queen Victoria knew how to conjure by
some still more potent and terrible obeah than even
Delgado's.

But Louis Delgado alone knew that the words were
pure Arabic, and that Edward Hawthorn grasped his arm
' in the name of Allah, the All-wise, the most Powerful ! '

At the sound of that mighty spell, a terrible one,
indeed, to the fierce old half-Christianised Mohammedan,
Delgado's arm, too, dropped powerless to his trembling

side, and he fell back, gnashing his teeth like a bull-dog
balked of a fight, into the general mass of plantation
negroes. There he stood, dazed and stunned apparently,
leaning up sulkily against the piazza post, but speaking
not a word to either party for good or for evil.

The lull was but for a minute; and Edward Hawthorn
saw at once that if he was to gain any permanent advantage by the momentary change of feeling in the fickle
negro mob, he must keep their attention distracted for a
while, till their savage passions had time to cool a little,
and the effect of this unwonted orgy of fire and bloodshed
had passed away before the influence of sober reflection.
A negro crowd is like a single creature of impulse—swayed
to and fro a hundred times more easily than even a
European mob by every momentary passing wave of anger
or of feeling.

'Take up Mr. Noel and Miss Dupuy,' he said aside,
in his cool, commanding tone, to the Orange Grove servants:—' Mr. Noel isn't dead—I see him breathing yet—
and lay them on a bed and look after them, while I speak
to these angry people.' Then he turned, mastering himself with an effort for that terrible crisis, and taking a
chair from the piazza, he mounted it quickly, and began to
speak in a loud voice, unbroken by a single tremor of fear,
like one addressing a public meeting, to the great sea of
wondering, upturned black faces, lighted up from behind in
lurid gleams by the red glare of the still blazing cane-
houses.

'My friends,' he said, holding his hand before him,
palm outward, in a mute appeal for silence and a fair
hearing, ' listen to me for a moment. I want to speak to
you: I want to help you to what you yourselves are
blindly seeking. I am here to-night as Queen Victoria's
delegate and representative. Queen Victoria has your
welfare and interest at heart; and she has sent me out to
this island to do equal justice between black man and
white man, and to see that no one oppresses another by
force or fraud, by lawlessness or cunning. As you all
know, I am in part a man of your own blood; and Queen
Victoria, in sending me out to judge between you, and in

appointing so many of your own race to posts of honour here in Trinidad, has shown her wish to favour no one particular class or colour to the detriment or humiliation of the others. But in doing as I see you have done to-night—in burning down factories, in attacking houses, in killing or trying to kill your own employers, and help-less women, and men who have done no crime against you except trying to protect your victims from your cruel vengeance—in doing this, my friends, you have not done wisely. That is not the way to get what you want from Queen Victoria.—What is it you want? Tell me that. That is the first thing. If it is anything reasonable, the Queen will grant it. What do you want from Queen Victoria?'

With one voice the whole crowd of lurid upturned black faces answered loudly and earnestly: ' Justice, justice!'

Edward paused a moment, with rhetorical skill, and looked down at the mob of shouting lips with a face half of sternness and half of benevolence. 'My friends,' he said again, 'you shall have justice. You haven't always had it in the past—that I know and regret; but you shall have it, trust me, henceforth in the future. Listen to me. I know you have often suffered injustice. Your rights have not been always respected, and your feelings have many times been ruthlessly trampled upon. Nobody sympa-thises with you more fully than I do. But just because I sympathise with you so greatly, I feel it my duty to warn you most earnestly against acting any longer as you have been acting this evening. I am your friend—you know I am your friend. From me, I trust you have never had anything less than equal justice.'

' Dat's true—dat's true!' rang in a murmuring wave of assent from the eager listening crowd of negroes.

' Well,' Edward went on, lowering his tone to more persuasive accents, ' be advised by me, then, and if you want to get what you ask from Queen Victoria, do as I tell you. Disperse to-night quietly and separately. Don't go off in a body together and talk with one another ex-citedly around your watch-fires about your wrongs and your grievances. Burn no more factories and cane-houses.

Attack no more helpless men and innocent women. Think
no more of your rights for the present. But go each man
to his own hut, and wait to see what Queen Victoria will
do for you.—If you continue foolishly to burn and riot,
shall I tell you in plain words what will happen to you?
The Governor will be obliged to bring out the soldiers and
the volunteers against you; they will call upon you, as I
call upon you now, in the Queen's name, to lay down
your pistols, and your guns, and your cutlasses; and if you
don't lay them down at once they'll fire upon you, and disperse
you easily. Don't be deceived. Don't believe that because
you are more numerous—because there are so many more
of you than of the white men—you could conquer them
and kill them by main force, if it ever came to open fighting. The soldiers, with their regular drill and their good
arms and their constant training, could shoot you all down
with the greatest ease, in spite of your numbers and your
pistols and your cutlasses. I don't say this to frighten
you or to threaten you; I say it as your friend, because I
don't want you foolishly to expose yourselves to such a
terrible butchery and slaughter.

A murmur went through the crowd once more, and
they looked dubiously and inquiringly towards Louis
Delgado. But the African gave no sign and made no
answer: he merely stood sullenly still by the post against
which he was leaning; so Edward hastened to reassure the
undecided mob of listening negroes by turning quickly to
the other side of the moot question.

'Now listen again,' he said, 'for what I'm going to
say to you now is very important. If you will disperse,
and go each to his own home, without any further trouble
or riot, I will undertake, myself, to go to England on
purpose for you, and tell Queen Victoria herself about all
your troubles. I will tell her that you haven't always been
justly treated, and I'll try to get new and better laws made
in future for you, under which you may secure more justice
than you sometimes get under present arrangements. Do
you understand me? If you go home at once, I promise
to go across the sea and speak to Queen Victoria herself on
your behalf, over in England.'

The view of British constitutional procedure implied in Edward Hawthorn's words was not perhaps strictly accurate ; but his negro hearers would hardly have felt so much impressed if he had offered to lay their grievances boldly at the foot of that impersonal entity, the Colonial Office ; while the idea that they were to have a direct spokesman, partly of their own blood, with the Queen herself, flattered their simple African susceptibilities and helped to cool their savage anger. Like children as they are, they began to smile and show their great white teeth in infantile satisfaction, as pleasantly as though they had never dreamt ten minutes earlier of hacking Harry Noel's body fiercely into little pieces ; and more than one voice cried out in hearty tones : ' Hoorrah for Mr. Hawtorn ! Him de black man fren'. Gib him a cheer, boys ! Him gwine to 'peak for us to Queen Victoria ! '

' Then promise me faithfully,' Edward said, holding out his hand once more before him, ' that you'll all go home this very minute and settle down quietly in your own houses.'

' We promise, sah,' a dozen voices answered eagerly.

Edward Hawthorn turned anxiously for a moment to Louis Delgado. ' My brother,' he said to him rapidly in Arabic, ' this is your doing. You must help me now to quiet the people you have first so fiercely and so foolishly excited. Assist me in dispersing them, and I will try to lighten for you the punishment which will surely be inflicted upon you as ringleader, when this is all over.'

But Delgado, propped in a stony attitude against the great wooden post of the piazza, answered still never a word. He stood there to all appearance in stolid and sullen indifference to all that was passing so vividly around him, with his white and bloodshot eyes staring vacantly into the blank darkness that stretched in front of him, behind the flickering light of the now collapsed and burntout cane-houses.

Edward touched him lightly on his bare arm. To his utter horror and amazement, though not cold, it was soft and corpse-like, as in the first hour of death, before rigidity and chilliness have begun to set in. He looked up into the

bloodshot eyes. Their staring balls seemed already glazed
and vacuous, utterly vacant of the fierce flashing light
that had gleamed from the pupils so awfully and savagely
but ten minutes before, as he brandished his cutlass with
frantic yells above Harry Noel's fallen body. Two of the
plantation negroes, attracted by Edward's evident recoil of
horror, came forward with simple curiosity, flinging down
their cutlasses, and touched the soft cheeks, not with the
reverent touch which a white man feels always due to the
sacredness of death, but harshly and rudely, as one might
any day touch a senseless piece of stone or timber.

Edward looked at them with a pallid face of mute
inquiry. The youngest of the two negroes drew back for a
second, overtaken apparently by a superstitious fear, and
murmured low in an awe-struck voice : 'Him dead, sah,
dead—stone dead. Dead dis ten minute, since ever you
begin to 'peak to de people, sah.'

He was indeed. His suppressed rage at the partial
failure of his deeply cherished scheme of vengeance on the
hated white men, coming so close upon his paroxysm of
triumph over the senseless bodies of Mr. Dupuy and Harry
Noel, had brought about a sudden fit of cardiac apoplexy.
The old African's savage heart had burst outright with
conflicting emotions. Leaning back upon the pillar for
support, as he felt the blood failing within him, he had died
suddenly and unobserved without a word or a cry, and had
stood there still, as men will often stand under similar
circumstances, propped up against the supporting pillar, in
the exact attitude in which death had first overtaken him.
In the very crisis of his victory and his defeat, he had been
called away suddenly to answer for his conduct before even
a higher tribunal than the one with which Edward Hawthorn had so gently and forbearingly threatened him.

The effect of this sudden catastrophe upon the impres-
sionable minds of the excited negroes was indeed immediate
and overwhelming. Lifting up their voices in loud wails
and keening, as at their midnight wakes, they cried
tremulously one after another : ' De Lard is against us—
de Lard is against us ! Ebbery man to your tents, O
Israel ! De Lard hab killed Delgado—hab killed Delgado

—hab smitten him down, for de murder him committed!' To their unquestioning antique faith, it was the visible judgment of heaven against their insurrection, the blood of Theodore Dupuy and Harry Noel crying out for vengeance from the floor of the piazza, like the blood of righteous Abel long before, crying out for vengeance from the soil of Eden.

More than one of them believed in his heart, too, that the mysterious words in the unknown language which Edward Hawthorn had muttered over the old African were the spell that had brought down upon him before their very eyes the unseen bolt of the invisible powers. Whether it was obeah, or whether it was imprecation, and solemn prayer to the God of heaven, they thought within themselves, in their dim, inarticulate, unspoken fashion, that 'Mr. Hawtorn word bring down de judgment dat very minute on Louis Delgado.'

In an incredibly short space of time, the great crowd of black faces had melted away as quickly as it came, and Edward Hawthorn was left alone in the piazza, with none but the terrified servants of the Orange Grove household to help him in his task or to listen to his orders. All that night long, across the dark gorge and the black mango grove, they could hear the terrified voices of the negroes in their huts singing hymns, and crying aloud in strange prayers to God in heaven that the guilt of this murder might not be visited upon their heads, as it had been visited before their very eyes that night on Louis Delgado. To the negro mind, the verdict of fate is the verdict of heaven.

'Take up his body, too, and lay it down on the sofa,' Edward said to Uncle 'Zekiel, still beside himself with terror at the manifold horrors of this tragical evening.

'I doan't can dare, sah,' Uncle 'Zekiel answered tremulously—'I doan't can dare lay me hand upon de corpse, I tellin' you, sah. De finger ob de Lard has smite Delgado. I doan't dare to lift an' carry him.'

'One of you boys, then, come and help me,' Edward cried, holding up the corpse with one hand to keep it from falling.

But not one of them dare move a single step nearer to the terrible awe-inspiring object.

At last, finding that no help was forthcoming on any hand, Edward lifted up the ghastly burden all by himself in his own arms, and laid it down reverently and gently on the piazza sofa. ' It is better so,' he murmured to himself slowly and pitifully. ' There will be no more blood on either side shed at any rate for this awful evening's sorry business.'

And then at length he had leisure to turn back into the house itself and make inquiries after Mr. Dupuy and Harry and Nora.

CHAPTER XL.

MARIAN was behind in the dining-room and bedrooms with Aunt Clemmy, helping to nurse and tend the sick and wounded as well as she could, in the midst of so much turmoil and danger. When she and Edward had been roused by the sudden glare of the burning cane-houses, reddening the horizon by Orange Grove, and casting weird and fitful shadows from all the mango trees in front of their little tangled garden, she had been afraid to remain behind alone at Mulberry, and had preferred facing the maddened rioters by her husband's side, to stopping by herself under such circumstances among the unfamiliar black servants in her own house. So they had ridden across hurriedly to the Dupuys' together, especially as Marian was no less timid on Nora's account than on her own ; and when they reached the little garden gate that led in by the back path, she had slipped up alone, unperceived by the mob, while Edward went round openly to the front door, and tried to appease the angry negroes.

The shouts and yells when she first arrived had proved indeed very frightening and distracting ; but after a time, she could guess, from the comparative silence which ensued, that Edward had succeeded in gaining a hearing : and then she and Aunt Clemmy turned with fast-beating hearts to look after the bleeding victims, one of whom at

least they gave up from the first as quite dead beyond the
reach of hope or recovery.

Nora was naturally the first to come to. She had
fainted only; and though, in the crush and press, she had
been trampled upon and very roughly handled by the barefooted negroes, she had got off, thanks to their shoeless
condition, with little worse than a few ugly cuts and
bruises. They laid her tenderly on her own bed, and bathed
her brows over and over again with Cologne water; till,
after a few minutes, she sat up again, pale and deathly to
look at, but proud and haughty and defiant as ever, with
her eyes burning very brightly, and an angry quiver playing
unchecked about her bloodless lips.

'Is he dead?' she asked calmly—as calmly as if it
were the most ordinary question on earth, but yet with a
curious tone of suppressed emotion, that even in that
terrible moment did not wholly escape Marian's quick
womanly observation.

'Your father?' Marian answered, in a low voice.—
'Dear, dear, you mustn't excite yourself now. You must
be quite quiet, perfectly quiet. You're not well enough to
stand any talking or excitement yet. You must wait to
hear about it all, darling, until you're a little better.'

Nora's lip curled a trifle as she answered almost disdainfully: 'I'm not going to lie here and let myself be
made an invalid of, while those creatures there are out
yonder without my leave still on the piazza. Let me get
up and see what has happened.—No; I didn't mean papa,
Marian; I know he's dead; I saw him lying hacked all to
pieces outside on the sofa. I meant Mr. Noel. Have they
killed him? Have they killed him? He's a brave man.
Have the wretches killed him?'

'We think not,' Marian answered dubiously. 'He's
in the next room, and two of the servants are there taking
care of him.'

Nora rose from the bed with a sudden bound, and stood
pale and white, all trembling before them. 'What are you
stopping here wasting your care upon me for, then?' she
asked half angrily. 'You *think* not—think not, indeed!
Is this a time to be thinking and hesitating? Why are

you looking after women who go and get fainting fits, like fools, at the wrong moment? I'm ashamed of myself, almost, for giving way visibly before the wretches—for letting them see I was half afraid of them. But I wasn't afraid of them for myself, though—not a bit of it, Marian : it was only for—for Mr. Noel.' She said it after a moment's brief hesitation, but without the faintest touch of girlish timidity or ill-timed reserve. Then she swept queen-like past Marian and Aunt Clemmy, in her white dinner dress—the same dress that she had worn when she was Marian's bridesmaid—and walked quickly but composedly, as if nothing had happened, into the next bedroom.

The two negresses had already taken off Harry's coat and waistcoat, and laid him on the bed with his shirt front all saturated with blood, and his forehead still bleeding violently, in spite of their efforts to stanch it unskilfully with a wet towel. He was lying there, when Nora entered, stretched out at full length, speechless and senseless, the blood even then oozing slowly, by intermittent gurgling throbs, from the open gash across his right temple. There was another deeper and even worse wound gurgling similarly upon his left elbow.

'They should have been here,' Nora cried; 'Marian and Clemmy should have been here, instead of looking after me, like fools, in yonder.—Is he dead, Nita? Is he dead? Tell me!'

'No, missy,' the girl answered, passively handing her the soaked towel. 'Him doan't dead yet; but him dyin', him dyin'. De blood comin' out ob him, spurt, spurt, spurt, so him can't lib long, not anyway. Him bledded to death already, I tinkin', a'most.'

Nora looked at the white face, and a few tears began at last to form slowly in her brimming eyelids. But she brushed them away quickly, before they had time to trickle down her blanched cheek, for her proud West Indian blood was up now, as much as the negroes' had been a few minutes earlier; and she twisted her handkerchief round a pocket pencil so as to form a hasty extemporised tourniquet, which she fastened bravely and resolutely with

intuitive skill above the open wound on the left elbow.
She had never seen such a thing before, and she couldn't
have said herself, for the life of her, how she knew it
would prove useful. She had no idea, even, that the little
jets in which the blood spurted out so rhythmically were
indicative of that most dangerous wound, a severed artery;
but she felt instinctively, somehow, that this was the right
thing to do, and she did it without flinching, as if she had
been used to dealing familiarly with dangerous wounds for
half her lifetime. Then she twisted the hasty instrument
tightly round till the artery was securely stopped, and the
little jets ceased entirely at each pulsation of the now
feeble and weakened heart.

'Run for the doctor, somebody!' she cried eagerly;
'run for the doctor, or he'll die outright before we can get
help for him!'

But Nita and Rose, on their knees beside the wounded
man, only cowered closer to the bedside, and shook with
terror as another cry rose on a sudden from outside from
the excited negroes. It was the cry they raised when they
found Delgado was really struck dead before their very eyes
by the visible and immediate judgment of the Almighty.

Nora looked down at them with profound contempt,
and merely said, in her resolute, scornful voice: 'What!
afraid even of your own people? Why, I'm not afraid of
them; I, who am a white woman, and whom they'd murder
now and hack to pieces, as soon as they'd look at me, if once
they could catch me, when their blood's up!—Marian,
Marian! you're a white woman; will you come with me?'

Marian trembled a little—she wasn't upheld through
that terrible scene by the ingrained hereditary pride of a
superior race before the blind wrath of the inferior,
bequeathed to Nora by her slave-owning ancestors; but she
answered with hardly a moment's hesitation: 'Yes, Nora.
If you wish it, I'll go with you.'

There is something in these conflicts of race with race
which raises the women of the higher blood for the time
being into something braver and stronger than women.
In England, Marian would never have dared to go out
alone in the face of such a raging tumultuous mob, even

of white people ; but in Trinidad, under the influence of
that terrible excitement, she found heart to put on her hat
once more, and step forth with Nora under the profound
shade of the spreading mango-trees, now hardly lighted up
at all at fitful intervals by the dying glow from the burntout embers of the smoking cane-houses.   They went down
groping their way by the garden path, and came out at last
upon the main bridle-road at the foot of the garden.   There
Marian drew back Nora timidly with a hand placed in quick
warning upon her white shoulder. ' Stand aside, dear,'
she whispered at her ear, pulling her back hastily within
the garden gate and under the dark shadow of the big star-
apple tree. ' They're coming down—they're coming down !
I hear them, I hear them !   O God, O God, I shouldn't
have come away !   They've killed Edward !   My darling,
my darling !   They've killed him—they've killed him ! '
    ' I wouldn't stand aside for myself,' Nora answered
half aloud, her eyes flashing proudly even in the shadowy
gloom of the garden. ' But to save Mr. Noel's life, to save
his life, I'll stand aside if you wish, Marian.'
    As they drew back into the dark shadow, even Nora
trembling and shivering a little at the tramp of so many
naked feet, some of the negroes passed close beside them
outside the fence on their way down from the piazza, where
they had just been electrified into sudden quietness by the
awful sight of Louis Delgado's dead body.   They were
talking earnestly and low among themselves, not, as before,
shrieking and yelling and gesticulating wildly, but conversing half below their breath in a solemn, mysterious,
awestruck fashion.
    ' De Lard be praise for Mr. Hawtorn ! ' one of them
said as he passed unseen close beside them. ' Him de
black man fren'.   We got nobody like him.   I no' would
hurt Mr. Hawtorn, de blessed man, not for de life ob me.'
    Marian's heart beat fast within her, but she said never
a word, and only pressed Nora's hand, which she held
convulsively within her own, harder and tighter than ever,
in her mute suspense and agony.
    Presently another group passed close by, and another
voice said tremulously : ' Louis Delgado dead—Louis Del-

gado dead! Mr. Hawthorn is wonderful man for true! Who'd have tought it, me brudder, who'd have tought it?'

'That's Martin Luther,' Nora cried almost aloud, unable any longer to retain her curiosity. 'I know him by his voice. He wouldn't hurt me.—Martin, Martin! what's that you're saying? Has Mr. Hawthorn shot Delgado?' As she spoke, with a fierce anticipatory triumph in her voice, she stepped out from the shadow of the gate on to the main bridle-path, in her white dress and with her pale face, clearly visible under the faint moonlight.

Martin flung up his arms like one stabbed to the heart, and shouted wildly: 'De missy, de missy! Dem done killed her on de piazza yonder, and her duppy comin' now already to scare us and trouble us!'

Even in that moment of awe and alarm, Nora laughed a little laugh of haughty contempt for the strong, big-built, hulking negro's superstitious terror. 'Martin!' she cried, darting after him quickly, as he ran away awestruck, and catching him by the shoulder with her light but palpable human grasp, 'don't you know me? I'm no duppy. It's me myself, Missy Nora, calling you. Here, feel my hand; you see I'm alive still; you see your people haven't killed me yet, even if you've killed your poor old master. Martin, tell me, what's this you're all saying about Mr. Hawthorn having shot Delgado?'

Martin, shaking violently in every limb, turned round and reassured himself slowly that it was really Nora and not her ghost that stood bodily before him. 'Ha, missy,' he answered good-humouredly, showing his great row of big white teeth, though still quaking visibly with terror, 'don't you be 'fraid; we wouldn't hurt you, not a man of us. But it doan't Mr. Hawtorn dat shot Delgado! It God Almighty! De Lard hab smitten him!'

'What!' Nora cried in surprise. 'He fell dead! Apoplexy or something, I suppose. The old villain! he deserved it, Martin.—And Mr. Hawthorn? How about Mr. Hawthorn? Have they hurt him? Have they killed him?'

'Mr. Hawtorn up to de house, missy, an' all de niggers

pray de Lard for true him lib for ebber, de blessed creature.'

'Why are you all coming away now, then ?' Nora asked
anxiously. 'Where are you going to ?'

'Mr. Hawtorn send us home,' Martin answered submissively ; 'an' we are all 'fraid, if we doan't go straight when
him tell us, we drop down dead wit Kora, Datan, an'
Abiram, an' lyin' Ananias, same like Delgado.'

'Marian,' Nora said decisively, 'go back to your husband. You ought to be with him.—Martin, you come
along with me, sir. Mr. Noel's dying. You've killed him,
you people, like you've killed my father. I've got to go
and fetch the doctor now to save him ; and you've got to
come with me and take care of me.'

'Oh, darling,' Marian interrupted nervously, 'you
mustn't go alone amongst all these angry, excited negroes
with nobody but him. Don't, don't ; I'll gladly go with
you !'

'Do as I tell you !' Nora cried in a tone of authority,
with a firm stamp of her petulant little foot. 'You ought
to be with him. You mustn't leave him. That's right,
dear. Now, then, Martin !'

'I 'fraid, Missy.'

'Afraid ! Nonsense. You're a pack of cowards. Am
I afraid ? and I'm a woman ! You ought to be ashamed
of yourself. Come along with me at once, and do as I tell
you.'

The terrified negro yielded grudgingly, and crept after
her in the true crouching African fashion, compelled
against his will to follow implicitly the mere bidding of
the stronger and more imperious nature.

They wound down the zigzag path together, under the
gaunt shadows of the overhanging bamboo clumps, waving
weirdly to and fro with the breeze in the feeble moonlight
—the strong man slouching along timorously, shaking and
starting with terror at every rustle of Nora's dress against
the bracken and the tree ferns ; the slight girl erect and
fearless, walking a pace or two in front of her faint-hearted
escort with proud self-reliance, and never pausing for a
single second to cast a cautious glance to right or left

among the tangled brushwood. The lights were now burning dimly in all the neighbouring negro cottages ; and far away down in the distance, the long rows of gas lamps at Port-of-Spain gleamed double with elongated oblique reflections in the calm water of the sleepy harbour.

They had got half-way down the lonely gully without meeting or passing a single soul, when, at a turn of the road where the bridle-path swept aside to avoid a rainy-season torrent, a horse came quickly upon them from in front, and the rapid click of a cocked pistol warned Nora of approaching danger.

' Who goes there ? ' cried a sharp voice with a marked Scotch accent from the gloom before her. ' Stop this minute, or I'll fire at you, you nigger ! '

With a thrill of delight, Nora recognised the longed-for voice—the very one she was seeking. It was Dr. Macfarlane, from beyond the gully, roused, like half the island, by the red glare from the Orange Grove cane-houses, and spurring up as fast as his horse could carry him, armed and on the alert, to the scene of the supposed insurrection.

' Don't shoot,' Nora answered coolly, holding her hand up in deprecation. ' A friend !—It's me, Dr. Macfarlane — Nora Dupuy, coming to meet you.'

' Miss Dupuy ! ' the doctor cried in astonishment. ' Then they'll not have shot *you*, at any rate, young leddy ! But what are you doing out here alone at this time o' nicht, I'm wondering ? Have you had to run for your life from Orange Grove from these cowardly insurgent nigger fellows ? '

' Run from *them !* ' Nora echoed contemptuously—' run from *them !* Dr. Macfarlane, I'd like to see it. No, no ; I'm too much of a Dupuy ever to do that, I promise you, doctor. They can murder me, but they can't frighten me. I was coming down to look for you, for poor Mr. Noel, who's lying dangerously wounded up at our house, with a wound on the arm and a terrible cut across the temple.'

' Coming alone —just in the vera midst of all this business—to fetch me to look after a wounded fellow ! ' the doctor ejaculated half to himself, with mingled astonishment and admiration. 'Why, the devil himsel' must be in the lassie!' But he jumped down from his horse with a quick movement, not ungallantly, and lifted Nora up in his big arms without a word, seating her sideways, before she could remonstrate, on the awkward saddle. 'Sit you there, Miss Dupuy,' he said kindly. 'Ye're a brave lassie, if ever there was one. I'll hold his head, and run alongside wi' you. We'll be up at the house again in ten minutes.'

'They've killed my father,' Nora said simply, beginning to break down now at last, after her unnatural exaltation of bravery and endurance, and bursting into a sudden flood of tears. 'He's lying at home all hacked to pieces with their dreadful cutlasses; and Mr. Noel's almost dead too; perhaps he'll be quite dead, doctor, before we can get there.'

CHAPTER XLI.

WHEN Nora and the doctor reached the door of Orange Grove, they found Edward Hawthorn waiting to receive them, and the servants already busy trying to remove as far as possible the signs of the wreck so lately effected by the wild rioters. Several neighbouring planters, who had come down from the hills above, stood in armed groups around the gate; and a few mounted black constables, hastily summoned to the spot by the fire, were helping to extinguish the smouldering ashes. Only Delgado's dead body lay untouched upon the sofa, stiff and motionless, for not one of the negroes dare venture to set hands upon it; and, in the room within, Marian sat still, looking anxiously at Harry Noel's pallid face and livid eyelids, and his bloodstained shirt, that yet heaved faintly and almost imperceptibly upon his broad bosom at each long slow-drawn inspiration.

'He isn't dead yet?' Nora asked, in a hushed voice of painful inquiry; and Marian answered under her breath, looking up at the bluff doctor: 'No; he's living still. He's breathing quite regularly, though very feebly.'

As for Macfarlane, he went to work at once with the cool business-like precision and rapidity of his practised profession, opening the blood-stained shirt in front, and putting his hand in through the silk vest to feel the heart that still beat faintly and evenly. ' He's lost a great deal of blood, no doubt, Mrs. Hawthorn,' he said cheerily; ' but he's a strong mon, an' he'll pull through yet, ye needna fash yersel'—thanks to whoever poot this bit handkerchief around his arm here. It's a guid enough tourniquet to use on an eemergency. —Was it you, Miss Dupuy, or Mrs. Hawthorn ? '

A round spot of vivid colour flashed for a moment into Nora's white cheek as she answered quietly : ' It was me, Dr. Macfarlane ! ' and then died out again as fast as it had come, when Macfarlane's eyes were once more removed from her burning face.

' Ye're a brave lassie, an' no mistake,' the doctor went on, removing the tourniquet, and stanching the fresh flow rapidly with a proper bandage, produced with mechanical routine from his coat pocket. ' Well, well, don't be afraid about him any longer. It's a big cut, an' a deep cut, an' it's just gone an' severed a guid big artery—an ugly business ; but ye've takken it in time ; an' your bandage has been most judeeciously applied ; so ye may rest assured that, with a little nursing, the young mon will soon be all right again, an' sound as ever. A cutlass is a nasty weepon to get a wound from, because these nigger fellows don't sharpen them up to a clean edge, as they ought to do rightly, but just hack an' mutilate a mon in the most outrageous an' unbusiness-like manner, instead of killing him outright like guid Christians, with a neat, sharp, workman-like inceesion. But we'll pull him through—we'll pull him through yet, I don't doubt it. An' if he lives, he may have the pleasure of knowing, young leddy, that it was the tourniquet ye made so cleverly that just saved him at the right moment.'

As Macfarlane finished dressing and tending Harry's wound, and Harry's eyes began to open again, slowly and glassily, for he was very faint with loss of blood, Nora, now that the excitement of that awful evening was fairly

over, seemed at last to realise within herself her great loss
with a sudden revulsion. Turning away passionately from
Harry's bedside, she rushed into the next room, where the
women-servants were already gathered around their master's body, keening and wailing as is their wont, with
strange hymns and incoherent songs, wherein stray scraps
of Hebrew psalms and Christian anthems are mingled
incongruously with weird surviving reminiscences of
African fetichism, and mystic symbols of aboriginal obeah.
Fully awake now to the blow that had fallen so suddenly
upon her, Nora flung herself in fierce despair by her
father's side, and kissed the speechless lips two or three
times over with wild remorse in her fresh agony of distress
and isolation. ' Father, father ! ' she cried aloud, in the
self-same long-drawn wail as the negresses around her,
' they've killed you, they've killed you ! my darling—my
darling ! '

' Dem kill you—dem kill you ! ' echoed Rose and Nita
and the other women in their wailing sing-song. ' But de
Lard ob hebben himself avenge you. De grabe yawnin'
wide dis ebenin' for Louis Delgado. De Lard smite him—
de Lard smite him ! '

' Get away, all you auld crones ! ' the doctor said,
coming in upon them suddenly with his hearty Scotch
voice, that seemed to break in too harshly on the weird
solemnity of the ghastly scene. ' Let me see how it was
they killed your master. He's dead, you say— stone dead,
is he ? Let me see—let me see, then.—Here you, there—
lift up his head, will you, lassie, and poot it down decently
on the pillow ! '

Nita did as she was told, mechanically, with a reproach-
ful glance from her big white-fringed eyes at the too
matter-of-fact and common-sense Scotchman, and then
sat down again, squatting upon the floor, moaning and
croning piteously to herself, as decorum demanded of her
under such circumstances.

The doctor looked closely at the clotted blood that hung
in ugly tangles on the poor old man's grey locks, and
whistled a little in a dubious undertone to himself, when
he saw the great gash that ran right across Mr. Dupuy's

left shoulder. 'An awkward cut,' he said slowly—'a vera severe an' awkward cut, I don't deny it. But I don't precisely see, mysel', why it need have positively killed him. The loss of blood needn't have been so vera excessive. He's hacked aboot terribly, puir auld gentleman, with their ugly cutlasses, though hardly enough to have done for a Dupuy, in my opeenion. They're vera tough subjects indeed to kill, all the Dupuys are.'

As he spoke, he leant down cautiously over the body, and listened for a minute or two attentively with his ear at the heart and lips. Then he held his finger lightly with close scrutiny before the motionless nostrils, and shook his head once or twice in a very solemn and ominous fashion. 'It's a most singular fact,' he said, with slow deliberation, looking over at Edward, 'and one full of important psychological implications that the members of every nationality I have ever had to deal with in the whole course of my professional experience—except only the Scottish people—have a most illogical an' rideeculous habit of jumping at conclusions without suffeecient data to go upon. The mon's not dead at all, I tell you—de'il a bit of it. He's breathing still, breathing veesibly.'

Nora leapt up at the word with another sudden access of wild energy. 'Breathing!' she cried—'breathing, doctor! Then he'll live still. He'll get better again, will he, my darling?'

'Now ye're jumping at conclusions a second time most unwarrantably,' Macfarlane answered, with true Scotch caution. 'I will na say positively he'll get better again, for that's a question that rests entirely in the hands o' the Almichty. But I do say the mon's breathing—not a doubt of it.'

The discovery inspired them all at once with fresh hope for Mr. Dupuy's safety. In a few minutes they had taken off his outer clothing and dressed his wounds; while Nora sat rocking herself to and fro excitedly in the American chair, her hands folded tight with interlacing fingers upon her lap, and her lips trembling with convulsive jerks, as she moaned in a low monotone to herself, between suspense and hope, after all the successive manifold terrors of that endless evening.

By-and-by the doctor turned to her kindly and gently.
'He'll do,' he said, in his most fatherly manner. 'Go to
bed, lassie, go to bed, I tell ye. Why, ye're bruised an'
beaten yersel' too, pretty awkwardly! Ye'll need rest. Go
to bed; an' he'll be better, we'll hope an' trust, to-morrow
morning.'

'I won't go to bed,' Nora said, firmly, 'as long as I
don't know whether he will live or not, Dr. Macfarlane.'

'Why, my lassie, that'll be a vera long watch for ye,
then, indeed, I promise you, for he'll no be well again for
many a long day yet, I'm thinking. But he'll do, I don't
doubt, with the Almichty's blessing. Go to bed, now, for
there'll be plenty to guard you. Mr. Hawthorn an' I will
stop here the nicht; and there's neebors enough coming
up every minute to hold the place against all the niggers
in the whole of Treenidad. The country's roused now;
the constabulary's alive; an' the governor 'll be sending
up the meelitary shortly to tak care of us while you're
sleeping. Go to bed at once, there's a guid lassie.'

Marian took her quietly by the arm and led her away,
once more half fainting, 'You'll stop with me, dear?'
Nora whispered; and Marian answered with a kiss: 'Yes,
my darling; I'll stop with you as long as you want me.'

'Wait a minute,' the good doctor called out after them.
'Ye'll need something short to mak' ye sleep after all this
excitement, I tak it, leddies. There's nothing in the
world so much recommended by the faculty under these
conditions as a guid stiff glass of auld Hieland whusky
with a bit lime-juice an' a lump o' shoogar in it.—Ye'll
have some whusky in the house, no doubt, won't you,
Uncle Ezeekiel?'

In a minute or two, Uncle 'Zekiel had brought the
whisky and the glasses and the fruit for the bit lime-juice,
and Macfarlane had duly concocted what he considered as
a proper dose for the 'young leddies in their present posee-
tion.' Edward noticed, too, that besides the whisky, the
juice, and the sugar, he poured furtively into each glass a
few drops from a small phial that he took out unperceived
by all the others from his waistcoat pocket. And as soon
as the two girls had gone off together, the doctor whispered

to him confidentially, with all the air of a most profound conspirator: 'The puir creatures wanted a little seddative to still their nerves, I conseeder, after all this unusual an' upsetting excitement, so I've just takken the leeberty to give them each a guid dose of morphia in their drap o' whusky, that'll mak' them both sleep as sound as a bairn till to-morrow morning.'

But all that night, the negroes watched and prayed loudly in their own huts with strange devotions, and the white men and the constables watched—with more oaths than prayers, after the white man's fashion—armed to the teeth around the open gate of Mr. Dupuy's front garden.

CHAPTER XLII.

NEXT morning, Tom Dupuy, Esquire, of Pimento Valley, Westmoreland, Trinidad, mounted his celebrated chestnut pony Sambo Gal at his own door, unchained his famous Cuban bloodhound Slot from his big kennel, and rode up, with cousinly and lover-like anxiety, to Orange Grove, to inquire after Nora's and her father's safety. Nora was up by the time he reached the house, pale and tired, and with a frightful headache; but she went to meet him at the front door, and dropped him a very low old-fashioned obeisance.

'Good-morning, Tom Dupuy!' she said, coldly. 'So you've come at last to look us up, have you? It's very good of you, I'm sure, very good of you. They tell me you didn't come last night, when half the gentlemen from all the country round rode up in hot haste with guns and pistols to take care of papa and me. But it's very good of you, to be sure, now the danger's well over, to come round in such a friendly fashion and drop us a card of kind inquiries.'

Even Tom Dupuy, born boor and fool as he was, flushed up crimson at that galling taunt from a woman's lips, 'Now that the danger's well over.' To do him justice,

Tom Dupuy was indeed no coward; that was the one
solitary vice of which no fighting Dupuy that ever lived
could with justice be suspected for a moment. He would
have faced and fought a thousand black rioters single-
handed, like a thousand devils, himself, in defence of his
beloved vacuum pans and dearly cherished saccharometers
and boiling-houses. His devotion to molasses would no
doubt have been proof against the very utmost terrors
of death itself. But the truth is that exact devotion in
question was the real cause of his apparent remissness on
the previous evening. All night long, Tom Dupuy had
been busy rousing and arming his immediate house-servants,
despatching messengers to Port-of-Spain for the aid of the
constabulary, and preparing to defend the cut canes with
the very last drop of his blood and the very last breath in
his stolid body. At the first sight of the conflagration at
Orange Grove, he guessed at once that ' the niggers had
risen; ' and he proceeded without a moment's delay to
fortify roughly Pimento Valley against the chance of a
similar attack. Now that he came to look back calmly
upon his heroic exertions, however, it did begin to strike
him somewhat forcibly that he had perhaps shown himself
slightly wanting in the affection of a cousin and the ardour
of a lover. He bit his lip awkwardly for a second, with a
sheepish look ; then he glanced up suddenly and said with
clumsy self-vindication : ' It isn't always those that deserve
the best of you that get the best praise or thanks, in this
world of ours, I fancy, Nora ! '

' I fail to understand you,' Nora answered with quiet
dignity.

' Why, just you look here, Nora; it's somehow like
this, I tell you plainly. Here was I last night down at
Pimento. I saw by the blaze that these nigger fellows
must have broken loose, and must be burning down the
Orange Grove cane-houses ; so there I stopped all night
long, working away as hard as I could work—no nigger
could have worked harder—trying to protect your father's
canes and the vacuum pans from these murdering, howling rebels. And now, when I come round here this morning to tell you, after having made sure the whole year's

crop at old Pimento, one of your fine English fiouts is all
the thanks I get from you, miss, for my night's labour.'

Nora laughed—laughed in spite of herself—laughed
aloud a simple, merry, girlish laugh of pure amusement—
it was so comical. There they had all stood last night in
imminent danger of their lives, and of what is dearer than
life itself, surrounded by a frantic, yelling mob of half-
demented, rum-maddened negroes—her father left for
dead upon the piazza steps, Harry Noel hacked to pieces with
cutlasses before her very eyes, herself trampled under foot
in her swoon upon the drawing-room floor by those naked
soles of negro rioters—and now this morning, Cousin Tom
comes up quietly when all was over to tell her at his ease
how he had taken the most approved precautions for the
protection of his beloved vacuum pans. Every time she
thought of it, Nora laughed again, with a fresh little outburst of merry laughter, more and more vehemently, just
as though her father were not at that very moment lying
within between life and death, as still and motionless as a
corpse, in his own bedroom.

There is nothing more fatal to the possible prospects of
a suitor, however hopeless, than to be openly laughed at
by the lady of his choice at a critical moment—nothing
more galling to a man under any circumstances than
patent ridicule from beautiful woman. Tom Dupuy grew
redder and redder every minute, and stammered and
stuttered in helpless speechlessness; and still Nora looked
at him and laughed, ' for all the world,' he thought to himself, ' as if I were just nobody else but the clown at the
theatre.'

But that was not indeed the stage on which Tom Dupuy
really performed the part of clown with such distinguished
success in his unconscious personation.

' How's your father this morning? ' he asked at last
gruffly, with an uneasy shuffle. ' I hear the niggers cut
him about awfully last night, and next door to killed him
with their beastly cutlasses.'

Nora drew herself up and checked her untimely
laughter with a sudden sense of the demands of the situation, as she answered once more in her coldest tone : ' My

father is getting on as well as we can expect, thank you,
Mr. Tom Dupuy. We are much obliged to you for your
kind inquiries. He slept the night pretty well, all things
considered, and is partially conscious again this morning.
He was very nearly killed last night, as you say ; and if it
hadn't been for Mr. Noel and Mr. Hawthorn, who kindly
came up at once and tried to protect us, he would have
been killed outright, and I with him. But Mr. Noel and
Mr. Hawthorn had happily no vacuum pans and no trash-
houses to engage their first and chief attention.'

Tom Dupuy sneered visibly. 'Hm!' he said. 'Two
coloured fellows! Upon my conscience! the Dupuys of
Trinidad must be coming down in the world, it seems,
when they have to rely for help in a nigger rising upon
two coloured fellows.'

'If they'd had to rely upon white men like you,' Nora
answered angrily, flushing crimson as she spoke, 'they'd
have been burnt last night upon the ashes of the cane-
house, and not a soul would have stirred a hand or foot to
save them or protect them.'

Tom laughed to himself a sharp, short, malicious
laugh. 'Ha, ha!' he said, 'my fine English-bred lady,
so that's the way the wind blows, is it? I may be a
fool, and I know you think me one '—Nora bowed immediately a sarcastic acquiescence—' but I'm not such a
fool as not to see through a woman's face into a woman's
mind like an open window. I heard that that woolly-
headed Hawthorn man had been over here and made a
most cowardly time-serving speech to the confounded
niggers, giving way to all their preposterous demands in
the most outrageous and ridiculous fashion ; but I didn't
hear that the other coloured fellow—your fine-spoken
English friend Noel '—he hissed the words out with all the
concentrated strength of his impotent hatred—' had been
up here too, to put his own finger into the pie when
the crust was burning. Just like his impudence! the
conceited coxcomb! '

'Mr. Noel is lying inside, in our own house here, this
very moment, dangerously wounded,' Nora cried, her face
now like a crimson peony; 'and he was cut down by

negroes last night, standing up bravely, alone and single-handed, with no weapon but a little riding-whip, facing those mad rebels like an angry tiger, and trying to protect me from their insults and their cutlasses ; while you, sir, were stopping snugly away down at Pimento Valley, looking carefully after your canes and your vacuum pans. Tom Dupuy, if you dare to say another word, now or ever, in my hearing against the man who tried to save my life from those wild wretches at the risk of his own, as sure as I'm standing here, sir, I give you fair notice I'll come up and slap your face for you myself, as soon as I'll look at you, you cowardly back-biter !—And now, Mr. Dupuy, good-morning, good-morning.'

Tom saw the game was fairly up and his hand out-witted. It was no use arguing with her any longer. ' When she's in this humour,' he said to himself philosophically, ' you might as well try to reason with a wounded lioness.' So he whistled carelessly for Slot to follow, lifted his hat as politely as he was able—he didn't pretend to all these fine new-fangled town-bred ways of Harry Noel's—jumped with awkward agility upon his chestnut pony, turned his horse's head in the direction of Pimento Valley, and delivered a parting Parthian shot from a safe distance, just as he got beyond the garden gateway. Good-bye, Miss Nora,' he said then savagely raising his hat a second time with sarcastic courtesy : ' good-bye for ever. This is our last meeting. And remember that I always said you'd finish in the end, for all your fine English education, by marrying a damned woolly-headed brown man ! '

CHAPTER XLIII.

ALL day long, Mr. Dupuy lay speechless and almost motionless on his bed, faint with loss of blood, and hovering between life and death, but gradually mending by imperceptible degrees, as Marian fancied. The brain had been terribly shaken, and there were some symptoms of

10

stunning and concussion; but the main trouble was merely
the excessive drain on the vascular system from the long-
continued and unchecked bleeding. About mid-day, he
became hot and feverish, with a full pulse, beating un-
steadily. Macfarlane, who had remained in the house all
night, ordered him at once a rough mixture of sal-volatile,
bismuth, and whisky. 'An' whatever ye do,' he said
emphatically, 'don't forget the whusky—a guid wine-
glassful in half a pint o' cold watter.'

Mr. Dupuy was raised in the bed to drink the mixture,
which he swallowed mechanically in a half-unconscious
fashion; and then a bandage of pounded ice was applied
to his forehead, and leeches were hastily sent for to Port-
of-Spain to reduce the inflammation. Long before the
leeches had time to arrive, however, Nora, who was watching by his bedside, observed that his eyes began to open
more frequently than before, and that gleams of reason
seemed to come over them every now and again for brief
intervals. 'Give him some more whusky,' Macfarlane
said in his decided tone; 'there's nothing like it, nothing
like it—in these cases—especially for a mon of Dupuy's
idioseencrasy.'

At that moment Mr. Dupuy's lips moved feebly, and he
tried to turn with an effort on the pillow.

'Hush, hush!' Nora cried; 'he wants to speak. He
has something to tell us. What is it he's saying? Listen,
listen!'

Mr. Dupuy's lips moved again, and a faint voice proceeded slowly from the depths of his bosom: 'Not
fit to hold a candle to old Trinidad rum, I tell you,
doctor.'

Macfarlane rubbed his hand against his thigh with
evident pleasure and satisfaction. 'He's wrong there,' he
murmured, 'undoubtedly wrong, as every judeecious person
could easily tell him; but no matter. He'll do now, when
once he's got life enough left in him to contradict one.
It always does a Dupuy guid to contradict other people.
Let it be rum, then—a guid wine-glassful of Mr. Tom's
best stilling.'

Almost as soon as the rum was swallowed, Mr. Dupuy

seemed to mend rapidly for the passing moment. He looked up and saw Nora. 'That's well, then,' he said with a sigh, recollecting suddenly the last night's adventures. 'So they didn't kill you, after all, Nora?'

Nora stooped down with unwonted tenderness and kissed him fervently. 'No, papa,' she said; 'they didn't; nor you either.'

Mr. Dupuy paused for a moment; then he looked up a second time, and asked, with extraordinary vehemence for an invalided man: 'Is this riot put down? Have they driven off the niggers? Have they taken the ringleaders? Have they hanged Delgado?'

'Hush, hush!' Nora cried, a little appalled in her cooler mood, after all that had happened, at this first savage outcry for vengeance. 'You mustn't talk, papa; you mustn't excite yourself. Yes, yes; the riot is put down, and Delgado—Delgado is dead. He has met with his due punishment.'

'That's well!' Mr. Dupuy exclaimed, with much gusto, in spite of his weakness, rubbing his hands feebly underneath the bed-clothes. 'Serves the villain right. I'm glad they've hanged him. Nothing on earth comes up to martial law in these emergencies; and hang 'em on the spot, say I, as fast as you catch 'em, red-handed! Flog 'em first, and hang 'em afterwards!'

Marian looked down at him speechless, with a shudder of horror; but Nora put her face between her hands, overwhelmed with awe, now her own passion had burnt itself out, at that terrible outburst of the old bad barbaric spirit of retaliation. 'Don't let him talk so, dear,' she cried to Marian. 'Oh, Marian, Marian, I'm so ashamed of myself, I'm so ashamed of us all—us Dupuys, I mean; I wish we were all more like you and Mr. Hawthorn.'

'You must na speak, Mr. Dupuy,' Macfarlane said, interposing gently, with his rough-and-ready Scotch tenderness. 'Ye're not strong enough for conversation yet, I'm thinking. Ye must just tak' a wee bit sleep till the fever's better. Ye've had a narrow escape of your life, my guid sir; an' ye must na excite yoursel' the minute ye're getting a trifle better.'

The old man lay silent for a few minutes longer; then he turned again to Nora, and without noticing Marian's presence, said more vehemently and more viciously than ever: ' I know who set them on to this, Nora. It wasn't their own doing; it was coloured instigation. They were put up to it—I know they were put up to it—by that scoundrel Hawthorn—a seditious, rascally, malevolent lawyer, if ever there was one. I hope they'll hang him too—he deserves it soundly—flog him and hang him as soon as they catch him ! '

' Oh, papa, papa ! ' Nora cried, growing hotter and redder in the face than ever, and clutching Marian's hand tightly in an agony of distress and shamefacedness, ' you don't know what you're saying ! You don't know what you owe to him ! It was Mr. Hawthorn who finally pacified and dispersed the negroes ; and if it hadn't been for his coolness and his bravery, we wouldn't one of us have been alive to say so this very minute ! '

Mr. Dupuy coughed uneasily, and muttered to himself once more in a vindictive undertone : ' Hang him when they catch him !—hang him when they catch him ! I'll speak to the governor about it myself, and prove to him conclusively that if it hadn't been for this fellow Hawthorn, the niggers 'd never have dreamed of kicking up such an infernal hullabaloo and bobbery ! '

' But, papa,' Nora began again, her eyes full of tears, ' you don't understand. You're all wrong about it. If it hadn't been for that dear, good, brave Mr. Hawthorn——'

Marian touched her lightly on the shoulder. ' Never mind about it, Nora, darling,' she whispered consolingly, with a womanly caress to the poor shrinking girl at her elbow ; ' don't trouble him with the story now. By-and-by, when he's better, he'll come to hear the facts ; and then he'll know what Edward's part was in the whole matter. Don't distress yourself about it, darling, now, after all that has happened. I know your father's feelings too well to take amiss anything he may happen to say in the heat of the moment.

' If you speak another word before six o'clock to-night, Dupuy,' Macfarlane put in with stern determination, ' I'll just clear every soul that knows ye oot o' the room at once, an' leave ye alone to the tender mercies of old Aunt Clemmy. Turn over on your side, mon, when your doctor tells ye to, an' try to get a little bit o' refreshing sleep before the evening.'

Mr. Dupuy obeyed in a feeble fashion; but he still muttered doggedly to himself as he turned over: ' Catch him and hang him! Prove it to the governor!'

As he spoke, Edward beckoned Marian out into the drawing-room through the open door, to show her a note which had just been brought to him by a mounted orderly. It was a few hasty lines, written in pencil that very morning by the governor himself, thanking Mr. Hawthorn in his official capacity for his brave and conciliatory conduct on the preceding evening, whereby a formidable and organised insurrection had been nipped in the bud, and a door left open for future inquiry, and redress of any possible just grievances on the part of the rioters and discontented negroes. ' It is to your firmness and address alone,' the governor wrote, ' that the white population of the island of Trinidad owes to-day its present security from fire and bloodshed.'

Meanwhile, preparations had been made for preventing any possible fresh outbreak of the riot that evening; and soldiers and policemen were arriving every moment at the smouldering site of the recent fire, and forming a regular plan of defence against the remote chance of a second rising. Not that any such precautions were really necessary; for the negroes, deprived of their head in Delgado, were left utterly without cohesion or organisation; and Edward's promise to go to England and see that their grievances were properly ventilated had had far more effect upon their trustful and excitable natures than the display of ten regiments of soldiers in marching order could possibly have produced. The natural laziness of the negro mind, combining with their confidence in the young judge, and their fervent faith in the justice of Providence under the most apparently incongruous circumstances, had made them all settle down at once into their usual listless *laissez-faire* condition, as soon as the spur of Delgado's fiery energy and exhortation had ceased to stimulate them. 'It all right,' they chattered passively among themselves. 'Mistah Hawtorn gwine to 'peak to Missis Queen fur de poor naygur ; and de Lard in hebben gwine to watch ober him, an' see him doan't suffer no more wrong at de heavy hand ob de proud buckra.'

When the time arrived to make preparations for the night's watching and nursing, Nora came to Marian once more with her spirit vexed by a sore trouble. 'My dear,' she said, 'this is a dreadful thing about poor Mr. Noel having to go on stopping here. It's very unfortunate he couldn't have been nursed through his illness at your house or at Captain Castello's. He'll be down in bed for at least a week or two, in all probability ; and it won't be possible to move him out of this until he's better.'

'Well, darling?' Marian answered, with an inquiring smile.

'Well, you see, Marian, it wouldn't be so awkward, of course, if poor papa wasn't ill too, because then, if I liked, I could go over and stop with you at Mulberry until Mr. Noel was quite recovered. But as I shall have to stay here, naturally, to nurse papa, why——'

'Why, what then, Nora?'

Nora hesitated. 'Why, you see, darling,' she went on timidly at last, 'people will say that as I've helped to nurse Mr. Noel through a serious illness——'

'Yes, dear?'

'Oh, Marian, don't be so stupid! Of course, in that case, everybody'll expect me—to—to—accept him.'

Marian looked down deep into her simple little girlish eyes with a curious smile of arch womanliness. 'And why not, Nora?' she asked at last with perfect simplicity.

Nora blushed. 'Marian—Marian—dear Marian,' she said at length, after a long pause, 'you are so good—you are so kind—you are so helpful to me. I wish I could say to you all I feel, but I can't ; and even if I did, you couldn't understand it—you couldn't fathom it. You don't know what it is, Marian, to be born a West Indian with such a terrible load of surviving prejudices. Oh, darling, darling, we are all so full of wicked, dreadful, unjust feelings ; I

wish I could be like you, dear, I wish to heaven I could ;
but I can't, I can't, I can't, somehow ! '

Marian stroked her white little hand with sisterly tenderness in perfect silence for a few minutes ; then she said,
rather reproachfully : ' So you wish Mr. Noel wasn't going
to be nursed under your father's roof, at all, Nora ! That's
a very poor return, isn't it, my darling, for all his bravery
and heroism and devotion ? '

Nora drew back like one stung suddenly by a venomous
creature, and putting her hand in haste on her breast, as if
it pained her terribly, answered, with a deep-drawn sigh :
' It isn't that, Marian —isn't that, darling.   You know
what it is, dear, as well as I do.   Don't say it's that, my
sweet; oh, don't say it's that, or you'll kill me, you'll kill
me, with remorse and anger !   You'll make me hate
myself, if you say I'm ungrateful.   But I'm not ungrateful,
Marian—I'm not ungrateful.   I admire him, and—and
love him ; yes, I love him, for the way he acted here last
evening.'   And as she spoke, she buried her head fervidly,
with shame and fear, in Marian's bosom.

Marian smoothed her hair tenderly for a few minutes
longer, this time again in profound silence, and then she
spoke once more very softly, almost at Nora's ear, in a low
whisper.   ' I went this morning into Mr. Noel's room,' she
said, ' darling, just when he was first beginning to recover
consciousness ; and as he saw me, he turned his eyes up to
me with a beseeching look, and his lips seemed to be
moving, as if he wanted ever so much to say something.
So I stooped down and listened to catch the words he was
trying to frame in his feverish fashion.   He said at first
just two words—" Miss Dupuy ; " and then he spoke again,
and said one only—" Nora."   I smiled, and nodded at him
to tell him it was all well; and he spoke again, quite
audibly : " Have they hurt her ?   Have they hurt her ? "
I said : " No ; she's as well as I am ! " and his eyes seemed
to grow larger as I said it, and filled with tears; and I
knew what he meant by them, Nora—I knew what he
meant by them.   A little later, he spoke to me again,
and he said : " Mrs. Hawthorn, I may be dying ; and if
I die, tell her—tell Nora—that—that—last night, when

she stood beside me there so bravely, I loved her, I loved her, I loved her better even than I had ever loved her ! " He won't die, Nora ; but still I'll break his confidence, darling, and tell it you this evening—Oh, Nora, Nora ! you say you wish to heaven you hadn't got all these dreadful wicked West Indian feelings. You're brave enough—I know that—no woman braver. Why don't you have the courage to break through them, then, and come away with Edward and me to England, and accept poor Mr. Noel, who would gladly give his very life a thousand times over for you, darling ? '

Nora burst into tears once more, and nestled, sobbing, closer and closer upon Marian's shoulder. ' My darling, my darling, she cried, I'm too, too wicked ! I only wish I could feel as you do ! '

CHAPTER XLIV.

THE days went slowly, slowly on, and Mr. Dupuy and Harry Noel both continued to recover steadily from their severe injuries. Marian came over every day to help with the nursing, and took charge for the most part, with Aunt Clemmy's aid, of the young Englishman ; while Nora's time was chiefly taken up in attending to her father's manifold necessities. Still at odd moments she did venture to help a little in taking care of poor Harry, whose gratitude for all her small attentions was absolutely unbounded, and very touching. True, she came comparatively seldom into the sickroom (for such in fact it was, the crushing blow on Harry's head having been followed by violent symptoms of internal injury to the brain, which made his case far more serious in the end than Mr. Dupuy's) ; but whenever he awoke up after a short doze, in his intervals of pain, he always found a fresh passion-flower, or a sweet white rosebud, or a graceful spray of clambering Martinique clematis, carefully placed in a tiny vase with pure water on the little table by the bedside ; and he knew well whose dainty fingers had picked the pretty blossoms and arranged them so deftly, with their delicate background of lace-like

wild West Indian maidenhair, in the tiny bouquets. More
than once, too, when Aunt Clemmy wasn't looking, he took
the white rosebuds out of the water for a single moment
and gazed at them tenderly with a wistful eye; and when,
one afternoon, Marian surprised him in the very act, as she
came in with his regulation cup of chicken broth at the half-
hour, she saw that the colour rushed suddenly even into his
brown and bloodless cheek, and his eyes fell like a boy's as
he replaced the buds with a guilty look in the vase beside
him. But she said nothing about the matter at the time,
only reserving it for Nora's private delectation in the little
boudoir half an hour later.

As Mr. Dupuy got better, one firm resolve seemed to
have imprinted itself indelibly upon his unbending nature—
the resolve to quit Trinidad for ever at the very earliest
moment when convalescence and Macfarlane would combine to allow him. He would even sell Orange Grove itself,
he said, and go over and live permanently for the rest of
his days in England. ' That is to say, in England for the
summer,' he observed casually to Nora; ' for I don't suppose any human being in his right senses would ever dream
of stopping in such a beastly climate through a whole
dreary English winter. In October, I shall always go to
Nice, or Pau, or Mentone, or some other of these new-
fashioned continental wintering-places that people go to
nowadays in Europe; some chance, I suppose, of seeing
the sun once and again there, at any rate. But one thing
I've quite decided upon : I won't live any longer in Trinidad.
I'm not afraid; but I object on principle to vivisection,
especially conducted with a blunt instrument. At my time
of life, a man naturally dislikes being cut up alive by those
horrible cutlasses. You and your cousin Tom may stop
here by yourselves and manage Pimento Valley, if you
choose; but I decline any longer to be used as the *corpus
vile* for a nigger experimentalist to exercise his skill upon.
It doesn't suit my taste, and I refuse to submit to it. The
fact is, Nora, my dear, the island isn't any longer a fit place
for a gentleman to live in. It was all very well in the old
days, before we got a pack of Exeter Hall demagogues sent
out here by the government of the day, on purpose to excite

our own servants to rebellion and insurrection against us. Nobody ever heard of the niggers rising or hacking one to pieces bodily in those days. But ever since this man Hawthorn, whose wife you're so thick with—a thing that no lady would have dreamt of countenancing in the days before these new-fangled doctrines came into fashion— ever since this man Hawthorn was sent out here, preaching his revolutionary cut-throat principles broadcast, the island hasn't been a fit place at all for a gentleman to live in ; and I've made up my mind to leave it at once and go over to England.'

Meanwhile, events had arisen which rendered it certain that the revolutionary demagogue himself, who had saved Mr. Dupuy's life and all the other white lives in the entire island, would also have to go to England at a short notice. Edward had intended, indeed, in pursuance of his hasty promise to the excited negroes, to resign his judgeship and return home, in order to confer with the Colonial Office on the subject of their grievances. But before he had time to settle his affairs and make arrangements for his approach- ing departure, a brisk interchange of messages had taken place between the Trinidad government and the home authorities. Meetings had been held in London at which the whole matter had been thoroughly ventilated ; questions had been asked and answered in Parliament ; and the English papers had called unanimously for a thorough sift- ing of the relations between the planters and the labourers throughout the whole of the West India Islands. In par- ticular, they had highly praised the courage and wisdom with which young Mr. Hawthorn had stepped into the breach at the critical moment, and singlehanded, averted a general massacre, by his timely influence with the infuriated rioters. More than one paper had suggested that Mr. Hawthorn should be forthwith recalled, to give evidence on the subject before a Select Committee ; and as a direct result of that suggestion, Edward shortly after received a message from the Colonial Secretary, summoning him to London immediately, with all despatch, on business con- nected with the recent rising of the negroes in Trinidad.

Mr. Dupuy had already chosen the date on which he

should sail; but when he heard that the man Hawthorn
had actually taken a passage by the same steamer, he
almost changed his mind, for the first time in his life, and
half determined to remain in the island, now that it was
to be freed at last from the polluting presence and influence
of this terrible fire-eating brown revolutionist. Perhaps,
he thought, when once Hawthorn was gone, Trinidad might
yet be a place fit for a gentleman to live in. The Dupuys
had inhabited Orange Grove, father and son, for nine
generations; and it would be a pity indeed if they were to
be driven away from the ancestral plantations by the
meddlesome interference of an upstart radical coloured
lawyer.

In this dubitative frame of mind, then, Mr. Dupuy, as
soon as ever Macfarlane would allow him to mount his
horse again, rode slowly down from Orange Grove to pay
a long-meditated call at Government House upon His
Excellency the Governor. In black frock coat and shiny
silk hat, as is the rigorous etiquette upon such occasions,
even under a blazing tropical noontide, he went his way
with a full heart, ready to pour forth the vials of his wrath
into the sympathetic ears of the Queen's representative
against this wretched intriguer Hawthorn, by whose
Machiavellian machinations (Mr. Dupuy was justly proud
in his own mind of that sonorous alliteration) the happy
and contented peasantry of the island of Trinidad had been
spurred and flogged and slowly roused into unwilling rebellion against their generous and paternal employers.

Judge of his amazement, therefore, when, after listening
patiently to his long and fierce tirade, Sir Adalbert rose
from his chair calmly, and said in a clear and distinct voice
these incredible words: ' Mr. Dupuy, you unfortunately
quite mistake the whole nature of the situation. This
abortive insurrection is not due to Mr. Hawthorn or to any
other one person whatever. It has long been brewing; we
have for months feared and anticipated it; and it is the
outcome of a widespread and general discontent among the
negroes themselves, sedulously fostered, we are afraid'—
here Mr. Dupuy's face began to brighten with joyous anticipation—' by the unwise and excessive severity of many

planters, both in their public capacity as magistrates, and
in their private capacity as employers of labour.' (Here
Mr. Dupuy's face first fell blankly, and then pursed itself
up suddenly in a perfectly comical expression of profound
dismay and intense astonishment.) ' It is to Mr. Hawthorn
alone,' the Governor went on, glancing severely at the
astounded planter, ' that many unwise proprietors of estates
in the island of Trinidad owe their escape from the not
wholly unprovoked anger of the insurgent negroes ; and so
highly do the home authorities value Mr. Hawthorn's
courage and judgment in this emergency, that they have
just summoned him back to England, to aid them with his
advice and experience in settling a new *modus vivendi* to be
shortly introduced between negroes and employers.'

Mr. Dupuy never quite understood how he managed to
reel out of the Governor's drawing-room without fainting,
from sheer astonishment and horror ; or how he managed
to restrain his legs from lifting up his toes automatically
against the sacred person of the Queen's representative.
But he did manage somehow to stagger down the steps in
a dazed and stupefied fashion, much as he had staggered
along the path when he felt Delgado hacking him about
the body at the blazing cane-houses ; and he rode back
home to Orange Grove, red in the face as an angry turkey-
cock, more convinced than ever in his own mind that
Trinidad was indeed no longer a fit place for any gentleman
of breeding to live in. And in spite of Edward's having
taken passage by the same ship, he determined to clear out
of the island, bag and baggage, at the earliest possible
opportunity.

As for Harry Noel, he, too, had engaged a berth quite
undesignedly in the self-same steamer. Even though he
had rushed up to Orange Grove in the first flush of the
danger, to protect Nora and her father, if possible, from
the frantic rioters, it had of course been a very awkward
position for him to find himself an unwilling and uninvited
guest in the house which he had last quitted under such
extremely unpleasant circumstances. Mr. Dupuy, indeed,
though he admitted, when he heard the whole story, that
Harry had no doubt behaved ' like a very decent young

fellow,' could not be prevailed upon to take any notice of
his unbidden presence, even by sending an occasional polite
message of inquiry about his slow recovery, from the adjoin-
ing bedroom. So Harry was naturally anxious to get away
from Orange Grove as quickly as possible, and he had made
up his mind that before he went he would not again ask
Nora to reconsider her determination. His chivalrous
nature shrank from the very appearance of trading upon
her gratitude for his brave efforts to save her on the evening of the outbreak; if she would not accept him for his
own sake, she should not accept him for the sake of the risk
he had run to win her.

The first day when Harry was permitted to move out
under the shade of the big star-apple tree upon the little
grass plot, where he sat in a cushioned bamboo chair beside
the clump of waving cannas, Nora came upon him suddenly,
as if by accident, from the Italian terrace, with a bunch of
beautiful pale-blue plumbago and a tall spike of scented
tuberose in her dainty, gloveless little fingers. ' Aren't they
beautiful, Mr. Noel ?' she said, holding them up to his admiring gaze—admiring them, it must be confessed, a trifle
obliquely. 'Did you ever in your life see anything so
wildly lovely in a stiff, tied-up, staircase conservatory over
yonder in dear old England ?'

' Never,' Harry Noel answered, with his eyes fixed rather
on her blushing face than on the luscious pale white tuberose. ' I shall carry away with me always the most
delightful reminiscences of beautiful Trinidad and of its
lovely—flowers.'

Nora noticed at once the significant little pause before
the last word, and blushed again, even deeper than ever.
' Carry away with you ?' she said regretfully, echoing his
words—' carry away with you ? Then do you mean to leave
the island immediately ?'

' Yes, Miss Dupuy—immediately; by the next steamer.
I've written off this very morning to the agents at the
harbour to engage my passage.'

Nora's heart beat violently within her. ' So soon !'
she said. ' How very curious ! And how very fortunate,
too, for I believe papa has taken berths for himself and me

by the very same steamer. He's gone to-day to call on
the Governor; and when he comes back, he's going to
decide at once whether or not we are to leave the island
immediately for ever.'

'Very fortunate? You said very fortunate? How very
kind of you! Then you're not altogether sorry, Miss
Dupuy, that we're going to be fellow-passengers together?'

'Mr. Noel, Mr. Noel! How can you doubt it?'

Harry's heart beat that moment almost as fast as Nora's
own. In spite of his good resolutions—which he had made
so very firmly too—he couldn't help ejaculating fervently:
'Then you forgive me, Miss Dupuy! You let bygones be
bygones! You're not angry with me any longer!'

'Angry with you, Mr. Noel—angry with you! You
were so kind, you were so brave! How could I ever again
be angry with you!'

Harry's face fell somewhat. After all, then, it was only
gratitude. 'It's very good of you to say so,' he faltered
out tremulously—'very good of you to say so. I—I—I
shall always remember—my—my visit to Orange Grove
with the greatest pleasure.'

'And so shall I,' Nora added in a low voice, hardly
breathing; and as she spoke, the tears filled her eyes to
overflowing.

Harry looked at her once more tenderly. How beautiful
and fresh and dainty she was, really! He looked at her,
and longed just once to kiss her. Nora's hand lay close to
his. He put out his own fingers, very tentatively, and just
touched it, almost as if by accident. Nora drew it half
away, but not suddenly. He touched it again, a little
more boldly this time, and Nora permitted him, unreprov-
ing. Then he looked hard into her averted tearful eyes,
and said tenderly the one word, 'Nora!'

Nora's hand responded faintly by a slight pressure, but
she answered nothing.

'Nora,' the young man cried again, with sudden energy,
'if it is love, take me, take me. But if it is only—only the
recollection of that terrible night, let me go, let me go, for
ever!'

Nora held his hand fast in hers with a tremulous grasp,

and whispered in his ear, almost inaudibly: 'Mr. Noel, it is love—it is love! I love you—I love you!'

When Macfarlane came his rounds that evening to see his patients he declared that Harry Noel's pulse was decidedly feverish, and that he must have been somehow over-exciting himself; so he ordered him back again ruthlessly to bed at once till further notice.

CHAPTER XLV.

WHEN Mr. Dupuy heard from his daughter's own lips the news of her engagement to Harry Noel, his wrath at first was absolutely unbounded; he stormed about the house, and raved and gesticulated. He refused ever to see Harry Noel again, or to admit of any proffered explanation, or to suffer Nora to attempt the defence of her own conduct. He was sure no defence was possible, and he wasn't going to listen to one either, whether or not. He even proposed to kick Harry out of doors forthwith for having thus taken advantage in the most abominable manner of his very peculiar and unusual circumstances. Whatever came, he would never dream of allowing Nora to marry such an extremely ungentlemanly and mean-spirited fellow.

But Mr. Dupuy didn't sufficiently calculate upon the fact that in this matter he had another Dupuy to deal with, and that that other Dupuy had the indomitable family will quite as strongly developed within her as he himself had. Nora stuck bravely to her point with the utmost resolution. As long as she was not yet of age, she said, she would obey her father in all reasonable matters; but as soon as she was twenty-one, Orange Grove or no Orange Grove, she would marry Harry Noel outright, so that was the end of it. And having delivered herself squarely of this profound determination, she said not a word more upon the subject, but left events to work out their own course in their own proper and natural fashion.

Now, Mr. Dupuy was an obstinate man; but his

obstinacy was of that vehement and demonstrative kind which grows fiercer and fiercer the more you say to it, but wears itself out, of pure inanition, when resolutely met by a firm and passive silent opposition. Though she was no psychologist, Nora had hit quite unconsciously and spontaneously upon this best possible line of action. She never attempted to contradict or gainsay her father, whenever he spoke to her angrily, in one of his passionate outbursts against Harry Noel; but she went her own way, quietly and unobtrusively, taking it for granted always, in a thousand little undemonstrative ways, that it was her obvious future rôle in life to marry at last her chosen lover. And as water by continual dropping wears a hole finally in the hardest stone, so Nora by constant quiet side-hints made her father gradually understand that she would really have Harry Noel for a husband, and no other. Bit by bit, Mr. Dupuy gave way, sullenly and grudgingly, convinced in his own mind that the world was being rapidly turned topsy-turvy, and that it was no use for a plain, solid, straightforward old gentleman any longer to presume single-handed upon stemming the ever-increasing flood of revolutionary levelling sentiment. It was some solace to his soul, as he yielded slowly inch by inch, to think that if for once in his life he had had to yield, it was at least to a born Dupuy, and not to any pulpy, weak-minded outsider whatever.

So in the end, before the steamer was ready to sail, he had been brought, not indeed to give his consent to Nora's marriage—for that was more than any one could reasonably have expected from a man of his character—but to recognise it somehow in an unofficial dogged fashion as quite inevitable. After all, the fellow was heir to a baronetcy, which is always an eminently respectable position; and his daughter in the end would be Lady Noel; and everybody said the young man had behaved admirably on the night of the riot; and over in England—well, over in England it's positively incredible how little right and proper feeling people have got upon these important racial matters.

But one thing I will *not* permit,' Mr. Dupuy said with

decisive curtness. 'Whether you marry this person Noel,
Nora, or whether you don't—a question on which it seems,
in this new-fangled order of things that's coming up nowadays, a father's feelings are not to be consulted—you shall
not marry him here in Trinidad. I will not allow the
grand old name and fame of the fighting Dupuys of Orange
Grove to be dragged through the mud with any young man
whatsoever, in this island. If you want to marry the man
Noel, miss, you shall marry him in England, where nobody
on earth will know anything at all about it.'

'Certainly, papa,' Nora answered most demurely. 'Mr.
Noel would naturally prefer the wedding to take place in
London, where his own family and friends could all be
present; and besides, of course there wouldn't be time to
get one's things ready either, before we leave the West
Indies.'

When the next steamer was prepared to sail, it carried
away a large contingent of well-known residents from the
island of Trinidad. On the deck, Edward and Marian
Hawthorn stood waving their handkerchiefs energetically
to their friends on the wharf, and to the great body of
negroes who had assembled in full force to give a parting
cheer to 'de black man fren', Mr. Hawtorn.' Harry Noel,
in a folding cane-chair, sat beside them, still pale and ill,
but bowing, it must be confessed, from time to time, a
rather ironical bow to his late assailants, at the cheers,
which were really meant, of course, for his more popular
friend and travelling companion. Close by stood Nora, not
sorry in her heart that she was to see the last that day of
the land of her fathers, where she had suffered so terribly
and dared so much. And close by, too, on the seat beside
the gunwale, sat Mr. and Mrs. Hawthorn the elder, induced
at last, by Edward's earnest solicitation, to quit Trinidad
for the evening of their days, and come to live hard by his
own new home in the mother country. As for Mr. Dupuy,
he had no patience with the open way in which that man
Hawthorn was waving his adieux so abominably to his
fellow-conspirators; so, by way of escaping from the un-
welcome demonstration, he was quietly ensconced below in

a corner of the saloon, enjoying a last parting cigar and a brandy cocktail with some of his old planter cronies, who were going back to shore by-and-by in the pilot boat. As a body, the little party downstairs were all agreed that when a man like our friend Dupuy here was positively driven out of the island by coloured agitators, Trinidad was no longer a place fit for any gentleman with the slightest self-respect to live in. The effect of this solemn declaration was only imperceptibly marred by the well-known fact that it had been announced with equal profundity of conviction, at intervals of about six months each, by ten generations of old Trinidad planters, ever since the earliest foundation of the Spanish colony in that island.

Just two months later, Mr. Dupuy was seated alone at his solitary lunch in the London club to which Harry Noel had temporarily introduced him as an honorary guest. It was the morning after Nora's wedding, and Mr. Dupuy was feeling naturally somewhat dull and lonely in that great unsympathetic world of London. His attention, however, was suddenly attracted by two young men at a neighbouring table, one of whom distinctly mentioned in an audible tone his new son-in-law's name, 'Harry Noel.' The master of Orange Grove drew himself up stiffly and listened with much curiosity to such scraps as he could manage to catch of their flippant conversation.

'Oh, yes,' one of them was saying, 'a very smart affair indeed, I can tell you. Old Sir Walter and Lady Noel down there from Lincolnshire, and half the smartest people in London at the wedding breakfast. Very fine fellow, Noel, and comes in to one of the finest estates in the whole of England. Pretty little woman, too, the bride—nice little girl, with such winning little baby features.'

'Ah, ha!' drawled out the other slowly. 'Pretty, is she? Ah, really. And, pray, who was she?'

Mr. Dupuy's bosom swelled with not unnatural paternal pride and pleasure as he anticipated the prompt answer from the wedding guest: 'One of the fighting Dupuys of Trinidad.'

But instead of replying in that perfectly reasonable and

intelligible fashion, the young man at the club responded
slowly : ' Well, upon my word, I don't exactly know who
she was, but somebody colonial, any way, I'm certain. I
fancy from Hong-Kong, or Penang, or Demerara, or somewhere.—No ; Trinidad—I remember now—it was certainly
either St. Kitts or Trinidad. Oh, Trinidad, of course, for
Mrs. Hawthorn, you know—Miss Ord that was—wife of
that awfully clever Cambridge fellow Hawthorn, who's just
been appointed to a permanent something-or-other-ship at
the Colonial Office—Mrs. Hawthorn knew her when she
was out there during that nigger row they've just been
having ; and she pointed me out the bride's father, a
snuffy-looking old gentleman in the sugar-planting line,
over in those parts, as far as I understood her. Old gentleman looked horribly out of it among so many smart London
people. Horizon apparently quite limited by rum and
sugar.—Oh, yes, it was a great catch for her, of course, I
needn't tell you ; but I understand this was the whole
story of it. She angled for him very cleverly ; and, by
Jove, she hooked him at last, and played him well, and now
she's landed him and fairly cooked him. It appears, he
went out there not long before this insurrection business
began, to look after some property they have in the island,
and he stopped with her father, who, I dare say, was
accustomed to dispensing a sort of rough-and-ready colonial
hospitality to all comers, gentle and simple. When the
row came, the snuffy old gentleman in the sugar-planting
line, as luck would have it, was the very first man whose
house was attacked—didn't pay his niggers regularly, they
tell me ; and this young lady, posing herself directly behind
poor Noel, compelled him, out of pure politeness, being a
chivalrous sort of man, to fight for her life, and beat off
the niggers single-handed for half an hour or so. Then he
gets cut down, it seems, with an ugly cutlass wound : she
falls fainting upon his body, for all the world like a Surrey
melodrama ; Hawthorn rushes in with drawn pistol and
strikes an attitude ; and the curtain falls : tableau. At
last, Hawthorn manages to disperse the niggers ; and my
young lady has the agreeable task of nursing Noel at her
father's house, through a slow convalescence. Deuced

clever, of course : makes him save her life first, and then
she helps to save his. Has him both ways, you see—devotion and gratitude. So, as I say, she lands him promptly :
and the consequence is, after a proper interval, this smart
affair that came off yesterday over at St. George's.

Once more the world reeled visibly before Mr. Dupuy's
eyes, and he rose up from that hospitable club table, leaving
his mutton cutlet and tomato sauce almost untasted. In
the heat of the moment, he was half inclined to go back
again immediately to his native Trinidad, and brave the
terrors of vivisection, rather than stop in this atrocious,
new-fangled, upsetting England, where the family honours
of the fighting Dupuys of Orange Grove were positively
reckoned at less than nothing. He restrained himself,
however, with a violent effort, and still condescends, from
summer to summer, fitfully to inhabit this chilly, damp,
and unappreciative island. But it is noticeable that he
talks much less frequently now of the Dupuy characteristics
than he did formerly (the population of Great Britain being
evidently rather bored than otherwise by his constant allu-
sions to those remarkable idiosyncrasies) ; and some of his
acquaintances have even observed that since the late
baronet's lamented decease, a few months since, he has
spoken more than once with apparent pride and delight of
' my son-in-law, Sir Harry Noel.'

It is a great consolation to Tom Dupuy to this day,
whenever anybody happens casually to mention his cousin
Nora in his presence, that he can rub his hands gently one
over the other before him, and murmur in his own peculiar
drawl : ' I always told you she'd end at last by marrying
some confounded woolly-headed brown man.'

THE END.

www.ingramcontent.com/pod-product-compliance
Lightning Source LLC
Chambersburg PA
CBHW021320250626
47155CB00002B/557